WYTCHFIRE

The Dragonkin Trilogy: One

MICHAEL MEYERHOFER

Wytchfire
The Dragonkin Trilogy™
A Red Adept Publishing Book

ISBN-13: 978-1-940215-28-0
ISBN-10: 1-940215-28-5

Red Adept Publishing, LLC
104 Bugenfield Court
Garner, NC 27529
http://RedAdeptPublishing.com/

Cover and Formatting: Streetlight Graphics

For Alysha Hoffa

PROLOGUE

FADARAH TURNED HIS TATTOOED FACE toward the granite walls of Syros, greatest of the Free Cities of the Simurgh Plains. He held the reins of his horse in one fist as he settled back in the saddle and took in the sight. Mid-morning light crested the city's crenellated battlements, shone through its white banners sewn with crossed longbows, and cast long, taut shadows over a forest made not from trees but from the raised arms of trebuchets. The sun burned in Fadarah's eyes, but he did not blink. He was, after all, a Shel'ai. What was the sun, if not fire?

But the soldiers arrayed in vast columns behind him were Human, and they winced as the sun climbed higher into the clear, cloudless sky, blazing in their faces. Those men knew what all good fighters had known since the dawn of time—to fight with the sun in your face was madness. Courage and armor meant nothing if you could not see.

Still, when Fadarah ordered them forward, the Throng obeyed without question. They had nothing to fear from Syros's archers and murder-holes, her broad battlements and stout, sealed gates. No, the Nightmare would take care of those.

Fadarah removed his gauntlets with deliberate slowness. Then he raised one fist and loosened his fingers. Tendrils of wytchfire burst to life above his open palm. The violet flames coursed the length of his arm. He felt a familiar, roiling heat. Though it titillated his senses, it left him unharmed. Those soldiers closest to him were merely Human, though. They blanched and drew away, already perspiring from heat as much as fear.

Concealing a smirk, Fadarah shouted, "Send forth my Nightmare!"

Fadarah rose, standing in the saddle of his huge, oxblood-colored horse. Even without his armor and the wytchfire coursing from his fingers, men might have fled at the sight of him. He stood at least seven feet tall, broad shouldered and muscled like an Olg, with intricate blue tattoos covering his arms and shaven head.

As his order took effect, his men reacted uneasily. Twenty thousand strong, bristling with spears and drawn blades, and clad in armor, they still feared magic. They feared Fadarah. But more than him, they feared the Nightmare.

Fadarah could not blame them. He feared it, too.

He closed his fist, extinguishing the wytchfire, then seized the reins of his horse so his soldiers would not see his hands shake when the Nightmare came forward. Even after so much time, even knowing that the Nightmare had once been a man—a friend—Fadarah could not entirely quench his fear. He clenched the reins of his horse until his knuckles turned white as the pupils of his eyes. Despite the bloodmare's training, the horse would have panicked had Fadarah not sent a paralyzing jolt of magic into the beast's mind.

Pity no one can do that for me. The Nightmare drew closer.

Fadarah heard shouting, even weeping, and sensed a wave of terror rolling through the ranks of his usually well-disciplined army. The men of the Throng had all seen the Nightmare at least once; many of them were conscripts from cities it had conquered. Even the most hardened soul could not stave off the panic for long. Fadarah imagined that some were already running while others fell to their knees, covering their eyes and ears. Fadarah wished he could follow suit.

Instead, he took a deep breath and turned in the saddle. He forced himself to look.

Through a great gap in the ranks slouched the Nightmare: a man-shaped thing twice as tall as he, but stooping on strong, twisted limbs. Black and burgundy scales covered its body, between which fire leaked like blood from open wounds. The eyes—yellow and dagger-thin—roiled with crazed malevolence.

Fadarah wanted to yank his mount to one side but resisted. The men of the Throng must not see him afraid of his own creation. With supreme effort, he gently tugged the reins, twitched his spurs, and urged his bloodmare sideways, farther and farther, until he was out of the Nightmare's path. The red horse balked and tried to move faster, but Fadarah gave no ground, maintaining a stoic demeanor as he repositioned himself in front of the northern half of his army.

Twelve Shel'ai flanked the Nightmare, all on foot, all wearing bone-white cloaks extravagantly sewn with crimson greatwolves. Fadarah made no motion to the twelve as they passed, nor they to him. To do so would have been disastrous. Controlling the Nightmare required their keenest concentration. If the twelve lost their focus, the Nightmare would free itself. It would incinerate not just Syros but the army in front of it, including the Shel'ai who had once been its friends. Fadarah tried to gaze upon the monstrosity shambling forward at the center of the twelve's broad circle but quickly wrenched his eyes away, sickened. *Iventine chose this. No one forced him, least of all me.*

As the Nightmare continued toward Syros, yoked by its Shel'ai handlers, Fadarah thought of the others: brave souls who, like Iventine, had voluntarily subjected themselves to the awful power hidden in the vaults of Cadavash, letting it mingle with the abilities they already had, turning them into Dragonkin. All slumbered in a separate camp, overseen by more Shel'ai whose job was not so much to guard the initiates but to make sure they did not wake in a delirium and turn everything in the vicinity to ash.

Fadarah shuddered. He prayed the other initiates—potential Nightmares in their own right—would never be needed. Then he wrested his attention back to the matters at hand. To prevent widespread panic and desertions, the rest of the Shel'ai commanded individual battalions throughout the host. The sight of the imposing sorcerers in bone-white cloaks usually squelched any rebellion before it started.

Still, only so much could be done about the horses. Thanks to Fadarah's magic, his bloodmare anxiously pawed the ground but did not bolt. Others were not so lucky. Steel spurs vainly raked the flanks of countless rounceys, drawing blood to no avail. Within moments, five broad, orderly rows of armored horsemen wavered like wheat in a harvest wind. Horses reared, casting scores of men to the ground. Other horses galloped off, hauling their hapless riders with them.

Fadarah glanced at Syros. Were the city's defenders emboldened by the sight of such upheaval? *Probably not, since Syros is the Nightmare's target.*

"Hold the line!" He drew his sword—an impressive two-hander, big enough for an Olg—and waved it high for emphasis. "Captains, stand by your battalions! Prepare to attack!" Then, shaking, he turned his full attention to the Nightmare.

The circle of Shel'ai had drawn their monstrosity to a halt, just beyond the range of Syros's famous archers. Those Shel'ai in front of the Nightmare withdrew, and the twelve formed a single row behind it. The Nightmare's ragged, wheezing breath filled the air, scalding it with heat as from a blacksmith's bellows. The beast faced the sunlit city. The harsh breathing grew louder, resounding with some awful sense of anticipation, like an attack dog anxious to slip its leash. For a long time, nothing moved. Then, Fadarah gave the order. The Shel'ai released their mental control. The leash came off.

Cries of panic spread across the high stone walls of Syros. Some of the city's defenders fled and dropped their weapons, abandoning their posts. Others found their courage and leapt into action. The Nightmare closed to within bow-range. Along the granite walls, hundreds of bowstrings shuddered. A broad, dark cloud rose against the sun.

The cloud bristled with enough arrows to shred an entire battalion of horsemen. Yet not one of them hit its mark. Hundreds of wooden shafts burst to cinders just before they might have struck, ignited by the intense heat rising in waves off the Nightmare's body.

Barreling through a blizzard of ash, the Nightmare continued its charge.

Syros's archers admirably managed three more volleys, but even their final, closest volley burst to cinders. Then, they did something even Fadarah had not anticipated.

All along the walls, men tipped great, sloshing cauldrons over the battlements. Water fell in fast, clear braids, flooding the plains at the base of the walls, transforming the earth into a swamp.

Fadarah smiled. "Clever," he admitted grudgingly.

The Nightmare hurtled forward. Its burning body met water, and steam rose in thick, gray clouds. For a moment, fog swallowed the high walls of Syros. Even the flaming Nightmare momentarily vanished in the hissing mist.

Fadarah heard cries of alarm, different from what he had heard before, and tensed. He used his magic to heighten his senses and extended his mind into the ranks behind him. He saw the problem right away. None of the conquered cities had ever tried this tactic before. The soldiers of the Throng feared it might work. With the Nightmare gone, they might have to fight with the sun in their eyes after all.

Then they heard the sounds. They echoed across the Simurgh Plains. Screams. The crack of ancient granite. The great shudder caused by tons of stone tumbling to earth. Then more screams.

Gods forgive us. Although the fog blocked Fadarah's sight, he could guess what was happening. He thrust his two-handed sword toward the sky. Sunrise flashed down its steely face like blood.

"The walls are breached! Syros has fallen!" He pointed his blade at the city. "Follow me!"

Raw exhilaration flooded his body. He led the charge himself. The army hesitated only a moment then roared to life and streamed after him. Cavalry, pikemen, archers. Shel'ai. All followed the Sorcerer-General as he rode toward the fog-shrouded city. Then the mist parted.

Syros's entire central wall was gone. Broken, blasted stones littered the plains. The gates had been reduced to puddles of wet ash. Dead men scattered the earth: archers, men-at-arms, Syros's reserves. Horns blared frantic declarations of surrender from the sections of wall left intact. No one had the heart to fight. Left with no option, armed men threw down their swords and surrendered, half expecting the Throng to cut them down anyway.

They didn't.

With the Nightmare gone—vanished—and the walls breached, Fadarah's soldiers greeted the survivors with pity. Throng captains sheathed their weapons and coordinated efforts to aid the injured, to prevent widespread rape and murder. They did not do this out of some rare inclination toward compassion; they were simply following Fadarah's orders.

Fadarah himself took no part in this. Instead, he watched as the twelve Shel'ai emerged, exhausted, from the ruins and fog. Dust and blood stained their bone-white cloaks, but their hoods were still drawn closed. It would not do for Humans to see the expression on their faces. But the men of the Throng were too busy looting or tending to injured, shocked prisoners to pay much attention to the twelve Shel'ai. So no Human saw what Fadarah saw: a thirteenth cloaked figure slumped amid the others, supported on each arm by one of the twelve. *Iventine...*

"Take him back to the camp. Hide him. Let me know if his condition worsens."

The other Shel'ai nodded, too tired to speak. As they passed, Fadarah caught a brief glimpse of Iventine's face. Ghastly, sunken cheeks. Wild, blood-shot eyes. He turned away.

By the time the Sorcerer-General retired to his tent, the sun was setting. He had sheathed his greatsword, for he no longer had the strength to hold it, but he took care to stand upright and breathe easily before his Human servants. He calmly accepted a goblet of cool wine then dispassionately ordered them away. When they were gone, he slumped into a chair. The ominous armor that made him look so imposing weighed him down incredibly, much too heavy for a Sylv.

But I am not a Sylv. They made that clear. He touched the tapered points of his ears. Then he attacked the complicated lattice of straps and buckles holding his armor in place, casting it piece by piece to the ground. This morning, he had watched in the mirror as his servants helped him don his plate mail: breast and backplates, pauldrons, gauntlets, greaves, and other pieces he could not name. The mirror had been left in place. Fadarah used it and removed the armor by himself. Doing so took a long time, but with each piece that fell, relief flooded his limbs. Half done, Fadarah flexed his fingers and massaged one sore shoulder. Then he studied his reflection. The Sorcerer-General's expression turned bitter.

The same blue tattoos that covered Fadarah's face and hands also covered the rest of his body, which was thickly muscled, as his father's must have been.

My father. Fadarah grinned sardonically.

His mother had been Wyldkin, one of those few renegade Sylv who lived beyond the majestic forests surrounding the World Tree— not because they were forced to, like those born with the dragonmist, but because they *wanted* to. She and her husband made their home somewhere between Sylvos and the land of the Olgrym. What exactly happened next, Fadarah did not know. But he could guess.

Wyldkin often ran from Olgrym, but sometimes they were caught anyway. The Olgrym must have slaughtered his mother's husband. Fadarah imagined them torturing him before devouring him raw. But that was nothing compared to what they did to his mother.

Fadarah shuddered. The Sylvs still told stories of female Wyldkin who kept small knives sheathed on the inside of a thigh—not for fighting but for slitting their own throats if the only other option was being taken prisoner by Olgrym. Fadarah did not know if his mother had carried such a knife, but he often thought that if she had, she should have used it.

True, he barely remembered her, but his mother must have been strong. She'd survived the Olgrym, hadn't she? She even escaped and returned to the Sylvs. There she gave birth—not to the child of her husband, the Sylvan baby she must have prayed was growing inside her—but to a brute. A half-Olg. Worse, he had the dragonmist in his eyes!

An abomination on two fronts.

Fadarah shook his head. His mother might have killed him to spare her own disgrace; she didn't. They lived in Sylvos instead, alongside the Sylvs. But even as a child, Fadarah sensed their suspicion. Their hatred. He sensed how it all must end.

Fadarah winced. He shook himself and then drew his sword. A fine length of exquisite kingsteel, fixed to a handle wrought of dragonbone. Many times, Fadarah had considered falling on it, just to end his torment. But that time, he quickly cast the sword aside. He knew he could not do that. His people needed him. Not the Sylvs, not the Olgrym, but the Shel'ai.

"My... people."

Fadarah laughed. He laughed for a long time. Then he wept. He pressed one hand to his mouth, not wanting anyone to hear. Still, his tattooed body jerked as though he were being stabbed.

CHAPTER ONE
THE EXILE

"MY NAME'S DAGATH." THE ROBBER grinned.

Rowen blinked away the blood dripping down half his face and met the robber's gaze. The wound was still too fresh to hurt, but his senses reeled. The robber towered over him, a big man with rotten teeth. He wore mismatched leather armor that he'd probably taken off previous victims, most of which looked too small and also cracked from poor upkeep, the buckles rusted through. Most striking was the fact that the robber was missing an eye but had not even bothered to cover the scarred socket with a patch.

Dagath paused, clearly amused by the look on Rowen's face. "Men ought to know the name of the man who's going to kill them. I'd ask yours, but I don't really give a damn." He gave his cudgel a few menacing practice swings. "You ready to go to the gods, boy?"

Rowen had struggled back onto his feet but could do little more. The blow to his head had caught him completely by surprise, stunning him long enough for a second, smaller robber to bind Rowen's hands behind his back. Rowen might have fought with his feet—on the Lotus Isles, he'd been taught to kick as well as punch—but it took all his willpower just to hold onto consciousness.

Breaking Dagath's gaze, Rowen looked around and spotted his shortsword lying nearby: a plain but elegant weapon with a waisted, Ivairian-style blade, all Rowen had left from his old life. Dagath scooped it up and whistled.

"Not bad. Probably sell for a nice price in one of the cities. Me, I prefer a good club." Dagath stabbed the shortsword into the earth and stepped so close that Rowen could smell the stink of the man's breath, like rotten meat bathed in sour milk. Rowen's eyes fell on his attacker's cudgel again.

But the robber did not strike, clearly content to enjoy the moment. He jabbed the tip of his cudgel into Rowen's chin and pushed his head to eye level. "What, no clever last words? No bribes?" He looked past Rowen at the second robber, still standing behind him. "This is a first!"

"Whatever coins I've got, I imagine you'll get soon enough," Rowen said, seething. "You've already got my sword. Besides that, all I've got left is in my pack. Go have a look."

Rowen nodded toward his satchel, which he'd dropped the moment he saw the small man lying on the road, feigning injury. Rowen had seen that trick before: a robber called for help, waited until some hapless traveler got close, then stuck a knife in his throat and took what he wanted. Rowen had been ready for that. But in his overconfidence, he had not seen Dagath sneaking up behind him.

Dagath turned, reflexively eyeing the pack. Gathering what strength he had left, Rowen pitched forward and drove his knee toward the robber's groin. With a look of only mild surprise, Dagath twisted and took the blow on his hip instead. Then he swung his cudgel into Rowen's knee.

Rowen bit his lip to keep from screaming and fell back down.

He wondered if he would lose consciousness after all. *Might be better that way.* But then he cursed and fought back the darkness nipping at his vision. Dagath upended the satchel onto the ground. Small Man, confident that Rowen was going nowhere, hurried forward to inspect the goods. Both looked disappointed.

Aside from a few articles of clothing, the satchel contained little more than a whetstone, sword-oil, a nearly empty waterskin, a rolled up scrap of parchment, his coin pouch, and two books. Dagath snatched up the coin pouch, yanked it open, and shook out its contents. He gave Rowen a withering look when only three copper coins tumbled out.

"This it, boy?" He threw them on the ground and used his cudgel to poke through the rest of Rowen's possessions.

Small Man retrieved the coins and inspected them. "I think these are Isle coins," he said quietly, holding up one to the afternoon light and inspecting the seal. "Looks like some kind of bird balancing on one foot."

A crane. Rowen kept silent. He had managed to roll onto his side, to keep the weight off his knee. Rowen's instincts had saved him, allowing him to pivot at the last second. He did not think Dagath's blow had smashed his kneecap, though the pain was making his eyes water.

Dagath frowned and snatched the coin from Small Man's grasp, inspecting it for himself. "You don't have to be an Isleman to have Isle coins, you dunce! They use 'em all over these days." He started to discard the copper coin then changed his mind and pocketed it instead.

"Or maybe he's an Isle Knight," Small Man offered. "Might be one giant ransom if he is!"

Dagath gave his accomplice so cold a look that, for a moment, Rowen wondered if Small Man's suggestion would be answered by Dagath's cudgel. Dagath pointed. "Does *that* look like an Isle Knight to you?" Before Small Man could answer, Dagath returned to where Rowen was still lying in pain. He prodded him with his cudgel. "Well, speak up, boy. You a Knight?"

Rowen's face turned almost the same color as the blood drying around his gashed forehead. "I'm no Knight. Never even been to the Isles." Shame surged through him, but he masked it with anger. "Get on with it. Either kill me or leave me, you bastard."

But Dagath's good eye sparkled. "You're lying." He went back to Rowen's goods and retrieved one of the books. He opened one then laughed coldly. "I can't read, but I know Lotus Isle scribbles when I see them." He threw the book to his accomplice. "You're too grubby to be a Knight, and you're too pale to be a native Isleman." He paused, sneering. "Know what I think?"

Rowen started to close his eyes then stopped himself, trying to meet Dagath's gaze without emotion. He offered no reply.

Nevertheless, Dagath laughed. He turned to his accomplice. "Know what we have here, Sneed? Another exile." He flashed Rowen another toothy, rotten grin. Sneed nodded, but Dagath explained anyway.

Just to taunt me... and gods know I deserve it!

"You see, once in a while, some dumb bastard gets it in his head to sail off to the Lotus Isles and be a Knight. Only they don't take kindly to mainlanders—so if you want to train, you have to pay. A lot." Dagath pretended to be lost in thought. "I bet this one was a sellsword... probably spent *years* saving up the coin!" He laughed again. "They took his money. Then, once they were tired of him, they kicked him out." He grabbed a handful of Rowen's unruly red hair, jerking up so Rowen was looking at him. "Am I right?"

Rowen said nothing. Dagath chuckled and returned to Sneed, who had retrieved the second book as well and was busy leafing through them.

"What are they?" Dagath asked him.

"Can't read more than a few words, but this one looks like a whole big list of rules." Sneed handed the thicker volume back to Dagath, who merely glanced at it then tossed it aside. "This *other* one"—Sneed half-smiled—"looks like poetry." He opened a page and held it up. "Pretty pictures, too. Colored ink. There's a handsome one of a dragon in here somewhere..." He started leafing through the pages again.

"They worth anything?"

Sneed shrugged. "Probably some priest in Lyos would buy them—or some rich ambassador from the Isles, if we can find one." He paused to think it over. "I bet each one's worth at least as much as that sword of his!"

Rowen recalled how, on the Isles, illustrated copies of the Codex Lotius could be bought from almost any street vendor for a few copper coins. As for the Codex Viticus, that arduous tome had been forced on him almost as soon as he arrived at Saikaido Temple. Rowen would be glad to be rid of it. *If I survive, that is.*

At the mention of Rowen's shortsword, Dagath had gone and retrieved it with his free hand. By then, the failed squire had sat up, straining vainly against his bonds.

"Don't bother. Sneed's not worth much, but at least he can

tie a decent knot." His smile looked almost genuine. "Almost feel like I should thank you, boy. Any last words? Maybe a plea to the Dragongod?"

Rowen had already tried to stand and failed, but he knew he had to try again. His mind scrambled for some kind of diversion. Then an idea formed. Though it was ludicrous, he had no choice.

"My father's a blacksmith in Harso, not far from here," he lied. "He's not rich, mind you, but he's got a few coins to rub together. *He was the one who paid for my training.* Gods know what he'll say when he finds out I got kicked out!" Rowen forced a smile. "Anyway, if it's ransom you're after, take me there."

Dagath scowled, clearly trying to decide if his captive was telling the truth. Thanks to years of training on the Isles, Rowen had the arms of a blacksmith, though everything else about him—unkempt hair, plain clothes, the fact that he was traveling alone—more closely resembled a sellsword. Dagath glanced down, studying Rowen's shortsword again. Though unadorned, the crossguard was brass, the blade high quality.

Kayden gave me that... The thought of his dead brother made Rowen wince, but he hoped Dagath mistook his grief for fear.

"He could be telling the truth," Sneed offered.

"Or he could be stalling, hoping he can get away—or wait us out until somebody comes along and rescues him." Dagath lifted the hand holding Rowen's shortsword and used one dirty thumbnail to scratch at his scarred eye socket. "That it, boy? You think some armored knight's gonna thunder in and save you?"

"No," Rowen said and meant it. He knew as well as his captors that they were too far from the coast, where they might be chanced upon by a patrol of Isle Knights. Lyos was still the closest of the Free Cities, but wanting to be left alone, Rowen had chosen to travel there via the most deserted road—a decision he was deeply regretting.

Dagath looked down at Rowen's shortsword again then glanced back at the books, visibly weighing the odds, trying to decide if he should be content with his already-impressive haul or push his luck and hope that Rowen himself could be ransomed.

This one's cruel, not stupid, Rowen realized. *He knows if he takes a ransom note to a town—whether I'm lying or not—he might wind up dead. Better he sticks with what he already has.*

But greed won out. "Fine, we'll try it your way. If you're telling it true, maybe you'll even have to keep the gods waiting awhile." Dagath lowered his weapons. "Sneed can write some, but it's best the note's in your scribbles. You know letters?"

Rowen nodded. "I can write."

Dagath smirked. "Figures." He gestured with his cudgel at Rowen's meager pile of possessions. "I don't want to tear up them books. Sneed, I saw parchment there. Bring it."

Rowen restrained a curse when he realized the scrap of parchment that Dagath was referring to. He wanted to argue but thought better of it. Sneed brought the scrap. He gave Rowen a faint, nearly reassuring smile as he handed the ancient-looking parchment to Dagath. *This one's different. He's a robber, sure, but not quite a cutthroat.*

Dagath kicked his injured knee to catch his attention. Rowen swore. Dagath said, "Scribble your father, tell him he pays twenty silvers or else he'll have to bury you in pieces."

Rowen knew better than to accept too quickly. "Twenty silvers is a lot. I told you, he's poor—"

"And I'm pretty. What of it? Every town needs a blacksmith. The villagers can pass around a gods-damned collection bowl if they need to."

"How will you get the letter to him?"

Dagath shrugged. "Sneed can take it."

Rowen saw his opportunity. "Then Sneed will bring the coin back himself?"

Dagath's expression changed. Rowen swallowed a smile. *You didn't think of that, you bastard!*

Sneed faced Dagath. "You can trust me..."

"Fohl's hells, I can!" Dagath interrupted with a snort. He fell silent. Rowen could imagine what he was thinking. If Sneed did not deliver the letter, then Dagath would have to do it. That would mean leaving Rowen in Sneed's care.

He guessed that Dagath had reached the same conclusion. "I'll take the scribble myself. Harso's not far." He turned to Sneed. "Gods hear me, if he's not here when I get back, I'll cut out your spine *and* keep your share."

Sneed's face paled. He tried to respond but stammered.

Dagath threw the parchment at Rowen's feet. He waved to Sneed again. "Untie his hands so he can write. But bind up his feet." He prodded Rowen with his own shortsword. "Guess I don't have to tell you what happens if you try anything cute."

Rowen shook his head.

Sneed bound Rowen's feet with a length of rope that Rowen had been using as a belt. Sneed's trembling hands fussed with the bonds securing his wrists. When the bonds went slack, Rowen resisted the impulse to throw an elbow at Sneed's jaw. He wouldn't get far with his legs still tied. He massaged his sore wrists then gingerly touched the gash on his forehead from Dagath's cudgel. Sneed withdrew meekly.

Dagath pointed at the parchment. "Write."

Rowen hesitated, eyeing the poor but familiar handwriting already covering one whole side of the parchment. "No ink."

Dagath frowned.

"If you start a fire, I can use the ash."

"You think I'm stupid, boy? Ash doesn't last." Dagath sneered. "Best we use blood."

Neither robber offered to bandage Rowen's slashed palm once the letter had been written. Instead, Dagath ordered Sneed to lash Rowen's wrists together again. By then, the sun was setting, bloodying the rolling hills to the west. The robbers dragged Rowen far off the road, untying his feet so they wouldn't have to carry him. They soon reached a copse of trees.

A paltry campsite indicated that the robbers must have been here before. Sneed bound Rowen's feet again. He had regained some of his strength, but the sword tip pressed to his throat dissuaded him from attempting escape. That time, they tied him with his back to a tree. Then Sneed built a fire and fixed a simple meal of porridge that smelled of burnt, mashed asparagus, none of which they shared with their captive.

Rowen tested his bonds and tried to ignore the growling in his stomach. Only three days had passed since he left the Lotus Isles, but he'd already been robbed and beaten, and his stomach was rumbling so ominously that he feared he was starving. He'd been well fed at Saikaido Temple, but once dismissed, he'd been forced to leave with only the few possessions he'd had when he arrived years before. It cost half his remaining coins to board the ship that ferried him across the Burnished Way, back to the mainland. He'd managed to buy some rations and a little lotus wine at a seaside village, but those had not lasted long. In fact, the only thing he had that remotely resembled foodstuffs was a pouch of sweetbitter leaves, chewed to keep teeth from rotting.

I should offer those to Dagath, Rowen thought spitefully.

When the highwaymen were done eating, Dagath forced Rowen to provide a detailed description of his father. *Just follow the sound of a ringing hammer,* Rowen wanted to say. He had already described the imaginary blacksmith twice, but he took care to keep the details the same. It might have been simpler to substitute a description of his true father, but Rowen barely remembered him. Still, Dagath appeared satisfied. With a final slew of threats, the burly killer set off into the night.

Despite the pain throbbing from his cut palm, Rowen had to stop himself from grinning. Since Dagath could not read, Rowen had considered detailing his subterfuge in the letter so that whoever saw it would know what kind of man Dagath was. However, he'd not wanted to risk Sneed making out enough of the letter to catch the deception, so instead, Rowen kept up the act, penning a pleading letter to a man who did not exist.

The act itself brought a pang of shame when Rowen remembered the knightly prohibition against lying for any reason. Then he reminded himself that he was not a knight. Besides, so far, lying had served him far better than his fighting prowess.

Now I just have to find a way to get out of here! The people of Harso would not come to his aid. He meant nothing to them and had only visited the town once, working as a merchant's bodyguard with his brother, though he doubted anyone would remember. *Still, I'm better off than I was before.*

He thought again of Saikaido Temple with its beautiful gardens overflowing with the sweet perfume of dogblossoms, its stores of cool lotus wine, and its extravagant tilting yard, overseen by perhaps the greatest weapons trainers in the world. *Maybe I'm not doing so well after all.*

Rowen tested his bonds again. He might saw the rope against the tree bark until he freed his hands and then easily free his legs, but he could do neither while Sneed was watching.

The small, balding man regarded him without expression, across the dwindling campfire. He sipped from a jug of wine. Rowen's fears had subsided enough to be replaced by pain. His forehead, knee, and palm filled him with dull pain, punctuated by jolts of agony when he moved, though he was certain that if he closed his eyes, he would fall asleep.

He resisted. Dagath would not return until midday if he returned at all. Sooner or later, no matter how nervous he was, Sneed was bound to fall asleep. Rowen wondered what he would do once he was free.

He was tempted to cut down Sneed then rearm himself and make for Harso—not just to reclaim his prized shortsword but to kill Dagath, if the bastard was still alive. The loss of the heirloom stung, but worse still was realization that so soon after leaving the Lotus Isles, Rowen had lost a fight to a common thug with little or no training.

Sneed's voice interrupted his grim ruminations. "That letter. Was it a trick?"

Rowen feigned surprise and shook his head.

Sneed laughed. "I'm not as dumb as I look. Maybe I don't know all my letters, but I can read faces well enough. If Dagath makes it back in one piece, you know he won't just kill you. He'll slice you into ribbons, make sure you die slow. I've seen it before."

Rowen thought the man shuddered. "You don't seem to like him much."

Sneed shrugged. "Man doesn't have to like what he does to stay alive." He took a long drink.

"How did you fall in with him?" Rowen did not especially care to hear the robber's life story, but he knew it would only help his chances of escape if he put the man at ease.

Sneed lowered the jar. "He's my half-brother." He sounded almost apologetic. "Different fathers, same whore of a mother. We're from Lyos, I guess you could say."

"The Dark Quarter?" Rowen doubted either man had been a true citizen of the wealthy city. More likely, they had grown up in the slums at the bottom of the hill. He searched his memory but did not recognize the man before him. *Then again, the Dark Quarter has more orphans and beggars than a graveyard has worms!*

Still, Sneed raised one eyebrow. "You too?" Rowen almost said yes before he remembered his lie about being from Harso. Luckily, Sneed did not seem to expect an answer. "Bad place to be a kid."

Rowen was inclined to agree. He had no interest in reliving such memories, though. "How many travelers have you robbed like this?"

Sneed winced. Rowen thought he would refuse to answer. Instead, Sneed said, "Maybe a dozen a year. Maybe more. If there's guards, we leave 'em alone. Dagath knows how to scrap, but he's not much for a fair fight." He took a longer drink of wine. "Folks from the north come down here, too. Ivairians, hair red as yours. Half-starved, unarmed. They're not much worth the trouble, but once in a while, they have some clothes or a trinket worth taking." He looked away and pretended to tend the fire. "Women and kids, too. Some of them, Dagath doesn't kill. Not right away..."

Memories of Rowen's own childhood in the slums flooded him, unbidden. He remembered hiding from the gangs with his brother, stealing to stay alive, doing whatever he could to stay out of sight of those who had no qualms about forcing certain vile acts upon boys as well as girls.

An old, raw terror sprang up inside him. It took all his willpower to keep from trying to break free of his bonds right then and there. Dimly, he remembered a passage from the Codex Lotius. *Singchai ushó fey*—no courage without fear—but the words brought no comfort.

A faint, sad smile played on Sneed's face. "It's a wretched world, ain't it?" He stabbed the fire with a knife. "So what was written on that letter? I mean, before."

24

Rowen started to lie then changed his mind. "It was a letter from my brother, telling me to come join him soon as I could."

Something in Rowen's tone made Sneed nod. "He dead?"

Rowen started to answer, but his throat constricted. He nodded instead. *I'm sorry, Kayden. I took too long.*

Sneed stabbed the fire again, as though he meant to smother the embers but then changed his mind and added another scrap of wood. "Was he a knight, too?"

Rowen tensed. "I'm not even a squire anymore, so I'm sure as hell not a knight!" He added, "But Kayden was. A good one."

Sneed stared off into the trees. "I wanted to be a knight when I was a kid. Would have been happy being a sellsword, too, I guess, but I never was much good in a fight." His expression turned eager. "If you want to teach me, maybe we can be sellswords together! I'll loosen your hands, and we can turn it on Dagath when he gets back."

Rowen tensed. He knew he only had to nod. Instead, he shook his head. "I'm done being a sellsword."

Sneed frowned and Rowen immediately regretted it. He blurted out the first thing that came to mind. "Being a knight's not all about fighting. There's reading and writing and laws, too. You have to learn them all."

Sneed took another pull of the wine jug. "Anything in those laws about playing hurt then stabbing whoever walks up to help you?" When Rowen did not answer, Sneed added his last scrap of wood to the campfire. "How'd you know it was a trick?"

Rowen was dangerously close to revealing that his story about being a blacksmith's son was a lie, though he suspected that Sneed already knew. "Kayden always said if you see a dying man, smell the air. If it don't smell like shit, he's faking."

Sneed laughed. "I'm glad I smell fresher than that, at least!" His expression sobered, and he stared out at the shadow-wrapped trees. "Here's what's bothering me, Squire. When you saw me laying there all groaning and wretched, you called out, said you weren't buying it, told me to get up and go."

Rowen nodded carefully, though he felt silly when he realized that Sneed was not looking.

"When I didn't move, you walked up and kicked me—though not half as hard as you could have, I bet. I heard you draw your sword. You missed Dagath hiding in that tree, a ways back with a green cloak over him. Still, you knew it was a trap. You could have stabbed me in the back and been done with it—only you didn't. Why?"

Rowen realized he had no answer.

Sneed nodded. "Would've made sense. Not one of the gods would have burned you for it. I'd have done it in your place. And here for all I know, we came out of those damn slums together."

He stood up—knife in one hand, wine in the other—and circled around the fire. He moved so purposefully that Rowen wondered for a moment if the robber meant to stab him.

"I figure you get this as well as anybody, Squire. Most times, you just do what you gotta to keep your blood in the right place." Sneed looked down. "Sometimes, though, you get to do what you want." He gave Rowen a final, dull look then simply walked away, vanishing into the night.

Is this a trick? Rowen wondered, too, if Sneed had only gone to fetch more firewood. But minutes passed, and the balding thief did not return.

Rowen wasted no more time. He worked his bonds against the tree, wincing when the motion sent jolts of pain through his slashed palm. At last, he broke free. His shoulders ached, but he hurried to free his legs as well. He rose shakily to his feet.

Sneed had left his satchel by the fire, but Dagath had scattered his meager possessions all over the camp. Rowen gathered them with his good hand. Without his shortsword, he had no weapons save his razor. *A pitiful weapon.*

He ripped two strips of cloth from his shirt. Since he had to do so with one hand, the cloth tore unevenly and too far, further souring his already-bedraggled appearance. But that, too, was a concern for another time. Rowen tied one strip of cloth around his palm as a bandage. Then he chose a suitable branch from the fire, wrapped the second strip of cloth at one end, and fashioned a makeshift torch. Though better than nothing, it still smoldered more than it burned.

He finished gathering his belongings, snatching up the Codex

Lotius and sliding it into his satchel. He glanced at the other volume—the one full of laws to which he was no longer bound—but left it where it lay. Then, heading away from both Dagath and Sneed, he hurried off through the trees into the night.

CHAPTER TWO

RUMORS OF WAR

ROWEN WALKED THROUGHOUT THE NIGHT, doubtful that Dagath would return so soon but unwilling to face the big man without a suitable weapon. He abandoned his torch when the fire burned almost down to his hand. Supposedly, the Shel'ai's strange, magical wytchfire burned without consuming fuel. *That would come in handy now.*

He remembered his brass-hilted shortsword—all he had left of Kayden—and considered circling back and trying to regain it. He trusted his fighting skills were a match for Dagath's, though his instincts had already failed him once. *Besides, I'm in no shape for a fight.*

Muttering a stream of curses, he continued on. Without his paltry torch, the way was slow going since Rowen had no desire to take a false step in the darkness and break his leg. Blue-black clouds veiled the stars and a sliver of moon. Even the starry swirl that was Armahg's Eye barely lit the outlines of trees and thickets, all of which roiled with shadows and convinced him that he was about to be confronted by everything from robbers to greatwolves.

So the sight of dawn cresting the broad, uninhabited hills of the Simurgh Plains brought a sense of relief, despite his exhaustion. Then he stopped and began cursing again. He had traveled mostly blind, hoping he was still heading in the general direction of Lyos. But he had gone farther east than he intended. In fact, he could faintly see the Burnished Way in the distance—a sun-washed span of amethyst water covered in plumes of fog.

Gods, I'm almost back where I started three days ago... and I don't even have my damn sword anymore! He shook his head. He wanted to set off at once, but he couldn't maintain that pace any longer. So he found a tree, put his back to it, and slept.

He had not slept long before hunger woke him. He searched his satchel but remembered that Dagath and Sneed had eaten what was left of his rations. Rowen scoured the area but saw no fruit trees, not even a stream from which to try and draw a fish, as he had days earlier. He pressed on and spotted a few urusks. Though they were the size of boars, the creatures were slow and docile, using their long snouts to root in the ground for insects. Rowen grimaced. He had practically lived off urusk meat in the Dark Quarter and had not forgotten its sour, acrid taste. *I'm not quite desperate enough for that. Not yet.*

He wished he had a bow. Few deer but plenty of wolves roamed these parts. He might fashion a crude spear or another torch to keep regular wolves at bay, but their greatwolf cousins would not be so easily dissuaded.

He considered a different danger. While the gash on his forehead had come from the blunt force of Dagath's cudgel, his wounded hand was another matter. He peeled back the strip of cloth he had used to bandage his sliced palm and grimaced at the swollen, bruised flesh. Despite his thirst, he used what little water remained in his waterskin to rinse his hand, cursing himself for not doing so earlier.

Gods, give me a fever if you have to, but don't make me have to cut off my own hand. He wondered how he would do so, without a sword. He remembered his razor, shuddered, and hurried on. Who could help him? The clerics of the goddess, Tier'Gothma, were renowned for their ability to treat wounds, but he was unlikely to find any in the few villages between here and Lyos. Besides, most required coin in exchange for their services.

Gods, is this how it ends? Dying either from fever or blood loss, alone on the plains—

He prayed for a stream where he might sate his thirst and more thoroughly wash his hand and rinse his blood-matted red hair, but the prayer went unanswered. Before long, the sun crisped the back of his neck. His steps faltered. He obsessively checked and rechecked his maimed hand. The skin was still purple—not yellow—but his fingers felt stiff and hurt terribly when he forced himself to flex them.

Rowen walked and walked until he came upon a farm. The place was far from impressive, consisting of little more than a small field and a lackluster mud hut. He was surprised to see men tending crops so late in the season but then realized that they must be harvesting paupers' root, as many poor people did. The nutritious stuff could be grown even in winter, though like urusk meat, the taste left much to be desired. "Like grain passed through the bowels of the gods," his brother used to say.

But they'll have water, at least. Rowen forced a friendly smile and waved to them. They tensed at his approach. The farmer and two boys who must have been his sons produced crude bows and spears.

"I mean you no harm," Rowen called out. "I'm not a robber, and I don't have the plague. I just want water, maybe some food. No charity. As the gods are my witness, I'll work for it—"

"Move on!" the farmer called.

Rowen caught an Ivairian accent in the man's voice. Maybe this family had abandoned their famine-ridden country for the Simurgh Plains, just as Rowen's family had so long ago.

"I only want some water," Rowen called back. "I'm hurt. I just need to clean my wound." He added, "I'm Ivairian... if that matters."

The farmer shouted again. One of the sons joined in, yelling a stream of curses Rowen could not understand through the accent. Rowen switched from Common to Ivairian Tongue, hoping to charm them with their native language, but they would hear none of it. When one of the farmer's sons fired an arrow into the dirt near Rowen's feet, its shaft quivering in the afternoon sun, he retreated.

Rowen weighed his options. He had spotted a little muddy stream behind the farmer's shack. He had no desire to creep up like a thief and risk his life for a mere drink of water, but circumstances left him no choice.

Rowen hid behind a line of yew trees, stomach growling, then made his way back to the farm. He chose an approach lined by low hills and mossy rocks and crawled on his hands and knees to keep out of sight. He risked a quick glance. The farmer and his sons were in the field again, though they stopped often and looked around. To his relief, they were looking in the wrong direction. Rowen kept crawling. He tried to favor his maimed hand, turning it so that the pebbles would not grind into his cut, but his eyes still watered from the pain. Dirt and mud caked his clothes. Finally, he reached the stream.

All shame momentarily vanished as he dipped his hands in the cool water. He drank greedily then washed his maimed hand as best he could. He rinsed his face next, working his fingers through his matted hair. Then he moved farther upstream and refilled his waterskin, half-expecting to feel an arrow in his back at any moment. He delayed leaving to try to rinse some of the grime from his arms and clothing, too.

Rowen shuddered. Staring back at him from the water was not the proud, aloof visage of a knight, nor even that of a squire, but a penniless, orphaned sellsword. Bitterly, he recalled a line from a Shao poem: *What madness, to become only what I had forsaken.*

He heard a cry of alarm. Almost grateful, he got up and ran. As he passed the edge of the field, he grabbed a stalk of ripened paupers' root and tugged it after him. Dirt flew, releasing the foot-long, twisted root into his grasp. Rowen heard the sound of an arrow whistling through the air and kept running, even after he was well out of bow range.

Late in the afternoon, Rowen came across a dead stag, rotting on the plains. The fantastic slashes in its hide told him that the deed had been done by greatwolves. He looked around but saw nothing. The meat was too rotten to eat, of course, and the stench was such that he had to cover his nose. Still, he lingered. He wished the dead animal were an urusk instead of a stag. Properly treated, urusks' backbones could be made into good—if gruesome—longbows. Then Rowen had another idea.

Well, it's better than nothing. Braving the smell and flies, he seized the decaying corpse by the antlers and, with great difficulty, managed to break off a formidable length of bone. Tearing another strip of cloth from his already tattered clothing, he wrapped one end to fashion a sort of handle.

His efforts to break off a bit of antler had left its head lying at a horrible angle, mouth agape. Rowen nudged it with his foot to straighten it. Rowen remembered the Shao custom, so favored by many of the Isle Knights, to offer a brief prayer of thanks to the spirit of any beast they harvested. He started to speak the words but then stopped himself.

"I'm not even a squire anymore," he reminded himself as he went on his way.

Rowen's fortunes took another upturn when, soon after leaving the stag's corpse, he reached a grove of fig trees. He had barely managed to keep down the bit of paupers' root, having no fire or spices to make it more palatable, so the figs were as welcome a sight as any Rowen could remember.

He ate savagely, filling his belly then harvesting the remaining figs into his satchel. Wild mushrooms grew at the base of the trees. Ignoring the mushrooms, he stopped to rest. He felt a little better. He had no coins or steel, but he had food enough to get him to Lyos. There, he might—

Might what? Rowen had no desire to go back to being a sellsword, but even if he did, in his current state, who would hire him? He considered finding a graveyard and robbing the dead, in the hopes that one of the corpses might be a sellsword buried with coins or patchwork armor, but the thought filled him with revulsion.

Besides, I doubt there's a single unlooted grave left anywhere. He was tempted again to turn around and go after Dagath—if the highwayman was still alive—but he remembered his reflection in the stream, and his anger slacked.

Better I just make for Lyos and put all this behind me. But how? One greatwolf, or another run-in with highwaymen, and I'm a dead man.

Then he remembered the cave. "Jinn's name," he swore, "could it still be there?"

Like most sellswords, Kayden and he had had no reliable place to stash their meager income. Most of what they earned went to food and drink and the occasional prostitute, or better weapons and clothes when they could afford it. From time to time, though, they had stashed whatever castoff possessions they could not sell in caves, knowing they could reclaim them if their fortunes took a turn for the worse. Provided no one else found them first, that is. One such cave was not far from here, near the town of Breccorry.

The goods stashed therein had hardly been worth preserving at the time: a few patchwork shirts and britches plus a small knife, a spearhead, and a shortsword flecked with rust. But that was then. Rowen caught his breath, remembering the handful of copper coins Kayden had stashed along with the clothes and weapons. What at the time had been just a fraction of their wages currently seemed like a fortune!

Rowen set out with newfound purpose. He checked the sun's position, calculating that he might be there by sundown if he hurried. He soon spotted another farm in the distance, this one no more impressive than the last. This time, though, he gave the place a wide berth and continued on without being spotted.

He stopped once to rest, draining most of his waterskin and forcing down more of the overripe figs, the latter of which did not taste quite so appealing since he no longer felt as though he was dying. Then, a while later, the grassy plains gave way to stray boulders. His pace quickened.

More and more boulders rose out of the earth, some as big as the mud hut he had seen earlier that day. It had been years, but Rowen found his bearings. One of the boulders, bigger than the rest, was concave on one side, as though some great giant had scooped out half its innards. He recognized it at once. Then he stopped in his tracks.

Faint tendrils of smoke rose from behind the boulder.

Rowen took a deep breath to steady himself. He must have been even more discombobulated than he thought, not to have already anticipated this. The cave was no secret. He and Kayden had sought shelter there before while in the company of other mercenaries, and other travelers had probably discovered it on their own. Still, Rowen doubted anyone would be able to find what his brother had left behind. *Kayden was always good at burying things.*

33

Rowen hesitated, weighing the possibility that he knew the cave's inhabitant. He had made enemies as well as friends in those days. He considered abandoning the notion of retrieving his old possessions and just heading for Lyos after all, but he decided against it. Between robbery, injury, and the shame he'd felt at the farm, he was tired of running.

Rowen cleared his throat and approached slowly. He even paused once to kick a few loose rocks with a loud clatter. When no one appeared to challenge him, he called out. "Hello! No need to spear me, friend. I'm not a robber or a demon. Just some cold, starving bastard who's lonely enough to think a cave would be good company."

He hoped that would earn a laugh, but no one answered. Rowen held his crude knife with one hand but kept it low, out of sight. He circled around and found the stranger's camp.

As he'd thought, a fire was burning. The warmth eased the autumn chill, as though inviting him to sit. Over the fire had been erected a spit on which a rabbit was cooking. Rowen's stomach growled. He squelched the impulse to wrench the half-cooked animal off the spit and devour it then and there. Instead, he looked around. No horse, but just inside the crude cave, he spotted a simple bedroll and a couple of satchels. Otherwise, the camp appeared to be abandoned.

Rowen saw something glint between the satchels. He stepped closer then whistled in disbelief at the source of the gleam: an enormous long-axe, its curved shaft carved of oak adorned with extravagant scrollwork, its blade bright and clearly well tended.

Rowen stared a moment longer, grinning, then straightened. He did not turn around. "Jalist?"

"Right behind you, jackass," a voice said.

"Figured as much."

Rowen turned slowly. He faced a barrel-chested man who, though a good foot shorter, sported arms nearly as thick as Rowen's legs. The man's skin had an odd, gray tinge to it, as though permanently veiled by shadow. His dark, nearly black eyes ranged over Rowen. He grasped a curious sword. Its blade was short but wide and heavy to make good use of the man's unusual strength. *Even if I had armor on, I bet he could shove that blade clean through my ribcage.*

34

"Jalist Hewn. Well met."

"Rowen Locke," the man answered, unsmiling.

"Since when were Dwarr so damn stealthy?"

Jalist ignored the jibe and eyed the crude knife in Rowen's hand. "You want to drop that bit of bone, or should I cut it out of your hand?"

Rowen slid the antler-knife into his belt instead. "Better?"

"It'll do," Jalist answered gruffly. The heavy shortsword came down. "Any chance you brought that bag of coins you owe me?"

"I'm afraid not."

Jalist grunted. "Didn't think so. I suppose you want to share my fire, though."

"So long as you stay on your side."

This time, Jalist half-smiled. "Don't worry, Locke. I like men, not boys." He gestured toward the fire, and Rowen sat.

"I'm glad it's you here and not Thass." Rowen smiled. "Or Will. He always stunk up the place."

Jalist sat opposite him at the fire. "And now he's stinking up the earth. Back of his head met a broadsword—some alley up in Phaegos about a year ago."

Rowen's smile vanished. "And Thass?"

"Gone south, I think. Said he was done with fighting. Didn't help that he lost half his right arm to infection." Jalist studied him, frowning. "What about you? Looks like you went back to living off paupers' root and burnt urusk. I thought you were saving up to follow your brother to the Isles!"

When Rowen did not answer, Jalist read his expression and grunted. "Looks like you had some trouble on the road."

"I thought I'd gotten better at watching my back. Apparently, the opposite's true."

Jalist shook his head. "You better not have gotten soft, Locke. You won't live long that way. Not these days."

Rowen bristled but then shrugged. The Dwarr sellsword had a point. "Things seem worse now. I was only gone a few years, but—"

"A lot's happened." Jalist turned the rabbit on its spit. The meat hissed and crackled. Rowen's stomach growled again. "Lots more sickness up north. Plagues here and there—especially last winter. Too many refugees, not enough food."

Rowen thought he should feel pity for his countrymen, but he had not been in Ivairia since he was a baby, when his family was still alive. "I heard about that on the Isles."

"Well, I'll wager you haven't heard the worst of it! Those Sylvs, the ones who can throw magic—"

"Shel'ai," Rowen said.

"Them. They've raised an army of some kind. Stories say they've got some kind of demon squatting with them. The Nightmare, they call it. They've overrun half the Free Cities so far. Everybody says they're going after Lyos, sooner or later. Looks like they mean to take all the Simurgh Plains!"

Rowen frowned. He'd heard that too, but he had a hard time believing such a thing, especially with the Dhargoth Peninsula just northwest of the Simurgh Plains. The Dhargots boasted an army as formidable as any on Ruun. Any force that disrupted the loose confederation of the Free Cities would have to brace for a potential invasion from the Dhargoth Empire.

Jalist said, "I know what you're thinking. But these sorcerers are mad for a fight. Sylvs, the Free Cities... seems like they want to take on the whole continent at once!"

Rowen smirked. "They say the Dhargots tried that once, too. Even with their war elephants, they didn't get far once the Free Cities banded together."

Jalist grunted. "Well, from what I hear, a few of those same cities are rubble now. Something's coming, Locke. Not like those little skirmishes we used to get hired into. Something bigger. I feel it in my bones."

Rowen shrugged. "Fair enough. What's your plan, then?"

"To get my short ass on the right side while there's still time. *That's* my plan!" Jalist turned the rabbit again. "I hear the sorcerers are hiring sellswords by the dozen. Pay sounds better than anything we ever made. I'm heading west to check it out." He scowled. "If you've got more brains than I recall, you'll come along."

Rowen considered the offer. It made sense. Still, he found himself shaking his head. "I'm done with that."

36

Jalist's scowl deepened. "What, being a mercenary? Honor is for the well fed, Locke. It's either this or go back to making a few coppers guarding some merchant who's just as likely to try and cheat you." When Rowen did not answer, Jalist said, "Well, it's your life to waste."

He plucked the rabbit from the fire then, almost as an afterthought, tore off a huge portion and offered it to Rowen, who accepted at once. Jalist watched Rowen devour his portion. The Dwarr laughed. "Gods, you're a sight!" He offered Rowen a wineskin. Rowen accepted with even greater enthusiasm, pleased to find that the Dwarr's taste in wine had not waned over the years.

They ate and drank in silence. Rowen considered mentioning the possessions he and his brother had stashed within the cave but then thought better of it. Jalist might not be a robber, but he had already been generous and might reasonably lay claim to whatever Rowen uncovered. *Besides, I still owe him a bag of coins from that drinking contest.*

Rowen warned Jalist about Dagath, in case the Dwarr was heading in that direction, but Jalist answered with a look of disgust. "That's an old trick, Locke. Can't believe you fell for it. But if I run into the bastard, I'll gut him and get your sword back—for a price."

When they had finished eating, Jalist offered to examine Rowen's maimed hand. The Dwarr produced a salve that soothed the sting and, he assured, would keep him from getting blood sickness. Jalist finished treating the wound then wrapped it in a fresh, clean cloth. "Should be fine in a couple days," he grumbled.

"I suppose I owe you for this, too," Rowen joked.

Jalist grunted but did not answer. The Dwarr wrapped himself in a cloak and lay down next to the smoldering fire, one strong hand resting on his long-axe. Within moments, the Dwarr was snoring. Rowen shook his head, still weighing the Dwarr's offer in his mind, then eventually fell asleep himself.

Rowen woke at dawn, but Jalist was already gone.

He spotted a shortsword lying on the ground nearby. He stretched then stood and went to examine the weapon. Though plain and rust-flecked, it was an adequate weapon—obviously a spare Jalist had left behind. Beside the shortsword lay three copper coins. A message had been scratched into the dirt in Common Tongue: "Good luck you damn fool."

Rowen smiled, more than a little surprised. He scooped up the coins, put them in his pocket, and examined the shortsword again. Though a far cry from what he'd lost to Dagath, the weapon was still a vast improvement over his crude antler-knife.

Rowen ducked inside the cave. He felt around in the darkness for a certain rock—a jagged bit of sandstone carved with a crude image of a wolf—then rolled it aside. He shoved dirt aside with his crude dagger, figuring he may as well utilize it for something before he threw it away. As he worked, he felt guilty for keeping his secret—especially since Jalist had left him weapons and three copper coins—but he forgot all that when his fingers touched fabric. Barely containing his excitement, he hauled up a thick wad of dirty cloth that turned out to be a few articles of clothing. Beneath them, still buried in the earth, he found five more copper coins—all cranáfi of the Lotus Isles—and the weapons he had been searching for.

The weapons disappointed him, though. Though wrapped in urusk skin, years of water had seeped in, and the knife, shortsword, and spearhead were all rusted through. Crestfallen, Rowen considered taking them anyway but then thought better of it and left them on the ground at the mouth of the cave. If someone wanted to risk blood sickness by handling them, that was their business. Rowen began to don the leather jerkin when he felt something crawling on him. He threw the garment away and saw that it had been transformed into a battleground between fleas and spiders. The other articles of clothing were likewise infested. He took the garments and threw them on the ashes of the fire. Then, girding the sword that Jalist had left for him, he stretched and made for the road to Lyos.

CHAPTER THREE
HRÁTHBAM

"BRECCORRY."

Rowen spoke the name of the familiar town and watched a red-gold sunset burnish three long, haphazard rows of thatched rooftops. Beyond the town, the great swell of Pallantine Hill dominated the northern horizon. Lyos was only three days away. Instead of relief, the realization filled him with dread. *I'm sorry, Kayden. I know I swore I'd never go back... but what choice do I have?*

He shook his head and fixed his gaze on the town before him. A few strangers glanced Rowen's way, frowned at his sword, then apparently decided he was harmless and walked on. Rowen was not sure whether to feel relieved or insulted. *What does the Codex Lotius say about dogblossom and honor blooming best from filth?*

Just off the wide dirt road to Lyos, Breccorry subsisted on the coin of travelers—just one of many struggling towns Rowen and Kayden had passed through during their time as mercenaries. The town had two competing blacksmith shops (neither of which appeared to be prospering), an emporium, a stable, a small house painted with a brazen mural of naked women in suggestive poses (the new brothel), and a dreary inn. He saw farms in the distance, plus a modest orchard, all crowded with a few dozen peasants in homespun clothes finishing their day's work.

Rowen visited the emporium first. His appearance drew stares, and the shopkeeper openly followed him to ensure that Rowen did not steal anything. Rowen flushed at the insult but reminded himself that, were he in the shopkeeper's place, he would do likewise.

Rowen glanced longingly at the weapons, particularly eyeing a brightly polished bastard sword locked inside a glass case, plus a pair of curved, brass-handled daggers with scrollwork covering the blades, but all cost ten times more than he had. He examined the armor next, drawn to a fine brigandine and a wide assortment of tooled leather armor, but these too were beyond his means. Finally, he chose a cheap tunic sewn with a lackadaisical rendition of the Lyos falcon. Then, ducking out of sight, he changed into his new tunic. The coarse wool garment scratched his skin, too tight in the arms and too big in the gut, but at least he looked more presentable. He left his torn, muddy tunic on the ground.

Rowen had intended to press on through Breccorry until nightfall, but he hesitated. He had all the weapons and supplies he needed and no horse, so he had no use for the smithies and stables. The brazen paintings on the wall of the brothel made his blood burn, but he could not afford a prostitute. Instead, his eyes lingered on the sun-bleached sign outside the inn. The sign showed a rough painting of a bloated, huge-eyed dragon curled around a mug of ale.

Rowen smiled slightly, scratching his red beard. He remembered the inn. Kayden and he had stayed there long ago. The inn doubled as the town brothel in those days, hosting a certain flaxen-haired beauty whose sweet acquaintance he'd made. She'd had a little Dwarrish blood in her, which had gifted her with a disproportionately large bosom. She also had some skill as a dancer and spoke of her intention to eventually leave Breccorry and head for Atheion to become a priestess of Dyoni.

It made sense. There in the luxury and beauty of the fabled sea city, among a sect of worshippers who saw pleasure as a vehicle for enlightenment, her talents would be in high demand. Rowen doubted she still lived in Breccorry—and could not afford her even if she did—but he might at least get a hot meal and a mug of cool ale.

Rowen touched the last few coins in his pocket. He bit his lip, warring with himself. He had not been thoroughly drunk since his expulsion from the Lotus Isles, and the desire remained as strong as ever. Common sense told him he should save his coin and press on.

Desire overcame common sense, and he made his way toward the inn.

As he drew nearer, he spotted what appeared to be a merchant's wagon unhitched just outside. Presumably, the horses were in the stables. The wagon was enclosed by a canopy preventing Rowen from seeing the goods inside. He turned back to the inn. Business had improved since he'd been here last.

The inn's shutters lay open, and the windows sported real glass instead of open air. He could even see oil lamps burning inside! So he was surprised when he opened the door and found the inn's common room nearly empty. There was a small, crackling fire in the hearth. A few farmers sat at one nearby table, talking in low, weary voices. At another table sat a thick-shouldered man whom Rowen guessed to be one of the town's blacksmiths. He sat alone, eating and drinking in sullen silence.

A bored, heavyset innkeeper stood behind the bar. The serving wench, probably the innkeeper's own gray-haired wife, came to greet him. Rowen smiled when he recognized her. She did not remember him, of course, but it made him feel better to see a familiar face. "What can I get you, young sir?"

Rowen hesitated. "How much is ale?"

The old woman raised one eyebrow skeptically. "Two coppers. We spice it with a secret recipe and keep it chilled in the basement. And there's still some good lamb stew, three coppers a bowl if you want it. We also have venison with potatoes and roasted onions for the same price." She lowered her voice slightly. "If coin's a problem, we've also got roasted urusk, just one copper a slab. My boy went hunting this morning. I could probably throw in a small potato or two if you don't cause us no trouble."

She eyed the sheathed sword at his side.

Rowen flushed. The old woman had not even bothered to tell him the price of a room for the night. He felt the coins in his pocket again. "I've eaten twice my share of urusk meat in this life. Bring me an ale and stew." He added, "You'll get no trouble from me." Rowen produced five coins and handed them over.

The old woman took his coins and tucked them into her apron. "Sit where you like. Still plenty of tables by the fire."

Rowen made his way toward the fire and took a seat at one of many empty tables, laying his satchel on the table's chipped, worn surface. Though Rowen did not mind the faint chill of early autumn—a product of Ivairian blood, some said—the warmth of the fire soothed him.

The old woman appeared a moment later with his ale, served in a wooden mug carved to resemble the drunken dragon pictured outside, and Rowen drank. He was not sure what the old woman meant about secret spices because the ale tasted bland and watery, especially in contrast to the heady, sweet lotus wines he had grown accustomed to on the Isles. But at least the ale was cool, and he was glad to have it.

When he realized he had already emptied half the mug, Rowen slowed and set it down, determined to savor what was left. He felt in his pocket again. All he had left was a single copper cranáf, not even enough to buy another mug, much less get good and drunk, as he wanted.

Rowen tried instead to concentrate on how good the stew would be. Though he doubted Breccorry's food would be much better than its ale, and certainly no better than the rabbit Jalist had shared, anything would be better than paupers' root. As he sat impatiently, he looked around the inn's common room and spotted another man, whom he had not noticed at first.

The man was sitting at a table right next to the fire, shaded by the stairwell above him, which presumably led up to the inn's guest rooms. The man's skin was as dark as the shadows around him. *He must be from Sorocco.*

Rowen had never actually visited that famous island city off Ruun's northeast coast, but its seafaring people dominated the entire world's silk trade, supposedly defending their own coasts with gigantic mirrors that could catch and magnify the sunlight until it set enemy ships aflame. Soroccan silk merchants were a common sight on the Lotus Isles, where some richer knights insisted upon something better than dyed linen or wool for their tabards. According to stories, Soroccan silk merchants had been a common sight in Ivairia too, before famines forced the Lancers to do away with such luxuries.

Rowen had met Soroccans before. As mercenaries, he and Kayden had made more than a few coins guarding merchants from one city of the Simurgh Plains to another. He smiled. *Maybe I won't have to go to Lyos after all.*

The Soroccan looked to be in his late thirties, taller and more broadly shouldered than Rowen, but with a softness to his build that spoke of years of sweet wines and easy living. He had thick, strong arms and a round belly mostly concealed by the folds of loose robes of black and violet silk. He wore gold rings and a gaudy medallion around his neck. A large Soroccan scimitar hung sheathed at the man's right side. While Rowen had met many who wore swords but had no real idea how to use them, something in the way the merchant's hands moved told Rowen that he was different.

No matter how good he is with a blade though, it's still strange that he doesn't have guards with him. Surely he could afford a few swordsmen for protection. Rowen's hopes grew. If this merchant was indeed alone, Rowen's services might be welcome. But mercenaries had to be as careful choosing their employers as did the merchants who hired them. Rowen continued his scrutiny.

The merchant's hair hung in dark, intricate braids. He sported a long, braided goatee and bright green eyes that flashed with mirth as he drank. Empty plates, bowls, and mugs crowded the merchant's table. Even alone, the man wore an easy grin that Rowen was not sure whether to attribute to drunkenness or good nature. He hoped, for bargaining's sake, that it might be both.

The man answered his scrutiny with a friendly nod.

Rowen barely spoke enough Soroccan to introduce himself, though he assumed the merchant must speak Common Tongue if he was doing business so many weeks' travel from home. Still, Rowen hesitated. He thought again of his plain attire and unruly red hair. He looked more like a gravedigger than a mercenary. *What sort of impression would I make like this?*

The old woman returned from the kitchen with Rowen's stew. She placed the bowl on the table, along with a worn wooden fork. Rowen was about to ask her about the merchant, but at that moment, the Soroccan motioned with his empty mug. The old woman hurried to the merchant's table instead. The two spoke briefly, too softly to hear, then the woman rushed off to get the merchant another ale. *Always the rich ones who get the best service.*

Rowen turned his attention to the stew. Unlike the bland ale, the stew smelled excellent, strongly peppered and heaped with lamb, potatoes, carrots, and sweet roasted onions. Rowen had not eaten since that morning, and he tore into the stew with a vengeance, emptying the entire bowl in minutes. Then he washed it down with the last of his ale. His head felt a bit swimmy from the ale, and his stomach warmed, but he was not yet sated.

He brought out the last coin in his pocket and pondered what to do next. More townsfolk crowded the inn. Talk and laughter rose in the night. Someone even brought out a mandolin and began to strum a simple, lively melody. Rowen saw the old woman talking to the innkeeper, both of them glancing in his direction. He flushed with shame when he guessed the meaning of their conversation.

The tables were filling up. If he wasn't buying, he would have to go.

The old woman approached him.

Rowen's stomach growled, despite the stew he had just eaten. He considered spending his last coin on the roasted urusk the old woman had mentioned before. He was not in the mood to leave, but the stew had been excellent, and he did not want to spoil its memory with the bitter, acrid taste of urusk meat, either.

The old woman set down a full mug of ale.

Rowen stared down at it thirstily. "I'm sorry. I can't pay for that."

"Don't have to." The old woman gestured toward the Soroccan merchant. "It's on him. He said to bring you more stew too, if you want it."

It took Rowen a few seconds to recover enough to nod.

The old woman left for the kitchen. Rowen turned toward the dark-skinned merchant and saw the man smiling. Rowen waved gratefully. The merchant responded with a light wave of his own then turned his attention back to his own drink.

The old woman reappeared with a second bowl of stew and set it down in front of Rowen. She brought bread as well. The ale had loosened Rowen's worries and quickened his appetite, and this second bowl of stew tasted even better than the first. This time, the stew came with fresh bread crusted with a sweet but unfamiliar spice. While Rowen ate, the old woman brought him a third mug.

"He says join him when you're done." She nodded toward the Soroccan. Rowen blinked, finished eating, then took the third mug of ale and rose unsteadily. He was not drunk yet, but his legs felt loose, and he nearly tripped as he made his way toward the merchant's table. As an afterthought, he fished a leaf of sweetbitter from his satchel, hastily chewed, and swallowed.

The man stood at his approach. He was taller than Rowen had guessed. The man extended one hand, his plump forearm decorated with gold bracelets, and shook Rowen's hand in a grip like iron.

"I trust you enjoyed your meal! The fare here is not extravagant, but Dyoni knows I've had worse since I left home." The man's voice was thick with the staccato accent of his people. He added, "Forgive me if this table is too close to the fire. The heat reminds me of home." Despite all the empty mugs on the merchant's table, he still sounded sober.

Rowen sat, spilling some of his own ale in the process. The Soroccan did not seem to notice. But Rowen saw that in addition to heaps of empty mugs and bowls, the man's table was littered with coins! Like most merchants, this man was prepared to travel anywhere. Most of the coins were copper, but Rowen saw a few silver cranáfi too, along with some bronze ones bearing the galleon insignia of Sorocco, even a handful of iron crowns from Dhargoth, stamped with the sigil of a dragon. Unlike the comical dragon painted on the sign outside the inn, though, the Dhargoth's dragon was a ghastly thing impaled on a long spear, its maw open and screaming.

The Soroccan said, "May I ask your name?"

"Rowen Locke."

The Soroccan merchant smiled. "I hear an Ivairian cadence. Are you as far from home as I am?"

Rowen hesitated. The ale had loosened his tongue, but he had no desire to share his entire history with a stranger. "Not quite. My family moved to the plains before I was born. I grew up in Lyos."

The Soroccan seemed to sense Rowen's unease and did not press.

Instead, he touched his own chest with one well-ringed hand. "I am Hráthbam Nassir Adjrâ-al-Habas." He bowed. "By Dyoni's grace, you may call me Hráthbam."

Rowen bowed too. *"Al mos haláka."*

Hráthbam's dark face broke into a wide grin. "You speak my language?"

"No better than a child of your lands," Rowen said. "I used to be a sellsword. I learned enough to get by."

Hráthbam grinned. "It is true: our children often have the vocabulary of mercenaries."

Rowen bristled then forced himself to smile back. He lifted his ale. "Thank you for this. And for the food."

"Of course. Call it an advance payment."

Did he already hire me, and I forgot? If so, I'm drunker than I thought!

The merchant laughed at Rowen's expression. "I need guards. I've been lodging here two days, hoping someone of mettle would pass through. You are the first I've seen wearing a sword." The Soroccan rubbed his green eyes. "I must apologize. I usually drink wine. Or hláshba. Anything else fogs my wits." He laughed and emptied his mug and then used one silk sleeve to wipe his mouth. "Straight to it, then. I hired two men when I passed through Phaegos, but they turned on me—would have cut my throat if I hadn't cut them first." Despite the statement, the mirth in his voice remained unchanged. "I'm tired of waiting. So I'll pay you what I took back from them: one hundred coppers. Two men's wage, at least. And all you have to do is keep me breathing and unbloodied for the next month. Maybe less if the road favors us. After that, if I still need you, we can talk."

Rowen's eyes widened. For that much, he would guard the man all the way to the Wintersea! Trying his best to appear unimpressed, he asked, "Where are you bound?"

Hráthbam raised his mug, found it empty, and set it down with a disappointed look. "That's the part you won't like. I'm going to Cadavash."

Rowen's surprise became instant trepidation. *The dragon graveyard...*

Before he could stop himself, he asked, "Since when did the dragon priests need silk?" He feared Hráthbam would take offense, but the Soroccan answered with a deep belly laugh that resounded through the inn and drew curious stares from the patrons.

"They don't," Hráthbam admitted. "But they *do* have something *I* need. Dragonbone. I want to buy as much I can, cart it off somewhere, and sell it. Maybe Atheion, depending on which direction I wake up facing." He added, "At the moment, you'll find my wagon all but empty: not one bolt of silk, if you have a heart for robbery."

Rowen's face flushed. "I'm no thief."

Hráthbam nodded soberly. "Of course not. Isle Knights rarely are."

It took Rowen a moment to form a reply. "I'm no Isle Knight. Not a squire, either."

Hráthbam shrugged and waved his hand, fat gold rings sparkling in the lamp-lit inn. "Squire, Knight... makes no difference to me, so long as you're worth your steel." His eyes narrowed. "You *are*, aren't you?"

"Yes! I mean..." Rowen hesitated. He remembered a passage from the Codex Lotius that characterized bragging as an act of dishonor. But Rowen had already been a fair swordsman before going to the Lotus Isles, almost as good as Kayden. The Isle Knights had made him better. In the tilting yards of Saikaido Temple, sparring with bamboo swords against the other squires, Rowen had won more matches than he'd lost.

"I'm good with steel. Good with my hands and feet, too, if the fight goes to ground. And I'm fair with a bow—although mine's still branched to a tree at the moment."

Hráthbam grinned, clearly appreciating the joke. "That settles it!" He tried to drink out of his empty mug again. "Standard contract, my friend: ten coppers now—the rest when the job's done."

"Didn't you say you paid your last guards all in advance?"

Hráthbam raised one eyebrow. "Yes, and look what it got me! Ten now, ninety later. That, my friend, is my final offer. Do you agree, or did I buy your ales for nothing?"

Rowen had never been to Cadavash, but its priests were infamous for their fanaticism. Rowen could not imagine that men who worshipped the ghosts of dead dragons would be willing to sell the very bones of their gods to a gaudy silk merchant. But one hundred copper cranáfi for a month's work was more than generous. Maybe Hráthbam would even extend his employment for another trip. Best of all, it meant Rowen could avoid going back to Lyos—at least for a while. He raised his mug. "Agreed."

"Excellent! I'll buy your room. We'll drink our fill and leave tomorrow at dawn."

Keep drinking like that, and you'll be lucky to make it out of your bed by sundown! Not that I'll be much better...

The old woman returned to the merchant's table and brought him and Hráthbam more ale. Without waiting for an invitation, she scooped up four copper coins off the table and tucked them into her stew-stained apron.

The merchant drank and talked nonstop, telling Rowen all about his travels through Phaegos, the mistake he'd made in hiring two charming wagon guards who later tried to strangle him, the fortune that could be made from the silk trade (if people knew what they were doing), and the wealth Hráthbam hoped to gain off dragonbone. Then, the Soroccan began describing the various attributes and peccadilloes of his wives and the annoyance of their own separate husbands.

Rowen was halfway through his fourth ale. "How many wives do you have?"

"Ten." Hráthbam held up both of his hands. His gold rings sparkled again. "One for each finger! When I have enough for each of my toes, I'll know it's time to stop."

He spoke more about his wives and children until Rowen was thoroughly confused by a seemingly endless series of long, foreign names. Then, the Soroccan changed topics completely.

"I should have mentioned this before. I'll have to test your mettle first. Nothing serious—just a little sparring to make sure you're worth your copper. Meet me outside the stables at dawn. And bring your sword!"

Rowen nodded through his confusion. Merchants commonly tested the fighting abilities of sellswords by pitting them in mock combat against one of their best guards, but Rowen had never known a merchant to engage in this combat himself. *Then again, if I'm his only guard, what choice does he have?*

Rowen sipped his fourth ale and tried to focus well enough to size up his opponent. The Soroccan, despite his padded build, must have been a skilled warrior once. Rowen believed his story about besting the guards who tried to kill him, but for all Hráthbam's obvious strength, he could not be very fast. And when it came to wielding steel, speed counted for more than strength. *Besides, if he keeps drinking like that, he won't even be able to lift his sword tomorrow!*

Rowen finished his fourth ale, paused a moment to comment on the mug's engraving of a drunken dragon, then nodded when Hráthbam mirthfully insisted on buying another round.

CHAPTER FOUR

THE DRAGON WAKES

MORNING SUNLIGHT STUNG ROWEN'S EYES as he stood outside the stables and tried to keep his balance. That was not easy, given how the earth rippled like water beneath his boots. "Gods!" Rowen swore, rubbing his eyes. "I'd like to know if that's spice they use in their ale or—"

A two-foot curve of sharp, naked steel flashed toward Rowen's neck. Wide-eyed, he ducked then backed away, clumsily unsheathing his own blade. Hráthbam advanced, laughing heartily.

"Come, my pale friend! Surely those chicken limbs can move faster than that!" Hráthbam's eyes shone clear, and his face looked well rested despite having helped Rowen polish off what he suspected was the Drunken Dragon's entire stock.

Rowen's face reddened, but he knew better than to respond with an insult of his own.

Hráthbam darted forward, nimble as a dancer despite his bulk, and swung his scimitar at Rowen's shoulder. Rowen raised his shortsword to block, barely remembering to keep his grip loose before the force of the Soroccan's blow sent a raw jolt through his arms. Rowen tried to push the scimitar down, but Hráthbam twisted free and lunged instead. Rowen managed to clumsily chop the blade out of the way, but it took all the strength he had.

I'm going to lose... Rowen shook his head to clear his thoughts.

The two circled each other. Rowen's face burned. Breccorry's early-risers stopped in the streets and doorways to watch the fight. Most were farmers; others, young women on their way to the brothel to begin their day's sordid work. The old innkeeper and his wife watched through the window of the Drunken Dragon. Rowen wondered if they were about to see him get chopped in half.

Hráthbam advanced again. They traded a rapid flurry of blows, then Rowen backpedaled again. This time, Hráthbam followed. The Soroccan gripped his scimitar with one hand while the other held up the hem of his pompous robes to keep him from tripping. Instead of boots, the merchant wore thin silk slippers. Rowen wondered how the man kept himself from yelping in pain whenever he stepped on a rock.

The rest of the merchant's clothing was just as preposterous. He wore a white turban today. Unlike the black and violet robes he had worn the previous night, his new ones were bright crimson. The color stung Rowen's eyes as badly as the morning sun.

"Gods, I have a headache! How are *you* so damned sharp?"

Hráthbam laughed heartily again. "Ten wives raises one's tolerance for pain, my friend!" He leveled his scimitar and lunged a second time. Rowen realized with shame that the Soroccan was going easy on him. A scimitar was no lunging weapon. Surely Hráthbam knew that.

If I want his respect, I have to put a stop to this. This time, instead of parrying, Rowen sidestepped, grabbed Hráthbam's sword arm to hold it immobile, then stepped in, angling his shortsword for Hráthbam's throat. He intended to stop short, just to get the blade close enough to prove his point.

But the Soroccan was too fast. He twisted away and kicked the back of Rowen's left knee, nearly sweeping his legs out from under him. By the time Rowen recovered his balance, the dreadful scimitar was sweeping toward him again.

Rowen cursed, blocked, then answered with a swing of his own. The two struggled back and forth, their swords clattering loudly in the morning air. As though sensing that Rowen had gained his composure, Hráthbam fought harder.

Sweat beaded on Rowen's forehead. "I thought... this was just a test!"

Hráthbam grinned. The scimitar whirled in his grip. "Are you telling me these paltry dance steps are the best an Isle Knight can offer?"

Rowen flushed then sprang to the attack. "I told you"—he feinted high, twisted his blade in midair, and nearly took Hráthbam's head off—"I am *not* a Knight!"

Hráthbam's face turned serious as Rowen drove the bigger man backward, toward the stable. Hráthbam caught the heel of one silk slipper on a rut and lost his footing. Rowen might have pressed the attack, but he caught his breath instead, giving his opponent plenty of time to recover.

"See?" Hráthbam noted. "Even enraged, the Isle Knight maintains his honor!"

Rowen flinched then realized too late that the merchant was only trying to distract him. The scimitar slashed, changed direction, lured Rowen's blade the wrong way, then changed back and slipped beneath his guard. Rowen grunted as the dull side of the scimitar slapped him hard in the gut. Then the scimitar flashed up. This time, the dull side cracked his right elbow.

Rowen cursed. He swung wildly to keep his opponent at bay. Then he backed up, his arm throbbing. *If he wanted to, he could have used the sharp side and cut me to pieces by now.*

"You should do something about that temper, my friend," Hráthbam advised, suddenly grave. "It disrupts your focus." He swung his scimitar in tight circles before him. "Tell me I am wrong, and by Dyoni's grace, I will apologize."

Rowen gritted his teeth but said nothing. He changed his shortsword to his left hand. His stomach ached, and numbness flooded his right arm. He wanted this contest to be over, but he knew he needed to redeem himself first. But that was not all. Suddenly, he wanted to kill this man!

Then, shamefully, he realized the Soroccan was right. On the Lotus Isles, Knights taught squires to channel their emotions, to clear their minds in the face of death. Rowen had absorbed much of the Isle Knights' tactics but still relied on anger.

What a fool I am! Rowen took a deep breath and released it. *Seek speed in slowness. Empty the mind. Breathe.*

Hráthbam charged. This time, Rowen dodged the blurring scimitar with ease. Then he stepped in and kicked the Soroccan in the side. He might have twisted his hips and generated enough force to break the man's ribs, but he held back. Rowen took a split second to focus then knocked the scimitar from Hráthbam's grasp, caught the hilt with his own numbed right hand, and tucked the curved blade beneath Hráthbam's chin.

Hráthbam's eyes widened. If he was troubled by having his own sword pressed against his throat, his smile said otherwise. "Dyoni's grace, my friend. Well done!"

Rowen blinked as though waking from a dream. "Forgive me..." He realized he was still holding Hráthbam's scimitar and clumsily passed it back. He bowed again.

Hráthbam sheathed his scimitar with a laugh. "Forgive you? Only if you promise you'll teach me how you did that!" Without waiting for a reply, the merchant went to attend to his wagon, muttering in Soroccan and rubbing his side.

The innkeeper and his wife gaped at Rowen through the window of the Drunken Dragon. Nearby, both of Breccorry's blacksmiths and the emporium owner stared at him, visibly impressed. Three young prostitutes smiled coyly from the doorway of the brothel. Rowen blushed further. Then he sheathed his shortsword and went to help his new master ready the horses.

At the same time, far away, dawn shone off the vast city of tents and cooking fires that distinguished the encampment of the Throng, sprung up in the shadow of another city walled in broken stone. Banners speckled the encampment, still throbbing with activity. Some armed men continued the well-orchestrated looting of Cassica while others, paradoxically, gathered and treated the fallen city's wounded. Amid the noise and bustle, a thin, hooded figure in a bone-white cloak shook his head with open derision.

Shade cursed the mud beneath his boots and the stench of wound and waste, wishing—not for the first time—that his master had marshaled the strength of other races: the Dwarr or maybe even Olgrym, with their macabre fondness for sometimes lighting themselves on fire before battle. Any race but Humans! *But then, I have always hated Humans.*

Olgrym could not help what they were. But Humans, while feebleminded, were still smart enough to know better. They had built cities, raised armies, and even written books. One of their ancient heroes—the Isle Knight, Fâyu Jinn—had even sworn allegiance to the Shel'ai and Sylvan rebels during the Shattering War.

Not that any of these men would remember that. Humans may be short-lived, but their memories were even shorter. The last, deciding blow of the Shattering War had been dealt ten centuries before. Not even Loslandril, the old Sylvan king, had been born yet. But Shade knew the stories—hard though they were to believe.

Nearly all the races had taken part in that war in one way or another. Some sided with the Dragonkin, seduced by their power. Among these were the Dwarr, Olgrym, and Humans. Ancient tomes even mentioned terrible, soulless creatures hewn from iron, into which the Dragonkin breathed life. But thanks to the Shel'ai, the Sylvs, and yes, even a few Humans who turned against their kind, the Dragonkin and their allies were driven back. *But that alliance is dead. So is Fâyu Jinn and his brand of knight—if they lived at all.*

Shade shook his head, scowling with open disgust as a squad of armored men passed. All were careful to bow, but Shade did not return the gesture. All Humans looked ugly in his eyes. They lumbered like oxen—even when sober, which was not often. Their thick, hairy limbs lacked grace, and their language sounded like the grunts of wild animals.

But this is what we have to work with. At least half the roster of the Throng was made up of conscripts from other conquered cities—men who joined the Throng in return for the Shel'ai sparing their families' lives. Soon the armies of Cassica would join them, too. The rest of the army was made up of mercenaries: a few Dwarr, who were little better, but mostly Humans.

The Shel'ai curled his lip. It sickened him to know that these uncouth Humans were willing to kill and die for nothing more than a few coins earned by gutting other men who spent their lives just as wastefully. *At least when we kill, we do so for good reason!*

Shade passed a stretch of field being used as a makeshift hospital. A hundred wounded lay there. Some of the men hailed from the Throng, bloodied and cleaved from isolated skirmishes, but most were soldiers from Cassica, injured when the Nightmare brought the wall down. Shade saw men with their faces burned black as tar, others with ghastly open wounds and shattered, protruding bones. The smell of blood and Human waste nearly gagged him.

Shade gritted his teeth, using his sleeve to try and mask the scent. Despite his disgust with these Humans, he resisted a sudden twist of pity by imagining that the injured and dying were Sylvs instead. *Like the ones who drove me out for what I am—for what I was born able to do.*

Shade quickened his pace. He did not have time to muse. He had been summoned. Hurrying deeper into the camp, he came to his master's tent.

In addition to a host of bodyguards, half a hundred white-and-crimson banners, all proudly displaying the sigil of a greatwolf, ringed the tent. The bodyguards stood nearly as still as the banners around them. Unlike the other men in the camp, these wore black from head to toe. Even their faces were covered, except for eyes as cold as stone.

Shade slowed. Five years since their inception, he still could not decide if the Unseen spoke to the power and rigid determination of the Shel'ai or instead illustrated their greatest folly. Groomed to be elite bodyguards and assassins, the Unseen were infamous. Loyal, yes, but they hardly had a choice, thanks to Shel'ai magic.

As Shade approached his master's tent, the Unseen knew better than to challenge him. None bowed or saluted either, which suited him fine. In fact, the Shel'ai had to admit that he preferred the blunt honesty of their hatred. Pushing aside the flap of the tent, he walked in.

Fadarah was seated at a great oaken desk, studying maps and reports. He stopped when Shade entered. Even plainly dressed, without raiment or his imposing blackened plate armor, the Sorcerer-General was a kingly figure. Shade fell to one knee.

Fadarah took him by the shoulders and pulled him up. "Welcome, Kith'el."

Shade winced. Though he no longer went by his given name,

Fadarah still used it from time to time. Shade might have protested, had it been anyone else. He quickly concealed his emotions, but Fadarah sensed them anyway.

"Why so grim, my child? Did we not win another great victory just a few days ago?"

Shade smiled thinly. Though he was tall, he still had to crane his neck to meet his master's gaze. "Yes, General. Thanks to you."

"Thanks to Iventine," Fadarah corrected. He returned to his seat—not the regal throne he deserved, Shade noted, but a simple wooden chair. "Have you seen him?"

Despite himself, Shade shuddered. "Yes, General. He sleeps. Four Shel'ai attend him in the southern subcamp, along with a full company of Unseen. He will not wake until you command it."

Fadarah nodded, but his expression remained troubled. "I sensed today that his power is still growing."

Shade hesitated. "As did I, General. Forgive me, but I'll say it again: if this continues, we may have to—"

Fadarah's eyes narrowed, silencing him. Despite his violet eyes, filled with dragonmist, his face flushed to a strange, ominous shade of gray—a product of his half-Olg blood. "We are not speaking of an animal. Iventine is still one of us—regardless of what we may be forced to do, in time."

Shade bowed. "Of course. Forgive me, General." He added, "Maybe if one of the other initiates—especially Silwren—could be awakened…"

Fadarah shook his head resolutely. "We have already seen what happens when an initiate wakes too early. We lost poor Iventine and El'rash'lin that way. We can't risk Silwren and the others too."

But Silwren is not like the others.

Fadarah turned his attention back to the reports on the table before him. "I summoned you because losses among the Throng remain lighter than usual. Only eighteen killed, thrice that wounded. Normally, this would be a cause for celebration. This time, it concerns me."

"Maybe rumors of the Nightmare's power sapped the courage of Cassica's defenders," Shade offered. "Word may have reached them after Syros, long before we got here."

Fadarah glanced up. "Undoubtedly. But General Brahasti has nearly finished rounding up Cassica's men-at-arms, and the numbers are light. Most dropped swords, and there are still some skirmishes, but Brahasti insists there's still at least one full brigade out there."

"Humans are infamous for deserting their compatriots in times of need, General."

Fadarah's eyes narrowed. "You do not think I should rely so heavily on Brahasti's advice, then." It was not a question.

"You lead this host, General. Not me. I bow to your wisdom."

"Thank you, but I did not request your endorsement. I asked for your opinion of Brahasti el Tarq."

The mention of the name made Shade's lip curl. "An army can have only one general. Besides, Brahasti is a Dhargot." He spat the word like a curse.

Fadarah smirked. "Brahasti is banished from the empire. I believe the Red Emperor threatened to have him impaled if he returned."

Shade did not laugh. "Then let the Red Emperor have him! We'd gain favor, and Brahasti would get what he deserves."

Fadarah shook his head. "We need Brahasti. For now, at least. But I sense there's more to your hatred than disagreement with his strategy."

Shade hesitated. Then in a low voice, he said, "Brahasti is a dog— even among Humans! He is a sadist who delights in torture and rape. Were it within my province, I would burn him to ashes and sleep well for it."

So strong was the Shel'ai's revulsion that, as he spoke, violet tendrils of wytchfire flickered to life, writhing and flitting about his fingertips. Shade flicked his hands, and the wytchfire disappeared. He blanched and bowed. "Forgive me, General."

Fadarah faced him, unfazed. "No Shel'ai need fear disagreeing with my decisions, Kith'el. You above all others know that." He sighed, leaning back in the chair, which strained to accommodate his muscular bulk. "I like the man no more than you do. I'll make you this promise: when Brahasti outlives his usefulness, you will be the one who sends him to be judged by the Light. And I suspect I'll sleep as well afterward as you will."

Shade bowed deeply. "Thank you, General."

Fadarah glanced at the reports again. "As for this missing brigade, it may be they deserted. But we should take care until this can be confirmed. Should this brigade return and attack us, they would not be so foolish as to assault the main camp. The hills to the south would be a perfect hiding place for them. I have dispatched scouts, but we should prepare, in the event that this missing brigade of men-at-arms attacks the subcamp to the south."

Shade caught his meaning. *That is where the initiates are!* "Silwren..." He whispered her name before he could stop himself.

Fadarah nodded. "She and the others must be protected at all costs. I do not want to risk the common men of the army learning about the initiates, so take only the Unseen with you. Their silence is assured. I have already ordered Captain Lethe to assemble a brigade and proceed to Iventine's tent, but we must guard the initiates' tent as well. Assume command of my bodyguards and go there at once. I will send more Unseen to relieve you as soon as I can."

"Your own bodyguards... Forgive me, General, but—"

"No need for concern. I summoned Que'ann from tending the wounded. She'll remain here and guard me until you return. Besides, I suspect I will be quite safe at the center of my own army."

Shade hesitated. "As you command, General." He bowed again and left the tent.

Assuming command of Fadarah's bodyguards—all handpicked from the ranks of the Unseen—he headed briskly for the southern subcamp. The Unseen followed without comment or complaint. Shade stalked through the main camp, his hood lowered. Armed men scurried to get out of his way. Shade led the Unseen past a line of sentries guarding the southern end of the main camp. At that moment, they were supervising the camp's fortifications—the digging of a ditch and the raising of a palisade.

Shade reflected on his master's plan to keep the Nightmare and the rest of the initiates in subcamps, separated from the main body of the Throng. Shade had argued that doing so made these subcamps prime targets for would-be guerrilla fighters from the cities they conquered. Fadarah had countered with a point Shade could not answer: what if the Nightmare awoke on its own? What if one of the initiates emerged from dream-sleep every bit as mad as Iventine? In a rampage, he might destroy half the army before the other Shel'ai could stop him! Those soldiers not killed would surely revolt, and all would be lost.

So the subcamps were placed under heavy guard—not just by Unseen but by Shel'ai too. Even against a far smaller number of Unseen, an entire brigade of Cassican men-at-arms would stand no chance once Shel'ai engaged in the battle too. Shade smirked. As far as he knew, there existed no armor on the continent that could shield its wearer against wytchfire.

They reached the southern subcamp, located a hundred yards from the rest of the Throng. Palisades ringed this camp as well, but here, all the sentries wore the black leather brigandines of the Unseen. Their armor bore the crimson greatwolf, and black silk cloths had been tied to conceal their faces. None saluted. Shade pointed, and those Unseen marching behind him joined the others encircling the initiates' tent, bolstering the sentry-lines. Shade approached the tent itself and bowed to the sorcerers standing outside.

Six Shel'ai stood guard, all dressed in bone-white cloaks like his own. They guarded the only entrance into the tent, stoic faces shadowed by hoods. They glanced impassively at the fresh squad of Unseen that Shade had brought with him.

"A brigade of Cassican men-at-arms may be hiding in the hills. Captain Lethe already guards Iventine's slumber. More Unseen will arrive here, too. I'll stay until then. Obviously, General Fadarah wants the initiates protected at all cost."

The six Shel'ai nodded. "Of course," one said. "Thank you, Lord Shade."

The Shel'ai who addressed him lowered her hood, revealing beautiful Sylvan features. She regarded Shade with open admiration. And something else.

Shade ignored this. "Nariel, what is the status of their sleep?"

Nariel's expression stiffened. "Unchanged."

Shade nodded. He was sorry to spurn this Shel'ai woman's affections, but that could not be helped. She knew, as did everyone, that his heart belonged to Silwren. He passed the sorcerers and went inside the tent.

Darkness cloaked the tent in which the initiates slept, even though no amount of light would disturb them. Shade summoned his wytchfire, raising his hands so that the magical flames flooded the whole tent with radiance. He told himself he did so only to light his path, but he had been here so many times he could have found his way to Silwren's side blindfolded.

No, there was something in the air—something he could not name—that drove a cold chill through his heart. The tent held three beds. These were not straw on wood but real beds, though the initiates could not possibly be aware of this small extravagance. Three figures lay untended: two men, one woman; all young, all Shel'ai; not dead but steeped in fitful, enchanted slumber. Two of the three Shel'ai—the men—were horribly disfigured, their skin swollen with sores, warts, and ghastly, barely healed burns. Yet the third, the woman, was whole.

Shade traced his hands in an intricate pattern, and the wytchfire separated from his fingertips to form two glowing spheres that rose in the air, continuing to light the tent even without his touch. Shade approached the woman.

He stared down at her, trying to see past the dreadful lack of color in her face. Hair the color of melted platinum spilled beneath her lithe figure in long, exquisite tresses. She looked small to him, but he smiled wistfully. Silwren was anything but fragile.

She had been only a child when her parents died. Unlike most parents of Shel'ai, hers had loved her in spite of the magic kindling her blood. In that, they were the exception that proved the rule. They tried to keep her in Sylvos, in the nurturing shadow of the World Tree, but their fellow Sylvs had other ideas. Silwren made cinders of her parents' killers then fled.

Shade stretched out his hand and brushed a soft curl of platinum hair from Silwren's eyes. Sylvs aged slowly; those born as Shel'ai aged more slowly still. Silwren had not changed at all in five years. He was not sure if that was a blessing or a curse. Like the other initiates, she often slept in fits, sometimes spasming, with wytchfire blossoming wildly from her hands so that only the quick action of her Shel'ai attendants prevented her from harming herself. So, too, did they feed and clean her, hoping that she would one day awaken and become their savior.

Silwren was lying still for the moment, but she had tossed the sheet from her body. Shade retrieved it and covered her. Silwren wore the same bone-white robes as the other Shel'ai, cut up the side for ease of movement and fighting, but subtle curves in the fabric revealed the womanly beauty of the figure beneath. Shade's eyes lingered on her bare thigh before he blushed with shame. He covered her with the sheet then touched her forehead with his fingertips.

The gesture was not merely an affectionate one. As he had countless times before, Shade used his magic to probe for some spark within her then-glacial mind to indicate that her recovery was more than a faint hope. He felt nothing.

Shade clenched his eyes, fighting back tears. Silwren had been in this unnatural sleep for nearly five years. Fadarah was probably right: to force her awake would mean turning her into something like the Nightmare. She needed to wake on her own.

But if it weren't for you, I never would have survived. How am I supposed to finish all this without you? He brushed her hair with the palm of his hand. *You saved me, even more than Fadarah did.*

Shade recalled his own history: abandoned on the plains as an infant, forsaken by parents who preferred to let starvation or wolves do what they did not have the stomach for. Instead, Shade had been rescued by another Shel'ai named Rhas'ero, a simple man of peace who thought that using his magic to cure the ills of Humans would allow them to be welcome in foreign lands.

For a time, it had worked. Rhas'ero and Shade—known then by a different name—made their home in a little Human village, not exactly welcomed but tolerated, using their magic to quicken crops and heal minor injuries, even driving off bandits with lethal washes of wytchfire from time to time. Then came a plague that Rhas'ero could not treat and, superstitious, the Humans turned on their very own benefactors. Only Shade escaped.

For years after Rhas'ero's death, Shade—still just a child—had wrought revenge on every Human he could find, killing so many of them that their faces blurred in his nightmares. By the time Fadarah found him, the naïve gentleness imparted by Rhas'ero was long dead. Shade had become an animal.

No, not an animal. A ghost. A shade. Shade half-smiled. He thought of how Fadarah had saved him from the mobs even as Silwren saved him from himself.

And how did I repay you? Shade winced as shame washed over him. He thought of the long hours throughout which Silwren had comforted him. For years, she had been unflagging in her belief that she could soothe his bloodlust and help him regain his humanity. They had become lovers, yes, but even then Shade had not treated her as he should have. By the time Silwren underwent her transformation, a wedge had already been driven between them.

But I will make amends. Just wake up, my love, and I will show you. I will be worthy of you. He brushed his fingertips through her platinum tresses again.

"I should not have let you do what I did not have the courage to do. Forgive me." He thought of the Nightmare and shuddered. *Is that what you'll become, when—if—you finally wake?*

He shook his head. "No," he whispered into the stillness of the tent. "Sleep as long as you can, my love. Wake as anything... but don't wake as *that*." He straightened the sheet and leaned in to kiss her forehead.

The jolt drove him backward, nearly blasting him off his feet. For a moment, stunned, he could only stare. Above him, the twin spheres of wytchfire he had conjured earlier began to flicker, as though some other wild, angry magic had just swept over them.

"Silwren?"

Before him, she lay as she had, breathing faintly, her face still pale as bone.

Slowly, he touched her forehead again—not with his lips this time, but his hand. Igniting his magic, he tentatively probed her thoughts, searching for her familiar spark of life. *Nothing...*

Shade closed his eyes, his hopes dashed. Fadarah had warned that Silwren and the other initiates might show false signs of recovery from time to time. He was just about to withdraw his hand when she scalded him again.

Stronger than the first, the jolt nearly blasted his mind into ruin. Shade reeled, recovered, then knelt beside her. His hands shook. Carefully, he extended his hand again. He did not touch her skin this time, but merely held his open palm above her forehead. His eyes widened. Deep within her mind, frail as a candle under thick ice, she was there. From the depths, still deep in that bottomless well, her mind was returning.

"Silwren!" he shouted joyously.

The sound of rustling cloth made him turn around. All six Shel'ai rushed into the tent. Shade stood to face them, the rarest of open smiles on his face. "It's Silwren! I felt—"

"We felt it too," Nariel said. "Even from out there." She cautiously splayed her fingers inches above Silwren's heart. Silwren's bosom rose and fell with slow, even breaths. "It's true. She's waking!"

In disbelief, another Shel'ai took her place. His fist uncurled over Silwren's body.

As rare as it was for Sylvs to flaunt their emotions, it was rarer still for Shel'ai. Their harsh lives did not permit it. But Shade felt no shame as tears of joy ran down his face.

Another Shel'ai said, "We must tell Fadarah!"

But Nariel scowled. "Wait. Something's wrong."

"I feel it too," said another. "Shade, she's waking too quickly!"

Shade pushed his way past them, fearfully probing Silwren's mind again. He had to know for himself. The tiny flicker that had been her deepest essence became a roaring blaze. Her mind was alive but wrought with ragged, incomprehensible energy. Her body shook.

"No," Shade whispered. "Not again, not her..."

"We have to stop this," someone said.

"Combine magic," Nariel suggested. "We seven can keep her asleep until—"

Harsh screams and the clatter of steel reached their ears. Shade knew at once what was happening. While the other Shel'ai swore and raced to the tent flap to confirm what they already feared, Shade was extending his consciousness beyond the tent, through the camp, seeking out the mind of his master. Unhampered by as ungainly a thing as verbal speech, their mental conversation required only the space of a few seconds. Then Shade broke the contact.

"Fadarah's on his way. We have to guard her until he arrives."

The other Shel'ai exchanged grim looks. They did not argue. To renew Silwren's magic-induced coma required their combined magic and concentration. But they had no time. Outside, men were dying.

Shade gritted his teeth. "Follow me." He strode from the tent. Wytchfire flared to full, terrible life at his fingertips.

At once, his eyes drank in the chaos. All around them, a pitched battle raged. The black-garbed fighters of the Unseen formed a tight circle around the tent, pikes and shortswords facing a full company of horsemen. Hundreds strong, they wore chain mail and tabards emblazoned with Cassica's intertwined serpents.

Howling men hacked each other with swords until the earth resembled the crimson of the setting sun above them. The savagery did not make him flinch. Nor did he intervene. To cast wytchfire into such a melee would only strike friend as well as foe—though Shade would hardly refer to the Unseen as his friends. Better to gather his strength, force himself to be patient, wait a little longer until all the Unseen had been slain. *Let them kill as many as they can. We'll kill the rest,* Shade vowed.

The other Shel'ai watched impassively. As the last Unseen fell and the furious men-at-arms closed in, thin fingers rose, unleashing streams of wytchfire. Fresh screams echoed across the plains. Horses reared up, spilling their hapless riders to the ground. Others were turned to cinders in the same fiery maelstrom that claimed their riders as seven grim-faced Shel'ai barred the path of hundreds.

Men on horses and on foot closed on them from three sides. Violet flames drove them back. Shade added his magic to the torrent, killing and killing. The men-at-arms recoiled, their faces slack with horror. Shade imagined they had heard tales of Sylvan magic, but none were prepared for this!

Shade singled out another rider. One hand blasted the man from his horse while the other unleashed a storm of flame that lit the earth and drove back the men behind him. He stood at the center of the

Shel'ai. On either side, his comrades fought with the same tenacity. They were winning. But it could not last.

One of the men-at-arms flung himself in front of his comrades, absorbing the worst of a firestorm, shielding the men behind him as he perished. Another threw a spear before he died. Shade screamed a rallying cry. The combined efforts of the Shel'ai drove the men-at-arms back again, but this time at a price. Two sorcerers lay dead, a third cut and bleeding.

"Hold them!" Shade cried. But even as he spoke, a terrible weariness flooded his brain, numbing his chest and limbs. The wytchfire he cast from his fingertips was like his own blood. If he cast too much of it, the men-at-arms would have no need to kill him after all.

None of the Shel'ai spoke after that. Brows knit with concentration as trembling hands cast more and more precious wytchfire from their bodies, thwarting charge after charge from the men-at-arms. Men hurled spears, but the sorcerers waved their hands, burning them in midair. Other men flung knives and swords or crawled on their bellies, hoping to avoid the deathly storm above them.

Then one of the Shel'ai gasped and fell. Shade turned to look. It was Nariel. Though her body bore no visible injury, she had simply exhausted herself beyond all limits.

Rage quickened Shade's senses. He did not cry out. Instead, he unleashed another torrent of wytchfire, then another. His comrades did the same. But they were too few. A wedge of men-at-arms broke through. Shade drove them back, so weakened by then that his vision blurred.

One Shel'ai perished. Then another, gravely wounded, gave Shade a glance of farewell.

The attack had stalled a moment. Shade thought of Silwren in the tent behind him. He would never see her again—but Fadarah and Que'ann were close. He sensed his master's reassuring words in his mind. They had more men with them. Silwren would live, as would the other initiates, because of this sacrifice.

Wide-eyed, reeling in heaps of ashes and acrid, burnt remains that had once been the better half of their brigade, the men-at-arms rallied one last time and charged. Shade thought that the men must know they had no hope of survival and guessed they had gone fey, only hoping to take as many Shel'ai as possible with them.

Another Shel'ai fell quickly, expending the last of his vital energy in a guttering wash of violet flames. The men-at-arms pressed on. Shade and the last Shel'ai beat them back. They knew they were beyond saving. All that mattered now were the initiates.

And then, at last, Fadarah arrived.

Pressing toward the tent, horsemen and footmen whirled suddenly to find fresh opponents streaming toward them. They were led, not by Humans, but by a towering man with fire streaming from his fingertips.

Shade's heart leapt. Through the chaos of the melee, he spotted his master. "Fadarah!" He struggled against the exhaustion he knew was about to claim his life.

He lost sight of the Sorcerer-General in the chaos of the melee. Then a staggering man-at-arms slew the faithful Shel'ai guarding Shade's back. Shade cast fistful after fistful of murderous fire and then reeled. A final, weak burst of flames escaped from his fingertips.

This is it. The moment of my death. Shade raised his hands. The next blast, he knew, would kill him.

A fresh cry caught his attention. The Sorcerer-General had claimed the horse of a fallen man-at-arms and was driving toward the tent, his great sword in one hand, fire streaming from the other. Men scattered before him. Shade had the wild thought that he might actually survive.

Beside him, deep within the pitch-darkness of the tent, something awful came to life. It howled once—a deafening cry that shook the earth, stunning friend and foe alike. The battle was forgotten as everyone turned, horrified, to see what could make such a sound.

Despite the danger, Shade turned his back on the fighting. "Silwren!" he cried, staggering forward. He threw aside the tent flap and was about to rush blindly into the darkness when white fire washed the world from his sight.

CHAPTER FIVE

A SQUIRE'S HONOR

AN AUTUMN BREEZE WHIPPED UP the grassy smell of the plains and flung Rowen's shaggy hair about as he left the town of Breccorry, riding in a wagon alongside Hráthbam Nassir Adjrâ-al-Habas. Glancing over his shoulder at the wagon's interior, he saw that the dark-skinned merchant had told the truth. The wagon contained nothing but foodstuffs, various weapons, and a few old, sealed trunks. Rowen wondered briefly if these battered trunks were filled with bolts of Soroccan silk. *Or more of his preposterous silk gowns!* Rowen resisted a grin.

He glanced at the weapons instead: Soroccan scimitars, a few Ivairian shortswords with waisted blades and man-shaped hilts, a battered round shield bearing a painted insignia faded past recognition, and a footman's pike. He also spotted a Queshi sickle-sword and remembered a brief time he'd spent with the nomadic horse masters of the Southern Basin, tending their herds of bloodmares. It had been a comparatively peaceful time in his life, and he had considered returning more than once.

Rowen continued scanning the wagon. He was relieved to see a pair of crossbows and even what looked like a Queshi composite bow. *Those will be a lot more useful than my sword if we're attacked by boars or greatwolves. Or bandits, for that matter.* Rowen would have preferred to have two or three more guards beside him, but Hráthbam had had no luck hiring more.

The Soroccan was a much better fighter than Rowen had

anticipated, though Rowen had proven he could hold his own against the bigger man. Between them, if they armed themselves first with bows and picked off as many targets as possible from a distance, they could take maybe half a dozen highwaymen at a time.

The wheels of the merchant's wagon jostled and buckled. This road was clearly rougher and less traveled than the road to Lyos, but the landscape had changed very little. The grassy Simurgh Plains extended in all directions, sloping sometimes in slight hills, speckled here and there with patches of forest.

Not many places to hide out here. If they were lucky, and they stayed sharp, they should be able to spot trouble coming from quite a distance. Rowen relaxed a little. He halfheartedly tuned back in to his boss's seemingly endless chatter.

Hráthbam had not stopped talking since they left Breccorry. He first introduced Rowen to the horses: a pair of plain but sturdy rounceys the merchant had named, simply, Left and Right. Left was an aging mare, Right her foal. While Left was slow, calm, and steady, Right was fast and easily agitated, so the horses often tried to pull the wagon in two different directions. Given how loosely Hráthbam held the reins, he was no expert when it came to horses.

Gods, I hope this isn't the man's first expedition! He remembered Hráthbam's story of hiring two men who later turned on him. Good, experienced merchants needed a knack for judging character. Likewise, Hráthbam should have known better than to pay the men all at once before their job was done. The Soroccan was lucky to be alive.

Another quick glance into the back of the wagon revealed the shoddiness of the trunks. Rowen returned his gaze to Hráthbam, lowering his eyes to the man's fat gold rings. He wondered if their luster had not simply been painted on.

Rowen's pulse quickened. Most of the coins he'd seen on Hráthbam's table at the Drunken Dragon had gone to pay for their food and ale. *What if he doesn't even have the coin to pay me, much less buy dragonbone from the priests at Cadavash?* He touched his sword hilt. He was willing to take what was owed him if need be, but what if Hráthbam simply did not have it?

Rowen forced himself to let go of his sword. Even if the Soroccan was not as rich as he appeared at first glance, he had still paid Rowen the first installment of his wage. Rowen now had ten copper cranáfi in his pocket, no paltry sum. If nothing else, Rowen's journey would lead him even farther from the Lotus Isles. Right now, that was enough.

Hráthbam had stopped talking and was staring at him as though waiting for something. "Sorry," he said, rubbing his eyes. "What was that?"

Hráthbam laughed. "You pale-faced Ivairians have the manners of boars!" he bellowed, not unkindly. "I asked what you thought about the gods."

Rowen hesitated. The question made him uncomfortable. He'd met priests in Lyos who worshipped the various gods and tried to convert him to their respective faiths. This had been especially prevalent after he and Kayden graduated from digging graves to working as mercenaries, and the priests realized that the brothers might make good temple guards. But Hráthbam was not a priest.

Which god did the Soroccans worship? Was it Maelmohr, the Firegod? No, that was the Dwarr. Tier'Gothma, the Goddess of Healing and Harvest? No, that did not sound right either. Nor could it be Fohl, the Undergod with his many burning hells, for no sane man worshipped him.

Rowen's headache reminded him of the merchant's love of drink, suggesting Dyoni, the God of Earthly Pleasures. But he saw no obvious emblem of faith carved into the man's rings or gaudy gold medallion. He gave up trying to deduce the best thing to say to worm his way out of this conversation and simply answered, "I try not to think about them very much."

"Truly? I thought you Isle Knights were supposed to be men of thought as well as steel!"

Rowen's face blushed to match his hair. "Told you, I'm not..." Reminding Hráthbam yet again that he was not an Isle Knight seemed pointless. "Most Isle Knights worship the Light," Rowen said instead. "*Worship* probably isn't the right word, I guess. They meditate, but they don't pray, exactly. They don't believe that the Light actually answers prayers. I mean, not that it ignores them either, but..." He felt foolish. "You should ask a priest if you want to know about the gods. I'm no philosopher."

Hráthbam nodded, adjusting his turban. "Nor am I. Don't look so worried, my friend. I am not trying to convert you. I was just wondering what you knew about Zet."

Rowen finally understood. The priests who dwelled in the graveyards of Cadavash worshipped Zet, the Dragongod. If they were going to do business with such men, it made sense to know what they were about. "Sorry," Rowen said, "I just get nervous whenever someone mentions the gods. Usually, that means they're about to tell me what an awful sinner I am."

"And how you'll sink into damnation unless they save your soul... for a price!" Hráthbam grinned and clapped Rowen on the shoulder. "That's not me, my friend. I understand the gods no better than I understand the stars." He gestured toward the faint, daytime star-swirl of Armahg's Eye. "You will not catch me pretending otherwise. I just ask because the Dragongod is unknown to my people. Maybe I'll get a better bargain from these priests if I can show some appreciation for their superstitions." He winked.

Rowen relaxed. He liked being back in the company of someone who shared his confusion about the enigmatic figures of a pantheon so many others seemed to believe in without question. "I don't know much about Zet either," he admitted. "In Lyos, some priests say Armahg made this world but Zet filled it with dragons. Only the dragons were too powerful. Or too beautiful, depending on who's telling you the story. So the other gods got angry."

Rowen felt ridiculous talking like this, but Hráthbam seemed interested. *At least so long as he's listening, he's not chattering about his wives, his children, the silk trade, and every other damn thing!*

"Some of the gods wanted to kill the dragons, but Zet stopped them. There was some kind of battle. Supposedly, the other gods killed Zet, but it took so much of their power that they weren't strong enough to wipe out all his dragons afterward."

"Couldn't the poor darlings just take a nap and recuperate?"

Rowen laughed. He liked this man's blasphemy. *Kayden would have liked him too.*

"You'd think so," he said, "but I guess that doesn't work with gods. Anyway, they came up with some kind of plan. They cast Zet's body down onto the world, where it burst open. All other life on this world emerged from his corpse."

Hráthbam grimaced. "Like maggots, you mean? Hardly a noble story!"

"Talk to another cult, and they'll probably tell you something different. That's just what the priests of Zet say, I think."

"What happened to the dragons?"

Rowen thought hard, trying to remember the rest of the tale. "Well, one of the races that wriggled out of Zet's corpse was the Dragonkin. Because they came from Zet, who made the dragons, they could control dragons, too. Only they craved more power, so they drained the dragons' life force somehow, used it to feed their own magic—which is what the gods wanted in the first place. In time, the dragons died out."

Hráthbam stroked his braided goatee. "My people tell a similar tale. Except in ours, the dragons turned to fighting each other."

Rowen said, "I've heard that, too. I think the followers of Maelmohr like that one."

"Strange how gospels change, depending on who's telling them!"

Rowen nodded. For hours after that, they traveled in silence. The wagon jostled as it rolled over the uneven road. The day was sunny but cool, and despite his weariness, Rowen was in good spirits. He rubbed his right elbow, which was still a little numb from the strike it had received from the blunt end of Hráthbam's scimitar. He had feared at first that his elbow was broken, but he could move his arm now with just a little pain. Likewise, he seemed to have recovered from the knot on his head that the robbers had given him, and Jalist's salve had all but healed his slashed palm.

As they traveled, legends of warring dragons dominated his thoughts. He imagined the scene: countless dragons battling each other in the sky, each one bending in the air like a fish underwater.

No one had seen a living dragon for close to a thousand years, but everyone knew for a fact that they had existed—at least on this continent. The great beasts' bones had been unearthed in fields from one end of Ruun to the other. He himself had once seen a gigantic, nearly complete skeleton of a dragon on display in the mansion of a rich man whom he had briefly served as guard. The skeletal dragon's eye sockets had stretched nearly as wide as he was tall.

Maybe dragons were still alive somewhere. Maybe they had merely fled from the Dragonkin to some remote corner of the world. The farthest he had ever ventured from Ruun was to the Lotus Isles, but he had seen ancient maps in Saikaido Temple that showed other continents beyond this one, mysterious lands about which he knew nothing. *Maybe someday, I'll go there. But I need coin first!*

Hráthbam continued to guide the wagon, tending the reins and staring out over the Simurgh Plains with patient curiosity. The two horses were causing some trouble, each trying to lead the wagon at a different speed. When Right petulantly nipped at Left's ear, Hráthbam scolded the horse in Soroccan. Then the merchant produced a flask, drank, and offered it to Rowen.

"Hair of the wolf, my friend. Have a drink!"

Rowen wanted to refuse, but he did not want to appear rude. He had worked for many merchants in the past, and he could remember none as personable as Hráthbam (let alone as good with a sword). Rowen ruefully accepted the flask and raised it to his lips. The pungent, sour smell overwhelmed his nostrils. It was hláshba—a powerful, Soroccan liquor made from fermented corn and potatoes. Even on good days, Rowen could not stomach the stuff. But he was still recovering from the night before, and the smell made him want to vomit.

Unable to speak except to curse in Ivairian, he shook his head and, as politely as he could, pushed the flask away. Hráthbam laughed, bright-eyed, and took another drink before he tucked the flask back into a pocket in his silk robes. Then he said, "And the Sylvs?"

Still struggling to regain his composure, it took Rowen a moment to realize that Hráthbam was resuming their conversation about divinity. "What do you mean?"

"My people say that the Dragonkin were the ancestors of Sylvs," Hráthbam said. "But no one seems to know how the Sylvs came about. Or why the Dragonkin disappeared." Rowen sensed that the Soroccan was speaking no longer from a desire to prepare for his dealings in Cadavash but out of genuine curiosity. "Do you?"

Rowen shrugged. "I've heard some pretty wild tales about that. Seems like each temple has its own version. Most of the stories make even less sense than what I just told you."

"And the Shel'ai?"

The mention of the sorcerers sent a chill down Rowen's spine. "Don't know much about them either, aside from tall tales of them stirring up famines and plagues," he admitted. "They're Sylvs, I think, except they're born with a bit of Dragonkin magic inside them. Something that makes their eyes purple, like the color of a bruise— but with misty white pupils instead of black. I hear the other Sylvs fear them. Usually, they kill them when they're born." He shuddered at this, hoping such stories of murdered infants were just stories. "Otherwise, they drive them out of the Wytchforest to torment the rest of us."

Rowen added, "Of course, they tell a completely different story on the Isles. Long ago, Fâyu Jinn—that's the man who founded the order—befriended both the Sylvs and the Shel'ai and enlisted their aid to fight the Dragonkin."

Hráthbam nodded slowly. "The Shattering War. My people speak of it, too."

"Not everybody believes that, though," Rowen continued. "I mean, the part about Fâyu Jinn asking the Sylvs for help. Some say that's blasphemy." He shrugged, trailing off. He remembered the rumors he'd heard on the Lotus Isles about trouble brewing in the west, something about the Shel'ai marshaling an army. He'd heard the same thing from Jalist. He wondered if Hráthbam knew such rumors, too. When pressed, though, Hráthbam seemed to know nothing of it. Rowen wondered if this was the first time the merchant had ever even left Sorocco. He considered asking the merchant about the legendary World Tree that supposedly grew at the heart of the Wytchforest, but if Hráthbam had not heard of it, he would only have to tell the story himself—and he knew nothing but vague mentions since no one he knew had ever gotten close enough to the Wytchforest to see it.

The two continued until sundown then camped next to a stream.

Rowen volunteered to tend the horses while Hráthbam prepared a Soroccan meal of heavily spiced vegetables and rice that was delicious but made Rowen sweat as though he'd spent all day in the tilting yards.

Hráthbam questioned whether or not they should stand guard but seemed none too interested in fulfilling that task himself. *Well, I'm the guard.* While Hráthbam slept in the wagon, Rowen stood watch, resting with his back to the campfire, sword in hand. He heard the howl of distant wolves—including one deeper, ominous howl that must have been a greatwolf. He tensed but trusted the fire would keep wild animals away.

The next day, seeing the dark circles under his eyes, Hráthbam invited him to sleep in the wagon while he drove the horses. Rowen accepted but slept little, unable to get used to the jostling of the wagon wheels over the rough road. Then, late in the afternoon, Hráthbam pulled the wagon to a stop and shouted for Rowen to join him.

Rowen hurried to the front of the wagon. He followed the man's gaze to the plains ahead of them. His own eyes widened.

"Gods!" Rowen's hand flew for his sword.

"Is that what I think it is?" Hráthbam asked. He held the reins to Left and Right with one hand. His other hand rested on his scimitar.

Rowen nodded grimly. "A greatwolf. Big one, too!"

"Looks like I'm seeing a regular wolf through a spyglass! We do not have such beasts on Sorocco." Hráthbam sounded fearful. "I suppose it's too much to hope that it isn't hungry."

"Greatwolves are *always* hungry." Rowen watched the greatwolf stare at them. Instead of charging, it approached very slowly, cautiously, its yellow eyes unblinking.

"Perhaps I should turn the wagon around. Do you think we could outrun it?"

Rowen glanced at Left and Right. The horses could smell what lay ahead of them and were pawing the ground and twisting, jostling the wagon. Rowen shook his head. "We'll have to try and scare it off." *Which might be easier said than done.*

He moved his hand away from his shortsword. Without waiting to ask permission, Rowen hurried into the back of the wagon. He grabbed the closest crossbow and passed it up to Hráthbam, along with a quiver of bolts. He was about to grab the second crossbow for himself when his eyes fell on the Queshi composite bow instead.

Made from fused bone and wood that took the better part of a year to cure, Queshi bows were short but incredibly powerful. Rowen had seen them send arrows through wooden shields and chain mail with ease. He had only a moment to inspect this one, but it appeared to be serviceable. He took it along with a quiver of solid, well-fletched arrows and rejoined Hráthbam at the front of the wagon.

The Soroccan merchant had already risen from his seat. He looked nervous, but his hands were steady as he spanned his crossbow and nocked a bolt. He held the reins of Left and Right under his boot. Lifting the crossbow to shoulder height, he tucked the weapon against his shoulder and sighted down the shaft.

"Don't fire yet," Rowen advised. "Maybe we'll get lucky, and the damn thing will leave us alone!" He drew an arrow from his quiver as he spoke, fit the arrow to his bowstring, and gave the composite bow a long test pull. He liked the smoothness of its draw, the raw power tensed at his fingertips. He relaxed the bowstring without loosing the arrow. For now, they would wait.

The greatwolf had not yet made up its mind. Thirty feet away, turned sideways, it blocked the entire road, studying them with yellow, dagger-thin eyes. Its jaws closed in a low growl. Sleek reddish fur ran the course of its well-muscled body. It looked like an ordinary wolf except that it had claws like a tiger and its hind legs were shorter— meaning that it charged not in a sprint but in long, powerful leaps. That made it harder to hit with an arrow. *Especially with shaking hands!*

Rowen took a deep breath to steady himself. "Just one arrow won't put that thing down." He gauged the distance between them and the greatwolf. He might get off two shots if he was lucky. Hráthbam's crossbow, because it took longer to load, would probably only manage one. After that, this would be a business for their swords.

Hráthbam swore, "Dyoni's bane, that thing is bigger than my third wife!"

Rowen said, "Greatwolves go after the strongest enemies first. It'll come for us first—not the horses."

Hráthbam glanced at him dubiously. "Surely it cannot leap *this* high!"

"Oh, it can. Believe me." Rowen drew his bow, heartened once again by its power. He could fire at the greatwolf now, before it attacked, while he still had plenty of time to aim. Or he could try to scare it off.

"I'll see if I can drive it away..."

He took careful aim. Rowen was no master archer, but he had practiced long hours in the tilting yards of Saikaido Temple, and a greatwolf was hardly a small target.

Rowen let the arrow fly. He grinned as the taut bow seemed to explode in his grasp, hurtling the arrow with deadly power. Then, just as quickly, his grin vanished. He had intended his aim to be shallow—just a warning shot—but the arrow flew farther and skidded off a rock. It grazed one of the greatwolf's massive paws.

The beast yelped. Then its yellow eyes drew thinner still. It charged.

Rowen swore and drew another arrow. Before he had time to nock it, he heard a tremendous *thwap* as Hráthbam fired his crossbow. Without waiting to see the results, the merchant braced the crossbow's stirrup with his foot and used his thick arms to haul the string back. Rowen was impressed by the Soroccan's speed, even as he fumbled with his own second shot.

Hráthbam's first crossbow bolt had caught the greatwolf midleap, sinking deep into its rear flank, right above the haunch. It was a good shot. The wolf's left rear leg was crippled now. It bounded more slowly, but it did not stop. It angled around the horses, flanking them, as though it meant to leap at Rowen's side.

Rowen hoped his second arrow would fix that. But the sight of the charging beast rattled his nerves. He rushed his aim and put his second arrow into the thick gristle and hide of the beast's right shoulder. The beast howled then charged faster than before.

No time for another shot. The composite bow slipped from his fingers as he drew his Dwarrish shortsword instead. Its blade suddenly looked ridiculous and puny in his grasp.

Beside him, Hráthbam was taking careful aim with his second crossbow bolt.

But the greatwolf hurtled closer. Left and Right panicked. Left balked, jerking the wagon to one side. Then Right reared up. Both Rowen and Hráthbam lost their balance, nearly tumbling off the wagon seat. The crossbow shuddered. Hráthbam's second bolt flew wild.

Rowen thought of the shield in the back of the wagon. *Why didn't I grab the shield?*

Then, the greatwolf leapt.

Its mouth flared open, revealing rows of fat teeth curved and sharp as Hráthbam's scimitar. Instinctively, Rowen braced his feet against the wagon seat and pushed hard, tumbling backward into the rear of the wagon. The greatwolf's paws, tipped with claws that could rip a man to shreds, struck the wagon to either side of Rowen's chest instead.

The wagon shook as though struck by a battering ram. The horses broke loose. Hráthbam, who had just drawn his scimitar, tumbled to the plains before he could use it. Then, Rowen's sight was blocked by a snarling blur of fur and teeth and thin, yellow eyes. On his back now, he shoved and kicked with his feet, cracking his head and shoulders against Hráthbam's trunks, trying to get away.

The greatwolf was huge, the wagon too narrow. The beast tensed its great bulk and shoved its way after him, knocking weapons and provisions aside. Frantically, Rowen hacked with his shortsword. He stabbed at the eyes. The greatwolf took the cuts on its snout then went for his throat.

Rowen stabbed again—this time, not at the yellow eyes but into the greatwolf's lunging maw. He meant to drive the blade up into the beast's brain, but his sword tip caught the wolf in the gums, just above its incisors. The greatwolf yelped and withdrew. Rowen tried to sit up. *Is this blood mine, or his?*

Outside, Hráthbam was swearing in Soroccan over the unmistakable growl of a mad, wounded animal. Fearful, Rowen stuck his head out of the wagon's canopy and saw Hráthbam, scimitar in hand, trying to fend off the injured beast.

Before Rowen could act, the wagon lurched beneath him. He fell, knocked his head, then struggled to rise again. Right had broken free, leaving Left still tangled in the reins, yoked to the wagon hitch. Right dashed away, but Left whinnied in terror and tried to scramble free again, hooves flailing, jarring the wagon every which way.

Rowen turned. Hráthbam stood ten feet away, turned sideways to make himself a smaller target, holding up the hem of his robes with his right hand to keep from tripping while his left hand whirled the scimitar in front of him. The merchant was playing it safe, only trying to keep the greatwolf at bay. Out here, on the open plains, the beast had all the room it needed to make full use of its ferocious strength and speed. But its mouth and snout bled from wounds dealt by Rowen's shortsword—plus a few new cuts left by the crisp blur of Hráthbam's scimitar. It still had an arrow in its shoulder, a crossbow bolt in its haunch. The wolf continued to bleed, growing weaker by the second, but remained formidable.

And now, thanks to me, it's being cautious. It circled Hráthbam with dreadful patience, snapping its bloody teeth. Hráthbam circled too, trying to keep his distance. Sweat poured down his face. He seemed to know better than to try the powerful, sweeping strike. A scimitar was made for swinging, not fencing. In the time it would take Hráthbam to recover from such a swing, the greatwolf could rip him in half. So the Soroccan lunged instead, answering the greatwolf's snapping jaws with quick jabs of his own.

"Locke, my excellent friend, perhaps you could lend some assistance here!"

Rowen grasped the nearest weapon—a footman's pike—and threw it.

The beast yelped, twisting so fast that the pike tumbled from the wound and landed on the bloody grass. Rowen's aim had been true, but the beast's hide was tougher than a leather brigandine. It would take more than that to stop it. Still, for a moment, the greatwolf forgot about the Soroccan and focused on Rowen instead.

No courage without fear... Rowen charged. He assailed the beast with everything he had, hacking with such intensity that the greatwolf recoiled. Then it leapt, jaws lunging.

Instead of flesh, it met the wooden shield now strapped to Rowen's left arm. The shield stopped the blow, but the force drove Rowen off his feet. All the breath exploded from his lungs.

The greatwolf stalked after him. Stunned, Rowen raised the shield to protect himself. The beast's paws slammed down, using its weight to pin the shield to Rowen's chest. The greatwolf's jaw loomed over him, trickling blood in Rowen's face.

"Aj thraci!" Hráthbam roared his battlecry and swung his mighty scimitar with both hands. The blade descended so fast that it made a sound like a cracking whip. The greatwolf's flank, already wounded by Rowen's pike, split open. Blood erupted from the wound. The greatwolf pivoted and opened Hráthbam's thigh with its claws.

Hráthbam swore and staggered back, silk robes bloody, dark face contorted by pain. The greatwolf went after Hráthbam now, the smell of the Soroccan's blood sweet in its nostrils. It tensed wounded haunches and leapt.

Hráthbam managed to get his scimitar between them. Instead of being impaled, the greatwolf's body struck the sword at an angle and drove it away. Then it bore the Soroccan to the ground with terrible force. Its teeth loomed over Hráthbam's head. But before it could strike, Rowen shoved his shortsword into the open wound left by Hráthbam's scimitar.

Rowen grunted as his blade jarred off bone. Blood soaked the hilt, making it slippery. Rowen lost his grip, regained it, and shoved the blade still deeper. The coppery smell of blood overwhelmed him. He lost his grip on his sword again as the greatwolf thrashed. Then he reached out blindly, found the pommel, and twisted with both hands.

The blade snapped.

The greatwolf gave a shrill yelp and tumbled to the earth. It shuddered then lay still.

Rowen fell too. Savage exhilaration turned suddenly to exhaustion. Gasping for air, he fumbled with the cracked shield still strapped to his arm, tossing away the fragments. Then he made his way to Hráthbam's side.

"Are you alive?"

The Soroccan's eyes clenched with pain. Gritting his teeth, he nodded. The greatwolf's hindquarters had landed on his ankles, but the merchant pushed his way clear. Then he fearfully examined his thigh. What he saw made him swear.

Rowen's stomach sank at the sight, too. For a moment, he was paralyzed. Then, shaking himself from his daze, he rushed to bandage and treat the awful wound.

There was too much of the greatwolf's blood on his own clothes, so he tore a clean strip from Hráthbam's robe instead. Hráthbam's flask leaned from one of the pockets. Rowen took the flask, opened it, and held it while Hráthbam took a long drink. Then he poured the rest of the hláshba over the wound.

Hráthbam went as rigid as the greatwolf, then slowly, he relaxed. "Such a waste... of good hláshba," he said with a forced grin. "Does it look as bad to your eyes as it does to mine?"

Rowen knotted a second then a third makeshift bandage around Hráthbam's wounded thigh. He pressed hard on the wound, causing the Soroccan to grit his teeth. This was not the first time Rowen had dealt with wounds, but this one was different. "I can't stop the bleeding."

Hráthbam nodded quickly. "I didn't expect you to. I am..." He paused. "There is no word for it in the Common Tongue. But my blood does not thicken as yours does."

Rowen felt a cold chill that had nothing to do with the breeze against his blood-wet face. He had seen this before, in the slums of the Dark Quarter: children who could not stop bleeding. For them, even a fistfight or a graze from a knife could be deadly, unless they kept proper ointments handy to staunch the blood flow.

"How... how do I treat this?"

Hráthbam shook his head. "Just bring me more hláshba. I want to be good and drunk when I meet the gods."

But Rowen refused. "No way even you were dumb enough to leave Sorocco without something to treat this. Now where is it?"

"In the wagon," Hráthbam said, finally. He shuddered. His eyes rolled before coming back into focus. "In the smallest trunk, the one painted with my people's sigil. A pouch full of green powder. Bring it... with water."

Rowen sprinted toward the wagon. Left had finally broken free. Both she and Right stood some distance away, watching. The wagon was on its side now, provisions spilled in all directions. It took an eternity for Rowen to locate the small chest painted with the emblem of a black galleon against a white sea. When at last he found it, the chest was sealed. Rowen grabbed the nearest weapon—a hatchet—and broke the lock. Inside the chest, he found cracked vials, soaked scrolls, and a small leather pouch.

He feared at first that the liquid from the cracked vials had soaked into the pouch, but inside he found a dry, foul-smelling powder the color of spring leaves. Rowen rummaged for a waterskin then hurried back to his master.

Hráthbam's dark face had paled. His eyes were closed. Rowen knelt on the bloody grass and shook him. Green eyes flickered opened. The Soroccan stared without comprehension.

"What do I do?" Rowen pressed. He showed Hráthbam the pouch. "Damn you, tell me what to do with this!"

Hráthbam's words slurred. "Two... pinches of the powder... right in the wound. Press hard. Then... just a little water. Bandage after."

Rowen nodded. Carefully, he removed the bloody silk bandages to find that the bleeding had not slowed. He was about to add the powder into the wound when he remembered stories of other men's and animals' blood causing further sickness to the wounded. He opened the waterskin and rinsed his hands as best he could. Then he rinsed Hráthbam's wound and sprinkled two pinches of the strange green powder directly into it.

He pressed hard. The Soroccan hissed, but Rowen did not let up. He leveled all his weight on the wound until he counted to one hundred, then he let up and rinsed the wound again.

This time, surprisingly, the wound foamed like the mouth of a rabid animal. Rowen added more powder then rinsed the wound but with less water this time. The bleeding slowed but did not stop.

Rowen kept more pressure on the wound. When finally the bleeding seemed to have ceased, he peeled off his own bloody tunic, noting in the process that his own injuries were just scratches, and wadded his tunic beneath Hráthbam's head as though it were a pillow.

He eyed the man's open wound and wondered if he shouldn't find a needle and thread to sew it shut. He was a fair hand at that, having treated Kayden's wounds and his own on the battlefield, but he did not want to leave the wound uncovered while he searched for what he needed.

He tore fresh strips of silk from Hráthbam's robes and once again bandaged the man's thigh, as tightly as he dared. Only then did he notice the Soroccan's eyes—closed, unmoving.

CHAPTER SIX

DRAGONKIN

F LAMES.

Shade could not see, could not move, could only feel crisp flames gnawing him down to the bone. With awful certainty, he realized it would not stop. It would never stop.

But then, it stopped.

Water—cool, deep, dark—enveloped him, soothing the pain into a memory. The water faded, became only air. He remembered Sylvos and the breathtaking height of the World Tree. He remembered his own name... then Fadarah... then Silwren. He opened his eyes.

Fadarah stood over him. The great man's tattooed face was taut with exhaustion, smeared with dirt and dried blood. Stripped to the waist, the big man's muscular torso—tattooed in Ogrish writing—was covered in sweat and a dissipating violet glow. Fadarah's eyes were closed, but he opened them as well and smiled.

"You nearly crossed over. Another moment, and we'd have lost you."

Shade tried to speak.

Fadarah shook his head. "Save your strength, my friend. The flames bit you deep. I have restored you, but you must rest now."

Shade blinked frantically, trying to will enough strength into his mind so that he might make sense of things. To know he was alive was not enough. What about Silwren?

Suddenly, Fadarah's voice echoed in his head even though his master's lips had not moved. *"Save your strength, my friend. We can mindspeak more easily."*

Shade cursed his own foolishness. *"General, is Silwren—"*

"Alive," Fadarah answered aloud, "but gone. I hoped that allowing her to emerge from her sleep on her own time would prevent madness. I was wrong. In her panic, she nearly destroyed you and everyone around her."

Shade tried to sit up.

Fadarah stopped him by pressing one great hand to his chest. "Peace, Kith'el! Save your strength. I don't have the power to heal you again, and there are others who need my attention this night."

For the first time, Shade realized that he was back in Fadarah's command tent, surrounded on all sides by burnt and injured Shel'ai. Others who had survived Silwren's awakening were tending to them, a violet glow enveloping their bodies. Instead of wytchfire, they summoned vaporous, healing energies and urged them into the broken forms of their comrades. Que'ann was with them, her wrinkled face taut with weariness and concentration as she moved about, seemingly set on healing everyone at once.

Shade remembered the six Shel'ai tasked with defending the initiates. Surely they were dead. But he had seen only Fadarah and Que'ann coming to their rescue. The other Shel'ai had been too far away, scattered throughout the camp. *"How were so many wounded?"*

Fadarah's brow furrowed. *"Silwren did not just attack those around her,"* the Sorcerer-General answered. *"As she fled, her rage sought out all others with magic in their blood. In her panic, she turned on herself—by turning on us."*

A terrible question formed in Shade's mind. *"The other initiates—"*

"Dead," Fadarah answered. *"Aerios, Cierrath... Silwren killed them both while they slept. They felt no pain, save what torment already roiled in their minds. Don't be afraid,"* he continued. *"We do not blame her. She's mad with pain worse than the rest of us can imagine. But we'll find her. Now rest. I must tend the others."*

Shade had a thousand questions, but he stopped himself. Fadarah squeezed his shoulder then left to tend the other wounded Shel'ai. Shade lay back and shut his eyes, battling the despair rising up within him.

El'rash'lin had already forsaken them. The Nightmare was

growing too powerful, too unstable. Now, death had claimed Aerios and Cierrath, and even Silwren was gone. How had it come to this? How long had he slept, and how far must Silwren have fled by now?

I will find her. Fadarah and the others must keep the army moving east, toward Lyos. It will take all of them to keep the Nightmare in check. But I'll find her. I will talk to her, reason with her, save her. I will bring her back!

The young Shel'ai took a deep breath and let it go. If he did not rest, he would die. And then, Silwren would be alone out there, ravaged and mad. Shade took a deep breath and released it. For now, he would wait. Besides, Silwren would be easy enough to find. Already, Shade could guess exactly where she was going.

"Cadavash..." He whispered the dreadful word, moments before he willed himself to sleep.

Hráthbam shuddered in his sleep-like stupor. Rowen knew at once the reason why. He sprinted to the wagon, gathered every cloak he could find, then rushed back and used them to cover his master. While doing so, he checked the bandages. *He's lost too much blood.*

He eyed the bloody grass and the dead greatwolf. The beast already reeked as though it had been rotting for days. He kicked its head. Then, grimacing, he grabbed its hind legs and hauled it away, muscles straining. He caught a faint glimpse of steel in the ruddy muck: the broken blade of his shortsword, still planted inside the greatwolf's ribcage. *That's two swords I've lost now.*

He searched the wagon for a needle and thread. The first trunk he opened overflowed with fine robes. Amid the heaps of silk, he found a satchel containing soap, several spools of thread, and a few needles. Some of the needles were thick enough to repair leather with the aid of a hammer, but Rowen found one slender enough for wounds. He chose the thinnest spool of thread and returned.

Rowen removed the silk bandages, rinsed the wound yet again, then meticulously sewed the man's thigh shut. Hráthbam barely stirred. Rowen remembered the long stream of curses his brother used to utter whenever Rowen sewed him up after a fight, be it on a battlefield or a tavern common room.

Rowen bandaged Hráthbam's wounds once again then checked for the big man's pulse. It fluttered weakly. The Soroccan was still shivering, so Rowen went to the nearest tree with a hatchet, hacked down a few dry branches, took the flint from his own satchel, and built a fire.

Left and Right had calmed down now, and they hesitantly drew closer to their injured master, stirring listlessly near the fire. The horses whinnied with concern. Rowen was stumbling with exhaustion, but he found oats and a brush in the wagon and cared for the horses. Finally, he allowed himself to sit and rest for a moment.

He happened to collapse facing west. The sky shone with the same vibrant color as Hráthbam's blood. Rowen shook himself from this thought then realized how hungry and thirsty he was.

He remembered food in the wagon, but he doubted he had the strength to rise any more. He ate some of the dry, tasteless rations from his satchel, drank from the waterskin, then slowly poured some water into his sleeping master's mouth. The Soroccan swallowed but did not stir, his dark skin colder than ever. Rowen added a few more branches to the fire.

Nothing more I can do, he told himself. He used the waterskin to rinse Hráthbam's blood from his hands. *I've stopped the bleeding, cleaned and sewn the wound, given him water. He's sleeping. It's in the gods' hands now.*

Rowen considered the irony of this, given their earlier, blasphemous discussion about the gods. Glancing up at the northern sky, he located Armahg's Eye, its light gaining brilliance as twilight blued the rest of the sky. Rowen looked up at Armahg's Eye and muttered the only prayer he knew. He said it several times. He did not expect anyone to listen.

A scream jolted Rowen from his sleep.

He bolted up, and for a moment, he did not know where he was. Twilight had darkened the clouds. Nearby, Left and Right pricked their ears, pawing the earth with fright. The campfire still burned, warm against his bare feet.

The awful sound had startled the wounded Soroccan, too. He tried to sit up. "Dyoni's bane... what was that?"

"Just a deer," Rowen lied, fumbling for his shortsword before he remembered it was gone. Rising shakily to his feet, he searched for another weapon. Nearby lay Hráthbam's heavy scimitar, the footman's pike—which he'd retrieved from the battlefield—and the Queshi composite bow. Rowen preferred the bow, but the quiver of arrows was still by the wagon. He grabbed the pike instead.

"Like hells," Hráthbam said, coughing. "Unless by 'deer,' you mean ornery succubus!"

Rowen ignored him. By the sound of the scream, he expected to see a flock of demons descending upon them. Dusk darkened the horizon as far as he could see. But the moon was waxing and the stars were out, and the pale glow of Armahg's Eye lit the hills and grasslands as Rowen's eyes searched for enemies.

"I must have been dreaming."

"More like a nightmare," Hráthbam said. He reached weakly for his scimitar. "And if you had it, my friend, so did I!"

Rowen kept the pike in hand as he returned to the wagon and found the arrows for the composite bow. He also grabbed Hráthbam's crossbow and quiver of bolts though he doubted the Soroccan was strong enough to use them. He returned to the campfire but sat with his back to the flames so his eyes would not be blinded by the light.

"How do you feel?" he asked.

Hráthbam whispered quietly, "Like I had my leg opened by a wolf the size of my third wife... then I bled half my guts on the cold, hard ground." He laughed thinly, the sound barely audible over the crackling of the campfire.

Rowen took the waterskin and helped the Soroccan drink as much as he could. "Do you realize that I could have killed you in Breccorry?"

Hráthbam paused. "Are you referring... to our little sparring match? If you managed... to scratch me, I'd have deserved it." He drank more then coughed.

Rowen lowered the waterskin, slipped one arm under the man's shoulders, and held him up until he was done coughing. "Sleep now," he said. "I'll keep watch."

"How... how are the horses?" Hráthbam asked instead. "Are they hurt? Did my third wife get them, too?"

"No," Rowen said, "they're just over there. If you could stand up, you'd see them. I think they're worried about you."

The merchant scoffed. "Don't bet on it, my friend! Especially Right. If she had teeth like that wolf, she'd have taken my head off a long time ago." Despite his words, the merchant's tone was filled with affection. "And the wagon?"

"Not as bad as you think," Rowen answered quickly. "Left tipped it over, but it'll be fine once we get it upright. A few things got banged and busted, but nothing serious." He added, "You should be more worried about yourself."

Hráthbam waved him off. "My people do not waste precious time on worry!" He laughed then winced with pain. "Is there any... hláshba left?"

"No," Rowen said. "But there's wine." He held the wineskin for the merchant again. "Just a little," he cautioned. "Take the edge off the pain, but too much is dangerous if you've lost a lot of blood."

"Now is hardly the time to scold me for drinking!"

Rowen sat with his back to the fire again, pike laid across his knees. The composite bow lay within easy reach, near a quiver of arrows. "You hired me to be your protector, didn't you? That hláshba stuff will rot your innards."

Hráthbam did not answer, shivering beneath the pile of cloaks. Rowen reached to one side and tossed a few more branches onto the fire.

"My wives bribed you to get me sober," the Soroccan grumbled at last. "Admit it."

"Freely," Rowen answered. "Now, sleep."

"I'll sleep soon enough, I fear. If 'sleep' is what you call it." He tried to sit up.

"Lie still, damn you! If you reopen that wound, I'll personally smash every last thing in the wagon!"

Hráthbam laughed weakly but gave in. "Talk," he grumbled. "If I can't... listen to my own prattle... at least I can listen to yours."

"What should we talk about? The gods, again?"

Hráthbam shook his head. "No, I think any questions I have about them... will be answered soon enough. Tell me... about the Isle Knights."

Rowen hesitated. "What about them?"

Hráthbam reached for the wineskin. Rowen helped the man drink again. After a moment, Hráthbam asked, "What made you... go to the Isles?"

"Mostly my brother, I guess," Rowen began uncertainly. "My parents were Ivairian. Far from rich but not quite poor, either. My father squired for some middling Lancer. But the famines ended all that. So we left Ivairia, moved to some nothing of a village north of Lyos..."

"Bandits?"

"More like rival, starving refugees. They killed my parents and... my sister too, once they'd finished with her."

"I am sorry, my friend."

Rowen shrugged. "I was only two or three. I don't really remember them." He clenched his fingers around the pike resting across his knees. "My brother, Kayden, was older. We would have died, too, but some Isle Knights happened by. They swept through the killers like fire through dry straw. They saved us. But the town was gone. So Kayden took me to Lyos. We grew up as orphans in the Dark Quarter."

"I have... heard of that place. Not a pleasant stage for a childhood."

Rowen snickered. "You could say that. If you don't starve or find yourself on the wrong end of somebody's knife, that's just the beginning. Certain things happen there... not just to women but to children, too.

"It wasn't all bad, though," Rowen added, anxious to change the topic. "Kayden took care of me as best he could—though he probably bloodied my nose more than anybody! We lived like rats at first, stealing food, but he kept me alive. And he talked about the Knights all the time. He never forgot how they saved us. When we were young, we survived by digging graves—and robbing them too, I'm ashamed to say." As he spoke, Rowen caught a whiff of the dead greatwolf and grimaced. "When we were old enough, we became sellswords. There's plenty of coin to be made among the Free Cities if you're willing to risk your skin for it. We went as far south as the deserts of Quesh, where they breed those red horses that ride faster than lightning." *I almost stayed there...* Rowen jabbed the fire with his pike. "On the way back, we stopped at Atheion, where everybody has copper-colored skin and all the houses float on rafts on Armahg's Tears. I've never seen a sea so big and clear." *Could have stayed there too, but Kayden always wanted to keep moving.* "For a while, Kayden talked about dragging us all the way up to Ivairia, finding a Lancer we could squire for—polish his armor and wipe his ass between tourneys."

This made Hráthbam smile weakly.

"But mainly, we just bounced between the Free Cities. Still, Kayden always said he wanted to go to the Lotus Isles and become a Knight of the Crane. The only real knighthood, he called it. I said he was crazy. The Shao almost never agree to train foreigners unless you could prove you had some tie to the older houses, like the first Knights who went there with Fâyu Jinn. But he went anyway. He saved up every coin for years—and took them from me when I let him—until he had enough to buy his way in. He trained with Aeko Shingawa herself. And by the gods, he did it. He became a Knight of the Crane."

Rowen stopped, wondering how much the Soroccan knew about the particulars of the Isle Knights. "That's the lowest of three orders, but I bet he could have been a Knight of the Stag in no time. They say they don't let foreigners rise higher, but Kayden would have changed that. Who knows? Maybe he even would have made Knight of the Lotus someday!"

Rowen stared down at his pike for a while, then out into the growing darkness. He pivoted and added more wood to the fire, feeding and feeding it until he was sweating.

He feared that Hráthbam would press him further about Kayden, but instead the Soroccan said, "I've seen those Shao sabers at work before,"—*adamunes*, Rowen thought but did not correct him—"even have one locked up in the wagon. After you... bury me, it's yours."

Rowen scowled. He was about to assure the merchant that he would survive his wound—or to point out that common practice among Isle

Knights actually forbade squires from owning adamunes—then he changed his mind. "It will be my honor."

Waving off his thanks, Hráthbam said, "If you want to be a Knight like your brother, what are you... doing here? Why aren't you on the Isles?"

Rowen almost wished he'd asked about Kayden instead.

"I was... expelled from training," he said. "It happens. Every half year, they dismiss certain squires they deem to be... unworthy. We started with two hundred. I made it until the fourth year. There were just thirty of us left. One more year, and I would have been knighted."

Hráthbam said, "After... how you dealt with that wolf, I can't imagine... it was for lack of skill! What kind... of training takes five whole years to master?"

"It's not just swords," Rowen answered. "They teach you reading and writing. Not just in Common Tongue but old Shao, too." Saying this reminded him of his conversation with the robber, Sneed. *What happened to you? Did you get away, or did Dagath hunt you down?*

Hráthbam smiled. "I bet... you learned everything they set in front of you. So why did they send you away?"

Rowen did not answer.

Hráthbam pressed, "Didn't they give you... any reason at all?"

"They don't have to. If the Knight in charge of your training touches your forehead with an empty scabbard, that's it. You're gone by morning, or you're dead."

He winced as he spoke. He had tried to expel that memory from his mind, but the sight of Aeko Shingawa with her almond eyes and long, dark braids—the same legendary Knight who had trained his brother, whom he had sought out for just that reason—grimly touching him with the empty scabbard still haunted him.

"Their mistake," Hráthbam said finally.

Rowen shrugged. His face burned red with shame. Nervously touching the pike again, he stared out into the darkness of the Simurgh Plains. The world had gone quiet. Whatever had caused that awful sound had vanished—probably died. Still, Rowen did not trust himself to sleep. The campfire blazed, almost unbearably hot, but Hráthbam went on shivering.

Rowen was about to add more wood, but he realized that they were out. He should rise, get the hatchet, and go trim a few more branches to burn. Instead, he sat in heavy silence, sleep tugging at his eyelids. Finally, he shook himself awake. With great effort, he rose to his feet and headed toward a cluster of thin, ragged-looking trees in the distance. He had already left them dismembered to fuel the fire; by the time he was done, they resembled trees less closely than they did thick spears thrust in the earth and abandoned beneath the dark sky.

Rowen stumbled back. He piled still more wood on the fire then sat. *I need to keep Hráthbam talking, keep him awake.*

"There are worse things than not being an Isle Knight, I suppose. Mercenaries live better than some. Besides, now I get to drink your wine and guard your sorry ass all the way to Cadavash!" He laughed in a way he hoped sounded convincing. "I meant to ask you at the inn—how did you know I'd been to the Isles?"

Hráthbam did not answer. Rowen wondered if the man had fallen asleep. He turned. The Soroccan's eyes were still open, bright green in the flickering firelight. Rowen started to repeat his question then stopped himself. He tossed the pike away and felt for the merchant's pulse. Then he bowed his head.

The fire went on crackling behind him. Not far away, cicadas began their night song. A cool breeze through a cluster of trees rustled a few autumn leaves from their branches. The horses, Left and Right, restlessly pawed the grassy earth in search of more oats. But Hráthbam Nassir Adjrâ-al-Habas was dead.

CHAPTER SEVEN
DRAGONKIN

ROWEN DID NOT WAIT UNTIL morning.

He closed Hráthbam's staring eyes and sat in a stupor for a long time, blank faced by the dying fire. Then he rose to his feet. He rummaged through the wagon for a shovel. The contents of the tipped wagon had been flung in all directions, and Rowen did not feel right going through the man's trunks, but he thought he remembered spotting a shovel in the back of the wagon. Finally, amid the jumble, he found what he needed.

He slumped back to Hráthbam's corpse. The man's silk robes now resembled a flamboyant burial shroud. The fire had nearly gone out, but the chill that swept through Rowen's body had nothing to do with the late autumn evening. Nevertheless, he stoked the campfire before he began to dig.

He chose a spot far from the road, beneath the dark boughs of a maple tree. The ground was soft there, the air fragrant with night-sap and good clean earth. Rowen blinked back exhaustion and thrust the blade of the shovel into the ground. By midnight, he had dug a hole deep enough to stand in up to his waist.

He worked on widening the grave next, focusing his anger into tossing shovelfuls of dark earth over his shoulder until, at last, he stopped. The grave looked big enough. Feeling foolish, Rowen tested it by lying down himself. He had to scrunch his knees to fit, and he remembered that Hráthbam was taller than he was. But if he bent the man's knees, it would work.

Rowen climbed out of the grave. It was time, but he could not bring himself to bury the man yet. He turned and saw Right nuzzling the dead Soroccan's body. Tears sprang to Rowen's eyes, but he blinked them away.

He thought about the dead greatwolf instead. Its body would attract scavengers who might catch Hráthbam's scent as well—even buried that deep. But Rowen was not about to dig a second grave for the greatwolf. So he went back to the wagon, rummaged around, and located several flasks filled, not with wine, but with a thick liquor nearly as putrid as hláshba. This, Rowen hoped, would burn.

He dragged the greatwolf farther still from his makeshift camp, across the road, as far as he could from Hráthbam's grave. Finally, cursing and sweating, he went to gather the flasks. He poured their contents into the beast's ruddy, blood-matted fur then glanced back toward Hráthbam. "Sorry to waste your stock, my friend." The sound of his own voice made him feel lonesome.

He let the strong liquor soak for a moment before he set it on fire. Then he gathered dry branches and added them to the fire made from the greatwolf's body, tying a cloth around his face to protect himself from the stench. Then, he returned to his own campfire. He shooed Right away. The horse's nuzzling had cocked Hráthbam's head to an awkward angle, and the merchant's jaw sagged.

Rowen shuddered. As gently as he could, he used the toe of his boot to straighten Hráthbam's head. "I'm sorry. I wish I could have done more."

Rowen suddenly felt absurd. He had barely known this man. After all the corpses he'd seen in battles, not to mention all the corpses whose graves he'd dug beyond Pallantine Hill outside Lyos, why should this death matter so much to him?

I could go through his pockets for coin. He squelched the thought, ashamed.

He left the shovel lying on the ground, grabbed the big man by his thick wrists, marshaled his strength, and slowly dragged the Soroccan toward the open grave. He had to stop often to rest, and he did not like how Hráthbam's slack arms fell to the earth when he released them, or the cold feel of his skin.

He hauled the Soroccan's body the rest of the way to the grave then stopped to rest one last time, intending to push him in and bury him as soon as he regained his strength. Thirsty, Rowen went back to the campfire, found the waterskin, then stopped.

Hráthbam's lips touched this last. Rowen remembered a Queshi tradition in which family members kissed the dead on the lips before he or she was given to the fire. He shuddered. Then he forced himself to drink what was left before he returned to his work. He looked down one last time at his former master. He was about to push him into the grave when a rustling sound echoed from behind him, in the direction of his makeshift camp.

Probably just the horses. Nevertheless, he reached for the pike and turned. Between the dark outlines of Left and Right, he spotted a man—stooped as though quite old, clad in a ratty cloak, gently patting the horses as though they were his own.

Rage flooded his senses. Hefting the pike, he stalked back toward the campfire. The stooped man turned at his approach. Instead of running, he patted Right's head as the horse nuzzled him.

"These horses mourn their master."

Rowen stopped. The man spoke Common, but his accent was melodic and strange. The man's hood obscured his features in shadows. Rowen pointed at him with the pike. "Would you rather they mourned you?"

The hooded man cocked his head to one side. "Are you in the habit of killing men you've only just met?"

Rowen's rage went slack. *Does he mean killing him, or is he asking if I killed Hráthbam?* "A greatwolf attacked us," he answered dumbly, gesturing toward the grave in the distance.

"I know." The stooped, hooded figure turned his attention to Left and stroked the rouncey's neck. "I was walking when I saw your fire. Or maybe I was dreaming. Can't say. But I felt something, thought you were... *her.* But you're just you. Just a Human. Yet here I am. Strange."

He's a madman. "What do you want?"

The stooped figure cocked his head again. Though Rowen could not make out the man's features, something in the gesture unsettled him. "To help you," the man said at last. "I'm supposed to, I think. Though I don't know what it will do to me."

Rowen answered the man's cryptic talk by holding up his hand. "See these blisters? Means you're late. I've already dug the grave. I just need to roll him in and cover him up. If you want to help with that, I'll pay you with food and a place by the fire—so long as you sit still and keep whatever nonsense your tongue is waggling to yourself!"

The stranger nodded. "How generous." He laughed. The sound sent a chill down Rowen's spine. "May I see your hands?"

Rowen frowned and backed up a step. "My what?"

"Your hands. Those things at the ends of your wrists with all the fingers on them. May I see?"

Rowen tensed his grip on the pike. "Listen, friend, I have no patience for madmen right now. If you want food, just take it and go."

The horses suddenly whinnied and drew back, as though sensing something terrible flash to life in the man before them. But the stooped figure's voice remained steady. "No patience for madmen? You may find that a liability in this world. All of us are mad. Some are just more honest about it."

Rowen leveled his pike at the stranger's chest, prodding him with just enough force to show he meant business without drawing blood. "Enough, old man. Pass on, or I'll burn your corpse right next to the greatwolf's!"

The stooped figure straightened. Rowen saw with surprise that the man easily matched his height. "I suppose I *am* older than you— by a good half-century, at least. But my people live a long, long time. So it's hard to say which of us is older, depending on how you mean the word."

Jalist once said you never turn your back on a madman. Should I kill him? "Listen, friend, I've warned you—"

The stooped figure raised one hand and touched the tip of Rowen's pike. As though wrenched by invisible hands, the weapon flew from Rowen's grasp and sailed end over end, landing somewhere in the darkness beyond the light of the campfire. Rowen's eyes widened. "How..."

"Beware men who call you *friend* while jabbing your chest with a pike," the madman said. "Now, can I have a look at those hands, or must I assault you with threats of my own?"

When Rowen did not move, the madman made a sharp, slashing motion with one hand. Rowen's hands thrust straight out, palms turned upward. He had no idea why, nor could he do otherwise. He struggled, but he could not gain control of his own arms.

"Now, let's see..."

The madman bent and examined Rowen's blistered palms. His skin was cold but his touch gentle. He clucked his tongue. "You should take better care of these hands, young man. Do you know that blood never truly washes off? If you know how to look, that is." He pressed his hands over Rowen's, tightening his grip. Rowen gasped. Despite his thin frame, the stooped man was frightfully strong. Rowen struggled to break free, to no avail. He wanted to aim a kick at the stranger's kneecaps, but his legs would not obey him, either. Rowen had the awful thought that he was as lifeless as Hráthbam.

But what stunned him most was the man's hands. They were covered in warts and scars, as were the man's bare wrists. His fingers were hideously twisted although he straightened the fingers to grab Rowen. Then, right before Rowen's eyes, a strange violet glow washed over the stooped figure's hands.

"Shel'ai..."

"Not quite. Not anymore." The stooped figure held him a moment longer then let go. Rowen felt some invisible force lift off his body, and suddenly he could move again.

"There! You see?"

The blisters were gone. Even the days-old cut dealt by Dagath had disappeared without a trace. Rowen was so stunned that it took him a moment to realize he could move his arms again. "I'm... dreaming..."

"Maybe we all are. Maybe that's all life is. Or not. Now, let's see about your friend." He passed Rowen and made his way toward Hráthbam's corpse. The ratty cloak rustled about his crooked frame as he shuffled forward into the night. He reminded Rowen of one of the crippled wretches who shambled through the Dark Quarter, begging for change. *But none of them can conjure magic!*

Rowen considered running. His fists clenched, and he followed after the crippled stranger, wishing he knew where the pike had gone. He remembered the composite bow but did not want to turn his back on the man long enough to find it.

By the time Rowen reached the maple tree, the stooped figure was slowly kneeling beside Hráthbam's corpse. The stranger inspected the man's wounded thigh through the gash in his robes left by the greatwolf's claws. He did not look up.

"This will hurt me," the stranger said in a low voice. "If I summon all that I'd need to heal this man, I don't know... what would happen to me after. Maybe I'll keep control. Maybe I won't. If not, there will be nothing left here but ashes. I'd tell you to take the horses and run, but the further he goes toward the Light, the harder this will be. You have to make the choice." He looked up. "Do you understand?"

Not a gods-damned word! "Yes," Rowen said instead.

The crooked figure seemed to take this as his answer and lowered his gaze to Hráthbam again. "Death is death. Every sane person knows that. Then again, death is also *not* death—depending, of course, on what you mean by *not*." He laughed curtly. "I have no idea what that means, but I know it's true." He took Hráthbam's cold, dark hands between his own. Rowen saw the stooped man's hideous flesh again.

Jinn's name, what is he doing? Rowen grabbed the only weapon within reach: the shovel. Holding it with both hands, he lifted it high. Moonlight shone off the dirt-speckled blade.

"You might want to wait a moment before bashing my head off," the stooped figure said. He still did not look up. "Your friend will thank you for it." The violet glow returned. But this time, it washed over the madman's entire body. Brighter and brighter it glowed, until Rowen was blinded. Light flooded the Simurgh Plains. Swearing, Rowen backed away, dropping the shovel to shield his eyes. He tried to hold his ground, but the glare drove him back until he lost his footing and fell, still pressing his fists to his eyes.

Moments later, the glow dimmed. Fearfully, Rowen lowered his hands. He was stunned for a moment, blinking in the dark, then he found and picked up the shovel again.

Ahead of him, the stooped figure rose slowly. He looked weaker now, unbalanced. As he took a step, he lurched and nearly fell. Rowen didn't know whether to help him or strike him. Then the hood fell from his face. Moonlight spilled down features every bit as hideous as the skin that covered the man's hands and wrists.

Rowen gasped, horrified. The stranger glanced up at him sharply. He quickly tugged his hood back up—but not before Rowen saw the man's eyes: deep violet save for the pupils, which were not black but white as mist.

The stooped figure turned away, looking at Hráthbam again. "You can try bashing me with the shovel again if you like. But I wouldn't suggest it. Your friend will be very hungry when he wakes. And confused. The latter is a blessing. Some things are best forgotten. Perhaps this whole night is one such example."

Gathering his ratty cloak about his stooped frame, the Shel'ai started to shuffle off then stopped and glanced back. "I think the Light has plans for us. But I could be wrong. I often am. Goodbye. Remember what I said about your hands." He shuffled toward the dark, easterly horizon.

Rowen started to follow when a low groan interrupted him. The body of the Soroccan merchant shuddered. Then, Hráthbam's eyes opened, green and full of life in the darkness.

The Soroccan stared. Then he saw the open grave beside him. His eyes fixed next on the shovel in Rowen's hand. Hráthbam shook himself. His voice hoarse, he said, "If you mean to bury me alive, you pale-faced, red-haired bastard, at least give me a drink first!"

Captain Lethe of the Unseen awoke with a stream of curses as someone yanked his tent open. Fresh sunlight streamed into his eyes. Shielding them with one hand, the captain reached for his sword. He drew the blade and might have taken the guard's head off before he recognized him.

Ruefully, he sheathed his weapon and closed his eyes again. "If you don't close that flap, I'll kill your mother and rape her ghost."

The guard paled. "I'm sorry, Captain, but General Fadarah sent me."

The captain's eyes stayed closed. "This army has been sitting in the same place for a week while the sorcerers tend their wounded. It will probably be sitting here another week before we start moving again. There's nothing to fight. What in Fohl's hells does that tattooed bastard want with me now?"

To speak with such open disdain about a Shel'ai—especially Fadarah—was unheard of even among the Unseen, who had more reason than any to hate the sorcerers. The guard said, "You are to meet Lord Shade at the east end of the camp. Fadarah has reassigned you to be his bodyguard."

Lethe sneered and opened one eye. "From what I hear, that one's killed ten times more men than I have. I doubt he needs a wet-nurse." He closed his eye. "Tell Fadarah to find somebody else."

"Forgive me, Captain, but General Fadarah said that if you do not go at once—"

Lethe chuckled. "Let me guess. If I don't scurry off like a good slave and serve the sorcerer as his lapdog, the mighty Fadarah will come drag me out himself, and I'll spend the rest of the day in unimaginable agony." He snickered, his eyes still closed. "Is that about right?"

The guard hesitated. "Actually, Captain, he said it would be *three* days this time."

Lethe gave the guard such a withering glance that the man reached for his sword. But Lethe merely rose, dressed, girded his weapons and leather armor, then stepped out to piss on the grass before quietly stalking away. As he did so, he imagined the guard who had awakened him turning to what must be his second task: locating the next Unseen officer in line, another cutthroat probably still drunk off wine and rape, and telling him he had just been promoted. *Poor bastard!*

As the former Captain of the Unseen stalked through the camp, soldiers hurried to get out of his way. Even unwashed and unshaven, Lethe was unmistakable in his black leather armor emblazoned with red greatwolves. As Lethe walked, he passed two Shel'ai in their bone-white cloaks and wished, as he always did, that he might simply step into their path and shove steel into their throats, angling it into their brains. Of course, that was impossible.

My own damn fault. Gods, why did I agree to this? Hurrying past the

Shel'ai, neither of which gave him a second glance, Lethe considered the complex web of magic that had been seared deep into his mind—as was the case for every Unseen warrior. While the Shel'ai required that all Unseen agreed to the Blood Thrall, it hardly seemed a fair choice since the only alternative had been death.

Used first as an assassin, Lethe had eliminated enemies of the Shel'ai from Dhargoth to Ivairia: rogue slavers, quarrelsome generals, and sellsword captains whose ambitions overshadowed their ability. Lethe had no idea how many he had killed. He only knew that he never failed, never lost. Not even once. Not even when he wanted to.

Lethe often thought that he had been transformed—thanks to the Blood Thrall—into the perfect attack dog. Still, he could not imagine any attack dog who spent so much time considering how satisfying it would be to crunch on the spines of its masters.

Lethe stalked the rest of the way through the camp then spotted Shade just outside the camp, seated on an impressive black destrier and dressed in his bone-white cloak and fighting robes, emblazoned with the crimson greatwolf. The Shel'ai impatiently held the reins of a pack-laden rouncey, along with a palfrey Lethe guessed was to be his mount. Shade threw him the reins to both animals, a short throw that gave Lethe no chance of catching them.

"You should not keep your masters waiting, Human."

Muffling a curse, Lethe mounted.

"I was awakened. I was summoned. Now, I am here."

Shade ignored the impudent response. "Your orders are simple. Command of the Unseen has been given over to your first officer for the time being. Tomorrow morning, this army breaks camp and presses on for Lyos. But we must ride ahead, find Silwren, and bring her back with all possible speed. Do you understand?"

Lethe was quiet for a moment. He had witnessed the creature Shade spoke of, just as the rest of the Throng had—an apparition, a dragon of moon-white fire—ripping across the sky, its scream chilling even the Unseen to the bone. That the thing bore little resemblance to the Nightmare did little to assuage the panic that had swept through the camp. Soon enough, the Shel'ai restored order. They swept through the camp, using magic to immobilize warrior after warrior, threatening to burn anyone else to cinders if they fled. The threat worked. Within hours, relative calm had been restored. The Shel'ai explained the event as some spell gone awry, nothing of consequence, but the Unseen knew better.

"Oh, I understand! One of your pets slipped her leash, and now—"

Shade waved his hand.

Raw pain exploded through Lethe's body. Even accustomed as he was to his torture, he still yelped when the agony of his Blood Thrall washed over him. Lethe struggled against it for a moment then toppled from his saddle. He fell hard, twitching, but did not even feel the impact. All he felt was the pain Shade wished upon him, pain in waves without end.

An illusion... The pain's not real, just an illusion...

But this helped him no more now than it had in the past. Once more, the agonies of the Blood Thrall flayed his mind until he wept. Then, at last, the pain vanished.

Shade said, "Get up."

Lethe obeyed, as though he were a dog.

Shade glowered at him. "Based on how well you've served the Sorcerer-General in the past, I thought you'd be more agreeable than this."

Still shaking, Lethe managed a response. "I serve those I fear. I do not fear *you*."

"Listen well, Human. I can harm you with impunity. Or, if you obey, I can reward you with what you seek most."

Lethe did not have to ask. He yearned for the same grace granted to all those Unseen who had perished in battle at Quorim, Syros, and Cassica. True, the Shel'ai presented the Unseen with this rare gift from time to time, but how could Lethe be sure that Shade meant what he said?

Shade smiled thinly. Lethe guessed that the Shel'ai was reading his mind. Lethe knew he should be used to such a violation, but still his face flushed with rage. He wanted to draw his sword and slash the smile from the Shel'ai's face, but he could sooner fly than accomplish such a thing.

"You know because I said so. If I give my word—even to one such as you—it is good. Now, get on your horse."

Lethe mounted the palfrey, holding the reins to the rouncey in his other hand. Satisfied, Shade turned his destrier away from the camp. "Follow." The Shel'ai started off without looking back. Angry and hopeful at the same time, Lethe had no choice but to obey.

She looked nothing like the Nightmare... Fadarah had not permitted himself to think this before, but he thought it now that he was alone in his tent. *True, the Well gave the Nightmare the same kind of power, but it did not turn him into a dragon. His appearance in battle is just our illusion, done to make him appear more terrifying.*

Yet he had seen it himself as Silwren rose from the camp, burning everything around her: though ghostly, her shape was unmistakably that of an ancient dragon: six-winged, scaled, graceful, and deadly.

The Light favors her. If she can harness the power, she might be even stronger than Iventine and El'rash'lin combined!

Of all the initiates, Silwren had been the most hesitant, persuaded less by selflessness than some kind of indignation resulting from a quarrel with her lover. Fadarah thought of Kith'el.

I should not let him call himself Shade anymore. That's the name he gave himself, the name of a killer. That's not who he is anymore. However, even as he thought this, Fadarah wondered if it was true. He remembered finding Shade on the westernmost corner of the Simurgh Plains: a boy, grinning wildly, even laughing as his hands turned a Human family to ashes. From what Fadarah could glean, these Humans had not been enemies per se, just a random clutch of dirty farmers who had the misfortune of being discovered by a vengeful child who could conjure fire.

El'rash'lin had warned him at the time, "That one is no better than a rabid animal. Right or wrong, kill him now before he destroys everything you're trying to build!"

Fadarah had sensed, even then, that Shade's magical abilities were nearly on par with his own. With Silwren's help, Fadarah had managed to civilize that child-killer, returning to Shade a measure of humanity.

But can I trust him to bring Silwren back? True, they were lovers once. But by the time she went to the Well, she had already begun to lose faith in him. Now, she has the power to annihilate an army. Until she regains her reason, she might kill him without a second thought.

Still, Shade was their best option for bringing Silwren back to the fold. He rubbed his eyes. His efforts to heal the wounded had left him exhausted. He needed to sleep, but there was no time for that. There was still a feeling of disorder in the camp. The men of the Throng needed to see him pacing about, strong and fearless—even if it was an act.

Fadarah straightened. He took a deep breath and let it go. As he did so, he touched the blue glyphs tattooed on his face in a language no one else in the camp could read: the names, in Olg, of all the Olg warriors and chieftains he had personally slain in his younger years. *Perhaps I am not so different than you are, Shade.*

As he left his tent, Fadarah wondered if one of the names had been the Olg who raped his Wyldkin mother. His father. He hoped so.

CHAPTER EIGHT

THE WINGED DEAD

UPON RISING, DIZZY AND FAMISHED, Hráthbam Nassir Adjrâ-al-Habas ate and drank even more than he had at the Inn of the Drunken Dragon in Breccorry, devouring dry rations and working his way through half a wineskin. Meanwhile, Rowen prepared a vegetable stew, which he flavored haphazardly with spices he found in the wagon: crushed peppercorn, salt, and some pungent red spice that made Rowen's eyes water but made Hráthbam grin as soon as he raised the wooden spoon to his lips.

Rowen still half-expected that he would wake any second from the strangest, most vivid dream of his life. But sunrise turned to late afternoon, and Rowen had still not come to his senses. *It happened. It all happened.*

Hráthbam did not believe at first that he had, in fact, died. But the wound—or lack thereof—proved Rowen's tale. The Soroccan could not have forgotten how the greatwolf's claws ripped a long gash in his thigh. Now, that wound was gone. No stitches, no scar.

Otherwise, only the greatwolf's charred body a little ways beyond the camp, plus the still-overturned wagon, remained to lend testimony to the events of the night before. The Soroccan only dimly remembered the battle and nothing after that until he awoke next to his own grave, Rowen standing over him, shovel in hand.

The Soroccan listened, captivated but skeptical, to Rowen's tale of the strange, disfigured madman who helped them. "That could not have been a Shel'ai," the merchant objected. "You said his face was hideous, but Sylv are supposed to be beautiful!"

"I know what I saw. His eyes were just like in the stories. As for the rest of him…" He shrugged helplessly. "If I'm lying, then how are you alive?"

"Maybe I'm not." Hráthbam scraped his wooden spoon to get at the last of the stew in his bowl then looked around. "No offense, but if I'm dead, you're part of a thoroughly disappointing afterlife." He stared into his bowl.

"What do you remember?"

Hráthbam looked up. "Of what?"

Rowen blushed. "Of being dead. The afterlife. Whatever happened to you."

Hráthbam tossed his bowl on the ground. "Not a thing." Something in his tone advised Rowen not to press the matter for the time being.

Rowen expected the merchant to be weak, but he was up once he finished the stew, rooting through the wagon and his scattered goods for hláshba. He grimaced when Rowen told him he'd used the last of it to burn the greatwolf.

"That was my private stock, not some common cooking oil. Some of those flasks cost me three silver cranáfi each!"

"If you paid three silver cranáfi for that swill, you were robbed. In the Dark Quarter, we used to brew better poisons than that for half a copper!"

They had pushed the wagon upright again, but two of the wooden wheels were cracked. Other merchants Rowen had traveled with knew enough to bring one or even two spare wagon wheels along with them, plus wood and nails for repairs. Hráthbam had none of these. This only reinforced Rowen's suspicion that his newly resurrected employer had little in the way of true merchanting experience. Rowen suggested they return to Breccorry and have the wagon repaired, but Hráthbam's map showed that Cadavash lay only half a day farther.

"Twice as long to get to Cadavash is just as bad as doubling back to Breccorry and starting over," Hráthbam pointed out. "The wheels aren't broken yet. We'll lighten the load and travel slowly."

If the wheels break tomorrow, before we get to Cadavash, we'll be in an even worse position! But he kept his mouth shut and respected Hráthbam's decision. And after all the strange goings-on of the past few days, if one or both of the wagon wheels broke before they reached the temple of the dragon-priests, that would hardly rival what they had already endured.

They lightened the wagon as much as they could by filling their satchels and loading much of the provisions in Left and Right's saddlebags. Rather than ride in the wagon and add to its weight, Hráthbam and Rowen walked instead. Rowen feared that the Soroccan might be too weak for this, but Hráthbam insisted he had never felt better in his life. Each of them took up position beside one of the rounceys. Rowen was glad when the Soroccan volunteered to keep an eye on Right, since the petulant horse was beginning to get on Rowen's nerves, pulling against the reins and nipping at anything that moved. Left was more agreeable, despite her newly laden saddlebags, and nuzzled Rowen's open hand as they walked. Rowen fed the horse a few oats from his satchel.

As they traveled, following the rough road westward along the Simurgh Plains, Rowen considered pressing Hráthbam about what it had been like to be dead, but something distant in the Soroccan's expression dissuaded him. He thought of the madman instead. He had no doubt that the man had used magic to restore Hráthbam's body and raise him to perfect health. But what kind of magic was capable of such a thing?

Rowen had heard barroom stories of Shel'ai throwing fire from their hands, engaging in deep meditation that allowed them to project their souls beyond their bodies, and speaking to each other using only their minds. He had always figured those stories to be nothing more than fairy tales. But even those abilities were a far cry from men who could raise the dead!

That man must not have been a Shel'ai. He had the eyes… but that kind of magic could only come from a Dragonkin. Rowen shook his head at the absurdity of this thought. The man had the ghostly eyes of a sorcerer, but his magic was simply too great to be anything less than a Dragonkin—which seemed equally impossible. Hadn't the Dragonkin vanished a thousand years ago, killed or banished from Ruun during the Shattering War?

Even if one had survived, why would he be here, at just the right time and place to help them? And what did he mean about danger, that if something went wrong, he'd lose control and we'd all die?

Rowen decided to search for answers elsewhere. Producing the weathered Codex Lotius, he scanned the pages as he walked, combing through oaths and poetry for some mention of the Shel'ai or their Dragonkin predecessors. After a while, bored, Hráthbam told him to read the words aloud. Embarrassed, Rowen did as he was ordered. The flowery speech, which Rowen had always loved to read, seemed mangled when he heard it in his own voice. He might have stopped, but Hráthbam urged him on, stopping him from time to time to ask a question about the Isle Knights. By and by, Rowen told how a wandering sellsword named Fâyu Jinn came to the Lotus Isles seeking training. How all the Shao masters refused him—all save one, who treated Fâyu Jinn like a son. How Fâyu Jinn, in turn, founded the Order of the Crane and persuaded the Shao masters to join with him, just in time to turn the tide of the Shattering War.

Hráthbam interrupted him. "The adamune! I may not be dead, but I still want you to have it." The Soroccan stopped the horses and vanished inside his wagon for a moment. Rowen heard the sound of trunks being opened and wares tossed every which way.

His pulse quickened. He had not seen or held an adamune since leaving the Lotus Isles. True, the Codex Lotius barred expelled squires from owning such splendid weapons, but who was to know? *If I can't be a Knight, at least I might look like one!*

When Hráthbam returned, Rowen's spirits sank. The grinning Soroccan did indeed hold an adamune, but the weapon looked far from impressive. The curved scabbard was made of cracked wood, wrapped in faded leather that looked like a good shake would send it falling to the earth in tatters. The hilt of the adamune was worse, bound in leather so stained and ratty that Rowen did not even want to touch it. But he was not about to refuse his employer's gift.

Forcing a smile, Rowen accepted the weapon. The sword's crosspiece—a brass oval and quillons designed to resemble interlocking crane and dragon wings, rising to grasp the blade—was horribly tarnished. He drew the sword a little and suppressed a groan.

The trouble with mainland swords was that the more you sharpened them, the weaker and more brittle they became—not true for adamunes. The favored weapons of the Isle Knights were forged from kingsteel, a blend of three metals joined in a secret way, sharpened to a razor's edge without sacrificing strength and resilience. The hammering and folding of the Shao forge masters left a fingerprint: deep, snow-white swirls buried deep in the metal.

Those swirls were nowhere evident in the blade he now held. True adamunes were impervious to rust, but rust had eaten parts of this blade clean through. He suspected the sword was just one of countless cheap imitations sold on the mainland. In such a state, this blade would surely shatter at the slightest strike, as though made of glass.

He inspected the sword more closely and saw a darker stain just above the crosspiece, along with an inscription he could barely make out. Though written in Shao, he had seen other imitation adamunes bearing Shao script as well: an attempt to make the cheap blades look more authentic.

"Fel-Nâya," he read aloud. He almost laughed.

"What does that mean?" Hráthbam asked.

"It's the sword's name, I think." Rowen tried to keep a straight face. "It means 'Knight's rage.' Or 'Knightswrath,' though I suspect the fire went out of this wrath a long time ago." He immediately regretted saying it. "A fine gift, though. I'm sure its name was well earned in its day."

Hráthbam shrugged. "Not much to look at, I know. It belonged to my father. He always said he won it in a dice game with a Sylv. We never believed him. But I figured even an antique adamune must be worth something to somebody! Gods know you deserve better, lad, but it's yours if you want it."

"I'll treasure it," Rowen lied. "This sword has history. Thank you." He bowed. Hráthbam took the horses' bridles and got the wagon moving again. Rowen waited until the merchant was looking away before he sighed with disappointment. He scrutinized his new weapon again. He realized he probably deserved no better.

Given their ill fortune thus far, Rowen had expected the cracked wagon wheels to split apart long before they reached Cadavash, or even for them to be attacked again by greatwolves or bandits, but luck favored them. They traveled without incident until the Simurgh Plains gave way to a gray, wasted circle of land in the distance.

Hráthbam looked disappointed. "Don't tell me that is Cadavash..."

"Maybe it's not as bad as it looks," Rowen offered.

"Something tells me it's *worse* than it looks!"

Rowen was inclined to agree. They slowed the wagon a moment and stopped to look. Ahead of them, the Simurgh Plains sank farther and farther before they eventually gave way to a gray, rocky fissure that resembled a great, open sore. Lean-tos filled with shabbily dressed pilgrims crowded the mouth of the fissure, shadowed by a gaudy temple. The temple walls and pillars looked as though they had originally been painted blood red and then were touched up whenever patches of color wore off, but the work had been done unevenly, so the temple had the appearance of being unintentionally two-tone. Priests congregated around it. They wore extravagant robes and jewelry that shone even from this distance with gold and precious stones.

"Business must be good," Rowen muttered.

Well-armed men patrolled the mouth of the fissure. Like the priests, all wore the green emblem of a man's body with a dragon's head and wings. Whenever one passed by, Rowen saw a fey look in their unnaturally wide eyes. He wondered if they were drugged, mad, or both.

"Watch yourself," he warned. "I don't like the look of the guards." He reached down and loosened his recently borrowed shortsword. Knightswrath was strapped across his back now—purely for appearances, since the sword was too long to draw that way, even if he wanted to. He wished he'd left it in the wagon, as it would only be in the way if a fight started.

"I see." Hráthbam loosened his scimitar then sighed. "Come, my friend. Let us do our business and be gone from here."

They started forward cautiously. The plains sank so rapidly

toward the fissure that Rowen's stomach lurched. He had to struggle to control the horses and keep the wagon from barreling on ahead of them. When they got closer to the fissure, Rowen heard a wailing that chilled him to the bone.

"Dyoni's bane, what are they up to?" Hráthbam asked.

Rowen gritted his teeth. "That's how they pray, I think." He pointed toward a cluster of priests. The men wept and lamented theatrically, tossing themselves upon the hard earth, often cutting their bodies against the rough stones. Rowen had met Zet worshippers before in Lyos, but never had he seen them behave like this. "I think they're crying for Zet. Or the dragons."

A squad of guards approached them, led by a young, green-robed priest with a cruel jaw and wide, mad eyes. Though the man was Human, he looked so fey that Rowen wondered for a moment if he hadn't just seen some entirely new race for the first time. The priest fixed them in a severe, unblinking look.

"Worship or trade?"

Hráthbam patted Right's neck to soothe the horse, who was suddenly more anxious than usual. "Trade."

The priest nodded. "Twenty copper cranáfi to approach the graveyard of the holy." He added, "Or if you're paying in iron crowns, *thirty*."

Hráthbam bristled at this. The priest's guards noticed, too. Several drew their swords. Rowen resisted the impulse to draw his own. Clearing his throat, he nodded slightly.

Hráthbam scowled, counted out twenty copper cranáfi, and passed them to the priest, who counted them again. "Follow." He turned on his heel and started toward the fissure. Half the guards fell in behind him. The rest waited, swords and pikes glinting in the daylight. Rowen guessed they would fall in behind the wagon. He did not like the thought of mad, armed men behind him, but it was too late.

As they drew closer to the fissure, the lamentation increased. Rowen resisted the impulse to plug his ears—in part because he feared the gesture might be taken as offensive, but also to keep his hands free in case the guards attacked. He and Hráthbam were no dunces when it came to swordplay, but what chance did they have against the ten armed men surrounding them—especially if Hráthbam took a wound without blood-powder or a Dragonkin handy to assist him? Besides, even if they cut their way through, dozens more were scattered along the fissure or pacing the painted stone steps of the gaudy temple.

"Looks like we'll have to take our chances," Hráthbam muttered, echoing Rowen's thoughts.

Rowen grunted in reply. Ahead of them, the priest and guards stopped. Rowen tensed. But they did not attack. Instead, the priest pointed. A broad stone stairwell descended into the depths of the fissure. Pilgrims crowded the stairs, often moving shoulder to shoulder. The fissure itself resembled a great, open mineshaft.

Rowen shuddered. A foul, sulfurous odor wafted from the fissure. But worst of all was the wailing. Here, the cries and screaming prayers of priests and pilgrims bounced off the high walls of stone, echoing frightfully. Rowen touched his short hilt, squeezing until his knuckles whitened. Pilgrims and priests jostled into him, and it took all his restraint not to shove them back.

Hráthbam caught his arm and whispered, "Dragon ivory be damned. Locke, let's get out of here!"

The priest held up his hand, stopping them. Rowen wondered if the priest had overheard or simply read the Soroccan's expression. "You may not leave before paying proper tribute to the winged dead." All around them, guards who had not already drawn their weapons did so.

Hráthbam scowled. Rowen feared the merchant was about to reference the twenty copper coins they had already paid in tribute. "Do the dragonbones come from this mine?" Hráthbam asked instead.

The mad priest smiled at the question. "Long ago, when the Dragonkin sucked dry the holy lifeforce of the winged ones, they buried their bones deep within the earth. We recover them. With tears and bloody hands, we lift back into sunlight the remnants of Zet's winged children."

And sell them.

The priest gave them so severe a look that Rowen feared he'd read his mind. Instead, the priest said, "You must leave your wagon."

Hráthbam scoffed. "Not likely." He quickly added, patting Right's neck, "This horse will go mad if she sees me go down there. She doesn't like to be left alone, you understand."

"Horses are not welcome in such a holy place. You can be assured that the guards will protect you from any thievery."

Hráthbam consented. They backed up the wagon as far as they could from the crowds and cries around the fissure, unhitched the wagon and tended the skittish horses, and turned them over to the nearest stable. Then, they reluctantly allowed the guards to lead them into the chilly bowels of the dragon graveyard.

The depths of Cadavash were even more disconcerting than the surface: a bizarre combination of temple and marketplace staged on the dark, dank floor of a huge, man-made fissure. Walls of dirt and rough-hewn stone bristled with the remnants of trees whose dead roots had been left in the earth.

The smell of sweat and lantern oil filled the air. Priests, pilgrims, and guards paced and wailed like madmen. Here and there, men, women, and even children were bleeding. A few held cloths to their wounds but most seemed ignorant of their own bloodshed. Rowen could not tell if their wounds had come from fighting or prostrating themselves on the stones before them. They passed a cluster of wide-eyed priests who tugged up their sleeves, feverishly chanted some kind of unintelligible prayer, and took turns ritualistically cutting themselves. Rowen shied away. Hráthbam did likewise. Rowen wondered if the merchant was wary of all those flashing knives, given his blood condition.

I should be watching him more closely. I'm his bodyguard. I'm not here to gawk.

So theatrical were the worshippers that it wasn't until he gazed past them that Rowen saw the gigantic dragonbones displayed in every direction—not just single bones, but full skeletons with outspread wings as wide as a farmer's field. Most of the dragons had two wings, but some had four. Then he saw the unfurled remnants of a six-winged dragon suspended on huge iron chains whose creaking could be heard even over the lamentation of the pilgrims clustered around it. The skeleton was completely intact, down to its leering skull and four limbs ending in scimitar-sized claws. *Jinn's name, that thing could have carried off two elephants at a time!*

The priest and guards who had led them into Cadavash had already lost interest in them and wandered back to the surface, but a different priest—an old man with half a hundred scars on his face—caught Rowen staring up at the ceiling and smiled wolfishly.

"Behold, Godsbane, the greatest of Zet's children!"

Hráthbam waited until the priest continued walking, then he leaned in. "I know that's something I'll tell my grandchildren about, but if you don't mind, I think I've seen enough."

Rowen wrested his gaze off the remains of Godsbane and forced himself to move on. He shifted his scrutiny from worshippers and dragonbones to all the merchants. Though easy to miss at first, given their comparatively subdued demeanor, there were plenty of them. All looked just as ill at ease as Rowen and Hráthbam, suggesting that they were equally new to this ghastly place. Rowen also saw food vendors, tradesmen, and prostitutes, nearly as mad as the priests around them, stumbling along in the twisted light of torches and the sound of tortured wailing.

"They're mad," Hráthbam hissed in his ear. "All of them!"

"Drugged, too, by the look of it. Let's just buy your damned ivory and go."

But that was easier said than done.

The priests of Zet demanded outlandish prices. On one dais, Rowen saw the horse-sized skull of a dragon for which a priest and his guards wanted more wealth than all the coin Rowen had ever held in his life! Even finger-length bits of bones cost double what Hráthbam had anticipated. But looking over the merchant's shoulder, Rowen had to admit that the ivory was impressive—stark-white in color but swirled with brilliant veins of red.

He could not exactly say why, but something about the bones spoke of power and lost history. The priest wrapped the wing bones in black cloth, which Hráthbam accepted. "You need more?"

Hráthbam hesitated. "Maybe. I'll have to charge a fortune for what I've got already, just to break even. If I can't find buyers willing to pay…"

Rowen heard a fresh chorus of wailing, saw a dazed child walk by with bloody arms, and fought the impulse to turn and run. Forcing a smile, he said, "I'm your servant. Lead on. You do your best to get rich, and I'll do what I can to keep you safe from all this."

Hráthbam smirked and answered with a jest that was drowned out by more wailing.

They continued to explore the market. The two men quickly realized, to their horror, that the depths of Cadavash extended much farther than they had anticipated. Crowded stairwells descended deeper and deeper into the earth. When Rowen stopped one of the priests and asked about this, the madman beamed.

"The true temple to the winged dead lies beneath your feet!" he said, louder than he needed to, then moved on, weeping.

Rowen and Hráthbam exchanged looks of trepidation. "Should we really go down there?" the Soroccan asked.

Rowen took a deep breath, one hand on the hilt of his borrowed shortsword. "We came this far. We may as well do this right." He added, as confidently as he could, "I told you, I'll keep you safe."

"Like you did against that damn greatwolf?" He clapped Rowen on the shoulder then started for the stairs.

Rowen and Hráthbam expected the subterranean levels of Cadavash to consist of dank caves and claustrophobic tunnels crowded with more fey-eyed dragon worshippers. But once again, what they found surprised and chilled them. The priest had spoken the truth.

The true Temple of the Winged Dead existed not on the surface but in the earth.

"Jinn's name," Rowen gasped, shaking his head. "This is a *city!*" He had heard stories of the Dwarrs building vast dwellings under the earth, hollowing out mountains for their homes, but he doubted even they would have approved of this.

Cadavash stretched in all directions: a dark, fire-lit metropolis of stone and gruesome winged monuments forsaken by the sun. Massive shafts cut in the stone allowed for a measure of fresh air, but despite these great feats of engineering, the air in Cadavash's subterrain remained dank and stale. Priests and guards stood everywhere, even more crazed than their brethren on the surface, alongside hollow-eyed merchants and tradesmen. More worshippers wailed and injured themselves in the name of their bizarre faith, some carving themselves with thin knives while others whipped themselves bloody with thick flails of knotted leather. But that was not what chilled Rowen's heart the most.

Both on the Lotus Isles and in Lyos, people had an open attitude toward prostitution. Cadavash took this to a frightful extreme. Women sold themselves—or were sold—then used on the open street. But the men's eyes burned with hatred, not lust. Again and again, Rowen was tempted to draw his shortsword and stab someone who deserved it. He did not have to look hard to see corpses here and there, ignored and untended, and he marveled that this place had not been overcome by disease. Tears stung his eyes.

Hráthbam said, "I thought I'd take a look around first then haul my wares down here and trade them, only I don't relish the idea of setting up a table in this place." When Rowen did not answer, he added, "Are you all right, my friend?"

"Let's just... finish and get out of here."

Hráthbam nodded in ready agreement.

The deeper they descended into Cadavash, the cheaper they could buy dragonbone. Hráthbam bought more wing bones then an expensive, larger bone nearly the length of Rowen's arm. Despite their foul surroundings, Hráthbam beamed.

"In Lyos, I bet I could sell that for five hundred silver cranáfi!"

Rowen had never seen such a sum, but he was not about to argue. Hráthbam trusted him to carry most of the cloth-wrapped ivory, while the Soroccan carried the longest shaft of dragonbone himself. Rowen was not offended. Hráthbam was already trusting him with a fortune. But Rowen was not about to run away with it. Even though he was not a Knight of the Crane, he was no thief—at least, not unless he had to be.

"That's nearly all the coin I have," Hráthbam said, then adding, "except for what I'll use to pay you, of course!" He stopped a passing dragon worshipper. "Is this the lowest level?"

The worshipper frowned. "Beneath you lies one last holy level. The *greatest* level, from which all but the anointed are forbidden!"

Hráthbam's eyes sparked with curiosity. Rowen groaned. "Maybe we've pressed our luck enough for one day."

Hráthbam hesitated a moment then agreed. The two quickly made their way out of the smoky, nightmarish subterrain, back to the comparative calm of the surface. They ascended the steps and made for the wagon. Rowen had never been so happy to see the sun, even though it was setting by now.

"Gods, I shudder to think how long we were down there," Hráthbam said.

"About four hours longer than any sane man would have done."

Hráthbam hurried back to the wagon. While nothing had been stolen and the horses were skittish but in good shape, Rowen cursed that he and Hráthbam had not had the foresight to have the wagon repaired while they were in Cadavash. They found a craftsman to repair the damaged wagon easily enough, but Rowen was disheartened to hear that the work would have to wait until the next morning. *Gods, do we really have to spend another night in this place?*

They found a cheap, comparatively sane inn near the stables, but Rowen advised Hráthbam to get a room while he remained behind to guard the wagon. Hráthbam wanted to keep the dragonbone with him in the room, but Rowen won out. Despite the number of patrolling guards—perhaps because of them—Cadavash was a rough place. It would serve nothing if both men got a good night's rest, only to find that their wagon and horses had been stolen the next morning.

Hráthbam brought him food and drink and then retired to his room in the inn. The craftsmen soon left as well, intending to finish their work in the morning. Rowen decided to sleep in the wagon, trusting that he would wake if anybody approached. Luckily, the screams and wailing of the dragon worshippers had died down although a chilling cry still ripped through the night from time to time, jolting Rowen from an uneasy slumber. Finally, Rowen gave up on sleep altogether. He lit a lantern but turned its wick low, listening to the lonesome sound of his own breathing.

Inside the wagon, he kept his borrowed shortsword within easy reach, along with a knife and the Queshi composite bow. His unease fended off sleep, but that suited him fine. Tired or no, he would feel better when they were gone from here. He tried to clear his mind by imagining what the morning would bring.

Hráthbam had his dragonbone. The merchant's next task would be to sell it. Lyos was still the closest city worthy of mention—a city Rowen knew all too well and couldn't avoid forever. If Hráthbam had a mind to extend their contract, Rowen could see the Soroccan safely to Lyos, guard him in the King's Market until his wares were sold, then decide what to do from there.

His pulse quickened. At least by then, he would have a pocketful of copper cranáfi! Hráthbam could probably be persuaded to sell Rowen the shortsword he'd borrowed—especially since he'd lost his last one trying to save Hráthbam from a greatwolf! He eyed the composite bow, appreciating its excellent workmanship. Doubtless, its price was beyond him.

I could just take it. It wouldn't be stealing, exactly. Don't I deserve some kind of reward for everything I've been through?

He chided himself. What would Aeko Shingawa say if she knew he was considering such a thing? What about Kayden? Sure, his brother had stolen plenty in his day, but hadn't that changed after he became an Isle Knight?

Besides, Hráthbam already gave me my prize! He glanced at Knightswrath, lying neglected and forgotten in the corner of the wagon. More out of boredom than curiosity, he picked up the sword and examined it further. He felt guilty for not feigning more gratitude over the gift, but the false adamune was practically worthless. The rusty sword was useless in a fight, which meant it would be nothing but a hindrance when Rowen had to carry it on his back from job to job, city to city.

Maybe I can sell it in Lyos. Not everyone on the Simurgh Plains admired the Isle Knights as much as he did, but surely he could find at least one pompous nobleman who might pay too much to have a rusty, imitation adamune hanging over his fireplace. Rowen snickered.

Then again, this is probably the closest thing to an adamune I'll ever own! He grasped the tattered, leather-wrapped hilt and unsheathed the blade. He gave it a few short swings—as much as the narrow wagon would allow—expecting to feel the blade shifting at the hilt:

a sure sign of a weak, half-tanged blade that would snap in battle. Instead, he found himself appreciating the sword's balance, how well it fit his hands.

"Fel-Nâya..." He smiled faintly and gave the Shao sword another short swing. He decided to see what the sword could do and climbed out of the wagon. The smell of straw and hay filled the dark stables, and he heard the even breathing of sleeping horses. The stable boy leaned against the wall, snoring and drunk. Glancing down at the stalls, Rowen saw Right and Left where they should be and then went outside, Knightswrath in hand. Though the night air chilled his bare chest, he liked how the cold quickened his pulse. Taking a few strides from the stables, Rowen took a deep breath and glanced up at the stars.

The moon shone nearly full near Armahg's Eye. The sight of the distant star-wash soothed the lingering blight left in his mind from what he'd seen in underground Cadavash. He calmed his senses then lifted Knightswrath with both hands and began the sha'tala.

The martial dance employed initially simple then increasingly complex circular steps and movements that simulated a Shao warrior being attacked from all sides. Rowen had never excelled at the exercise—he always felt self-conscious performing it under the scrutinizing gaze of his trainers on the Lotus Isles—but he enjoyed how the warrior's dance stretched his muscles, sharpened his balance, and aligned his senses.

Several passing guards wearing the green tunics and emblems similar to the priests of Zet stopped in the streets to watch him. Rowen could not read their expressions in the dark, nor did he care anymore. He was deep in his sha'tala now, entranced, nearing that state Shao warriors often described as being alertly asleep.

Despite a rush of exhilaration, Rowen kept his breathing slow and deep. Knightswrath whirled faster and faster in his grasp. To Rowen's surprise, the sword's balance was superb. He could not see its rusty blade in the darkness, so he forgot its disrepair and began to feel oddly as though the sword had been made for him.

He quickened his pace, performing the sha'tala faster than he ever had before. Moonlight spilled past his wild red hair, down his bare arms, and played off the naked, whirling sword as it slipped and flashed through the night air. His heart leapt. He lost himself in his exercise, only to find himself anew.

At last, he finished his sha'tala and lowered Knightswrath to his side, as though sheathing it in an imaginary scabbard. He bowed to his equally imaginary defeated opponents. Then he saw that he'd attracted a larger crowd than he'd realized. They stared at him in stunned silence. A few applauded.

Suddenly self-conscious again, Rowen blushed, nodded to them, then started back toward the stables. As he did so, he glanced down at Knightswrath. He stopped. During his sha'tala, the ratty leather wrapped around the hilt had come loose. Rowen had torn it off without looking, unwinding and casting it away as he moved. Now, for the first time, he realized what he was holding.

"Jinn's name..." The pommel was exquisitely carved dragonbone. It bore the familiar iconography of the Isle Knights—the crane, the stag, the crimson lotus flower—as well as other designs: a nursing mother, an armored man standing by a stream, a woman with fire flying from her hands. Rust had flaked away from the crosspiece—or vanished—revealing further, painstaking details of the crane and dragon wings rising to grasp the blade.

I must be losing my mind. Or dreaming! Knightswrath's blade remained rusty as ever, but the red swirls in the dragonbone pommel meant the hilt was worth a fortune. Rowen considered selling it. For some reason, the thought filled him with shame. Shaking his head, he took a single step into the stables when a familiar scream froze him in his tracks.

A single, blood-chilling cry. Female. Not quite Human, but not animal, either. The same cry that had echoed across the night-shrouded Simurgh Plains only days before, the night Hráthbam lay dying. The same night the mysterious, disfigured Shel'ai had appeared out of nowhere to bring the slain Soroccan back from the dead.

"Jinn's name..." Rowen barely had time to speak before the darkness blossomed into blinding white fire. He turned—wincing from the brightness—just in time to see a ball of scalding-white flame plummet from the heavens. It fell upon the Simurgh Plains, beyond the outskirts of Cadavash, crashed without sound, then disappeared. For a moment, no one moved. Then, panic ensued.

Guards ran to get the priests, calling at the top of their lungs. Drunk and weary dragon worshippers stumbled from temples and inns, their eyes wide with fright. Behind him, the horses in the stables were going berserk. He picked out Left's and Right's whinnies among the cacophony. He was about to rush inside to soothe them before they injured themselves—or each other—but something stopped him. He stood immobile for a moment, his heart beating in his throat. Then, clutching the hilt of Knightswrath, he ran in the direction of the vanished flames. As he moved, the sword's hilt seemed to warm in his hands.

CHAPTER NINE

BATTLE IN THE
TEMPLE DEPTHS

NOT FAR FROM CADAVASH, LETHE turned in the direction of the awful cry frosting the night air.

The rider beside him threw back the hood of a white-and-crimson cloak and faced the vanished sound with a look of relief. "It's as I thought. Silwren makes for Namundvar's Well." He gestured for Lethe to follow and started forward. "Hurry! We're close."

Lethe scowled. Having seen all too often what the Nightmare could do, he was in no hurry to approach a similar creature. But Shade's promise spurred him on.

"If I help him catch her, he'll let me die..."

He smiled faintly. No more murders, no more torture. No more Shel'ai. All he had to do was follow orders one last time. He could do that. Snapping the reins, he followed his master, loosening his sword as he rode.

The Simurgh Plains swarmed with armed men, crazed dragon worshippers—whose theatrics had suddenly been replaced by true terror—and one ex-squire from the Lotus Isles. Rowen still held Knightswrath in his hands, but he wondered what good an imitation adamune would do against a dragon.

"If it *is* a dragon," he reminded himself. *But what else could it be... unless it's a Dragonkin?*

All around him, the wretched priests of Zet whispered feverishly. A great fire had fallen from the sky, leaving a great swath of the plains blackened and smoldering. Surely, their gods had returned! But why? Were they angered by the temple, by the very worshippers who sold the bones of the ancient, winged dead? Should the priests commit mass suicide to appease their deities, or had the dragons instead come back to reward them for their patience and faith?

The priests were so busy debating that none seemed to realize the obvious: they saw no dragon—just burnt, smoke-wreathed plains and cold night air. Rowen tried to keep his distance from the dragon worshippers. Unlike their exaggerated lamentations in the depths of Cadavash, their panic was genuine. Soon, they would become violent. They might very well turn on each other—or upon any stranger they didn't recognize, whom they could conveniently blame for their dragon disappearing as quickly as it appeared.

"And I am just such a stranger," Rowen muttered. He turned back toward Cadavash. "Dragon ivory be damned! Time to find Hráthbam and get out of here."

Rowen knew the way, but his legs betrayed him. Instead of toward the inn and the wagon, he found himself running deeper into Cadavash, toward the gorge and the wretched temple within.

Jinn's name, have I gone mad? What am I doing? But Knightswrath's hilt grew warmer, the farther he went. He considered returning to the wagon, but curiosity got the better of him. He reminded himself that it was not wise for an armed stranger to run at night into the sacred temple of fanatics. Reversing Knightswrath in his grasp, he slid the rusty blade into his belt and hurried on.

Lethe reined in, scowling at the noise and chaos in the distance. "You said nothing about dragon worshippers."

Shade whirled back to face him, violet eyes taut with impatience. "You'll do as I command! Besides, what do a few fanatics matter?"

"They will think she's a god. They'll worship her. Or kill her, depending on how mad they are."

Shade's fists clenched, wytchfire rising unbidden from his closed fingers. "We will not let that happen."

Lethe nodded. "As you say. But there will be hundreds—"

"Then we will *kill* hundreds! I have no time for cowardice. Now follow... or stay here in agony!"

Lethe obeyed, casting a murderous look at the Shel'ai as he rode behind him. *Not cowardice, you damn fool! I'm just not in the mood to slay madmen until sunrise, just so you can have your pretty Dragonkin back.*

But he kept silent. He reminded himself that the more enemies he faced, the more likely one would manage to kill him. Then, there would be no need for Shade to make good on his vow. *And maybe, in that last moment before death, I can throw a blade in the general direction of that haughty bastard's neck!*

Lethe grinned. He urged his horse on more quickly until he was riding at his master's side.

To Rowen's great relief, the dragon temple was nearly deserted. Most of the guards, priests, and worshippers had already rushed aboveground, anxious to see what the great disturbance was all about. Those who remained spoke in cold, anxious whispers, too preoccupied to notice Rowen as he slowed his pace, lowered his head, and passed as casually as he could.

Where on earth am I going... and why? His feet seemed to know the course better than his mind. To his dismay, they were leading him deeper and deeper into Cadavash, down one dark, torch-lit stairwell after another. He could still turn and run if he wanted, but he had the odd sense that Knightswrath *wanted* him to keep going—as though through the sword, someone or something had called for help.

As much as the temple had frightened him during the day, it was worse now. The silence unnerved him. Torchlight and shadows played off macabre carvings on the stone walls. The smell of death hung thick in the air, punctuated by the honored bones of dead dragons hung here and there, usually guarded but now abandoned as everyone else made for the surface. Nearby lay bodies. Some, he figured, were drunks. But others, he knew, must be worshippers who had gone too far in their lamentations and now lay dead because of it.

He realized he was now at the deepest level he and Hráthbam had explored earlier. The crowds were gone, but unlike the previous levels, this one was not abandoned. Here and there, a few guards and priests cast suspicious glances at him. Rowen tried to appease them by staring reverently at his surroundings. He remembered what the worshipper had told them before: only a select few were permitted to enter the deepest level of Cadavash.

But with all the commotion on the surface, maybe the guards... Ahead of him, a gothic stairwell descended into a great mouth of darkness. Unlike the previous stairwells, this one was flanked by armed guards. Two of them.

No such luck.

The guards rose to attention at the sight of Rowen. The ex-squire resisted the impulse to draw his sword, telling himself how absurd he must look—a bare-chested, armed man with unkempt red hair, stumbling around the lower vaults of their sacred temple in the middle of the night—and smiled at them instead. "Greetings, brothers. I don't suppose you could tell me what all the fuss is about?" He pointed toward the ceiling. "Sounds like everyone on the surface has lost their wits!"

One of the guards said, "None but the anointed are permitted in the deep vaults. Go, or it'll cost your life."

"Surely, brothers, there's no harm in—"

The guard who had spoken stepped forward and placed a gauntleted hand on his chest to stop him. "I said turn back, or I'll cut your—"

Rowen's uppercut struck the guard full on the chin and sent him tumbling backward, senseless, rolling loudly down the stairs into darkness.

Rowen swore over the noise then turned to face the second guard. This man was younger, his eyes wide, and he made the mistake of trying to draw his sword.

"Too close for that," Rowen chided. He grabbed the guard's sword hand and held him immobile then dropped the man with a savage kick to the knee. He covered the guard's mouth to muffle his scream. One swift blow from his edge of his hand to the back of the guard's neck drove him to the floor, unconscious.

Rowen heard footfalls behind him and turned. He cursed again. Two others raced down the stairs toward him, alerted by the commotion—a priest and a guard. The priest's eyes widened. He issued a quick order to the guard, turned, and ran to get help. The guard, meanwhile, drew his sword and charged.

No choice... Rowen drew his sword, too. "Stop! We don't have to—"

But the guards of Cadavash were only a little less fanatical than the priests who employed them. Here was a stranger, an interloper seeking to defile their sacred temple. Here was a chance to stop him, to honor the spirits of the winged dead, to earn riches and perhaps even immortality in the pantheon of the heavens. The guard leapt at the chance.

Rowen braced to meet him, holding Knightswrath with both hands. *Let's hope this damned, rusty sword doesn't shatter on me!* The guard swung. Rowen sidestepped, narrowly avoided falling down the stairwell, and answered with a swift cut of his own. But the guard was a better swordsman than Rowen had anticipated. He dodged the cut then swung for Rowen's midriff. No time to dodge. Rowen had to block.

He expected the rusty adamune to shatter, but Knightswrath turned the guard's blade with ease. No time to feel relief—Rowen feigned a cut at the guard's thigh. When the man moved to block, Rowen cut for his neck instead. The guard's eyes widened... a split-second before Rowen turned the blade and struck him with the flat instead. Again, Rowen expected his blade to shatter. It didn't. But it struck the guard with enough force to knock him out.

Rowen took a deep breath and let it go. More guards would be there in seconds. He had to run, hide, maybe incapacitate another guard and take his uniform, then make his way back to the surface.

He turned to the stairwell again. The darkness chilled him even more than his guilt. Then, lifting Knightswrath, he started downward.

"Where is she?" Lethe demanded in a seething whisper. He resisted the impulse to draw his sword as armed fanatics filled the night. "No way we'll find her in *this*!"

Shade closed his eyes in concentration. When he opened them, he pointed. "There."

Lethe sneered. "I was afraid you'd say that."

The former Captain of the Unseen followed his master toward the gorge. Though he'd never visited this wretched temple before, he'd heard stories about it—none of them pleasant. It looked as though most of the worshippers were spilling out into the streets, milling around the smaller temple on the surface, trying to figure out what had happened.

But there still could be plenty of guards below the surface. And gods only know what we'll find once we reach Namundvar's Well!

Lethe said, "We'll never get out of this place alive." Fighting back a wild grin, he quickened his pace to keep up with his master.

Darkness reigned over the lowest depths of Cadavash. Rowen stumbled in the pitch blackness and nearly tripped over something: the guard he'd knocked down. He figured the man had been knocked unconscious. He felt in the dark for a pulse but found none. The man's neck was broken.

Bad luck. Rowen whispered a short, Shao prayer over the corpse. Guilt twisted inside him. Finally, Rowen wrenched himself away and continued.

Faint, dim light shone from a single lantern hanging in the distance, down at the end of a long corridor. Rowen had expected another vast, open area similar to the previous levels of Cadavash. Instead, he found a hallway barely wide enough for a single man to pass through. He tried to proceed cautiously until he heard shouts and booted footsteps above him. The guards were coming.

"Damn..." Rowen ran blindly through the darkness, nearly tripping twice before he reached the lantern. It was bolted to the wall, but Rowen used Knightswrath—its hilt still warmer than before—to pry it free. He raised the wick. The growing light spilled across ghastly carvings on the walls, even more macabre than the ones he'd seen before. Here, a man was being disemboweled by winged beasts. There, a laughing woman appeared to be feeding her own children into a dragon's open maw. Rowen shuddered and pressed on.

The corridor turned left then led to another stairwell, this one just as narrow as the hallway. At the bottom of the stairs, he found a locked door. Rowen pushed, testing its weight. Solid oak. He would need a battering ram to break this down.

Even a Knight of the Crane might give up now, Rowen told himself. *But I am not a Knight...*

He sheathed Knightswrath in his belt again. Then, he tore the thin metal handle from the lantern, bending it and reshaping it until he could slide it into the keyhole. Memories of his childhood in Lyos returned to him. There, he and his brother had learned to do what was necessary in order to survive. In the hierarchy of their sins, Rowen knew that picking a lock was not so terrible.

Not so difficult, either. Rowen jostled the metal wire and heard the rewarding click of the lock mechanism. He bent the wire again and slid it back into place in the lantern, holding the lantern high by its reformed handle as he pushed the door open.

There, he found an antechamber filled with dust and relics. No guards, no priests. No dragon. Rowen closed and locked the door behind him then investigated the chamber as quickly as he could. He found another locked door at the far end. Rowen knew the lantern's wire handle would break if he tried to reshape it again, and he couldn't very well carry a hot lantern without a handle! Broiling with impatience, he scouted around and discovered a dry torch. He used the lantern to light the torch and tried to remove the wire handle from the lantern again.

The wire broke in his fingers, as he'd feared it would. But he salvaged a short, straight piece and slid it slowly into the lock mechanism. He'd hardly begun when he heard shouts and footsteps behind him. The guards were at the door.

He dropped the wire and reached for his sword, holding Knightswrath in one hand and his blazing torch in the other. Both sent waves of heat up his arms. But the door at the far end of the antechamber did not open. Muffled shouts echoed, right before the door shuddered. They were trying to break it down.

Rowen shook himself from his daze, leaned Knightswrath against the wall, and went back to work. He'd dropped his makeshift lockpick, but after a few precious moments, he retrieved it from the dusty floor and slid it back into the lock.

Another booming thump echoed behind him. Rowen's heart leapt in his throat. Given enough time, the guards would break the door down. He had to get out of there. He had to get his own door open.

"Then what? I'm trapped in the bottom of this damned temple, out of my mind, probably about to get—"

The lock interrupted him with a loud click. Rowen stood. He slid the lockpick into his belt, retrieved his sword, and pushed the door open.

He expected to find an enormous chamber containing whatever person or thing had summoned him here in the first place. Instead, he saw a tiny, dark room not much bigger than a closet. No doors, no stairwells, not even a single carving on the wall. Behind him, wood splintered.

I'm a dead man...

Shade and Lethe descended deeper and deeper into Cadavash, all the way to the fourth level, before they were stopped in a corridor. Both men had kept their hoods drawn the entire time, but when three guards appeared to question them, led by a wild-eyed priest, they lowered their hoods. Both knew they had no chance of talking their way out of this.

The priest's eyes narrowed at Lethe's cold gaze and scarred face. Then he looked at Shade. His eyes widened. "Are you a Sylv?"

"No."

"But your face—"

Shade lifted his hands. Wytchfire sprang from his fingertips, washing over the priest and his guards. They fell, screaming and burning.

Cursing, Lethe drew his shortsword and finished them off. "If you're going to kill them, kill them!"

Shade did not answer. The dark-cloaked Shel'ai strode forward. Two more guards appeared, their faces stunned. Shade dispatched them without hesitation, unleashing enough wytchfire to reduce them to ashes before they could scream. "Better?"

Lethe seethed. "If Silwren came down here, shouldn't we be following a whole trail of ashes?"

"Her powers are greater than mine, Human. She can avoid being seen, if she wishes."

"Avoid *killing*, you mean!"

Shade was quiet a moment, his eyes closed in concentration. When he opened them again, he pointed. "As shall we. There is a locked door and a secret stairwell beyond that dais. Few men in Cadavash know of it. That will lead us down to Namundvar's Well." He started forward.

Lethe followed, bloody shortsword in hand. "And my death," he pressed.

Shade answered without slowing. "And your death."

CHAPTER TEN
NAMUNDVAR'S WELL

ROWEN DESPERATELY SEARCHED THE ANTECHAMBER for escape, at least for a place to hide, but found nothing. Only two doors: the one behind him, which led nowhere, and the one at least a dozen guards were about to break through. Panic seized him. *Gods, why did I come down here?*

He considered giving up, but he had already slain two men. Worse yet, he'd broken into the sacred temple of the dragon worshippers!

Surrendering would likely only get me killed out of revenge. And probably tortured first. He shuddered. *Maybe Hráthbam will save me.* But one man would not be enough to rescue him from all the guards of Cadavash. Besides, this was Rowen's fault, not Hráthbam's. Rowen took a deep breath, trying to steady himself. He held Knightswrath before him, fixing his gaze on the door in the distance.

The crash and shudder intensified. He had no idea what the guards were using to break the door down—a statue, perhaps—but more than the weight of men was driving against it. In seconds, it would be over.

No courage without fear... Rowen hoped the Isle Knights' credo would hearten him. But what was coming, he knew, would not be a battle. It would be a slaughter he had brought upon himself.

Another crash made him take a reflexive step backward. He was nearly inside the tiny chamber now. He could hide inside, close and lock the door behind him, but the guards would never fall for that. Still, it might buy him time.

He took another step backward, his boots scraping along the

dusty stone floor. He was inside the chamber. Then, strangely, the floor sagged beneath him.

Rowen nearly wept with relief. Stepping out of the tiny chamber, he turned and knelt, brushing aside a thick layer of dust with his hand. Underneath the dust lay a hidden trapdoor. It was locked. No time to use the lockpick. Straightening, he kicked the trapdoor with everything he had. It did not budge. Rowen kicked it again without result. Desperate, he moved entirely into the tiny room and closed the door behind him. The ceiling was too low for a torch, so he cast it away and stood in darkness. He positioned himself on top of the trapdoor and jumped as high as he could.

The weight of his body crashed down upon the trapdoor beneath him, but it did not give. Rowen steadied himself and jumped again. That time, the trapdoor shattered, and Rowen plummeted through.

Lethe started to laugh.

They'd found the long, secret stairwell, sure enough, but at the bottom they were greeted by a blank wall. No door, no markings, nothing. "Looks like a dead end," he said.

Shade closed his eyes again. That time, a violet glow sprang up about him, enveloping his entire body. Reflexively, Lethe stepped back. Shade slowly extended one hand, touching the blank wall. The stone wall shimmered like a desert mirage then vanished altogether.

Lethe stared in amazement. Then he cursed.

Before them lay an antechamber, lit by torches. The chamber was filled with armed men.

The guards turned, blinking as Shade stepped through what had been solid stone just moments before. Some raised their weapons. Others started to kneel, perhaps intending to worship. Shade gave them no chance.

Lethe winced. He could feel the awful heat on his face as its sheer intensity momentarily blinded him. But that was nothing compared to the screams. Furious, he followed Shade into the antechamber.

The Shel'ai stood alone, stone faced. All the guards were dead.

"You didn't have to do that," Lethe said. "You are a Shel'ai! You've been here before. They might have groveled at your feet if you'd commanded it!"

"I am not here to bandy words with would-be worshippers. I'm here to save Silwren." Shade pointed toward a door in the distance. "There." He waved his hand, and an invisible force yanked the door open.

Rowen feared for a moment that he had broken his leg in the fall. He tried to move and bit back a scream. He fumbled in the dark as his warm, wet blood soaked through the thigh of his pants. A shard of wood had stabbed him during the fall. Gritting his teeth, Rowen pulled it out. He bit back another scream then waded through the cloud of pain in his head and groped blindly in the darkness.

He stood at the beginning of another narrow corridor. It led in only one direction. Rowen found Knightswrath on the ground, struggled to his feet, and started forward. He placed his weight on his good leg and prepared to use his sword as a crutch if necessary. He heard commotion behind and above him. The guards had broken the door down. They were in the antechamber now.

It will only take them a minute or two to find me. Summoning his strength, he moved faster, hugging the hall with one arm while he used the other to grope in the darkness ahead of him. The corridor ended abruptly. He probed to the left and right and found another hallway in each direction. He wondered only for a moment which path to take. Facing the corridor to the right, he touched Knightswrath's hilt. It felt cool. Still gripping the hilt, he turned left—and immediately withdrew his hand when the hilt nearly burned him.

Somewhere on the surface, the Soroccan merchant probably searched for him. Rowen shook his head. *Hráthbam, just what kind of demon trinket did you give me?*

He'd only gone a few steps when the screams of dying men echoed from the chambers above him. Rowen froze for a moment then surrendered all thoughts of caution and ran left, headlong into the darkness.

Shade lit their way by conjuring tendrils of wytchfire that wrapped and tangled around his wrist, leaving him unharmed but transforming his arm into a living torch. They proceeded down the corridor until Shade stopped in his tracks, so abruptly that Lethe nearly ran into him.

"She's close. Silwren..." He turned. "Hear me well, Human. She does not answer my mind speak. That means she's frightened, probably hurt. When we find her, stay back and keep silent, or the torments—"

"Or the torments you'll unleash will be like nothing I can imagine," Lethe finished. "I am quite familiar with Shel'ai threats." He gestured to the corridor ahead of them. "After you, m'lord."

Shade's expression tightened with fury, but the Shel'ai was in far too much of a hurry to stop and punish the assassin now. Shade felt Silwren's essence more strongly now.

"Silwren, my love, I'm here." Shade mind spoke the words but received no reply. He sensed that she was conscious, that she heard him but did not understand. Beneath her confusion, he sensed terror. But what was she afraid of? Surely, not of him. Herself, then. She feared power so great that it threatened to devour her from the inside out, to rot her memory and her senses if she used it—her body, if she did not.

"Do not be afraid, Silwren," he told her. *"The power's too great—I know—but we will help you. Do you hear me? I made you a promise long ago, and I swear, I've come to honor it. I'll save you from this madness, my love. And you will save me."*

At the end of the corridor, Rowen discovered an open doorway. Light blazed from within. *Where there's light, there might be guards.* He drew Knightswrath and entered slowly. But his newfound sense of caution quickly dissipated in the face of the breathtaking chamber before him.

This chamber was the size of a village, with vaulted ceilings and gigantic pillars carved with intricate runes. Unlike the filth of the rest of Cadavash, the floors here were clean marble covered with carvings and intricate paintings. The walls bore lit torches in brass brackets, but Rowen saw at once that these were not ordinary torches. They produced no smoke, and instead of crackling flames, they yielded a soft white glow. Rowen, wondering a moment who might have lit them, realized that the answer might be no one.

He studied the floor paintings instead. None, he saw with relief, resembled the grisly carvings of the temple floors above. Dragons of all colors did nothing more menacing than sleep or spread their wings—two, four, even six—among painted clouds. He spied other figures, too: all naked, dancing or making love, some resting on the green banks of a blue-white river. They looked Human but for their lithe bodies and more delicate, exotic features. *Are these Sylvs?*

He tried to remember the priestly legends he'd heard as a child, plus the myths he'd been taught while training on the Lotus Isles. Hadn't the Sylvs come *after* the dragons vanished? These figures must be the ancestors of the Sylvs, then. The Dragonkin.

Rowen frowned. Hadn't the Dragonkin *stolen* their power from the dragons, draining them of their godly essence until the winged beasts dried up and vanished like water in a desert? Why, then, did these paintings show the two living in harmony?

But this was no time for pondering. The guards must be closing in by now. He thought, too, of the scream he'd heard on the surface—the same as the one he'd heard that crazed night on the plains, after the battle with the greatwolf, when the deformed Shel'ai appeared to raise Hráthbam from the dead.

A dragon, if that's what it was, something great and awful that would probably destroy him. Rowen tried to recall a passage from the Codex Lotius to give him courage, but all the words seemed to have fled his mind. Finally, he lifted Knightswrath into a guarded position before himself and headed deeper into the chamber.

Hráthbam Nassir Adjrâ-al-Habas's first thought, when the fireball fell from the sky and burst into nothingness upon the plains, was that he had drunk too much hláshba, having indulged after the good fortune of finding an inn that served it in the first place. His second thought, once the inn emptied and priests and armed men fell into panic, shrieking that the dragons had returned, was that he had to find Rowen Locke and escape.

Left and Right pawed at their stalls, nervous but unharmed. The young squire, however, had vanished. Hráthbam frowned. The shortsword he had lent to the squire lay inside the wagon, along with his cloak. Wherever Rowen was, he was probably unarmed. *Except for that decrepit adamune I gave him. Gods forbid he try and use it!*

He had his wagon, his horses, his coin, and his dragonbone. Better yet, he had his life, which was saying something, given the chaos starting to spread through Cadavash. The best thing to do was to get out of here while he still could. If the squire was dumb enough to wander off in a place like this, he was in Dyoni's hands.

The stable boy was gone, so he readied the wagon himself. Left accepted the harness willingly, as though anxious to be gone from here, but Right nipped at his fingers. Hráthbam scolded the mare and pretended he was about to strike. The horse recoiled.

"We'll have none of that, Right. I want to get out of here as bad as you!"

Right gave in, and the merchant finished yoking them to the wagon. Then he climbed into his seat, adjusting his scimitar before he sat down. As an afterthought, he fetched a crossbow from the back of the wagon and kept it loaded. He doubted the guards would stop a simple merchant disembarking from the outskirts of the temple town, but on nights like this, it made sense to be cautious.

Hráthbam sat immobile in his seat, holding the reins, listening to the shouts outside the stable. He could make out snippets of what was being said. Most of it amounted to nothing more than the panic and rejoicing of fanatics who thought one of their long-dead gods had just plummeted out of the sky. But he heard whispers of some sort of disturbance in the temple, too. Fighting in the lower levels. Men dead, guards in a panic. *And Locke right in the middle of it, I bet!*

Still, he did not move. After a few minutes, Right pawed the ground nervously while Left craned her neck to look at him.

"Don't look at me like that, girl. I know what you're thinking, and I'll have none of it." Hráthbam started to snap the reins, then stopped himself. He cursed and hopped down from his seat. "Damn you, Left!" He tied off the reins and left the stable alone. Covering his scimitar with the folds of his extravagant robes, he slipped through the crowds, most of which seemed to be fleeing the gorge, and wondered if they had more sense than he did.

At the end of the vast chamber, Rowen tripped over a slain priest of Zet. Straightening, he saw four more—all dead. He examined the bodies. Most had died wide-eyed, but their bodies bore no obvious wounds. Whatever had slain them had not used steel to do it.

Ahead of him, a few broad marble stairs led up to a small interior chamber containing more carvings, tapestries, and what looked like a well. Beside the well lay a motionless figure.

Rowen ascended the stairs and entered the room, looking left and right for assassins, but he saw no place for a killer to hide. His pulse quickened.

At his feet, a nude woman face lay down on the marble floor. Long hair spilled around her luxurious platinum tresses. Her bare, pale skin shone bright in the strange torchlight. He knelt beside her, his head spinning. Knightswrath nearly burned his palm as he laid it on the floor within easy reach. He reached for the young woman's shoulder.

He gently turned her over, and the breath caught in his throat. He could tell by her almond-shaped eyelids and angular features that she was not Human. He glanced back at the floor paintings.

A Sylv? He shook his head, trying to steady himself. He saw her breasts rise and fall and realized she was still alive. A pulse fluttered faintly beneath his fingertips.

She's alive—but not for long.

He searched her body for wounds. But like the slain priests of Zet, she bore no obvious injuries. He frowned. *How in Jinn's name did she get down here?*

"Look inside the well."

Rowen leapt to his feet, snatching up Knightswrath as he whirled toward the speaker. A stooped figure in a ratty cloak, hood drawn, stared at him from the steps just a few feet away. Two hands covered in sores and welts rose to the hood and lowered it.

Rowen recoiled from the ghastly, familiar face. "You..."

A faint, sad smile played across deformed but angular Sylvan features. "A poor way to greet an old friend. But given more pressing matters, I'll forgive you." He clumsily ascended the stairs.

Rowen drew back a step, raising his sword. "Stay back," he warned.

The Shel'ai cocked his head, regarding him curiously. "Are you defending yourself... or the girl?"

Rowen glanced down at the woman, still motionless at his feet. "Both," he said.

The Shel'ai smiled at his answer. "Good. The Light chose wisely. Now, look in the damn well."

Rowen kept his eyes locked on the figure before him. *He could kill me with a wave of his hand. If he attacks, I must be quick.*

The cloaked figure smiled again. "Yes, Human, I could kill you with a wave of my hand. But I won't. Need I remind you that I saved your friend's life?"

Rowen's eyes widened. "You can read my thoughts..."

"Only because you think so loudly." The Shel'ai glanced behind him then focused his gaze on Rowen again. The former squire shuddered as the man's ghost-white pupils bore right through him. "My patience exceeds our time, I'm afraid. Now look where I told you before I have to force you."

This time, something in the man's voice left no room for refusal. Rowen turned, confused, and glanced into the well. "I see darkness and water. Is this your idea of—"

Out of the corner of his eye, he saw the Shel'ai wave his hand. Rowen feared that he was about to be blasted into cinders. Instead, something wrenched his gaze back to the well. He could not look away.

It's just a well. It's just water...

Then, as though a curtain fell away from his vision, he saw the well for what it truly was—not a well at all, but a window. His eyes widened.

"Gods..."

Light washed over him. Despite its intensity, he did not blink. The light flowed into him, filling him utterly. He forgot his name, forgot everything. For a moment, Rowen knew peace. Then it was gone.

Rowen recoiled. "What... what have you shown me?"

The Shel'ai's taut features seemed to soften. "You *know* what I've shown you. A better question is *why*. But I have no time to answer." He glanced over one shoulder. "Someone is coming... someone I must face alone. If I can, I will find you later and answer all your questions. Now take Silwren and go."

But Rowen did not move. "Who is this woman? Why should I help her?"

"Because we both already know you're going to, Isle Knight. Because you're twice the man you think. Because I'm entrusting the hope of all races into your sole care and protection. Now, stop staring and go!"

Even without touching Knightswrath's hilt, Rowen felt waves of heat roiling off the sword. He considered running, but the crippled man was right—his honor would not allow it. Before he knew what he was doing, he gathered up the fallen woman in his arms. Her skin felt so hot that he nearly dropped her. Blushing, he faced the deformed Shel'ai and asked, "How do we get out of here?"

The Shel'ai did not answer, nor did he need to. Even as Rowen gathered the unconscious woman in his arms, all around him, the world began to shimmer.

"El'rash'lin!" Shade spat the word and broke into a run, sprinting down the narrow corridor and turning out of sight before Lethe could ask what he meant. As the Shel'ai left, he took his wytchfire with him, and Lethe was plunged into darkness. Cursing, he ran after his master, groping blindly down the stone hallway until he spied the wytchfire again, blazing in the distance.

By the time Lethe caught up, Shade stood at the center of an enormous chamber, seething, both hands clenched into fiery fists. Lethe saw another figure using the wall of a stone well to push himself up. The figure wore a ratty, stained cloak. But it was his face—blistered, covered in sores—that sent a chill down Lethe's spine. "Gods, what is that?"

Shade took a step toward the deformed figure, wytchfire crackling around his wrists as though he were poised to unleash it. "Where did you send her?"

The deformed figure smiled faintly, straightened, took a few inelegant steps down a short series of stairs, and stood before Shade. "Not far enough, I suspect."

Shade howled in rage and engulfed the man in violet flames. Lethe's eyes widened. He had never seen a Shel'ai unleash so much power at once.

But more amazing still, when the flames dissipated, the deformed man stood unharmed. "We should talk."

"We have talked too much already." His voice resounded with hate but something else as well.

Lethe smiled. *Lord Shade of the Shel'ai, second in power only to Fadarah... afraid?* But Shade wasn't just afraid. He was exhausted, too. The Shel'ai had just unleashed nearly all of his magic at once, yet his opponent stood unfazed. *If this one kills Shade, then I can die, too!*

But the deformed sorcerer did not attack. "Leave her alone, Kith'el. This has gone on long enough. Don't you see that she came here to give it back? She doesn't *want* it, you fool!"

Shade said, "She can't give it back. She can *never* give it back! Fadarah warned her. She's just confused. But she accepted the risk. Disbelieve in her if you wish. But I never will."

The deformed sorcerer shook his head. "You believe in her like a soldier believes in his sword. Call that *love* if you want to. I don't."

Shade shuddered—from rage or hurt, Lethe could not tell—then turned and stalked back the way they'd come. Lethe followed, so stunned by the anticlimax that it took him a moment to feel despair. *Looks like I won't be dying today after all.*

CHAPTER ELEVEN

ON THE ROAD TO LYOS

S UNRISE BROKE OVER THE AMETHYST waves of the Burnished
Way and unrolled across the Simurgh Plains. Hráthbam's
wagon was already well on its way, following the same rough
northerly road it had been following all night. The horses sweated
from exhaustion. When Hráthbam nodded off at the reins, Rowen
nudged him. They had no way of knowing what had happened in
Cadavash after their escape. He wondered if the clerics of Zet were
still employing their guards to scour the temple depths for intruders
or if they had extended their search to the plains beyond.

*We have a head start, but that won't last long if they come after us on
warhorses. Gods know our trail is plain enough. Then again, what reason
would they have to follow us?*

Rowen rubbed his tired eyes. The events of last night seemed as
confusing and unbelievable as ever. Somehow, the deformed sorcerer
had magicked him and the unconscious woman out of the temple, just
outside the gorge. They appeared amidst a crowd of terrified dragon
worshippers, violet mist dissipating from their bodies. Eyes widened.
Women screamed. Men howled. Some fell and worshipped. Others
reached for weapons. Still hugging Silwren against him, momentarily
forgetting the awkwardness of their bare skin touching, Rowen
had tried shoving his way through the crowds. When that seemed
impossible, he considered drawing Knightswrath and cutting his way
out. Luckily, Hráthbam appeared.

Incredulous, the Soroccan acted quickly, wrapping the naked

Sylvan woman in his own oversized robe and carrying her back to the wagon while Rowen drew his sword and followed, warning the crowds to stay back. Somehow, they reached the wagon unharmed then fled Cadavash as quickly as they could. Crowds started to follow, shouting and wailing, until Rowen fired a crossbow bolt into the earth.

Throughout it all, Silwren had not stirred. Though she still breathed, they could not wake her. Rowen had already shaken her and considered shouting in her ear before Hráthbam stopped him, reminding him that a startled Shel'ai might not be their greatest ally.

Rowen glanced over his shoulder at the beautiful woman still locked in troubled sleep in the back of the wagon. He sensed somehow that she was the cause of all of this. The scream. The flames. *But she's no dragon. So what is she?*

At last, Rowen sighed and hauled in on the reins. "Enough. Let's stop and rest."

Hráthbam nodded wordlessly. He half hopped, half fell off the wagon and stretched. "No need to set up camp. I'll sleep quite happily on the ground." Settling his great weight on the earth, Hráthbam wrapped himself in his cloak. "Wake me when the world makes sense again."

Rowen climbed out of the wagon and stretched. "You may have to sleep more than a day for that," he grumbled and then saw that his employer was already fast asleep. Rowen unhitched the wagon then brushed and fed the horses. Right and Left nudged him with affection, as though relieved to be far from Cadavash.

"It's over," he reassured them. "Whatever that was, it's over." Rowen brushed them a while longer then gathered firewood. They did not need a fire, nor did he wish to give off their location to any pursuers, but he doubted he could sleep yet and knew they'd need the wood eventually.

As he worked, he eyed the wagon, imagining the lithe, platinum-haired figure inside, still asleep in Hráthbam's robe. He remembered the sight of her in Cadavash, how her beauty had momentarily banished even the horrors of that wretched place. Shaking himself, he gathered more firewood than they could possibly need, keeping a watch on the southern horizon in case the priests of Zet were pursuing them after all. *But there are always others to watch out for,* Rowen reminded himself.

With Hráthbam asleep, it was up to Rowen to guard their makeshift camp, but he could not possibly stay awake for long. With his limbs growing heavier by the minute, Rowen returned with the last batch of firewood, tied the horses to the wagon, and built a small fire anyway, hoping that would deter predators. Then, after retrieving Hráthbam's crossbow from the wagon seat, he sat facing south and closed his eyes.

He wanted a blanket, but he did not want to be so comfortable that he would not wake at the slightest sound, so he resigned himself to a warrior's sleep instead, telling himself that he would wake every few minutes to check for danger. But the moment he closed his eyes, exhaustion overtook him, and he tumbled headlong into nightmares.

Rowen woke with a start. He fumbled for his sword and looked around, uncertain where he was. Dark plains spread before him. Above, the sky was clear and star filled, Armahg's Eye blazing with brilliant indifference.

"Easy, my friend," Hráthbam called out to him. The Soroccan sat by the fire, adding seasoning to a pot of bubbling, sweet-smelling stew. "It's night. We're safe. So long as you're still willing to trust my cooking, that is."

Rowen rose stiffly, only a little heartened at the thought of more of Hráthbam's spiced vegetables and rice, and joined him by the fire. Hráthbam had dragged two chests from the wagon to use as chairs. As soon as Rowen sat, the merchant offered him a bowl of stew as well.

He placed Knightswrath on the ground beside him. As he did so, he felt a hint of warmth emanating from the hilt. *Just like in Cadavash.*

Could Silwren's presence be causing it somehow? He thought of stories he'd heard about men who could feel the presence of underground water through tiny vibrations in sticks they called divining rods. He wondered if Knightswrath acted the same way in the presence of magic. Frowning, he unsheathed the blade a little and stared down at the rust.

Whoever heard of a rusted magic sword? He slammed the blade back in its sheath and turned his attention to his bowl of stew.

"There's wine," Hráthbam offered, gesturing. "I'd ask you what kind of nightmares had you bellyaching in your sleep, but if they were anything like mine, I doubt you want to speak of them."

"You had them, too?"

"Dragons, fire, dead men..." Hráthbam nodded. "I wonder if it's just coincidence or some kind of warning from the gods."

"I would not have taken you for a believer in omens and prophecies."

Hráthbam chuckled. "Nor I, had the past few days never happened." He gestured. "She's awake, by the way."

Rowen tensed. *You could have told me sooner!* "The wytch?"

"Wytch, Shel'ai, Sylv, Dragon, Dragonkin, Goddess... whatever you want to call her. She woke up a little before you did."

Rowen lowered his voice. "Did she... speak?"

Hráthbam shook his head. "Hasn't left the wagon, either. But I heard her wake up while I was sitting here... *felt* her might be more like it! Like someone stabbed my heart with a red-hot poker." He took an empty bowl and filled it with stew, jabbing a crude wooden fork into the brightly spiced mass. "Take this to her if you like."

Rowen took the bowl but hesitated. "Not sure you pay me enough for that."

"Not sure it's my responsibility to feed every demon you rescue, either."

Rowen winced. "Understood." He stood and reluctantly made his way toward the wagon. He made it halfway before he regretted not bringing his sword.

The campfire illuminated her face as she sat cross-legged and still at the mouth of the wagon, watching him. Rowen shuddered. Her eyes were like those of the disfigured Shel'ai, the pupils not black but white as sun-bleached bone. Rowen felt dread creep through him.

Steeling himself, he bowed slightly. "Good evening, my lady." He held out the bowl of stew. "Are you hungry?"

She watched him closely but did not answer. She'd wrapped her body in one of Hráthbam's robes—this one so dark blue that it was almost black.

"Do you... understand me? Can you speak my language?"

The woman said, "I speak all languages." Firelight played through her platinum tresses as she slowly accepted the bowl of steaming stew from Rowen's hands.

Her voice was soft and beautifully cadenced but edged too with something that frightened him. Rowen forced a smile. "Good. I'm afraid my Sylvan is a bit rusty."

The woman did not respond to his joke. She ate slowly, her face expressionless. If she liked or despised the taste of the stew, she gave no indication of it. Rowen wanted to leave, but he could not wrest his eyes off her.

"There's wine," he managed. "Would you like some?"

Taking her silence as an answer, he went and fetched one of the wineskins, avoiding Hráthbam's scowl as he did so. He brought her the wine. She accepted it and drank without comment.

"Do you... know where you are?"

She chewed, swallowed, and answered stoically. "I am beyond Sylvos, far from the World Tree, in the Wyldlands." Her eyes settled on him. Rowen tried to focus on the violet irises instead of the white pupils. "The land of Humans. I assume my kind are still not welcome here."

Rowen nodded uncomfortably. "We found you in Cadavash. My name is Rowen Locke. That's Hráthbam. There's more, but he'll have to tell you the rest of his name himself."

Hráthbam watched closely from the fire but offered no greeting of his own.

"The other one mentioned your name, but I'm afraid I missed it," Rowen said.

The woman faced him, eyes narrowing.

Rowen drew back a step.

"The other one?"

"Yes... the other one. Like you. Well, *not* like you, exactly. He had white pupils like yours, and he could work magic, but he was covered in scars and sores. He was dressed like a beggar, all hunched over—"

"El'rash'lin," she interrupted. "His name is El'rash'lin."

Rowen nodded. "And your name?"

145

"Silwren," she said. "That much, at least, I still remember."

Rowen frowned. "What do you mean?"

Silwren tugged the silk robe around her body and said nothing.

"Can you tell us what you were doing in Cadavash, at least? Or why you summoned me?"

"I did not summon you," Silwren answered curtly. "Even a Human does not deserve to be endangered for no reason."

Rowen hesitated. Should he push her further?

Silwren had apparently finished with her supper, because she returned the bowl. Then she said, "I have no more answers... and probably more questions than you ever will. Let me sleep until dawn, if it pleases you, then I will be gone."

She climbed into the back of the wagon, taking the wineskin with her.

Rowen's relief turned to curiosity. "Where... where will you go at dawn?"

She was quiet for so long that he thought she meant to ignore him. When she finally answered, he immediately wished he had never asked. Turning her ghostly eyes to face him, she answered his question with a single word: "Lyos."

Despite their intentions to leave that night, as soon as they were rested and fed, neither Rowen nor Hráthbam Nassir Adjrâ-al-Habas could summon the courage to hitch up the wagon and start off again while Silwren was sleeping. Rowen still hoped that El'rash'lin might appear as he'd promised to answer at least some of the questions plaguing him.

But there was no sign of the sorcerer. So they milled about and spoke in whispers as the night wore thin around them, drawing conjectures about what the Shel'ai woman intended to do once she reached Lyos.

"My brother always said only fools believe in coincidence," Rowen whispered. "Of all the people she could run into, why me, who happened to grow up in the same city she's heading to?"

"A lot of people grow up in Lyos," Hráthbam reminded him.

146

"Besides, you said the other one could read your thoughts. Maybe that's just what she did—although I'll be damned if I can guess why!"

It was on the tip of his tongue to speak of the well, but he had no idea how to describe the experience, and the very thought of it nearly brought tears to his eyes. Whether they were tears of anguish, he could not say.

He stared into the campfire instead. "She said she didn't summon me," he said at last. "*Something* led me down into Cadavash, led me straight to her, but she says it wasn't her."

Hráthbam shrugged. "Maybe she's lying."

"You think she's lying about where she's going, too?"

"It doesn't really matter. Let's say she *does* go to Lyos. They'll kill her the moment they see what she is!" He took a long drink of hláshba. "Shel'ai or no, she won't last ten seconds against a few hundred armed men, and probably a mob besides."

"Never seen a Shel'ai before," Rowen admitted, "but she seemed different somehow. So did El'rash'lin. More like Dragonkin—whatever they used to be. I don't think a mob could stop them."

"Then you're worried about her torching your home the way this other one, this Nightmare, is burning cities in the west?"

Rowen sneered. "If she wants to burn down the Dark Quarter, I'll hand her the torch!" He remembered the fire that fell from the sky. "If she needs one, that is." He glanced at the wagon, imagined the figure sleeping within, and wondered if the delicate-looking young woman really had that sort of power. "I suppose the real question, then, is whether we try and stop her or applaud her."

Hráthbam's eyes narrowed. "Indeed." He stabbed the fire with the drawn blade of his scimitar. "Well, neither one of us has tried to kill her yet, so it seems we've made up our minds on *that*, at least."

"Ignoring her isn't the same as helping her."

Hráthbam shrugged. "Seems we've already done that, too. Or did I imagine you risking your neck—and mine—to get her out of Cadavash?"

Rowen's stomach sank. "You're right." He bowed slightly. "For what it's worth, you have my apology."

Hráthbam scoffed. "Fohl's hells, it's my neck to risk. My choice."

147

He stabbed the fire again. "What I meant is you already seem... well, I'd say *taken* with her, but maybe *ensnared* is a better word!" The Soroccan did not laugh.

Rowen didn't laugh either. "My brother always said I was dull-witted. Maybe he was right."

"I doubt that," Hráthbam said. "Dimwits don't see trouble coming. That's why they can't help getting themselves killed. But you, my friend, seem just thick-skulled enough to see it coming then walk right into it anyway!"

Rowen's temper flared. He stood, fists clenched, biting back an angry retort, and stalked away.

Dawn brought no sign of trouble from Cadavash. Rowen would have preferred to see a column of angry dragon priests bearing down on them than face what was to come. Both he and Hráthbam, still awake, saw Silwren emerge from the wagon. She wore one of Hráthbam's extravagant gowns, belted and folded so it would fit her. But the gown was still much too large for her thin frame, and despite himself, Rowen laughed at the sight of her.

Silwren glanced toward the sound, eyes narrowing, but instead of offering a rebuke, she blushed.

As she passed the horses, Rowen expected them to shy away from her, but they regarded her as though she were no more obtrusive than the grass beneath their hooves or the faint morning breeze blowing through the trees in the distance.

Hráthbam frowned. "Where is she going?"

Rowen blinked in surprise. "East, I guess."

Hráthbam scoffed. "You're welcome," he muttered after her. "Let's get going, then."

But Rowen was already moving. Before he realized what he was doing, he ran after the Shel'ai and blocked her path. "Wait! Where are you going?"

"I told you last night."

"So you did. But you didn't say why."

"I was not aware I had to."

Rowen steadied himself. "You will if you intend to get past me." He moved his hand to his sword hilt.

Silwren studied him a moment and then laughed. Not unkindly, she said, "Forgive me, Human, if I doubt the sincerity of your threat." She stepped past him and continued on.

Rowen's face burned. Hráthbam laughed. Cursing, Rowen glared at the merchant. Then he turned to face Silwren but saw her back instead.

"Lyos is *my* city!" he called after her.

Silwren turned, half smiling. "I took you for a fool, not a king."

"There's stories of someone... *something*... like you burning cities in the west. If those stories are about you, if you intend—"

"I'm not the one they call the Nightmare if that's what you're asking."

Rowen swallowed hard. "Just the same, I was born in Lyos. If you mean its people harm, I can't let you go." Fixing the bravest expression he could muster, he drew Knightswrath and prayed the rusty blade would not fail him. As he did so, he winced when he felt the hilt nearly hot enough to burn him. "I don't *want* to kill you," he added. "I just want to understand what in Fohl's hells is happening here!"

Kill her? Gods, I probably couldn't even get close before she burned me to ashes!

But Silwren did not attack. Her expression sobered. "You would do well to fear for your people, Rowen Locke. But not because of me. I go to Lyos to warn them." She bowed slightly, then turned and walked away.

Rowen stood a moment, dumbfounded, then returned to Hráthbam and the campfire.

Hráthbam said, "Let it go, Locke. Better this way. Don't forget, my friend, we have dragonbone to sell!"

Rowen tensed. "Where do you want to take it?"

"Somewhere pretty and far away. Atheion, maybe. I'd like to see those streets made of water."

I would too. "Bad idea," he heard himself say. "Atheion's full of simple folk. They don't even wear jewelry. You won't get a good price there."

Hráthbam frowned. "So simple that they live in floating houses?"

Rowen kept a straight face. "They hate dragons. As much as those worshippers at Cadavash love them—or love their bones, at least—the folk in Atheion hate them. Some ancient legend about one of the last dragons killing their king." *Gods, I'm a bad liar! He'll see right through this!*

Hráthbam was quiet for a while then shrugged. "You're the wandering fool, not me. Where would *you* go?"

Rowen chose his words carefully. "I'd say Cassica, but that's close to Syros—and Syros has probably already fallen to the Shel'ai and that demon of theirs." *I'm telling the truth about that, at least.*

He thought of Jalist going to join the Throng but pushed the Dwarr from his mind. "That doesn't leave many options," Hráthbam grumbled. "I suppose Phaegos—"

"Lyos is closer." Rowen pretended not to notice the Soroccan's scowl. "Forget Silwren. Forget demons and Shel'ai and all that nonsense. You're right. She's just one woman. And anyway, Lyos has the biggest market I've ever seen. Lots of rich, fancy bastards who like spending their dead parents' money. And it's closer to Sorocco, besides. You ride all the way west, you might get caught up by these Shel'ai and lose everything. Make it to Atheion, and you've still got to come back. Finish your business at Lyos, though, and you're just a few days from the coast."

Hráthbam mulled it over. "The sooner I can put all this madness behind me and sail home to the warmth of pretty wives, the better." He gestured absently. "Fair enough. We'll make for Lyos instead. May as well fix some breakfast first, though. Give that wytch some time to get well ahead of us and maybe forget you just pulled a sword on her."

Rowen smothered a grin. "Agreed. But no more stew."

"Don't jest about Soroccan stew, my friend," Hráthbam answered, stoking the fire. "It's just the thing for thickening a soft skull."

CHAPTER TWELVE

ROUSING THE THRONG

FADARAH SIGHED.

The great war camp had been broiling on the Simurgh Plains for days now, a stain no amount of sunlight or rainfall could purge. Cassica lay sacked in the distance, its city walls still blackened from the Nightmare's onslaught. But things had calmed since then. Cassica's surviving men-at-arms had joined the Throng—some voluntarily, others less so. The Shel'ai wisely divided the newest members of the Throng, stationing them so that all served with strangers, in case they still fostered notions of rebellion. Farmers were free to return to the fields and bring in crops, provided that a substantial portion of the yield went to feeding Fadarah's hungry soldiers.

The army had barely moved since the attack. Men stirred amid a great sea of tents, smoke, and waste, all of it ringed in a protective palisade.

Fadarah had heard some of the Shel'ai whispering, "It is not good to keep the army so close to Cassica. The sight of the broken city might yet incite a rebellion!" He could not entirely disagree. Still, the Throng was the least of his worries at the moment.

Just past sunrise, he knelt in his tent. He had sent his servants away even though he had yet to don his armor. His great half-Olg frame knelt in the center of the tent, eyes closed as though in prayer. But the faint violet glow enveloping his body hinted at a level of magical exertion not usually seen with mindspeak.

"General... I have failed you." Shade's voice echoed in his mind, drawing a scowl to Fadarah's tattooed face.

"Kith'el, to mindspeak over such a great distance—"

"My Human thrall can protect me if needs be." A pause. *"Master, I lost her. I tracked her to Cadavash, to Namundvar's Well. But then..."*

Fadarah's frown deepened although his eyes remained closed, deep in concentration. *"Did she attack you?"*

"No, Master. She was unconscious. But El'rash'lin was with her."

Fadarah's open hands clenched into fists. The glow around his body turned a deeper shade of purple, almost black. *"He teleported her away from you?"*

Shade answered, *"Yes. I can't believe he had that much power! Almost as much as Iventine—"*

"What was she doing in Cadavash?"

"El'rash'lin claims she went there to try and be rid of her powers."

"Do you believe him?"

Shade did not answer.

Fadarah said, *"Don't judge her too harshly. She's not in her right mind. In such a state, any of us might do as she has done—myself included."*

Shade did not reply for such a long time that Fadarah feared his pupil had succumbed to exhaustion. Then Shade asked, *"What are your orders, General? Shall I return to the army?"*

"No. Hurry ahead to Lyos. Gauge the city's strength, as we discussed." He added, *"And I would not be surprised if you find Silwren there. If so, appeal to her if you can, but do not risk yourself needlessly. Remember, as painful as this may be, she probably hates both of us right now. But that, too, will be remedied."*

"I understand."

"But rest first," Fadarah insisted. *"If all goes well, the Throng will reach Lyos in three weeks."*

Lest Shade be tempted to continue, Fadarah emerged from his trance, ending their discussion. He opened his eyes. He continued kneeling for a moment. Then he called for his servants. "Bring my armor. And wake my captains," he said. "We march east in two hours."

Pallantine Hill rose from the Simurgh Plains like a gigantic, mossy fist in the late afternoon sun. As Hráthbam and Rowen drew nearer, their ears caught a cacophonous mix of shouts and drunken laughter. Hráthbam stopped the wagon. He stared into the distance for a moment.

Hráthbam's face broke into a smile. "Well, I see no flames wreathing the battlements. Seems the pretty wytch was merciful."

"Unless she's not here yet."

"She *should* be. Something tells me she made better time than we did."

Rowen nodded absently. At the moment, Silwren was the farthest thing from his mind. *Home.* "Let's get this over with," he muttered.

Hráthbam silently flicked the reins. Left and Right stirred, looking annoyed that their rest had been disrupted so soon, and began to pull the heavy wagon toward the city of Lyos.

Peasants and carts choked King's Bend—the wide, cobblestone road that wound up to the great hilltop, hauling goods and people to and from the city. The road had been deliberately fashioned in a winding manner so that any army charging the summit would be exhausted by the time they reached the walls and, all the while, would be fodder for bowmen lining the parapets above.

Trees lined the trail, their leaves dried by autumn. The musk of the city washed over him, overwhelming him for a moment: sweat, whiffs of floral perfume, the tang of foreign spices and sweet, charred meat. Rather than breathe through his mouth, Rowen inhaled deeply. The act made his eyes water, but it clogged his senses—an old trick he'd learned in the Dark Quarter. He told Hráthbam to do the same.

"No need," the Soroccan answered. "I've visited cities before, my friend. Besides, you haven't felt your senses roil until you've been to a hláshba brewery." Nevertheless, the Soroccan dabbed his watery eyes with one sleeve.

As when Rowen was last here, countless vendors had set up stands everywhere along King's Bend beneath the shade of the trees, selling silvery-blooded fish and rainbow-shelled crabs hauled in from the coast, next to bolts of rough leather and bows fashioned from shafts of urusk bone. Other items vied for attention: bolts of fine, watery silk from Sorocco; string-tied stacks of sweetbitter leaves; beautiful, blue-white seashells drawn from the oft-frozen Wintersea; poor imitations of the long-handled adamunes of the Isle Knights, their curved blades forged not from folded kingsteel but common iron; even clay pots packed with darksoil, the legendary stuff of the Dwarrs to the south, who grew their food in caves without need for sunlight.

He even saw obscene paintings and drawings from Dhargoth, their purpose as obvious as their popularity. The sight of these reminded Rowen that he had not been with a woman in a long time—in a brothel or otherwise—but he blushed and pushed the thought from his mind. Rowen suggested Hráthbam remove his jewelry—several thick, gaudy rings and a brass choker fixed with precious stones—but the Soroccan refused. "If I were buying, I'd be dressed like you. But when I'm selling, I fetch a better price when it looks like I don't need the coin."

Rowen rolled his eyes. As a merchant driving a wagon, Hráthbam would already be a prime target for cutpurses. "My job would be far easier if you wouldn't draw thieves and murderers like ants to honey."

"That's why I have you to protect me! Well, and this, too." He rattled his scimitar for emphasis. "Between all that, they'd have to cut my hands off to get my rings!"

"Trust me, they would," Rowen muttered.

Hráthbam's grin vanished. Convinced by Rowen's stark tone, he removed his jewelry and tucked it piece by piece into the pockets of today's pompous silk gown, this one a deep burgundy trimmed in purple. "Satisfied?"

Rowen considered suggesting that the merchant put on different clothes as well, but he decided not to press his luck. He nodded.

Hráthbam asked, "Do you still think we'll find your pretty young wytch in there?"

The question caught Rowen off guard. "If she really did come here, I can't imagine they'd let her live... though from what I've seen, I don't think Shel'ai die easily."

Despite the bustle, the crowds appeared far too calm for having executed a magic-wielding wytch only a day or two ago. He tried to clear his head and focus on the matters at hand.

Midday found the Red Watch out in full force. Pikemen patrolled on foot and horseback, dressed mostly in leather brigandines or the occasional chain mail hauberk, over which they wore faded scarlet tabards stitched with the black falcon of Lyos. Though crowds here behaved far more civilly than in the Dark Quarter, the Red Watch had its hands full trying to maintain order, breaking up the occasional fight and apprehending cutpurses whenever they could.

The sight of the guards prompted a strange, instinctual reaction within him. His fists clenched. His pulse quickened. As a boy, he'd hated and feared the guards, who had standing orders to beat any urchin from the slums caught trying to steal from the city above. Some guards had been known to take that punishment further. Many times, sprinting with a stolen loaf of bread under his shirt, dodging through streets—half blind with panic—with a guard or two just steps behind, Rowen had been lucky to escape with both hands intact.

He tried to calm his temper, reminding himself that the guards were just men charged with a nearly impossible task. At best, they could do little more than hold the criminal elements of the Dark Quarter to a stalemate. Besides, although no one in the slums wanted to admit it, the Red Watch did much to dissuade more than a few of the more sinister gangs that prowled the Dark Quarter, searching for orphaned children.

Rowen paused a moment as a wave of dreadful memories washed over him: leering men with false smiles, worse than animals, whom he'd learned early on to avoid, despite their promises of coins and free food.

Jinn's name, what madness brought me back here? He thought of Silwren. He thought of the Well. He thought of what he had seen there, in the depths of Cadavash—less a vision than a feeling of wholeness fused simultaneously with a loss of identity, something he still did not quite understand.

But Silwren understands. Somehow, through Knightswrath, he had been drawn to her. She could help him make sense of that, not to mention what he'd seen in the Well. Besides, with his contract with Hráthbam nearing its end, he had nowhere else to go.

Hráthbam slowed the horses, sensing Rowen's unease, but Rowen waved him on without a word. Soon, they were caught up by the traffic flowing up and down the great hill. The market smell—an amalgamation of spice, burnt meats, sweat, and dung—closed in again, along with the raucous crowds around them. Left and Right were clearly agitated by so many strangers jostling about—guards in armor, rich men and women in silk sarongs, peasants in rags—but they obeyed their master's commands for once. Rowen, meanwhile, was grateful that he was sitting in the wagon, but he had to resist the temptation to tug his tunic over his nose to protect himself from the smell of the crowds. He should have been used to it, but his time in the clean civility of the Lotus Isles must have softened his senses.

"Dyoni's bane!" Hráthbam's voice was muffled. Rowen felt a mixture of amusement and relief that his employer had covered his face with a silk rag. "How do people live amid such filth?" the Soroccan demanded. He gestured, incredulous, at a line of people immodestly relieving themselves just off the trail. "Have your kind never heard of privies?"

Rowen laughed curtly, biting back a reference to Hráthbam's earlier mention of hláshba breweries. "We have some in the city, alongside the bathhouses. But the poor aren't welcome up there."

Rowen felt the wagon jostle. He cursed and looked over his shoulder, into the canopy. Sure enough, a thief had hopped onto the back of the wagon: a young man, frightfully thin with eyes like a wild animal. The thief had no notion of the fortune in dragon-ivory concealed under a pile of cloaks. He simply reached out with both hands and grabbed the nearest objects—a hatchet and a knapsack of dried foodstuffs—and was about to jump off the back of the wagon.

Rowen caught the man by the ankle. The man kicked but Rowen did not let go. A certain hold and twist he'd learned on the Isles would snap the thief's leg at the knee. Instead of using it, he shook the man by his tattered shirt.

"Open your hands."

A hatchet fell to the wagon floor with a heavy clang. A knapsack followed. Rowen released him. The man rabbited out the back of the wagon and vanished back into the crowds.

"Are you whole, or did you just catch a knife between the ribs?"

Hráthbam asked, straining to hold the reins and look over his shoulder at the same time.

"I'm fine. Just a thief." He sat beside Hráthbam at the head of the wagon again but turned sideways so he could keep a better watch on the rear.

"A thief? Looked more like a half-starved lizard to me!"

"Probably was," Rowen admitted. "Half starved, that is."

Hráthbam's expression soured. "Now I wish you'd let him take what he wanted."

"Some merchant you are!"

Hráthbam shrugged, eyes straight ahead. "I *inherited* my fortunes, Locke. If ever you thought otherwise, now's the time for amends. Were you to say I'm too soft hearted to be a merchant, you and my wives would have that in common."

Surprised, Rowen said nothing.

They'd gone halfway up King's Bend now. Rowen's eyes strayed southward, toward the spiderweb of thin, worn paths breaking off the main road and leading back down the summit toward the grim, smoky slums. The Dark Quarter. These paths were even more rowdy than King's Bend, filled mostly with beggars, cutpurses, and prostitutes.

One of the latter, a pale young woman clearly naked beneath a translucent gown trimmed in lace and pearls, sidled up to the wagon. She was wearing a long, extravagant wig of knee-length dark curls, and her eyes were heavily painted in ochre. A burly, expressionless man—probably her protector—followed a step behind. The prostitute caught Rowen's eye.

"Want to see the gods, big man? I'll have you screaming their names for fifty cranáfi!"

Rowen blushed, grateful that Hráthbam sped the wagon past her.

"Gods, she's just a child!" Hráthbam swore.

Rowen winced. "The poor will do what they must to survive. Age doesn't enter into it. Believe me." Reflexively, he moved his hand to Knightswrath's dragonbone hilt. The hilt was cool now—not like it had been in the depths of Cadavash—but it reassured him nonetheless.

Rowen scanned the wagon one last time for thieves and returned his attention to the Red Watch. They were close enough to the summit now to dissuade most would-be criminals. That only made Rowen more anxious because it meant they would have to deal with the city guards soon.

The great walls of Lyos loomed over them now, bristling with battlements, black-and-scarlet banners, and bored, pacing soldiers. Just ahead lay a broad, open gateway and a raised portcullis. The portcullis glinted in the sunlight, though here and there, rust speckled the iron. Nearby, a dozen pikemen made a token effort to control the flow of traffic in and out of Lyos. Rowen noticed without surprise that the guards turned away beggars but welcomed merchant wagons—for a price. Rowen saw coins exchange hands, copper glinting in the midday sun.

"May as well take out your coin purse," Rowen said. "They'll tax you to enter the city. More like a bribe, really. But pay it, or else they'll confiscate your wagon."

Hráthbam's glower made it clear that he did not think much of the suggestion, but having never been to Lyos, he took Rowen's advice.

"And say nothing of the dragonbone," Rowen added, "or else they'll think you're rich and charge you twice as much!"

"It's a good thing you made me take off my rings, then."

Their wagon fell into line behind a column of other merchants. Most of the other merchant wagons bristled with stone-faced mercenaries. The sight of so many grizzled warriors in stout, expensive brigandines reminded Rowen of his own days as a hired sword. He'd had armor then, good weapons, and plenty of coin for food and comforts.

All of which I sold to buy my way into the Lotus Isles—for all the good that got me!

Rowen's face burned until he imagined it matched the shade of the unruly red hair that had been the object of so much teasing from the other aspiring squires on the Isles.

After what felt like an eternity, their turn came. A scowling, middle-aged pikeman wearing an officer's crest on his tabard walked over, gave Rowen a cursory glance, then asked Hráthbam a few quick questions about their business in the city. Hráthbam answered, saying nothing of the dragonbone. Instead, the Soroccan said he had come to Lyos to sell spices. The officer nodded absently, clearly uninterested.

Then he demanded a fistful of copper cranáfi. Once Hráthbam reluctantly handed them over, the officer delivered a bored, endlessly rehearsed speech about how they would find the King's Market and the nearest inn. Then, he waved them into Lyos.

Rowen felt a pain in his right hand. He realized he'd been clenching his sword's hilt so hard that his fingers cramped, his knuckles white as the bones underneath. He opened his fingers.

I'm sorry, Kayden.

Then, the sounds of the city washed over him.

CHAPTER THIRTEEN
A KIND OF HOMECOMING

T HE INSIDE OF THE GREAT city, mercifully, bore little resemblance to the dirty, disarrayed crowds and paltry street vendors set up along King's Bend. Lyos itself was almost exactly as Rowen remembered it: beautiful, well manicured, and woefully insincere. Still, the sight of the groomed trees, exotic gardens, and running fountains was a welcome respite from the open road, to say nothing of his brief glimpse of the slums he had once called home at the base of the hill.

Here, inside the city, cobblestone paths and marble walkways framed wrought-wood shops and small, quaint homes built from bricks of white mud. Around the homes, children played in small yards near mothers spinning wool or tending gardens. Here and there, broad clay basins caught rainwater that could, in turn, be used for public washing.

In the distance sat the aerie: the high, slender tower stocked with birders and their messenger pigeons. The king used the pigeons for diplomacy, his captains to convey information in times of war. The poor could use them to communicate with faraway friends and relatives, too—for a hefty price. Rowen had received the message from Kayden that way, just as word of his death had arrived on gray wings.

Rowen shook his head, trying to scatter his thoughts. As he'd told Hráthbam, Lyos had privies and bathhouses aplenty, drawing water from the Burnished Way via a marvelous, covered aqueduct that fed a massive underground pool deep inside the hill, this in turn feeding wells and water screws throughout the city. But many of the bathhouses had fallen into disrepair over the years, and only the wealthiest citizens of Lyos could afford to regularly frequent those that remained.

Hráthbam slowed to let a small crowd pass: street washers and men with carts paid to collect and empty chamber pots—the poorest people of the inner city, only a little better off than the slumdwellers of the Dark Quarter. Mostly children and young women, half nude, they made slow, lackadaisical rounds with buckets and rags.

Not far away, a young mother bathed her small child before she casually removed her own plain sarong and bathed herself, washing the garden dirt from her hands, her dark hair held up by a comb of bone.

Rowen's face flushed. The sight of the pretty young mother excited him far more than that of the prostitutes who moved amid the Dark Quarter like vultures. He felt ashamed, suddenly reminded of his bedraggled appearance. He resolved to trim his hair and beard and bathe as soon as Hráthbam was settled at the inn or the King's Market—whichever the Soroccan chose first.

He was about to ask when Hráthbam said, "The way you spoke of this city, I expected to see children roasting dead rats for supper!"

"They do. Just not here. At the base of the hill, in the slums. Here, things are better. But I spent most of my time in the Dark Quarter."

Hráthbam nodded absently, his green eyes drinking in the sights around him. He waved to a group of merchants who walked past, all of them dressed in simple cloth wraps. The men scowled back and said nothing.

"Put your jewelry back on," Rowen suggested. "They'll happily greet you then!"

Though Rowen was half joking, Hráthbam obeyed. Then he guided the wagon through the streets toward the King's Market. A growing din reminded them of the chaos of King's Bend, but upon their arrival, they saw that the market was clearly in a better state. A seemingly endless sea of merchant tables had been set up inside a huge open area at the center of the city, prompting trade of all kinds: not just wheat and turnips from nearby farmlands, but also lemons and cloves from Ivairia; capers, silk, and dried fish from Sorocco; water clocks and sundials from Atheion; even potions and powders sold by copper-skinned women from Quesh in their bell-trimmed hoods and veils. Thanks to the proximity of privies and clean water, the market smelled less of filth than spice, leather, and cooked meat. Though Rowen had already eaten some of Hráthbam's stew only hours earlier, his stomach growled.

Judging by the number of pacing uniforms, the bulk of the Red Watch had been deployed here to oversee trade and keep order, leaving relatively few to patrol elsewhere. Hráthbam chuckled, mirroring his thoughts. "No wonder things are such a mess outside the gates!"

"Kayden always said swords go where the money is. Do you want to set up in the market now or find an inn?"

Hráthbam looked at him as though he'd gone insane. "To the market, you dunce! I have a fortune in precious ivory to sell!"

Rowen concealed his disappointment. He'd hoped that his employer would choose the latter, although he had not really expected him to do so. Rowen dismounted from the wagon and led the way. They advanced with great difficulty through the crowded square until they found an empty spot where the previous vendor had just left. They claimed it at once. Rowen unhitched the horses and led them behind the wagon, tying them in the shade of a poplar, away from the crowds but still close enough that he could watch over them.

Hráthbam, meanwhile, hurried to unload the wagon. The merchant dragged down a table and chair by himself, covered the table with a bright silk cloth sewn with the maritime iconography of his homeland, and began displaying his new assortment of dragonbone.

Rowen watched, arms crossed, Knightswrath close at hand. He doubted thieves would be bold with so many guards nearby, but he quickly felt hard pressed trying to keep an eye on Hráthbam's wares *and* the horses tethered in the distance at the same time.

As expected, the crimson-swirled shafts of dragonbone sold— but slowly, and not for nearly as much as Hráthbam was expecting. Rowen quickly guessed why and cursed himself for not anticipating this earlier. Only a few days' travel separated Cadavash from Lyos. Wealthier merchants must have already conceived of Hráthbam's plan months or even years before. As rare as dragonbone might be in the world at large, the markets of Lyos had plenty of it. After a few hours, Hráthbam was forced to steadily lower his prices until Rowen feared the big man was about to cry.

Rowen ignored the temptation to console him, his own patience wearing thin. His eyes scanned the crowds, on the lookout not just for would-be thieves but for a mist-eyed young woman with platinum tresses as well.

He cursed himself. *If she really did come here, would she be wandering around the market where anybody could see her?* Still, he found himself catching his breath each time he spotted golden hair in the distance, only to be disappointed.

Rowen considered asking the Red Watch about her, but that would only get him branded as a lunatic. He might simply listen to the gossip of the city folk around him, but he had already strained his ears listening for some mention of a mist-eyed wytch found wandering the city, to no avail.

Maybe she changed her mind. He did not know whether to feel relieved or disappointed.

By the time the sun was sinking beyond the western battlements, flashing orange through the gardens and marble walkways of Lyos, Rowen realized a hard truth: she was not there. Something must have happened. Or else she'd simply changed her mind. Or she'd lied.

He sighed. He and Hráthbam exchanged glances. The Soroccan's disappointment clearly matched his own, albeit for different reasons. The market was clearing now. Without a word, they sullenly loaded the few remaining scraps of dragonbone and the rest of Hráthbam's wares into the wagon, rehitched the horses, then made for the nearest inn.

Luck was not with them. The first three inns they checked had no rooms, and all three of them looked too expensive for Hráthbam's sour mood, anyway. The merchant finally settled on a decidedly cheaper and more dismal inn with a name Rowen could not pronounce, located in a small section of the eastern city that appeared to be just slightly better off than the Dark Quarter. The inn had a stable with a guard though, and Rowen hoped that he might at least sleep on a real bed

163

tonight. But if Hráthbam intended to buy his room or at least allow Rowen to spend a few of the ten copper cranáfi in his pocket so he could buy a room himself, he gave no indication of it.

Rowen, temper frayed, finally pressed the matter. Hráthbam glowered at him then insisted he sleep in the wagon. They had stabled the horses but been forced to leave the wagon outside. Though the stable guard assured them it would be safe, Hráthbam did not like the look of the man—an imposing but unscrupulous-seeming fellow who was missing three fingers and half an ear, common punishments for thieving.

Rowen was inclined to agree, but he kept this to himself. Ruefully, he made his way into the stables to check on the horses. When he was certain they'd been properly cared for, he returned to the wagon. Above him, Armahg's Eye shone faintly through a veil of blue-black clouds: a bad omen among almost any people he'd known.

A chill ruled the air, and Rowen shivered. Hráthbam had at least thought to send out a serving wench with some bland fish stew and watery ale for him, but this did little to protect him from the chill. Rowen tried to pass the time by striking up a conversation with the stable boy and the guard—the only other two people nearby—but neither answered with more than a grunt. After a while, Rowen deduced that the stable boy was mute while the stable guard was another story and simply seemed to lack manners as well as digits. *Best keep my eye on that one.*

Sleep evaded him, and he had no heart to practice his sha'tala. He tried to read the Codex Lotius, but this too gave him no comfort. He thought of Sneed again. Rowen wondered what had compelled him to leave the Codex Viticus behind; Sneed could not even read it and had rather seemed to prefer the Codex Lotius with its colorful illustrations. Rowen told himself that he'd left the ponderous tome as a reward, but now, he wished he'd kept it so he could sell it himself.

When this is done, maybe I'll track down Dagath after all! Gods know I won't have anything better to do.

Then he thought of Jalist. Rowen hoped he'd reached the Throng and joined them without incident if that was really what his friend wanted to do.

Maybe I should have gone with him. Ah, but then I wouldn't have a rusty sword and memories that are probably slowly driving me crazy!

Rowen picked up Knightswrath and studied its exquisitely-carved hilt again. He wondered if he should sell it after all. He also wondered if Hráthbam would still have given it to him had the merchant known about the dragonbone hidden under the hilt's ratty leather.

Rowen cursed himself for thinking this. The Soroccan was a far cry better than any other man Rowen had ever worked for. And if the merchant kept his word, Rowen would still have ninety more copper cranáfi in his pocket before this was all over. Silwren be damned. If he never saw her again, if he never truly understood what he'd seen in that strange well in the deepest levels of Cadavash, at least he'd have enough coin to start over somewhere.

Rowen permitted himself the fantasy of buying a good sword, some leather armor, maybe even a horse. Then he'd at least be back where he'd been before he gave up being a mercenary and went to the Lotus Isles in the first place.

But that's not what I wanted. He'd thought many times about going north and squiring for an Ivairian Lancer, but everyone knew the realm had been wracked by famines and unrest for decades. He doubted he'd have much luck. He could always return to the Lotus Isles with a false name and try to train at a different temple—once he had enough coin to buy his admittance again—but the laws of the Knighthood were nothing to scoff at. If he was recognized, he'd be put to death.

As he lay in the wagon, tired more from despair than physical exhaustion, he rested one hand on Knightswrath's hilt again. This time, he thought he felt a flicker of heat in the hilt but, half asleep, he took it for a figment of his imagination.

CHAPTER FOURTEEN

THE BLOOD THRALL

S HADE REINED IN HIS HORSE, gesturing for Lethe to do the same. On the road ahead, someone called for help. Shade could not tell much about the little man's appearance, save that he lay crumpled in a torn cloak, his voice unmistakably Human.

"Help, m'lords! Bandits took my horse, cut my leg…" The man trailed off, as though weeping.

Shade was tempted to ride by, but only a day ago, he'd incinerated a dragon priest and a few guards who recognized them from Cadavash. Lethe had openly accused Shade of murder, saying the Shel'ai could just as easily have incapacitated them. Shade decided that now was as good a time as any to demonstrate that he could be merciful, too.

"See to his wounds. Leave him food and water as well."

Instead of looking surprised, Lethe winced, visibly pained as he rode ahead.

Why would he argue about helping someone in need? "Hold," Shade called out. He rode to where Lethe had paused. "I thought you would approve of this. What's the problem?"

"It's a trap," Lethe said. "I've seen this before. That man probably has a knife hidden somewhere."

The little man overheard them. He sat up a little. "No, m'lords, I swear! I'm just—"

Shade burned the prostrate man into the earth. Lethe stared, aghast. Shade attacked so quickly that their pack horse bolted. He extended his mind into that of the animal, compelling it to return.

Then he turned his attention back to Lethe. "Why the grim face, Human? You said yourself it was a trap. He might have killed the next traveler who happened by."

"Oh, I don't object to you killing them," Lethe countered, "just how much you enjoyed it."

Shade considered answering the rebuke with an invocation of Lethe's Blood Thrall but then changed his mind and let the matter drop. "I know how much you Humans crave riches. If you want to search him for valuables, I'll wait."

Though Shade meant it as a rebuke, Lethe dismounted and approached the charred corpse. Shade cursed at the delay but decided to feign indifference. Covering his nose with one hand, the assassin prodded the corpse then rifled through a knapsack lying nearby. Lethe frowned. He pulled something out of the knapsack—a book. The assassin paled.

"What is that?"

"Nothing," Lethe said. He slid the book back into the knapsack, dropped it on the ground, and returned to his horse.

"Nothing of value?" Shade prodded.

Lethe shook his head. "I crave death, not riches. Until then, Sorcerer, I've got everything I need."

"Too bad you had to warn me it was a trap, then. You might have gotten what you wanted."

They pressed on, stopping only when the horses could go no farther. They passed a handful of travelers, but all of them had the good sense to shy away from the Shel'ai and his fearsome bodyguard, some cursing or making superstitious signs of warding as they did so. Shade dared to hope they'd make it all the way to Lyos without further incident. Then, a half-dozen bandits crested the hill, directly in their path.

Rough-looking men, all of them carried swords, and one even carried a repeating crossbow. The crossbow caught Shade's eye. He had seen such weapons a few times before. Supposedly, they were an invention of the Dwarrs. Fitted on top with a stock that contained ten or so crossbow bolts, the weapon was fired using a lever that drew back the bow, dropped a bolt into place, and fired it all in one pull.

While not especially accurate or powerful, repeating crossbows made up for this in speed. *Might be a good addition to the Throng.*

Shade judged by the laughter that the bandits were expecting an easy mark. They did not know a Shel'ai of the Throng when they saw one, simply mistaking Shade for some foppish priest or nobleman.

"Let's have them coin purses," their leader said, reining up not far ahead of them.

Shade stared straight ahead and made no reply to the bandit leader's orders. The smell of the bandits' unwashed bodies had preceded them just as surely as the sound of their poorly shod horses.

"Did you hear me?" the bandit leader called out. "Toss over the purses! And you"—he pointed at Lethe—"drop all them weapons!"

Still, Shade did not answer. The bandit leader drew his sword. The other bandits did the same. The bandit leader howled and led the charge, gripping the reins with his pike-hand, his rusty bastard sword whirling overhead.

Shade lifted his hands, slender fingers splayed at the oncoming men. Violet flames exploded from his fingertips, blasting the bandit leader clean out of his saddle. His body struck the ground and burst like a bag of cinders.

In the awful stillness that followed, Shade changed his aim.

More wytchfire unfurled from his wrists and crackled from his hands, taking a second man from his saddle. Then a third. Forgotten, the Dwarr crossbow tumbled onto the plains, burning. Shade sighed with regret.

The remaining bandits' eyes widened. Horrified, they yanked on their horses' reins and tried to flee. Probably none, Shade thought with bemusement, had ever seen magic before. He hesitated. On the one hand, allowing the bandits to escape meant they would spread word of the horrible power of the Shel'ai—always a good thing in Shade's eyes. On the other hand, he and Lethe would have to be on guard when they camped that night, just in case the bandits found their courage and returned for revenge.

Shade said, "Take them."

Lethe chased the bandits straight into the setting sun. The bloody glare made him wince. His pulse leapt in his throat. He did not particularly wish to kill anyone today, but the Blood Thrall would wreak agony on him if he disobeyed.

He dispassionately drew both of his shortswords, leaning low and bracing himself in the saddle with his knees. He raked his palfrey's flanks with his spurs. The bandits were terrified, flying away at breakneck speed, but Lethe's mount was better. It took only a few moments for him to close the distance. When he caught them, he gave no battle cry.

The bandits glanced over their shoulders and saw him. Lethe wondered if they were relieved, seeing a man pursuing them and not his fire-conjuring devil of a master. This thought amused him as the first bandit turned, swung clumsily, and suddenly found himself without a head.

The last two bandits whirled to face him, too. When they saw how effortlessly Lethe had dispatched their comrade, they hesitated. They might have tried to flee again, but Lethe was already on top of them.

He drove his horse straight into one, blocked the man's wild swing, then shoved him out of the saddle. He faced the third. This bandit stabbed conservatively at Lethe's face, trying to hold him at bay. Then, the bandit swung for Lethe's horse. *Nice try.* He cut the blade and the hand that wielded it from the bandit's body.

The bandit howled, leaning so far away in his saddle that he was just beyond range of Lethe's shortswords. The man cried for mercy. Lethe thought of the book he'd left on the plains—of the laws therein, stating that mercy must always be granted when requested. Cursing, Lethe urged his mount closer. He used the bandit's tactic against him. One shortsword flashed down in a brutal swing, cutting the bandit's horse out from under him.

But then, as the horse crashed to the plains, the beast flailed wildly with its hooves, tangling them in the legs of Lethe's own palfrey. Blood had left the grass slippery. Lethe's mount lost its footing.

Lethe flung himself clear. He struck the ground hard, rolled, and tried to come up, but his foot caught a divot in the earth, and raw pain lanced through his leg. A strange elation filled him, despite the pain. *My leg's broken. Two bandits left. If I let them kill me—*

No sooner did he have this thought than new, far more terrible pain washed over him. His master had given him orders to kill these bandits. The Blood Thrall tapped directly into his brain and his heart. Though it could be activated by a Shel'ai, it had a will of its own, too. If Lethe did not do everything in his power to carry out his orders, the Blood Thrall punished him.

Still, if the bandits could kill him quickly enough, Lethe might be able to bear the torment long enough to earn himself the sweet release of death. But suddenly, the world moved at the pace of melting ice.

Through a blur of tears and pain, he could see the bandit he'd unhorsed earlier moving to help the one whose hand he'd taken. Both readied their swords. Lethe could make out the rage on their faces and knew they meant to kill him. But they moved like snails. The awful sundown sparkled off drawn steel as though the sun had also frozen in place. The Blood Thrall roiled through him, inflicting layer upon layer of torment. He would suffer the equivalent of years before the bandits actually slew him.

Lethe gave up. He would have to fight. He'd lost one sword in the fall, but he raised the other. Instantly, all pain but that of his broken leg disappeared, and the flow of time returned to normal. The bandits barreled toward him. One reeled from pain and blood loss but held a knife in his remaining hand. Lethe could not stand, could not move anything but his sword arm, but that was enough.

The shortsword danced before him, seemingly everywhere at once. He held the bandits at bay then feigned a mistake, leaving himself open. The one-handed bandit lurched immediately for Lethe's side. Instead, puzzled, he found himself weaponless, impaled hilt-deep on a shortsword.

Lethe grinned. *This is it.* He'd fought as well as he could. He'd tried to kill all the bandits, but he'd lost one sword and stuck the other in this dying man's gullet. There was no way he could wrench it free or draw another weapon before the last bandit finished him off. The Blood Thrall had no reason to torment him.

Lethe closed his eyes. *By the Light… thank you. At last!*

Violet flames caught the final bandit in the back, washing over his body with heat intense enough to sear Lethe's cheek. He opened his eyes in time to see the force of his master's magic propel the howling bandit through the air, scattering his body like ash.

Shade rode toward him and dismounted. The Shel'ai was smiling. "What would the rest of the Unseen say if they could see their great captain bested by a mere three brigands?"

Lethe stared back, speechless. He nearly wept. *So close... I was so close!*

Shade knelt to examine his leg. "You broke your ankle. This will not do." He lifted the leg of Lethe's trousers, revealing a swell of angry, purple skin. Bone jutted through. Lethe winced—more from the sight than from the pain.

Shade laid his hand over the ghastly wound. Without warning, he shoved the bone back in. Lethe bit back a scream. Shade squeezed the wound. Heat flowed from the Shel'ai's hand. The wound tingled, followed by a brief but maddening itch, then more heat. The pain subsided. By the time Shade removed his hand, only a faint bruise remained.

Shade knelt to rest. The Shel'ai's hood was thrown back, revealing his pale skin and hair. For all his urgency to find the Dragonkin, Shade was smiling.

Lethe recalled all the stories he'd heard, that Shade had spent years killing Humans as revenge for the slaying of some other Shel'ai. Lethe eyed the Shel'ai's exposed throat. He wanted to jam a blade into it. Instinctively, one hand moved to his weapons belt. But no sooner had he touched the hilt of a knife than the Blood Thrall washed over him again.

CHAPTER FIFTEEN
THE NEWEST GUARD

I
T SEEMED TO ROWEN THAT Hráthbam, at least, woke in better spirits. He brought Rowen a bowl of spiced porridge, water, and a plate of sliced apples in the morning. The merchant announced his intention to sell the remaining contents of his wagon in the King's Market that afternoon. Rowen ate without comment and then accepted the sweetbitter leaf the merchant passed him. He chewed and kept it in his mouth until the mix of the plant's burning juices and his own saliva made him wince, then spat it out.

Hráthbam wore his most bombastic silken robe yet: a silver-and-golden thing sewn with an intricate pattern of interlocking leaves and scimitars, plus a rather comical rendition of a purple lion tipping back what looked like a bottle of wine. The pouring wine was represented by a trail of scarlet gemstones.

Gold and silver rings bound the Soroccan's goatee, too. He had apparently exchanged his scimitar's plain scabbard for a more extravagant one wrought of stained mahogany inlaid with carvings that depicted the fanciful myth of Dyoni seducing Fohl the Undergod only to leave him engorged and wanting, as revenge for his disrespect of her priestesses.

Perhaps the merchant's good humor was a façade, but Rowen was not about to question it. He insisted on readying the wagon all by himself, allowing Hráthbam another moment to flirt with a pair of Lyosi tradeswomen. Tall and lithe, both had dark hair and deeply tanned skin. Though they batted their eyelashes and feigned fascination in Hráthbam's accent and biceps, Rowen sensed they were just trying to charm him into lowering his prices. He missed the conclusion of their dealings, but when he returned, Hráthbam was smiling.

"I might be the only man who enjoys being robbed from time to time."

Rowen was about to ask for details, but a pang of jealousy prompted him to stay quiet. They drove the wagon to the King's Market. Rowen unhitched the team. This time, Rowen told Hráthbam to refrain from unloading the wagon until he'd personally entrusted Left and Right to the nearest stable. Then Rowen returned as quickly as possible and helped the merchant set up his displays.

Hráthbam had already sold most of his dragonbone, but he still had all manner of weapons, silk, liquor, and other trinkets. In fact, what Rowen had mistaken earlier for chests full of junk actually seemed to sell better than the dragonbone. The Queshi sickle-sword and the Ivairian-style shortswords sold quickly, something of a novelty in a street market where most merchants preferred to sell cheap imitations of Isle Knights' adamunes.

Rowen had secretly been hoping to buy the Queshi composite bow for himself, but a hunter happened along who shared Rowen's appreciation for the bow's fine, powerful curves. After only a token attempt at reducing Hráthbam's outlandish asking price, the hunter bought it. Rowen swore.

The silk sold as well, plus trinkets the merchant had brought with him from Sorocco. By midday, Hráthbam's table stood half empty. Rowen realized his newfound friend would almost certainly leave the next day, his wares sold, the job done. Hráthbam, on the other hand, was all smiles. He offered Rowen a handful of copper cranáfi and told him to fetch both of them some lunch and ales. The Soroccan insisted he would be all right, hefting his scimitar for emphasis.

"Just so you know, Locke, that sorcerer appears to have healed my blood as well!"

Rowen frowned at the abrupt comment. "What?"

Hráthbam laughed. "I nicked myself a few days back, preparing that stew you like so much. I fetched the powder, figured the bleeding wouldn't stop—but it did." He shrugged. "Apparently, being hauled back from death brings additional benefits!"

Rowen's eyes widened. Speechless, he took the coins then went to fetch lunch. If the resurrection magic had altered Hráthbam so much, he wondered if the magic El'rash'lin had used to teleport him out of Cadavash had done something else to him—something he had not perceived yet.

He rejected the first few food vendors he saw, judging by the gray hue of the meat they were selling that it had been improperly treated and left out too long in the sun. He remembered what he'd heard of the Soroccans' peculiar diet: they preferred vegetables and fruits over meat, but if necessary, they would eat the flesh of land animals. They would not consume the flesh of birds, which they associated with the sea and therefore considered holy. Rowen was confident that Hráthbam's tastes were motivated less by belief than habit, though.

He bought food and ale, for the first time forgetting to scan the crowds for a sign of tapered ears and long, platinum tresses, then returned. He found Hráthbam grinning even more broadly, his table empty but for a few trinkets of jewelry. What's more, two young women—twin sisters, by the look of them—were fawning over the merchant. Both women wore gowns with all the substance of colored clouds.

Unlike other cities, Lyos had long since adopted the Lotus Isles' open-minded view on prostitution, largely regulated and overseen by the well-schooled clerics of Dyoni. But their affection was an act—just business, like shoeing a horse or repairing a busted piece of armor. While not evil, the act held no substance. And substance, it seemed, was what he was forever doomed to crave.

Still, he reminded himself, he was just a wagon guard. What made him uncomfortable was irrelevant.

Hráthbam gave Rowen a hearty greeting, accepted the food as though he had completely forgotten what food was, then handed one of the girls a handful of copper cranáfi. He winked at Rowen. To the young woman, he said, "The good Knight here finds himself far removed from the comforts of his temple. Might you help him find it?"

The woman smiled. "Of course!" she purred. She took Rowen's arm with teasing affection, using one hand to trace his chest through his clothes before snaking boldly downward, brushing his thigh before she lifted it again. At her touch, his blood burned despite her insincerity. For a moment, he hated himself for it. Then he surrendered. He offered Hráthbam the remainder of the coins he'd been given before. The Soroccan waved them off.

"I'll be here when you return." Hráthbam glanced at the wagon. "Well, I'll be *nearby*, at least!"

Face burning, Rowen pocketed the remaining few copper cranáfi then followed the young woman. She guided him by the hand toward a nearby inn. Forgotten, the food he'd just purchased grew cold and inedible on the empty table, lost in the daily commotion of the world around it.

Rowen rose slowly from the bed, hoping not to wake the prostitute. He went to the window of the dusty room in the upstairs of the inn. It was nearly sunset. Orange light filtered through the battlements and fringed the tops of houses and walkways. He sighed. His second day in Lyos. Naked, weary, he stretched.

"So, are you really an Isle Knight?"

Rowen was glad he wasn't facing her. "No. I was just a squire."

"So you cleaned your master's armor and carried his lances and such?"

Rowen concealed a smile. "You're thinking of the Lancers, up in Ivairia. The Isle Knights are a bit different, more like fighting monks. They care for their own steel. It's part of their discipline. Squires are basically just advanced students... like acolytes, I guess." He shrugged. "Anyway, I left the Isles before I finished training." He blushed further. He remembered his brother saying that he lied as well as he danced.

"Liar!" she teased, echoing his thoughts. "It's all right," she added. "Lots of squires end up here, m'lord. No shame in that. I could name a dozen if I had a mind to."

Rowen did not like being called a lord. "I bet you could." He

175

glanced at her in time to see her wince. "Sorry." He returned to the bed but shifted awkwardly.

She looked at him and smiled. She had a pretty face, round with a small nose and full lips. Her breasts were also full and more than his hands could grasp—the way he liked it, oddly perfect but for a scar on the side of one that looked to have been made by a knife.

He had half a mind to ask her about the scar, but he decided not to. He liked her. He wasn't sure if it was his loneliness or the ache in his loins or the blackberry wine they'd shared earlier, poured from a skin that Hráthbam had given her.

She squeezed his hand. "Relax, Sir Knight. I have skin like armor. I promise."

For some reason, the words touched him. He wanted her to stay, but she kissed him playfully then rose from the bed. Rowen was sure his face matched his hair again as he watched her dress in a burgundy sarong trimmed in white lace.

She glanced over her shoulder at him. "Have you ever thought about joining the Red Watch?"

Rowen laughed. "An orphan from the Dark Quarter joining the Red Watch..."

She smiled. "*I* came from the Dark Quarter, I'll have you know! I like to say it toughened me. Maybe it didn't, maybe scars are just scars, but it's a nice idea." She lifted her arms over her head and wriggled into her gown. It sank past the faint, serpentine outline of her spine, past her pleasingly full buttocks, to her bronze ankles. "Anyway, the Red Watch ain't all bad. But I'd understand if you want to get away from here, what with the war coming."

Rowen tensed. "What do you mean?"

She frowned at him. "You should listen to rumors more!" She continued talking as she dressed. "I got to know an officer of the Watch a while back. He said they'd gotten reports about that sorcerer's army. The Throng, I think they call it. Anyway, they're moving east. Weird thing is, he said they're not even bothering to guard their rear—whatever that means!" She winked at him. "He said they'll probably take a stab at Cassica if they haven't already."

Rowen forced himself to smile. "Their army's even bigger than the one here at Lyos. My brother and I sold our swords there a long time ago. If this so-called Throng marches on Cassica, they'll get slaughtered!"

The woman was dressed now. "If you say so, Sir Knight." She stretched, playfully arching her back and accentuating her bosom through the tightly-tied sarong. "I have to go. You can stay for a while and sleep, but can you be gone before dark?"

He caught her meaning. "Yes... of course."

She kissed his forehead then vanished out the door. Only then did Rowen wish he'd thought to ask her name. He considered sleeping. Instead, he thought of what the woman had said. It occurred to him that Cassica was far away. If it had already been attacked—had already fallen—word might not have reached Lyos yet.

By the time Rowen returned to the King's Market, twilight had spread through the whole of the city like some nobleman's thick, blue rug. Rowen found Hráthbam where the table had been. The table and chair had already been loaded into the wagon, the horses hitched. On the ground lay Rowen's few, meager possessions, neatly stacked. Hráthbam now wore a plain traveling cloak over his pompous silk robes. When he saw Rowen, he grinned and held out his hand. *"Fa'taj dá fiél-tha."*

Rowen blinked in surprise. Reflexively, he shook Hráthbam's hand. "What are you thanking me for?"

"For keeping me alive," Hráthbam laughed, "although I suppose you had a little help!" He pressed a coin purse into Rowen's hand. "Ninety coppers. To tell it true, I thought about making another trip to Cadavash, but the coin doesn't seem to be in dragonbone after all." He shrugged lightly. "Anyway, I thought about hiring you to see me safely to the docks off Sorocco, but something told me you'd be staying in Lyos."

Rowen frowned. "I have no reason to stay here."

Hráthbam's expression sobered. "Could have fooled me." For a long time, neither spoke. Then Hráthbam lowered his voice. "My friend, should we meet again in this life, perhaps we will each have the courage to tell the other what we have seen."

Before Rowen could reply, Hráthbam shook his hand again. Then, silently, he climbed into the wagon and steered it through the King's Market, down the cobblestone streets, past the open gates of Lyos, down the muck-trodden path of King's Bend, and beyond, out of Rowen's life.

Rowen stood in the King's Market for a while, uncertain, wind rustling his tangled red hair. Then, as darkness shrouded the city, penetrated only by the occasional flicker of lamps and torches, he headed for the nearest tavern. Hunger gnawed his stomach. And for once, coins filled his pockets. He ate his fill of bread and thick, spiced stew, plus a slab of charred, peppered salmon, then drank until a thick fog settled inside his head. At last, alone in a room crowded with strangers and a lively melody played by a brightly dressed troupe of minstrels, he pondered what to do next.

Was it true that Cassica was in danger? He'd heard such rumors but had put little stock in them. Just as Syros was famous for its archers, Cassica was known for the skill of its men-at-arms. But what use were such things against magic?

He listened to the common room's chatter, hot with whispers of battle. Some even insisted that Cassica had already fallen. A few spoke fearfully of the possibility that the Throng would march on Lyos next, but most dismissed this. With these, Rowen was inclined to agree. After all, assuming Cassica had been taken, what was the point of seizing such a great city, only to relinquish it to the Dhargots?

The Dhargots had been massing their legions for years: charioteers, phalanxes swelled by conscripts and slaves, highly trained war elephants, all poised to expand their bloody empire from the western peninsula across the Simurgh Plains. Rowen himself—along with his brother, Jalist, and a handful of others—had worked both for and against Dhargots in the past. He detested fighting alongside them. Their sanction of slavery and their penchant for disemboweling captured enemies thoroughly sickened him. But fighting against them was worse. For all their chilling cruelty, the Dhargots boasted discipline that rivaled even the Isle Knights'. And just as greatwolves always hungered for flesh, the Dhargots always hungered to expand their territories, take slaves, gain riches, and sow fear. If this General Fadarah was smart enough to conquer so many of the Free Cities of the Simurgh Plains, surely he must recognize that so overextending his lines only welcomed the Dhargots to sweep up behind him!

No, Lyos is safe—even if Cassica is already gone. We're too close to the Isles, too friendly with the Knights.

But Silwren's words nagged at his mind. She had said that Lyos was in danger. Rowen did not know her, did not even know if he could trust her, but he sensed she was telling the truth.

She'll be here—sooner or later. I just have to decide what I'll do when she gets here!

But what would he do in the meantime? Glancing across the tavern, he saw a squad of guards from the Red Watch engaged in a drinking contest, guzzling their mugs so quickly that ale spread like bloodstains down their red tabards. An answer came to him. He ordered another ale.

Rowen had found a room at a modest inn called Dyoni's Bane. The inn's name reminded him that Hráthbam had used the phrase more than once. Rowen cursed himself for not asking what it meant while he had the chance. He tried asking the serving girls there, but none of them seemed able to understand what he was saying. So he went to his room and slept instead.

He woke to sunlight streaming through the eastern window, into his eyes. He resisted for a while but then roused and dressed himself, forced himself to chew some sweetbitter for his breath, splashed his face with water from the basin laid outside his door, and made his way down to the streets. He adjusted Knightswrath on his hip, wishing he'd taken the time to trim his beard or cut his hair first. But he did not want to wait any longer. He thought of the decision he'd made the night before. It seemed no more asinine now than it had then, which he took as a good sign. He asked around, and all the guards he spoke to directed him toward the gates. So Rowen made his way out to King's Bend.

He spotted a weathered-looking sergeant, dressed in a red tabard emblazoned with a black falcon. He approached the man, saying simply that he wanted a job. The sergeant scowled at him then waved him toward the captain of the Red Watch. The captain was just exiting the privy, a tired scowl on his face.

"Captain Ferocles, another recruit!" the sergeant called.

The captain—a barrel-chested man with short-cut dark hair, a thick beard, and skin suntanned the color of leather—sized up Rowen with a quick glance. Then he said, "Hired." The captain turned and barked orders at the nearest soldiers, as though he'd already forgotten Rowen was there.

"Cassius, get your lazy asses over to Beggar's Drop. Epheus said another drunk fell—or jumped—off the ledge last night. This one was a merchant's kid, so now we have to pretend to care about stopping dumb bastards from killing themselves." He turned to a different man of the Red Watch. "Poska, since you were so kind as to show up late for duty, you get the pleasure of emptying the buckets." He gestured to the privies. The other soldiers laughed.

Rowen shifted from foot to foot, unsure what to do. Finally, he cleared his throat. Neither the captain nor the sergeant looked up. The captain removed a flask from another soldier's hand just as the man was about to drink, drank it himself, then passed the flask back. Then he turned to Rowen. "What in Fohl's hells are you still doing here?"

Rowen blinked in surprise at the man's gruff tone. "Begging your pardon, Captain... thank you, but what am I supposed to do now?"

Captain Ferocles stared at him for a moment then burst into laughter. The nearby men of the Red Watch chuckled, too, and Rowen felt his face turn the color of their tabards. "Why, try not to get your guts carved out, of course!" the captain said. "What's your name?"

Rowen bowed in the fashion he'd learned on the Lotus Isles. "My name is Rowen Locke."

The captain rolled his eyes. "Lovely. Another brooding washout from the Isles!" His statement drew more laughter. Rowen's fists clenched at the insult. "It's pretty simple, Locke. You'll be paid ten copper cranáfi from the tax coffers on the last day of every week in which you don't get yourself killed. Die, and we'll pay the balance to your family instead—if you have any."

The other soldiers snickered at this.

"In the meantime, report to Quartermaster Phews in the barracks for your uniform. He'll also set up your shift schedule and fix you up with a bunk—rather, a board with some straw on it. Once you're dressed, haul your pompous ass back here and get to work!"

The captain gestured to King's Bend. "We'll start you out here. What we do, boy, is keep order here as best we can. Simple as that. If you see a fight, break it up. If you see a pickpocket, grab him. Don't kill anyone you don't have to. Don't bash anyone you don't have to. If I find out you've broken either of these rules, I'll kill you myself." The captain yawned. "Over there, just off the bluff, is the Dark Quarter—" He stopped himself and squinted, scrutinizing Rowen again. "But you already know that, don't you?"

Rowen nodded, surprised.

"Figured as much. You have that look." The captain continued. "Well, in case you've been away, I'll fill you in. Not a damn thing's changed. The gangs still control the Quarter—which is just fine by us, since we're outnumbered and underpaid. So stay out of the Quarter unless I tell you otherwise. When you're in the city, whether you're on duty or not, keep yourself armed. Keep your eyes open. Men sneak up from the Quarter sometimes and look for women or children to... you know." He grimaced meaningfully. "If you catch them doing that, or trying to, do us all a favor and cut the man's throat. So long as you have a good reason and a reliable witness, and I'm not suspicious, I won't ask questions." He yawned again. "Speaking of questions, do you have any? The correct answer is no."

Caught off guard, Rowen hesitated a moment then shook his head accordingly.

The captain said, "Good. Oh, and one more thing, we practice every day with weapons and bare hands. All of us, even me. You look like you can handle yourself, but some of those bastards in the Quarter fight every bit as good as those Knights you trained with. So stay sharp. Miss drills because you're drunk, in bed with a whore, or any other reason that doesn't involve you recuperating from a stab wound, and you're through. Understood?"

Rowen nodded. Captain Ferocles waved him off, as though forgetting him again. Rowen had no idea where the barracks were, nor could he even remember the name of the quartermaster, but he knew better than to ask.

He hurried through the gates. A metallic creak made him look up at a raised portcullis followed by a column of murder-holes. The captain called after him, "I'd welcome you, boy, but wherever you were before this, you were probably better off!" Rowen guessed that must be an old joke by now, but once again, the other soldiers broke into laughter.

Rowen's first week in Lyos made him wonder if he might have been better off leaving after all. As Captain Ferocles had said, nothing much had changed.

As much as Rowen detested the cutthroats and would-be rapists, he especially loathed dealing with all the half-starved thieves. Some looked even more destitute than the man who had tried to rob Hráthbam's wagon outside the city gates. Technically, Rowen's duty was to apprehend these desperate souls and turn them over to Red Watch interrogators, ignoring their pleas for release.

This thought chilled Rowen's blood, for he had seen the results of such things as a boy. Since the thieves rarely had valuable information to share, the interrogations often degenerated into rote punishment, usually a flogging followed by a severed finger or a notched ear. On matters like this, no clear laws existed, and no one in the Red Watch seemed inclined to press for change.

Unwilling to see that kind of punishment visited upon those who most often wished only to feed themselves and their families— something he'd done himself more than once—Rowen contented himself with merely apprehending thieves and returning what was stolen. Besides that, he broke up fights when necessary and generally minded his own business.

The work wore on him, dreary and nerve-racking. Still, even when his shifts ended at sundown, he could not bring himself to leave a place where he knew his uncharacteristic temperance and quick eyes were sorely needed. So he would stay and try to help the other soldiers maintain order as best he could. He thought this might earn their favor. Instead, this earned him nothing but a bloody nose from a drunken brawler's fist and, from his fellow soldiers, the reputation of being a showy fool.

Before long, Rowen abandoned this practice. Better instead to settle himself in the nearest tavern. So, partly out of homage to his absent friend—gone now for two weeks—he returned again and again to Dyoni's Bane. Often, he visited the inn while still dressed in his faded scarlet uniform, the blackness of the falcon masking the ale stains on his sleeve.

One day, as Rowen downed another flagon of warm ale, he glanced down at his tabard with sardonic appreciation. He'd noticed the first time he dressed in his new uniform that if the restitching was any indication, no less than three soldiers had probably worn—and died in—this tabard before him. Likewise, the leather armor he'd been given left much to be desired: heavy but poorly balanced, thicker at some points than others, and poorly treated besides. It had reeked so badly of blood and stale sweat when he donned it that at first, he'd gone to bathe twice before he realized the stench was not his own.

Rowen missed the light but stronger armor of the Isle Knights, each piece capable of near-blinding brilliance when polished, even though he'd been allowed to wear it only a few times during training. He squinted at the insignia of a falcon on his breast until he could imagine it was a crane instead. "I shouldn't be here," he muttered, his slurred voice lost in the noise of the crowded tavern.

Two weeks had passed with no sign of Silwren. So far, he'd saved almost nothing since all his meager earnings went toward staying at an inn. Though he preferred being alone, he considered simply moving into the barracks—which were free—then leaving Lyos for good once he'd saved enough coin. More and more, he wanted to head west, perhaps toward Cassica.

Maybe Jalist was right. I should have joined the Throng. He did not relish the thought of fighting for the Shel'ai, but what did it matter? Five years ago, would he ever have even considered joining the same Red Watch that had beaten and killed more than a few of his acquaintances when he was a boy?

Maybe El'rash'lin, that strange, deformed man, would appear to make sense out of this madness. Hadn't the sorcerer saved Hráthbam from death after their battle with the greatwolf—then appeared again and magicked Rowen right out of the depths of Cadavash? One moment, he was deep inside the dragon priests' temple. The next, he was out in the open, beyond the gorge and the mad priests within, still holding Silwren in his arms.

He thought of the Well and shuddered. *Maybe it was all a dream. Maybe I've just lost my mind!*

He tried to recall what he'd seen upon gazing into the Well—but it had not been so much a vision as a perception, a momentary feeling of wholeness. He'd heard Isle Knights refer to such a state as *emptiness*. Before, he'd always been unable to understand how such a thing could be positive. At the Well, though, he'd momentarily transcended all his fears and doubts, even the encumbrance of his own identity, and in their place, felt only joy. *And now it's gone. Maybe it's just best I forget it... if I can.*

He waved for another ale. When it arrived, he drank deeply. As he set the mug down, he thought of the drills.

If Rowen was not well-liked on duty, he at least received a measure of grudging respect from the other soldiers during each day's training. As Captain Ferocles said, all soldiers of the Red Watch were required to train during at least one of each day's drills, free at least to choose the drill that best matched their guard shift. Though nobody kept records, the captain was present at every drill, and somehow, even with hundreds of soldiers to oversee, he could tell at once who had not participated in training.

In his first week with the Red Watch, Rowen witnessed half a dozen fellow soldiers dismissed for this reason. He quickly learned that among the soldiers of the Red Watch, Captain Ferocles was infamous for not only his temper but also his sharp memory. This, at least, might work in his favor.

Whether with wooden swords or bare hands, Rowen held his own. Some of the other soldiers had themselves been squires on the Lotus Isles; they too seemed reluctantly impressed. Rowen hoped his skill might also earn him the respect of the captain, which would ease his time in Lyos—regardless of how long a time that ended up being. But if the captain noticed, he gave no indication of it. In fact, he had not spoken to Rowen since their terse exchange at the city gates.

Rowen was brooding on this when Sergeant Epheus entered the tavern and sat down beside him. The sergeant had a build similar to Rowen's, with a close-cropped beard and long, dark hair pulled back into a ponytail so tight his hair looked like a black skullcap. Like Rowen, the sergeant was a former squire of the Lotus Isles, although his own failure to become an Isle Knight had taken place seven years before Rowen's. Like other such men in the Red Watch, the sergeant had no wish to talk about it. But unlike the other soldiers, the sergeant was at least willing to speak to him.

Epheus asked, "How's the ale here?"

"Warm and flat... but cheap."

The sergeant snickered. "Figures." He waved for a drink. "You know, there are a lot of better places in Lyos to get drunk. You should try the White Chimera, just up the street. That's where most of the Red Watch goes. Good whores there—including some skinny, dark-eyed Isle women. Not to mention a few Dwarrs, if you prefer 'em with oversized tits and rumps."

"Something tells me I'm not very welcome there."

"Probably not. But don't take it personal. New faces don't get much respect at first."

"How long's *at first*?"

Epheus shrugged. "A few months, I guess."

Rowen drank. "Then what?"

"Well, enough of the ones who have been here longer than you get killed, and suddenly, you're a veteran!" The sergeant chuckled and slapped Rowen on the shoulder. "Don't worry about it." The sergeant took the mug that was handed to him across the bar and drained half of it in one long swallow. Then he grimaced. "You're right. My horse's piss probably tastes better."

185

The barkeeper glared at him but said nothing.

"I hear you grew up here, before the Isles," the sergeant said nonchalantly.

Rowen nodded. He was hesitant to speak of his past, but he did not want to appear rude to the only person here who had showed him a sign of friendship. "My brother and I grew up in the Dark Quarter after our parents died."

Sergeant Epheus whistled softly. "Another Quarter-man! Just what we need." He finished his ale then waved for another. "Barkeeper, one more of your worst!" He chuckled at the barkeeper's glare. "Where's your brother now—still trimming throats down here?"

"Gone." Rowen raised his mug to drink but found it empty. "He went to the Isles a few years before I did."

"Two in the same family, huh? Where did he go after they rejected him?"

Rowen bristled. "They didn't. He became a Knight. He made it."

The sergeant's expression sobered. "I didn't think that was actually possible."

"It's not. Not really. But Kayden did it anyway." Rowen waved for another mug.

"Then what?"

Rowen realized what the sergeant was asking. He pretended to be inspecting his empty mug.

"How did he die?" the sergeant asked finally.

"Don't know," Rowen answered. "I wasn't there. The Knights say it was just an accident, though. He fell off his horse and dashed his brains on a rock." Rowen almost laughed, imagining how Kayden might have reacted had he foreseen such a senseless, ignoble end.

"Have you heard about those Sylvan wytches?"

Rowen frowned. "The what?"

"That's what we call them here," the sergeant said. "Shel'ai, I guess they're called elsewhere. Sylvs who can craft spells." The sergeant grimaced as he spoke, this time not from the bad taste of his ale. "Rumor is they've raised an army in the west."

Rowen thought of Jalist and rubbed his eyes. The ale was beginning to catch up with him. "An army of Shel'ai?"

"No, Humans. Mercenaries, mostly. Plus conscripts from whatever village or city they thrash. There are other stories, too, about some sort of creature. Not a wytch but something they made. Some kind of demon. They use it like an attack dog. They say nothing can kill it."

Rowen was surprised to see the sergeant shudder. What would have been farfetched a month ago, before Cadavash, now loomed as an all-too-real fear.

The sergeant asked, "Have you ever seen one?"

"A Shel'ai?"

The sergeant nodded.

Rowen thought of Silwren and El'rash'lin. "No."

"Me, neither. Nor a Sylv, for that matter. But I hear they look the same—except for the eyes. Sylv eyes are blue. But wytch eyes are purple. Only the pupils aren't black. They're *white*! Dragonmist, they call it."

Rowen shrugged. "Superstitions told by old men with ugly wives."

"I hope so. Because if it ain't, not much anybody's gonna be able to do about it. With none of these plains cities willing to stand together, I bet a strong enough army could sweep across the whole Simurgh Plains if it wanted."

"As soon as they reached the coast—*if* they reached the coast—they'd have the Knights to deal with."

"Boy, did someone brain you while I wasn't looking? The Lotus Isles are a dung heap! Weren't you there long enough to see that?"

Rowen tensed. "Why do you say that?"

The sergeant sneered. "Relax, Locke. You went there for the same reason I did. Probably your brother, too. You thought you were going to find honor there. But that doesn't exist outside of fairy tales. Not here, not there, not anywhere."

The sergeant waved something in front of Rowen's face. Irritated, Rowen slapped the hand away. The sergeant chuckled and tossed a copper cranáf on the bar before him. "Look at that insignia, boy," he said. "A damn crane. Not a falcon. Why do you suppose that is?"

Rowen had never bothered to consider that before.

The sergeant said, "Just a bunch of hypocrites! Didn't you ever stop to wonder why the poor never become Isle Knights but the rich do? Do you really think you deserved to be shooed off like a stray dog, after all that training? Did I?" He scoffed. "The Knights took us in so they could take our coin. Then they let us go. We may as well have handed our coins to one of those wandering tonic peddlers, for all the good it did us."

Rowen gritted his teeth. "That's not true."

"Locke, why do you think the Dark Quarter exists in the first place? Don't you think King Pelleas would raze it if he could?"

"Every city has its slums."

"Cities on the Lotus Isles don't."

Rowen shrugged. "Maybe he doesn't care. Or maybe he can't afford enough men."

The sergeant laughed. "With all these taxes, all this trade?" He shook his head. "Don't be so gods-damned naïve! I've served under three kings in my lifetime. Pelleas is as good as any. Do you think he *likes* his precious city ringed by slums like a jewel dropped in dung? No, you can blame the knights for that."

Rowen rubbed his eyes again. "What are you talking about?"

"Are you telling me you don't know?" When Rowen shook his head, the sergeant answered with a condescending laugh. "Locke, haven't you ever wondered why every damn city on this half of the plains uses the same coin? How do you think the Isles can afford such big keeps and fancy armor? They tax the so-called Free Cities from Lyos to Cassica! In return, they promise protection. But if you see Isle Knights patrol the roads once in two months, you're lucky. Twice, and it's probably *your* town they're getting ready to plunder!" He laughed. "There's something the captain says. A saying, I guess you could call it. 'If you're in trouble, pray for a Knight. If one shows up, hide your daughters and your jewels until he goes away.'"

Rowen stared in disbelief. "That's not true. If it were, I'd have heard about it a long time ago."

The sergeant scoffed. "It's a secret... of sorts. No king wants his people to know he doesn't even rule his own city! Better we think they keep the gold for themselves than give it up for nothing." The sergeant paused then added thoughtfully, "Well, not *nothing*, I guess. In exchange for what the Isle Knights call *tributes*, Lyos doesn't burn.

Only difference is, it's *their* swords they're sparing us from!" He shrugged. "The secret used to be easier to keep before the Knights got this greedy. Now—"

The room was spinning. "Prove it. Give me proof..."

The sergeant waved the coin again. "Ever been to Phaegos, a couple days northeast of here?"

Rowen thought of the Sister City, nestled against Artisan Bay near vineyards and good soil. Phaegos had been pillaged, robbed house to house, but left standing. Word was that now, four years later, the city still struggled to recover. "They were planning to invade the Isles. The Knights heard about it and struck first. What of it?"

The sergeant glowered. "Ah, yes. The mighty Phaegian army: poets, fishermen, and brothel dancers. Hardly a blade among them! But they stopped paying the tributes. So the Knights dealt with them."

"I heard—"

"You heard what the Knights *wanted* you to hear." The sergeant finished his ale and stood, tossing a handful of copper cranáfi onto the counter. "Believe what you want, Locke." The sergeant rose and walked away.

Rowen saw the sergeant through the window, probably walking up the street toward the White Chimera. Rowen's fists clenched. He could not believe what Epheus had said, nor could he imagine why the man would lie. Maybe Epheus was simply wrong. Weren't the bandits who attacked Rowen's own village defeated by Isle Knights?

But how many times since then had he even seen a Knight before he ventured to the Isles? How many times in his whole life had he seen a single patrol on the mainland? How much of his knowledge of them had been based purely on stories?

Rowen's rage slackened. Nausea roiled in his gut. He hoped it was only the putrid ale he was drinking. Cursing, he ordered another.

CHAPTER SIXTEEN
HARD CHOICES

E L'RASH'LIN FOUND HER JUST WHERE he knew he would: on the edge of the parapets, overlooking the palace at the spot the city's people called Beggar's Drop. She was kneeling—either in prayer or meditation, he could not tell. Platinum curls spilled down her back, all the way to the dirty walkway.

El'rash'lin said, "I figured you'd left Lyos a long time ago. Gone south, maybe."

Silwren did not answer. El'rash'lin extended his mind into hers. He felt her trepidation and wondered how long she had been wandering the city, invoking enough Dragonkin magic to render her invisible to Human eyes. Moonlight and the soft, steady glow of Armahg's Eye illuminated her curls and then his scarred hand as he reached for her. At the sight of his own deformed flesh contrasting with her beauty, he withdrew his hand.

Finally she said, "Have you come for counsel or comfort?"

"I doubt you can offer me any more wisdom or comfort than I can offer you. Such truths are well past lamentation, though." He eyed the sleeping palace in the distance. "I came to see which option you currently favor."

She opened her eyes. "Two options? I didn't know we had so many."

El'rash'lin gestured to the white stones and moon-washed rooftops around them. "To save them"—he laughed thinly again—"or kill them."

"Or do nothing," Silwren interjected.

El'rash'lin grew thoughtful. "Yes, apathy is always an option. I'm sure even Fadarah would agree to that."

Silwren stood so slowly that it seemed to El'rash'lin she floated onto her feet. The pupils of her eyes flared like iced starlight. "You know it makes no difference. The Dhargots will take the plains. The Isle Knights will fight the Dhargots, which means they *won't* be able to help the Sylvs fight the Olgrym—even if they wanted to, which I doubt. Either now or later, Lyos will burn just as surely as will the World Tree."

"Something might still be done," El'rash'lin insisted. "If you didn't believe that, you wouldn't have come here."

"Not belief, my friend. Foolish hope. And that died once I looked into these people's minds."

"It took you weeks to look into their minds? You could have done that in seconds."

Silwren's eyes narrowed. "What are you implying?"

"Just that I've never known a Dragonkin to wander aimless and invisible through a city she'd given up on."

Silwren almost smiled. "Have you known many Dragonkin?"

"Just three, if you count myself. Of all of us, you're prettiest." El'rash'lin hoped the jest would add to her momentary flash of humor, but already, he could feel her mood shifting.

"We tried it your way, old friend. You saved a Human from the grave, showed another one how to look into Namundvar's Well, into the Light itself. Their response? They pretend it never happened. We hoped for too much from Humans. The people of Lyos will be no different."

El'rash'lin shook his head, his voice gentle but insistent. "I did not summon that man into Cadavash. I did not force him to look into Namundvar's Well. Neither did you. Something else brought him there."

Silwren glowered at him. "Faith breeds more murderers than heroes. You know that as well as I do."

Are you sure you know that lesson? You nearly married Shade, after all. El'rash'lin hesitated. "There's a *fourth* option. Another choice. We both know it."

Silwren shuddered. "I will not consider that. I won't."

He started to reach for her arm, but she pulled away.

Her eyes flared with rage. "Would *you* do it? Would *you* destroy your own kind?"

"Perhaps I should," El'rash'lin answered. "You forget, you've been asleep for years. But I woke soon after Iventine. I've seen their sins with my own eyes: what they've done, how they've changed. The Blood Thrall, the burning cities, the executions—"

"I don't excuse their sins," Silwren said. "I felt them while I slept. I could hardly believe it. Especially Shade. I know his capacity for cruelty better than anyone. He shared his memories with me, all those Humans he killed when he was younger..." She winced. "But that, at least, I could understand. The invocation of the Blood Thrall was pure madness!"

"Our whole *cause* is madness now," El'rash'lin said. "It's not just Fadarah and Shade. I tried to reach Iventine, to see if there's anything of who he was left in there..."

Silwren looked at him expectantly, but El'rash'lin shook his head. After a moment, Silwren said, "You know the same thing will happen to us if we use this new power to stop them. And to save Humans, no less! To save those who despise us."

"Olgrym despise us, too," El'rash'lin countered. "Yet they respect power. Fadarah will yoke them, use them against the Sylvs... kill two birds with one arrow, as the saying goes."

Silwren's jaw tightened. "Are you suggesting now that we enslave these Humans to help us stop Fadarah, that we raise a Throng of our own?"

"No." El'rash'lin winced. His hideous features tightened further. "I'd prefer to save them, I think. One of us must. If you won't, I will. We both know I'm stronger, by the look of what it's done to me, but you have the superior will."

Silwren said nothing. Then she began to tremble. El'rash'lin thought at first that she was about to cry. Instead, she screamed—not in anguish, but with raw rage. Magic ignited around her. Angry, violet flames flared to life, roiling off her body, blotting out the light of the heavens.

She screamed a second time. This time, an inhuman cry of madness. Too late, El'rash'lin looked into her mind and saw what she meant to do. He grasped for her hand. She blazed past him instead and plummeted headlong over the parapet edge, into the unforgiving night.

The awful scream sliced through the night air, jolting Rowen from his dreams. The barracks shook. Heart pounding, he fumbled for Knightswrath then cursed when the hilt burned him. He drew it anyway, wondering if the heat meant magic was close by.

Confusion filled the barracks. Most of the soldiers, like him, had fallen asleep drunk. They sat up now, blinking away sleep. All could tell, despite their fogged senses, that something terrible had just happened.

Guards from the night watch burst in, all talking at once. They had seen something—a sudden, searing light—plummet from the battlements near Beggar's Drop, all the way to the base of Pallantine Hill. The slums were burning.

All around him, men leapt up and reached for weapons and armor. They ran half dressed out into the streets, expecting to find all of Lyos reduced to an inferno. Rowen moved more slowly. His hands shook. The scream had seared into his ears, just as it had that night on the Simurgh Plains...

Rowen struggled into his leather armor, fumbling with buckles and straps that suddenly seemed twice as complicated, then tugged on his boots and helm and girded his weapons. In addition to Knightswrath, he now carried one of the plain longswords issued to the Red Watch. Wrought of mediocre steel, unimpressive but sturdy, it still felt odd in hands accustomed to the heft of Ivairian-style shortswords or, more recently, the curved practice swords of the Shao. *It'll kill someone if I shove it through their guts. That's all that matters.*

Captain Ferocles appeared. "Get your tabards on!" he roared. "You're soldiers, not snot-faced peasants! I will personally truncheon every last bastard who leaves these barracks without his uniform!"

Rowen swore. He returned to his bunk for his faded scarlet tabard, even as other soldiers were donning weapons and armor as fast as they could, including those who had rushed outside but were returning for their gear. Bleary eyed, most demanded answers no one had yet, turning this way and that, disoriented by the clamor of panicked yelling and the faint smell of smoke.

"Form riot squads, double-step!" the captain roared, pacing furiously. The big man's drawn sword gleamed, clearly of finer quality than Rowen's blade. Within minutes, the entire barracks had been mobilized in neat columns in the night air. The people of Lyos were spilling into the streets as well, just as confused as the soldiers.

Not far away, Captain Ferocles spoke in hushed tones with his sergeants. A moment later, the sergeants disbanded, each taking command of a different squad.

His eyes bloodshot, Sergeant Epheus took command of Rowen's squad. He held a blazing torch in each hand, one of which he passed to the nearest soldier. "This way, lads," he said. "Keep close and stay in formation. If you spot a demon, kindly point before you start pissing yourself."

The final remark brought scattered laughter. The squad set out at a brisk march. On either side, the rest of the Red Watch dispersed in all directions. Some marched double-time toward the palace of King Pelleas while others tried to maintain order in the streets of Lyos.

Numbly, Rowen realized that just his squad of ten men—only half of which he knew by name—were heading to the Dark Quarter. Sergeant Epheus called over his shoulder, "Stay sharp, men! But keep those blades in their scabbards until I tell you otherwise!"

A few men who had drawn their weapons sheathed them now as the squad raced down the road, out the open gates of the inner city. Here, the sergeant paused just long enough to order the gates sealed behind them. The squad turned sharply, heading down one of the worn trails that led down the hill, into the Dark Quarter below.

Rowen scanned the horizon. Smoke veiled the stars, but no flames defied the surrounding night. Even from this distance, he could see the Dark Quarter alive with commotion, filled with men and women just as panicked and confused as the people of Lyos. Except these people were armed.

194

So far, Rowen's duties had kept him in the city, mercifully distant from the slums of his youth. That was over now. The slums horrified him. What he knew they'd find, though, frightened him more. He wiped his sweaty palms on his trousers, knowing it would not do to lose his grip on his sword in the middle of a fight.

Sergeant Epheus slowed and turned to face the soldiers. "The men say they saw a screaming fireball land in the Dark Quarter. Now, I may be dense as an ale keg, but I'm pretty sure fire doesn't scream. So we're dealing with... something else." Rowen detected unease in the sergeant's voice. "We're just going to poke around, see what our eyes can see, then report back to the captain. Understand?"

Rowen thought of Silwren, wondering if his pulse quickened out of fear or dread, but nodded with the others.

Ahead of them lay a haphazard sprawl of taverns and shanties, all reeking of waste, charred meat, and cheap tobacco, as different from the inner city as could be. Though smoke lingered in the air, nothing appeared to be burning. Armed men, women, and filthy children crowded closer at their approach. For once, though, the inhabitants of the Dark Quarter seemed to welcome the sight of the Red Watch. The crowds parted to let them pass. Rowen was glad he was wearing his helm and gladder still that it was night. He did not think it likely that anyone left in the slums would know him from the old days, but he had no wish to be recognized, given slumdwellers' special hatred for fellow residents of the Dark Quarter who joined the Red Watch.

As the men marched in brisk formation, Rowen pulled his tabard over his face—not just to further conceal his identity but to avoid the stench. While the residents of the Dark Quarter knew enough to dispose of corpses by burning them, lest the entire place fall victim to plague, there were limits to what fire could do. Corpses and waste—both Human and animal—were common sights in the Dark Quarter.

What little order could be seen in the Dark Quarter's construction pointed to wild concentric rings of poorly made structures, enclosing an open field that served as the slumdwellers' market, unaffectionately called Dogbane Circle. Rowen gleaned from the shouting that the fireball had descended there. Given the surrounding reek, one soldier after another vomited, forced to keep moving even as they clutched their guts and tried to wipe their faces.

"Damn!" Sergeant Epheus tugged up his tabard, covering his nose just as Rowen had done. "Double-quick!" he called to the Red Watch, his voice muffled. "Let's get this done and be out of here."

As they marched, the crowd continued to press in on them, pushing them along inexorably. Rowen's hand moved to Knightswrath. He felt ridiculous for bringing the tarnished adamune in the first place. He told himself that he'd only brought it along to keep it from being stolen. Yet the hilt was warmer than ever, and he was torn between wanting to draw the sword, despite his sergeant's orders that they keep their weapons sheathed, and wrenching his hand away. He chose the latter.

Meanwhile, the sergeant was busy asking questions of the nearest slumdwellers as they marched. In all the commotion, everyone spoke at once. Rowen made out what one wide-eyed woman was saying: "She just fell out of the sky like a gods-damned stone!"

"A stone on fire," someone amended.

"She's a demon!" cried another voice. "Zet's daughter. It must be! Another dead god cast down from the heavens!"

Sergeant Epheus tried in vain to draw details from the crowd then finally gave up. "Show us."

The crowd surged toward Dogbane Circle. Rowen tensed at the sight of even more drawn weapons. But the men of the Red Watch seemed to be the least of the slumdwellers' worries.

"A demon!" they cried, over and over.

As they marched, Epheus glanced back at Rowen. The sergeant looked pale. Rowen thought of the conversation they'd had in the tavern: talk of a ferocious demon employed by the Shel'ai. Surely, the sergeant would see Silwren and assume that demon had come here. *And what will I do if he wants to kill her?*

They reached Dogbane Circle. Here, all the rough streets in the slums converged, forming a great open space ringed by crude taverns and brothels. The crowds had grown so thick by now that the Red Watch had to shove their way through. The gangs prowled in full force, each grubby man openly wearing on his bare shoulder or arm a crude tattoo marking his loyalty: the Skull-Breakers, the Bloody Asps, the Crazy Knifemen.

Rowen had the wild thought that perhaps this had all been a trick to lure down men of the Red Watch and kill them. After all, despite the smoke lingering in the air, he saw no actual burning buildings anywhere around them. Then he remembered the scream. The gang leaders issued orders. Crowds parted to let them pass.

Rowen half hoped to find a gigantic, crimson beast with scales and horns. Instead, a familiar woman lay on her back in the filthy square, her white gown all but burned away, though the skin beneath shown pale and unharmed. Cinders smoldered all around her.

The soldiers exchanged glances of surprise that momentarily crested their panic and confusion. Long tresses like melted platinum spilled beneath the woman's half-nude body. Though stunning, her tapered ears and angular features made it clear she was not Human. Though her eyes remained closed, the slight rise and fall of her breasts made it clear she was breathing.

Sergeant Epheus reached her first. Rowen followed. Everyone else kept their distance. A hush fell over the crowd.

The sergeant felt for a pulse. Then he pushed open one of her eyelids. The ghost-white pupil made him flinch, recoiling as though he'd touched a hot stove. "I feared as much." The sergeant drew his knife. "Best make this quick, before she wakes up!"

Rowen grabbed his arm. "What are you doing?"

Sergeant Epheus jerked away. "I'm going to peel an apple in case she's hungry when she wakes up. What in the gods' names do you think I'm going to do?" He lifted the knife.

Rowen seized him again. "No."

Epheus scowled. "Locke, remember what I said about the demon? This could be it!" He gestured at her body with his knife. "We have to do this. If you can't stomach the thought of gutting a pretty wytch, step back and let me finish this myself."

"No," Rowen repeated. "We're taking her with us, back up to Lyos. That's what we're going to do. If you try anything different, I'll punch you in the windpipe so hard you'll be dead before you hit the ground."

The sergeant cocked his head, unafraid, as though he'd just been threatened by an unruly child.

Rowen broke the gaze first and eyed the surrounding crowds. He sensed the tension building, the hush replaced by angry muttering as the slumdwellers grew tired of waiting to see what would happen next. "We have to get her out of here before she's raped!"

Sergeant Epheus was speechless for a moment. "*Raped?* Locke, if these people had sense, they'd have gutted her already!" He raised the knife again. Rowen grabbed his arm and wrenched it backward, twisting the knife out of the sergeant's grasp. The knife clattered to the ground. The sergeant broke free and drew his sword. Rowen drew Knightswrath. Stunned, the other soldiers made no move to intervene.

"So much for punching me in the windpipe."

"Your arm was in the way," Rowen answered. He gripped Knightswrath with both hands, the tarnished blade trembling in the night air. The hilt burned so hotly now that his hands should have been seared, but oddly, the heat caused him little pain.

"Locke," the sergeant said with surprising calm, "she's bewytched you. Sheathe that blade, step back, and I'll forget this ever happened."

Rowen hesitated. Telling the sergeant he knew Silwren would only further erode his credibility. Instead, he asked, "What if she's *not* the demon we've heard about? What if the Shel'ai really are coming to Lyos next? She must know their plans! We could interrogate her."

The sergeant hesitated. His sword dipped a little. Rowen was getting through to him.

"Let's just take her back up to Lyos. We can lock her away. Wytch or no, she's just one woman! What can she possibly do against an entire garrison? We'll question her, find out what she knows. Maybe what she tells us could save lives. But if we kill her, we gain nothing."

The muttering of the crowd became an angry clamor. If the Red Watch wasn't willing to kill the wytch, they were. The crowds began to close in. Springing into action, the other soldiers formed a protective ring around their sergeant and, inadvertently, the woman lying at his feet.

Rowen pressed on. He could not be certain that the sergeant had even heard him over the noise. But Epheus glanced coldly at the woman. He lowered his sword. He stepped closer and growled, "Fine, Locke. *You* carry her. And if this crowd turns on us, or she wakes and blasts us to ashes, I'll follow you down to Fohl's hells and box your ears. Hear me?" He gave Rowen a shove.

Sheathing Knightswrath, Rowen gathered Silwren in his arms. Her skin felt like a blacksmith's forge, but he hugged her close anyway, his heart pounding. Sergeant Epheus started toward King's Bend. Rowen followed. The reluctant soldiers of the Red Watch encircled them as the crowd pressed in on all sides.

CHAPTER SEVENTEEN

TRIALS

R OWEN LOCKE WONDERED IF HE was about to be hanged.
The sun had barely risen. He stood unarmed in the office
of Captain Ferocles, just above the barracks. The captain's
face was furrowed with anger, fixed for the moment on a piece
of parchment. On the captain's desk lay a drawn dagger, its blade
gleaming cold and dull in the morning light angling through the
captain's window. Rowen tried not to look at the dagger. Instead, he
focused on the noise outside.

Even inside, he could hear that all of Lyos was in an uproar. Despite
attempts to keep Silwren's arrival secret, word had already spread from
the Dark Quarter, and now angry crowds bristled outside the palace
of King Pelleas, at the eastern edge of the inner city, demanding that
she be released to a growing mob.

Thanks to rumors planted by none other than Captain Ferocles
himself that the wytch was being kept in a secret location, the mobs
had no idea that she had simply been locked away in the basement of
the jailhouse. That gave them time to decide what to do with her. But
it also required the captain to reassign nearly half the Red Watch to
protect the palace, which made him none too happy.

Rowen swallowed hard, sweating in his leather armor. He had
finally told his story: how he had met El'rash'lin on the plains, how
he found Silwren in Cadavash and saved her, only to watch her leave
with the stated intent of warning Lyos of danger. He had told them of
everything except his dizzying glimpse into the Well, into the Light

itself: a glimpse that had filled him with joy and reassurance at the time but had since left him so lamenting its absence that he refused to let himself think about it. Nor did he mention how Knightswrath, the rusty sword given to him by Hráthbam, seemed to warm in the presence of magic, even to draw him somehow.

Rowen hoped his candor in all other matters might save him, especially if they believed what he'd said about El'rash'lin's selfless action on the plains. But as he finished his tale, their frowns made it clear that they did not believe a word of it. He could feel the cold eyes of Sergeant Epheus, who was sitting in a chair off to one side. Captain Ferocles finally looked up, stone faced, from the parchment before him. The captain asked, "Do you know what this is?"

"No, sir." Rowen was glad that he was still standing at attention, his shaking hands clasped behind him, hidden from view.

"It is an order for your immediate expulsion from the Red Watch—plus a recommendation from your squad commander, Sergeant Epheus, that I have you executed for insubordination and striking an officer."

Rowen's jaw dropped. He had expected expulsion from the Red Watch. But he had spent the night in the jailhouse harboring the vague hope that he would merely be beaten instead of killed. He might have escaped from the barracks and fled Lyos, but he'd stayed for Silwren—though he could not say why, since he suspected they would kill her soon enough. *Not that I can blame them.*

Captain Ferocles leaned toward him. "How do you plead to these charges, Locke? Do you understand what I've just told you?"

Rowen managed a nod. "Yes, Captain."

The captain threw up his hands impatiently. "Well, then? Say something, whelp!"

Rowen steadied himself and began. "Captain, I intended no disrespect—"

"You drew steel against your sergeant," the captain interrupted. "You don't even have a gods-damned rank yet, and you defied his orders in front of about a hundred witnesses."

Rowen glanced reflexively at Sergeant Epheus. The sergeant returned the look with murderous calm, arms folded. Rowen shuddered and faced the captain again. "Sir... may I explain?"

The captain snorted and leaned back in his chair. "I wish *somebody* would! So far, all I know is that a damned fireball fell out of the heavens like the flaming corpse of Zet himself! Now I have a Sylv wytch in my stockades, four hundred angry townspeople marching on the palace, and a king mad with questions I can't answer." He pointed to the sergeant. "Epheus tells me he wanted to cut this woman's throat right then and there. That very well might have prevented all this. You stopped him. Why?"

Rowen sighed. "I'm sorry, Captain. I don't know."

His answer caught the captain off guard. Ferocles stared at him for a moment, incredulous. Then he laughed. "At least tell me it was because she's beautiful, Locke. Or by the Light, I'll hang you myself."

Despite his fear, Rowen smiled. "Captain, I swear I meant no harm. But we've all heard stories about the Shel'ai marshalling an army in the west. This woman... Silwren... she said she was coming here to warn you. She said the entire city was in danger. If she was evil, she could have killed me with ease. But she didn't." He shrugged, helpless to explain further.

Captain Ferocles scrutinized him for a moment. Then he set the one parchment aside in favor of another one lying beneath it. "I got this report a few hours ago. Before I tell you what it says, Locke, I have a question. Have you ever been to Cassica?"

This time, it was Rowen's turn to be caught off guard. "Yes. Years ago, when my brother and I were sellswords."

"Years ago?" The captain sneered. "What were you, twelve?"

Rowen blushed. "We started early."

"And what do you remember?"

Rowen could not fathom what this had to do with his imminent execution, but he was not about to question the delay. "Cassica's not bad. A city like any other. We might have taken work there, but their king doesn't take kindly to mercenaries. Or brothels, as I recall."

Ferocles ignored the joke. "What of their army?"

Rowen shrugged. "Not much in the way of cavalry—ground's too rough around there to graze horses—but Cassica's men-at-arms are near the best I've seen. No disrespect to the Red Watch, of course."

"And the Dhargots?"

Rowen thought for a moment, remembering the Dhargots' well-disciplined phalanxes with their interlocked tower shields, their devilish catapults hurling clay jars of burning pitch that seeped into the chinks of armor and roasted men alive, so that afterward, they looked like bread left to burn in the oven. And, of course, their gigantic war-elephants: moving fortresses, virtually indestructible, tons of muscle and bone and fury carrying chariot-like saddles crowded with archers. And all of it emblazoned with the Dhargots' chilling sigil: a dragon impaled on a spear.

Rowen said, "I fought both with them and against them. With them was better. Their phalanxes are more or less indestructible. They fight with chariots and archers, too. And those elephants of theirs are a nightmare all to themselves. There's always stories about the Dhargots wanting to sweep down and conquer the Simurgh Plains, but the Free Cities keep them at bay, especially Syros. So the Dhargots mainly just fight each other and terrify foreign villages. Even elephants aren't much use against stone walls."

Ferocles glanced at Sergeant Epheus again then back at Rowen. "Then it might interest you to know," he began, "that the rumors are true. Cassica has fallen. And Syros too, maybe a couple weeks before."

Rowen's eyes widened. "The Dhargots?"

"No. To my great surprise, it looks like Dhargoth had nothing to do with it. According to my scout, whose messenger bird arrived just this morning, it was the Shel'ai. Or more accurately, it was this patchwork army they've raised. And"—he grimaced—"this demon of theirs. The army itself is mostly hired swords, plus conscripts from all the places they've conquered. But this demon is something else. Swords won't cut it. Arrows don't pierce it. It shoulders through stone walls like they were made of twigs. They say the Shel'ai control it. And now, thanks to you, we have one of them in our jails." He smiled slightly. "I suppose I should thank you."

Captain Ferocles picked up the first parchment—the one containing Sergeant Epheus's recommendation to have Rowen executed—and tore it in half. From his chair, Sergeant Epheus fixed a cold stare on both of them.

Ferocles's low voice commanded Rowen's full attention. "This is where we stand, Locke. Rumors of Cassica have already spread through the city. In another day or two, no matter how hard I try to keep this secret, everyone will know. Meanwhile, two weeks' march from here lies an army at least five or six times the size of the Red Watch in its entirety—an army bolstered by sorcery, which I don't pretend to understand. If they march on Lyos, we'll have to surrender. King Pelleas knows this. That's why the wytch is still alive. We need to know why she's here and exactly what her wretched kind are planning."

The captain pointed at Epheus again. "The good sergeant thinks we should wring the information out of her, maybe throw in some rape and red-hot tongs. I'm inclined to agree." He smirked at Rowen. "Don't look so surprised, Locke. I'll do what I must to save this city. But we'll try diplomacy first. That's where you come in."

Rowen swallowed hard. "What would you have me do, Captain?"

Ferocles answered, "*Talk* to her. Offer her whatever she wants. Tell her you're her friend. Tell her you'll have her released. Get her to fall in love with you. Honestly, I don't give a damn how you do it. Just get her to talk." He sighed. "You're probably the only one who doesn't want her dead. That's why I'm sending you first. But if this doesn't work, I'll visit her myself." He tapped the knife before him. "Do we understand each other?"

Rowen cleared his throat. "Yes, Captain."

"Good. A detail of guards is waiting outside. They'll escort you to the jailhouse. The better you fare at this, the more likely I am to forget what happened in the Dark Quarter."

Rowen said, "Thank you, Captain." He saluted and turned to go.

"Another thing, Locke. Since half my men want you dead for defending a wytch, we're moving your lodgings to the jailhouse. Don't worry, you're not a prisoner. Not exactly. But if you try to leave Lyos, my men have orders to kill you. In fact, right now, my orders are about the *only* thing keeping them from tearing you limb from limb. So if I were you, when you meet this wytch, I'd be very gods-damned charming."

Chaos swamped the cobblestone streets and marble walkways of Lyos.

Rowen pieced together what had happened from snippets of conversation he overheard between the guards walking on either side of him. Mobs had formed, word having spread by then that the fireball fallen from the heavens just the previous night was, in fact, a Sylvan wytch come to kill them. Many demanded that the wytch be brought out immediately and executed in the King's Market.

Still others sought only to use the abrupt unrest in the city as an excuse to loot and burn whatever they could. With most of the Red Watch busy trying to keep order in the city, gangs of the Dark Quarter had no trouble slipping into the city to wreak their own brand of havoc. Adding fuel to this was the growing whisper that three mighty cities—Quorim, Syros, and Cassica—had already fallen to a rampaging army of sorcerers.

The smell of smoke reached Rowen's nostrils. Supposedly, the temples of Tier'Gothma were already filling with the wounded and dying. The city streets bore a startling resemblance to those of the Dark Quarter. In less than a day, Lyos had been transformed into a city besieged from within. He shuddered.

I have to get out of here! But that was impossible. Scowling soldiers flanked him on all sides, hurrying him along. Rowen's Lyosi longsword had been confiscated, but surprisingly, Ferocles had returned Knightswrath to him. Rowen figured the captain did not think the rusty blade posed much threat to anyone, let alone half a dozen armed men who squarely blamed him for what was happening in their city.

Maybe they're right, Rowen thought ruefully. He clenched his fists, growing so tense that the guards bristled around him, thinking he was about to strike.

Rowen forced himself to relax. On the Lotus Isles, the Knights had taught him to respect even one's enemies. Now, thanks to Sergeant Epheus, Rowen was beginning to distrust the very order he'd wanted so desperately to join. Did the Knights who had trained him even believe in the very code of honor and piety they preached? *But that doesn't mean the code itself is wrong.*

Acrid smoke stung his eyes, making them water. They were passing a burning inn. Dyoni's Bane. Half the inn was already wreathed in scarlet flames, which a squad of soldiers was trying in vain to extinguish. They called for help, but the nearest citizens of Lyos were busy trying to save their own homes. The men escorting Rowen to the jailhouse hesitated.

"Go," Rowen said. "Go help them. I won't run."

But the soldiers did not believe him. Instead, their corporal issued a quick order. Three Red Watch soldiers ran to the inn to help their fellows while the other three stayed with Rowen. These three drew their swords.

The corporal spat. "By all means, try to run!"

Another joined in. "My wife and son are out there. If anything happens to them, I'm coming for you."

Rowen met his gaze. "I'd do the same."

His answer caught them off guard. The corporal shoved him, and Rowen started toward the jailhouse again. Moments later, they reached a squat, gray, two-story structure with few windows and only one set of gates, these guarded by armed men who looked as though they would rather be anywhere else.

Rowen wondered if these men had families in Lyos, too. If so, surely they longed to be with their loved ones now, to protect them from the spreading violence of the mobs, despite whatever orders kept them here. But with all the rioters and looters being brought in, the jailhouse was more chaotic than anywhere else in the city. *Another thing that's probably my fault.*

"This is him," the corporal announced gruffly, signaling the guards. He prodded Rowen in the back with his sword, hard enough to pierce cloth and skin. Rowen managed, with great effort, not to cry out as he felt a little of his own blood run down the small of his back. He knew the wound could not be deep and he would only make things worse by acknowledging it.

The corporal said, "I know you'd like to swap his bones with his organs, but the captain says leave him alone."

The jailhouse guards scowled at Rowen. One spat on the ground at his feet. But they led him inside.

The jailhouse reeked of sweat, blood, and urine. Shouting men— many of them drunk—filled every inch of space in the cells. The men shouted to be released, but they also quarreled with each other. Jailhouse guards tried to keep order by breaking up fights, but they were hopelessly understaffed. As Rowen was led past the cells, he thought he saw at least one corpse being trampled and looted by cellmates.

"The wytch is downstairs," a jailhouse guard said. "We've kept that level clear. Your quarters are in the cell next to hers. If it stinks, that's just because we all took turns using it as a privy. You're welcome for not locking you in."

Rowen knew better than to reply. The jailhouse guards led him down a narrow set of stairs, into the dim, dank basement. One of them pointed. "The wytch is down at the end of the corridor. You're on your own down here."

The sounds of fighting echoed from the jailhouse cells above. The guards hurried up the stairs, leaving Rowen untended. He tried to ignore the reek of wet, filthy straw as he looked down the dim, torch-lit corridor.

Though it made sense for the guards to leave the cells down here empty, he almost preferred the noise and violence to this silence as he made his way toward the Shel'ai woman's cell, one hand on his sword hilt. He wondered if she would kill him or transform him into a beast or an insect through some matter of devilry.

Then he saw her. Despite his fear, his eyes widened, and he felt a sudden pang of lust.

She had discarded the remnants of her burnt gown. Her exotic tresses fell about her nude shoulders as she rose from her knees, as though she'd just been praying or meditating, and faced him with violet eyes. Her dragonmist pupils sent a chill down his spine.

Surprised that she made no effort to cover herself, Rowen forced himself to keep his eyes on hers. "Did they... hurt you?"

"You mean, did they rape me?" the sorceress said with bemusement. The melodic quality of her Sylvan voice startled him though he had heard it before. "No. I saw in their minds that a few considered it, but they were too busy being afraid."

Rowen looked away, searching for something she could wear. "I'm sorry for the stench down here. I'll see if I can find you something."

207

He wished he wore a cloak so that he could give it to her. His own cell looked as filthy as the guards promised, but in another empty cell some distance from theirs, he found a relatively clean blanket forgotten amid the straw. He brought it to her. He hesitated, realizing as he offered it how shabby it looked. But Silwren accepted the blanket through the cell bars and wrapped it around her shoulders.

"Thank you." She was quiet for a moment. "You are the one who saved me."

Rowen nodded dumbly. "If you want to call it that. I came to Lyos, thinking I'd find you here. You said you were coming to warn the city. Did you?"

"They would not have listened."

Rowen frowned. "So why are you here? What were you doing up on Beggar's Drop?" Now that she was covered, his arousal was turning to rage. "Can't you hear what's happening out there? People are dying because of you!"

"They are dying because of their own fear and stupidity. I pose no threat to them. I swear this upon the Light."

Rowen swallowed his temper. "But others do. Others of your kind."

She nodded. "As others of *your* kind would do *me* harm. Are you suggesting I burn you to cinders solely on the basis of your appearance?"

Rowen drew back a step. "I'm not threatening you. I'm trying to help."

Silwren faced him a moment longer, then turned. "We fight those who hate us. We fight to save ourselves. Would you do differently?"

"Don't fence with me, wytch. Either you let me help you or you let them kill you. Which will it be?"

Instead of answering, she knelt again, resuming her meditation.

Rowen snapped. He struck the bars of her cell, ignoring the pain that lanced through his knuckles. "What have we ever done to the Shel'ai? Whatever's happened is between you and the Sylvs!" When she did not answer, he said, "What about the Free Cities your kind have already smashed? This is not defense. It's conquest! It's murder!"

Silwren faced him, her gaze hardening. "Name one place, Human. Take your time. Think hard. Name one place in all of Ruun where the Shel'ai would be welcomed. Do that, and we will go there." She paused. "We are not a separate race, as you might think. We are Sylvs. Only we are born with magic in our blood, a throwback to the days of the Dragonkin. For that, we are banished from Sylvos and the World Tree... that place you call the Wytchforest—a kingdom itself forged of magic."

The way she trembled made Rowen's rage go slack. He backed up, wondering if he'd gone too far and she was about to kill him. Instead, she continued.

"At birth, you were given the color of your hair and the roots of your temper. We were given magic. We had no more say in this than you did. But for what we are, the Sylvs hate us. And you Humans are no better. If you think it's only the Sylvs who have shed our blood, you are wrong."

Rowen had traveled throughout many of the kingdoms of Ruun, and never had he found one that regarded the Shel'ai as anything but a frightful abomination, comparable to the wicked Dragonkin of old. While the Lotus Isles had a kinder view, that was due mainly to fairytales that few even believed anymore.

"Even if that were true," Rowen protested, "Ruun is just one continent. Isn't there a whole world beyond? Find a forest of your own. Find a desert if you want. Live there. The other races will leave you alone."

Silwren snickered. "It's always someone else who must give up their home, isn't it? Besides, we've tried. Always, we are followed. *Hunted*."

Rowen scowled. "So your kind's answer is to kill everyone who might possibly threaten
you?"

Silwren's voice grew quiet. "It will not come to that."

This is getting nowhere. But what else can I do? Rowen glanced into the open cell that was to be his new home. The cell contained an overturned chamber pot, a small washing basin, a straw bed, and a chair. His few, meager possessions had already been delivered there. The guards had taken the liberty of pissing on them.

Rowen grabbed the chair, placed it outside the closed door of Silwren's cell, and sat down. "I have more questions."

"I know. Your mind is open to me."

Rowen winced at the thought that she'd been reading his mind all along. He tried to clear his thoughts. "No more talk of Lyos for now. Just tell me what you are. I've heard stories of your kind working feats of magic, but nothing like what you and your friend have done. You're not just a Shel'ai, are you?"

Silwren eyed him curiously. A slow, sad smile formed on her lips. "El'rash'lin believes the Light guides our actions, that the Light even guided you to me. I do not. I wonder which of us is right." She continued, "There were five of us. All born as Shel'ai, exiled from Sylvos and the World Tree, rescued from the wild by Fadarah. The name itself is a Sylvan word. It means *father*." She looked away. "Fadarah knew that Shel'ai magic alone would not save us from our enemies. Our power has limits. Cast too much wytchfire, or speak too long with just our minds, and we risk death from exhaustion. Fadarah understood. We needed power that could *not* be exhausted, something greater than any of the Shel'ai wield. We needed the magic of—"

"The Dragonkin," Rowen finished.

Silwren nodded. "There is a place, Human. An ancient place where one may gaze directly into the Light. But Fadarah learned... we could do much more than that."

A great sadness filled him at the mention of the Well. He thought of the peace he'd felt for just that one moment—a peace and clarity unlike anything he'd ever experienced, all the more maddening now for its lack. "Tell me. Help me understand what I saw there..."

He saw that same sadness reflected in the mist-white pupils of Silwren's eyes as she said, "More often than not, gifts are curses."

He thought she would say more, but she did not. Finally, Rowen rose to his feet. Countless questions still raced through his mind, but he doubted he'd get more answers at the moment. "I have to go for now. But you have my word, you won't be mistreated. I'll return as soon as I can." He added, "I'll bring you some clothes."

Silwren did not answer, seeming instead to return to her meditation. As Rowen turned to go, he saw her trembling. She'd let the shabby blanket slip, revealing the bare curve of her spine, all the way down to the dimples at the small of her back. He realized she was crying.

He took a step toward her but stopped himself. Shaking his head, he hurried up the stairs.

Far to the west, Shade was kneeling, too, surrounded by a wispy, violet haze of magic. He and his reluctant bodyguard were still well ahead of the Throng, only three days from Lyos. He had no doubt now where Silwren was, but her refusal to mindspeak with him left him more and more troubled. Shade could not believe that she would betray them. So that morning, in the middle of the Simurgh Plains, he had called a halt, knelt on the grass, and willed himself into a deep, magical trance.

Unencumbered by his physical body, his essence sped on alone, faint as a wisp of vapor speeding toward the red, rising sun. In this state, he could sense much more strongly the wake left by Silwren's flight, as if she had scorched the very air through which she traveled. He had hoped she was trying to work some sort of deception. Maybe she'd turned southward instead, to begin the second stage of their campaign on her own.

But that, he knew, was absurd. As his essence neared Lyos, he sensed her even more strongly than before, a growing spark of unmistakable light and power. It would not take him long to find her now, to see her. Then she reared before him—not a creature of flesh but of spirit, perceived by him as white hot and winged. Her gaze bore no expression as she regarded him for a moment.

Then she struck—a jolt of raw power that jarred him to the core. Shade's essence reeled, thrown back faster than should have been possible. He thought he would fade like mist, but then he felt flesh and bones closing around his ethereal nerves, painfully reconnecting him to a living body.

By the time he opened his eyes, the violet glow had dimmed around him. He knelt, momentarily unable to move through a combination of pain and exhaustion. Gradually, he regained his senses. He stood, exhausted but fuming, and returned to his horse.

Lethe obediently handed him the reins. The assassin was still mounted, idly holding the reins to the rouncey laden with their supplies, and curled his lip with open derision. "Were you praying?" he asked mockingly.

"Not a very proper tone to use with one's master, let alone one who saved your life."

Lethe's lips quivered with rage. "Forgive me. I tend to forget your boundless compassion, Master."

"What you saw is called divination. What it sees, I see. But there are risks." He wiped his nose, saw blood. "Even if all goes well, the spell is taxing. I can only cast it once a month, and it will leave my magic weakened for the rest of the day." He snickered. "It will be up to you to protect me, Human."

"Oh, you have nothing to fear from me. Your curse makes sure of that."

Shade fought back a wave of exhaustion—both physical and mental—and laughed. "So it does." He flicked the reins and started off, using what energy he had left to hold himself upright in the saddle. He thought of Silwren's essence rearing up before him, how coldly and effortlessly she had batted him away from the city. *My love, what are you doing?*

To distract himself, he fixed his attention on his bodyguard. "How does it feel to answer to the Blood Thrall's every command?"

Lethe winced. "You asked, so I have to tell you. Whatever orders you give, I have to follow. If I don't, pain like nothing you could imagine fills me until you decide otherwise. If I try to kill a Shel'ai— and believe me, I've tried—the pain drops me before I even get my dagger drawn." The assassin spat. "Even when we Unseen obey, the curse is still there, always there, like a wasp inside our ears. Waiting, ready to sting."

"You make an unlikely victim, Human. You made a choice. You *chose* this. You should accept the consequences without these daily, theatrical lamentations."

"You call that a choice?"

Shade shrugged. "Were you not so untrustworthy, Human, the Blood Thrall would not have been necessary. Nor would you even notice it. It's your own pride you should be snarling at, not me."

212

Lethe looked at his fingernails. "Your kind has a strange definition of compassion."

"And yours has a strange definition of honor." Shade yawned. "This is tedious. I have no intention of wasting breath on one whose sins, were they bones, would fill all the graveyards of the world."

The two men rode on in silence. The day wore on, long and monotonous, with Shade permitting them to stop and rest only a handful of times. The Shel'ai himself was nearly blind with exhaustion now, his body sapped both physically and mentally by his divining trance that morning, but each step brought him closer to Silwren. He could make out Pallantine Hill in the distance now. Just a few more days, and they would reach Lyos. Shade would find Silwren there, reason with her, and bring her back to Fadarah before it was too late.

What can she be thinking? Shade wondered again. *Bad enough that she lashed out and killed the other initiates!*

"We've gone far enough for one day," he said to Lethe. "Strike camp and start a fire." As he spoke, the Shel'ai realized with alarm that the assassin slumped with exhaustion in his saddle, despite the Blood Thrall's ability to enhance each Unseen warrior's ferocity and endurance as well as ensuring their loyalty.

Lethe said, "I don't suppose you'll tell me where we're headed?"

"Lyos, one of the Free Cities to the east. Silwren has gone there. That's all you need to know for now." He dismounted. He wondered why Lethe's eyes widened with fear.

"I can't... I can't go there."

Shade frowned. "Would you prefer to spend the rest of your days twitching in agony?" But the assassin seemed unfazed by the threat. Puzzled, Shade did something he almost never did. He used his magic to probe an Unseen's thoughts.

He needed only a moment to understand. Breaking his mental connection, he stared at the assassin with newfound pity. For a moment, he considered sending Lethe back to the Throng, but that would displease Fadarah. Besides, Lethe might still be of use, and finding Silwren remained his first priority. But the pity remained.

"I'll make you a promise, Human. See me safely to Lyos, and you'll be released. The Blood Thrall can be lifted without killing you—but

I *will* kill you, if that's what you desire. This I swear upon the trees of my homeland, to the gods, to the Light."

Lethe glanced at him but did not answer. Shade did not have to probe the assassin's thoughts to tell that the man did not believe him. He started to give the assassin the reins to his destrier but stopped himself. He decided that for this one night, he could care for his horse himself.

CHAPTER EIGHTEEN
RELUCTANT ALLIES

EKO SHINGAWA SLOWED TO A halt as Pallantine Hill rose at last on the horizon, lording over the Simurgh Plains, which shone bright and wild in the afternoon sun. Lyos was faintly visible now as well. The city crowned the hill's summit while its slums darkened its base.

The other Knights around her stirred restlessly in the saddles of their palfreys, some of them towing the reins of rounceys and destriers, the latter of which were much too prized and valuable to be used except in battle. The Isle Knights were followed by wagons driven by Islemen, squires charged with the duty of hauling the Knights' provisions and extra armor. All had pressed hard to reach the city. Now, after four days of riding, they couldn't wait to put the trip behind them.

But their captain took his time, staring at distant Lyos with a look of disgust. "It would be too much to hope that old Pelleas has finally done something about the filth in his city." He waved a fly from his face. "Such is the nature of mainlanders, I suppose."

Aeko tugged at her tabard. "Are you referring to the Dark Quarter, my lord?"

The Knight-Captain scowled at her. "Tell me, Commander Shingawa, is this where you lecture me on the dangers of imposing value judgments on others I do not know?"

Aeko Shingawa knew better than to respond. She'd grown accustomed to the captain's rebukes and knew full well the reason behind them. The captain was in his early forties, well built, with handsome, aristocratic features including dark eyes that could be either charming or malicious, depending on his mood. He was used to young, female Knights competing for his favor. But Aeko had no intention of playing that game.

A few of the other Knights chuckled behind her, but most laughed only because it was expected of them. Especially among the younger Isle Knights—most of whom were Knights of the Crane, the lowest of the three orders—genuine respect for Captain Ammerhel was in short supply.

Aeko glanced at her captain's attire. While Crovis Ammerhel wore an azure tabard similar to her own and those of the other knights, emblazoned with the emblem of a balancing crane, he also wore an additional insignia: a lotus flower.

How, by the Light, do bastards like Crovis get to be Knights of the Lotus? Of course, she knew better than to ask this question aloud, no matter how many times she posed it to herself in private. Ammerhel might be as un-Shaolike a surname as any she'd heard, but Crovis could still trace his lineage back to one of the first mainland warriors who'd founded the Knighthood with Fâyu Jinn, so many centuries ago. What's more, Crovis would almost certainly be Grand Marshal once old Bokuden died.

Perhaps sooner. She shuddered and glanced down reflexively at her tabard. She wore the emblem of a noble stag—still quite an accomplishment for a woman, let alone one in her late twenties, but she would never be promoted higher.

"Begging your pardon, Captain," she said. "I meant no offense."

Crovis laughed. "None taken, Commander. The young are often too idealistic for their own good. It seems pious to view slumdwellers as equal to nobles, but experience teaches otherwise."

What Crovis had just said directly contradicted the Codex Lotius and the principles of the entire Knighthood, meaning she was honor-bound to bring him up on charges or even challenge him to single combat. But Aeko would not do that. *If I challenged every Knight who deserved it, my sword arm would never rest!* "Shall we be on our way, Captain?"

Crovis seemed to ignore her, his eyes following the motion of a fly. His right hand shot out and caught the insect midair. He crushed it in his gauntleted fist. "Ah, yes. I suppose the sooner we relieve this wretched city of its wytch, the sooner we can go home."

He signaled, and the column of Knights started forward again.

"Thank you," King Pelleas told the messenger who had just informed him of the Knights' arrival. He glanced at the gigantic map unrolled to cover half the table, and forced a smile to hide an abrupt feeling of dread. He told the servants to usher them in. Then, sensing the gaze of his captains, he lifted his wine goblet and drank away his grimace.

In all the years of his reign, despite a fortune paid to the Isle Knights in tribute and taxes, King Pelleas had only called upon their aid a handful of times. He hated paying them, seeing as how the Knights actually did very little to ensure the safety of Lyos. Also, it left him counting coppers and borrowing from other plainsmen nobles just to keep all of Lyos from deteriorating into the Dark Quarter.

But more than that, King Pelleas detested calling upon the aid of the Lotus Isles because it gave them exactly what they wanted: a chance to show off their prowess, to excuse their unfair taxes and tributes and maybe even raise them. But these were desperate times. Captain Ferocles already had his hands full trying to quell the city's near-riotous population and keep order. What chance did the tirelessly loyal captain have against an army of mercenaries five times the size of the Red Watch, not to mention a cadre of demon-conjuring sorcerers? They needed the Knights, whether they liked it or not.

Nevertheless, Pelleas swore under his breath when the doors to his council chamber opened and the king's least favorite Knight walked in. "Wonderful," he mumbled. "I send for Bokuden and he sends me Ammerhel instead!"

Judging by their frowns, Ferocles and his sons visibly shared his disappointment. They, too, watched the smartly armored figures walk toward them, each Knight wearing a superb, long-handled sword wrought of kingsteel.

Ferocles leaned toward him. "Looks like someone wants to make Grand Marshal, Sire. And this is just the neat little war he needs."

King Pelleas whispered back, "Indeed," and rose from his chair, signaling a shift to necessary formality. His advisors rose as well, faces stoic. In a loud voice, the king greeted Sir Ammerhel and the Knight's somber retinue. "Welcome, Sir Ammerhel! It has been too long, my old friend."

The haughty Knight of the Lotus fell to one knee before the king's great, semicircular council table. The other Knights did the same. Almost as soon as the Knight's knee touched the stone floor, it rose again, less a sign of respect than a stumble. "It has, Sire. Allow me to introduce my subordinates: Aeko Shingawa, Knight of the Stag; and Paltrick Vossmore, Knight of the Crane."

Pelleas nodded quickly at Vossmore then faced Aeko and gave her a genuine smile. "Lady Shingawa's name is known to us." He caught himself. "Should we call you Sir or Lady? We do not see many female fighters on the plains."

Some of the other Knights stifled laughter, but Aeko answered graciously. "Either will suffice, Sire."

Pelleas nodded again. "Lady Shingawa, then. The peasant who became a Knight. Welcome."

Sir Ammerhel's eyes flashed with rage at this. The same qualities for which Commander Shingawa was famous had made her an object of scorn in Ammerhel's eyes—which was all Pelleas needed to admire her. It didn't hurt that she was beautiful.

But then, he admitted to himself, he'd always had a weakness for Islewomen. Like other natives of the Lotus Isles, Aeko had exotic, burnished skin and hauntingly dark, almond-shaped eyes. Her long hair—luxurious and black—reminded him of a night sky washed clean of stars. Probably for the sake of convenience, she wore it in an intricate braid that spilled off her shoulder as she bowed.

"Thank you, Sire," Aeko answered politely. If she caught the spark of interest in the king's eyes, her own expression did not acknowledge it. But as she turned her gaze to acknowledge his advisors, a look of surprise passed over her face.

He followed her gaze to the same soldier with unkempt red hair whom Ferocles had charged with interrogating the Sylvan wytch. Ferocles had suggested permitting him to attend the council, just in case he had some additional perspective on their Shel'ai prisoner.

What was the man's name again? Ah, yes. Locke. The name was Ivairian, but this man was clearly no northman Lancer. Captain Ferocles said the man had actually grown up as a Lyosi orphan— probably in the Dark Quarter, for that matter...

Pelleas needed only a moment longer to figure out the rest. Lyos had no shortage of washouts with dreams of becoming Knights. Aeko Shingawa must have been one of the soldier's former teachers. His suspicion was confirmed when the same surprise registered on the young man's face, a moment before he blushed and looked away. This intrigued him, despite everything else on his mind. Pelleas understood failure. Hadn't he himself failed, like all his forefathers, to free Lyos from the Isle Knights?

The soldier's red hair made Pelleas think of Typherius, his hotheaded youngest son, still struggling to get the city of Phaegos back onto its feet. Typherius had refused to attend this council. Pelleas could not blame him.

The king did not want to waste time introducing all of the officers, advisors, and temple priests present, not to mention the representatives of the various city guilds, so he introduced only his three other sons and Captain Ferocles, then bade the Knights sit down and join them. At least the priests and priestesses of Dyoni had elected not to attend. The Isle Knights would not have taken kindly to sharing a war council with a sect of half-naked men and women who were drunk more often than not.

"We had just convened to discuss strategy," Pelleas said. "Your timing could hardly be improved."

Crovis Ammerhel cleared his throat. "You might have done better to wait a little longer, Sire. Matters of war are best left to us."

Pelleas's sons, Captain Ferocles, and the others stirred at this insult, but he ignored it. "Of course, your prowess in such matters is well known. But I only dispatched my request to Marshal Bokuden a few days ago. I had not counted on you being so punctual."

"Your letter said the need was urgent, Sire. The Order of the Crane does not abandon its protectorates to the ravages of mercenaries and sorcerers. Not now, not ever."

Given what I know of the Knighthood, was that meant to be heartening? King Pelleas sighed. Already, this council was going to be even more unpleasant than expected. "May I inquire, Sir Ammerhel, how many Knights you have with you?"

Sir Ammerhel's expression stiffened. "I bring one full company of my best swords: two hundred anointed Knights of the Isles. Plus several hundred squires, of course."

Before Pelleas could stop him, Captain Ferocles burst out, "Two hundred Knights? You fool, we need *ten times* that number!"

Sir Ammerhel gave the captain a withering look then raised one eyebrow at the king, as though indicating he should exercise better control over his subordinates. "Two hundred is all that could be raised in such a short time. Rest assured that a second, larger force is being raised even now. They can relieve us in sixteen days, should their presence be required." He added, "We have already strained the precepts of the Codex Viticus by bringing squires who have not yet earned their adamunes, but again, your plea sounded urgent, and the Knighthood does not abandon its allies."

Captain Ferocles pointed at the map covering half the table. "But—"

Pelleas cut him off. "There has been considerable unrest in Lyos of late. I have imposed both danger and strain on the good captain and his men. You must forgive him. You spoke of a second army of Knights coming to relieve us. I am sure the captain shares my gratitude as well as my concern that this sorcerers' army—the Throng, as they call it—will reach Lyos long before this relief force arrives."

Sir Ammerhel sighed in obvious exasperation. The Knight glanced down at the map as well, eyeing the various markers corresponding to the approaching mercenary army—some of which already covered Cassica, Syros, and Quorim. Sir Ammerhel stood and drew a knife. Men frowned at the sight of steel drawn in presence of the king, but the Knight only stabbed it into the map, at the northwestern peninsula corresponding to the Dhargoth Empire.

"*This* is why you would all be better off leaving matters of war and strategy to us," Crovis Ammerhel said in gentle rebuke. "I fear you've wasted your time and created a great deal of panic for nothing. All that is required to win this war is the ability to read a map. As you can see, the sorcerers have whipped this hired army of theirs back and forth across the plains, hounding every Free City they could. They've taken Syros, Quorim, Cassica, probably a hundred other towns along the way. Now, they're heading for Lyos. You fear them, but with all respect, fear has made you blind." He smiled. "The sorcerers move too quickly! They've taken more land than they can possibly hold—even if they were to hire twice as many mercenaries as they have now! Such a strategy is self-defeating."

Sir Ammerhel waited for a response. When he did not get one, he indicated the knife, still thrust into the map at the Dhargoth Peninsula. The venerated Isle Knight sounded like a parent lecturing an ignorant, disobedient child. "For decades, the Dhargots have wanted to expand their empire beyond the peninsula, but what you call the Free Cities held them back. No more. Scouts have reported that this Fadarah does not even have the good sense to leave behind a considerable rearguard to defend the lands he's taken! That means the Dhargots can sweep east and seize half the Simurgh Plains whenever they want. They are probably already mobilizing to do so."

He yanked his knife from the table—leaving a gaping tear in the map. "Have no fear, good King. In a few days, the sorcerers will have no choice but to retreat or risk losing everything they've gained. Come winter, they'll be neck deep in their own dead, trying to reclaim the same territories they took before. All we have to do is hold. We don't have to beat them. The Dhargots will do it for us."

Sir Paltrick Vossmore desperately tried to imitate the smug expression of his commanding officer. Aeko, on the other hand, met the king's gaze with sympathy, though he sensed she still agreed with Ammerhel's assessment.

Pelleas said, "Let's suppose you are correct, Sir Ammerhel, as I hope you are. Say the sorcerers really have committed such an obvious tactical blunder. Even if the Dhargots are now marching onto the Simurgh Plains, I'm afraid you've forgotten two things."

Crovis Ammerhel raised one eyebrow.

"The demon," Pelleas began. "Whatever the sorcerers have conjured up. I have many reports of it demolishing whole cities in seconds, with little or no help from the Throng itself—"

"Rubbish," Sir Ammerhel interrupted. "Magic is an abomination. The Light would never allow such a terrible affront to exist in this world. What you call reports are mere lies spread by this Fadarah to demoralize you."

Pelleas hesitated. Out of the corner of his eye, priests and priestesses to the various deities nodded in agreement. "And the Shel'ai woman we have prisoner—"

"The wytch is just another diversion, Sire. The sorcerers probably sent her ahead to frighten and confuse us. You should have her executed immediately."

Pelleas saw Rowen Locke tense.

"Maybe you're right," Pelleas's eldest son, Heritus, interjected. "But what if you're wrong? There are hints that this wytch has turned against her own kind and come to warn us."

"My son speaks out of turn, but he has a point," Pelleas said quickly. "Probably this wytch is a liar and an abomination, as you say. But what if she *can* be made into an ally?"

Sir Ammerhel shrugged. "It makes no difference. We would be damned in the eyes of the Light if we accepted help from a wytch. As the Codex Lotius says, 'One cannot take on the countenance of one's enemy without becoming that enemy.'"

King Pelleas felt tensions rise still further. "Perhaps we have discussed enough strategy for one day," he said. "You and your Knights must be tired from your long journey. Please accept my full hospitality."

"Thank you," Crovis Ammerhel said. "I should probably inspect your troops, Sire, in the unlikelihood that there is a battle after all."

Aeko scowled openly at her captain. Pelleas kicked Heritus beneath the table to keep him from responding. "Captain Ferocles will see to that. We make no claims to the fame and skill of the Knighthood. But I think you will find, Captain, that the skill and valor of the Red Watch far exceeds what you are expecting."

Sir Ammerhel answered with a condescending grin and strode out of the chamber, boots and spurs echoing against the cold flagstone. Sir Paltrick Vossmore hurried after. Aeko moved more slowly, glancing over her shoulder at Rowen Locke again.

Now, the real question—do I dismiss the council and draw attention to the fact that Ammerhel left without permission, or sit here and listen to the rest of them argue about things we can't change?

"All of you, begone. I must retire for a while and sleep. We will reconvene tomorrow morning to continue fussing over maps." Before anyone could object, the king rose quickly and left the chamber, his anxious sons in tow.

Aeko Shingawa lingered by the doorway. The council chamber emptied until only she and Rowen Locke remained. She smiled at him. "Locke, it *is* you!"

Rowen hesitantly approached her. He bowed awkwardly. "Commander."

Aeko laughed. Then she moved forward and embraced him. "What are you doing here?" She smiled at his uniform. "You only just left the Isles, and you're already an officer!"

Rowen blushed. "The rank means nothing. Ferocles just promoted me because he said the other men were less likely to strangle an officer. And I imagine I'll only keep the rank—and my life—if I convince Silwren to talk."

"You've been interrogating her?"

"You could call it that, I suppose. I ask questions. She gives answers I don't pretend to understand, which I pass on to the others, who understand them even less." He rubbed his eyes. "Really, I'm just trying to keep them from torturing her."

"I am sorry." Aeko glanced at the falcon on his tabard. "Perhaps... we should speak of this? I meant to find you on the Isles, but you left before I could reach you."

"I know. I... I needed to get out of there. I couldn't stand how the others looked at me. The ones who hadn't... failed." Rowen's voice broke. He took a moment to steady himself. "You owe me no explanation, Commander."

He fidgeted, but Aeko barred his path. She glanced around, making sure they were alone, then lowered her voice anyway. "Rowen, you were one of twenty-seven squires dismissed that morning. If you want the Light's truth, barely a dozen of those actually deserved it." She squeezed his arm. "You were *not* one of the latter."

Rowen jerked his arm away. "Three years, Commander! Every day for three years, I trained as hard as any man could. Tell me, what great offense did I commit?" Rowen's fingers curled into fists.

Aeko held up her hands, trying to calm him. "There are many requirements for Knighthood, Locke. Skill at arms is only one of them..." She hesitated. "Lord Ammerhel has final say over which squires are dismissed from Saikaido Temple and which ones are made into Knights. I can argue with him—and believe me, I do—but in the end, it's his decision."

Rowen scoffed. "Too many rich men's sons needed to be knighted ahead of me. Is that what you're saying?"

"In essence, yes."

He blinked. "So much for the Codex Lotius."

He started to stalk away, but Aeko grabbed his arm. "Rowen, don't be a fool. Beneath all that posturing, words are just words. You can't expect the knights to base their lives around ancient writings they don't have the time or inclination to interpret!"

Rowen stared at her, speechless, then wrenched free and hurried away, his boots ringing off the cold stone.

Aeko knew she'd gone too far. If she wanted to keep her rank as a Knight of the Stag, she needed to be more careful. What she had said might be true—especially among the older Knights—but no one dared speak such things aloud.

Never mind that Crovis probably agrees with me. She sighed. Truth did not matter. This was politics, for which she had no stomach. But she'd seen other Knights banished or transferred to obscurity for opposing Crovis Ammerhel and his ilk. Aeko might be popular among the poorer knights, but they could do little against Crovis. Besides, for every young Knight of the Crane who admired her, there was another like Paltrick Vossmore.

Rowen, I did you a favor. The Knighthood is not what it used to be.

Not anymore—if it ever was. Lowering her head, she hurried to catch up with the other Knights. By then, Sir Ammerhel must have been cursing her name.

Rowen blinked back tears as he walked briskly from the palace, heading for the jailhouse. He was glad that Captain Ferocles finally trusted him enough to let him travel alone, for he did not think he could have withstood the other guards jeering at him.

I was wrong. Everything Epheus and the others had said about the Knights was true. He thought of Sir Ammerhel again. While Rowen had lived on the Lotus Isles, he saw the man a handful of times, always at a distance. At the time, Ammerhel left him awed. Strong, charismatic, and confident, the man boasted of legendary skill in combat. Men followed Ammerhel, trusted him with their lives. Rowen remembered how desperately he wanted that same sort of respect for himself. But he knew that was impossible now.

But what about Aeko? Hadn't she also been poor once, like him? Wasn't she the same Knight who trained Kayden? Rowen smiled faintly, remembering the letter his brother must have paid a fortune to send him. The letter spoke glowingly of the Knighthood. But even Aeko was not what she seemed.

No, the Knighthood can wither and die for all I care! Let the sorcerers and their demon come. Let them bring down the walls of Lyos if it means at least a few of these vainglorious bastards will be taken out of the world.

Rowen drew Knightswrath and considered casting it away. He stopped himself. *No,* he thought, *I'll sell it, raise what I can, and leave all this rot behind me.*

The jailhouse guards saluted halfheartedly as Rowen approached them. His promotion did not sit well with the men, but they knew as well as he did that all the promotions in the world were meaningless if Captain Ferocles changed his mind. If Rowen failed to extract the necessary information from the city's famous prisoner, they'd kill him.

One of the guards chortled as he finished his salute. Rowen did not care. He returned the gesture with the same insincerity, thought to himself that at least the jailhouse and the city seemed quieter now that the Knights had arrived, then made his way down the dank stone stairs to Silwren's cell.

At least they cleaned up the place. He had spoken with Silwren several times now, bringing her food and a clean set of clothes, including a pale, Lyosi sarong, but he still could not get used to the lingering reek that always struck him when he went down to the basement level. Nor could he grow accustomed to the slight jump of his heart whenever he saw her.

Gods, I'm a fool. She's as foreign to me as the stars—and probably dangerous as poison, besides. Except I'm not afraid of her anymore. He wondered if that was a good omen or a bad one. He reached the bottom of the stairs and started down the corridor. Then he stopped. Someone else stood at the end of the corridor—a short, stooped figure in a dark cloak.

Rowen drew his sword. Aside from Rowen, Captain Ferocles, and the king himself, no one else was permitted down on the basement level of the jailhouse. Nor could he imagine anyone brave enough to get that close to her, anyway. Rowen barreled down the corridor, sword raised. He did not shout for the guards. Rage overwhelmed him, and all he wanted to do was kill this assassin himself.

The cloaked figure turned to face him. Scarred, wart-covered hands lifted to throw back the dark hood, allowing the yellow flicker of torchlight to illuminate familiar, sad eyes and a face even more sore-covered than he remembered.

Rowen's sword was already in motion. He grunted and wrenched it higher, angling the blade away from El'rash'lin's neck. Knightswrath's rusty edge whirled over the man's head and sparked off the iron bars of Silwren's cell instead.

El'rash'lin glanced down, unflinching, and stepped on a few sparks before they could ignite the straw strewn across the floor. "You Humans have a strange way of treating those who try to save you."

Rowen saw Silwren unharmed, staring back at him with her usual unblinking expression. He sighed with relief, then turned back to El'rash'lin. "How did you get down here?"

The disfigured sorcerer smiled faintly. "Of all the questions on your mind, that one seems the least important."

Rowen aimed his sword at the sorcerer's throat. "You sure?"

El'rash'lin met his gaze, unafraid. So piercing was the Shel'ai's stare that Rowen drew back a step. "If you wish to slay me, Human, I will not stop you." El'rash'lin's twisted lips broke into a disconcerting smile. "Truth be told, I would welcome it."

Rowen's stomach soured. He sheathed his sword. "Why are you here?"

"A better question."

Rowen threw up his hands in exasperation. "Can your kind ever speak plain?"

Unblinking, El'rash'lin said, "Plain it is, Human. I came here to die."

The Shel'ai lurched then caught himself. He pointed to the chair left outside Silwren's cell. When Rowen did not take it, El'rash'lin sat instead.

When the sorcerer spoke again, Rowen was alarmed by the weakness in his voice. "Like Silwren, I know what Fadarah is planning. Once, I agreed with him. Not now. We came to stop it. But the magic is too much. It festers, driving us mad. The more we feed it, the more it consumes. If we face the Nightmare... even if he doesn't destroy us, the magic will." He grinned sardonically. "You see what it has done to me. It ravaged Iventine, too. It changed him into what you know as the Nightmare. In time, it will do the same to Silwren."

Rowen said, "Wait, I don't understand..."

El'rash'lin sighed and faced Silwren. Rowen had the strange feeling that they were talking to each other, though neither of them made a sound. Then, El'rash'lin faced him again. "I will give you the answers you seek. But you may not like them." He coughed. "Do you have the courage?"

Something in the sorcerer's voice filled Rowen with fear. He looked at Silwren, trying in vain to interpret the veiled look in her eyes. Then, he gave El'rash'lin a nod.

El'rash'lin stood. The stooped figure stretched to full height, towering over Rowen. One twisted limb extended, bent fingers touching Rowen's forehead. Rowen resisted the impulse to recoil from the cold of El'rash'lin's touch. El'rash'lin closed his eyes, and a violet glow enveloped his body.

"Wait, what—"All around Rowen, the world collapsed.

CHAPTER NINETEEN

THE WYTCHFOREST

O
NE BY ONE, MEMORIES DISSOLVED from him like dew beneath an oppressive wash of sunlight. All that he was fell away from him. He panicked, plummeting headlong into blackness. He tried to scream, but he had no voice.

Emptiness.

Then, slowly, new memories filled the void. They felt like his own: images of azure-eyed parents staring at him with revulsion; the taunts of other children with long, tapered ears; the lonesome solace of tree-shade, far from the others, deep in a forest so vast that the stars almost seemed nearer than the treetops.

This is the Wytchforest. My home.

A dim voice warned him that this could not be true—then that voice fell away. He had forgotten his own name. Then, he remembered. El'rash'lin. His name was El'rash'lin. He winced. The name meant "cursed one."

Why am I cursed? What have I done? Why do they hate me?

In the forest again, alone, he ran as quickly as his young legs could take him. The trees alone understood him. Not safe even among his own family, at least he might be safe among the trees.

Twilight darkened the boughs, spreading a thick web of shadows through the undergrowth. He could not see the stars anymore. He lost his way. Then he found it. He ran harder... then slowed to a stop.

In the clearing ahead of him lay a pool—deep blue water, so unstirred that it might have been made of glass. Nervously, he drew closer. He saw reflections in the pool. The constellations, the moon, the foggy white swirl of Armahg's Eye.

Then he saw himself: just a boy, slim faced, pale haired. What was so different about him? Then he saw his eyes—not azure like the others but purple, like the last moment of twilight before nightfall. Purple, like a bruise.

There's something else...

He stirred. His heart leapt in his throat. Was this a trick of the water, the stars reflecting of its surface? The pupils of his eyes were white! He frowned.

Is that all? Is that really so terrible?

He must be missing something. He needed a better look. Instinctively, he raised one hand. A tingling heat kindled within him, starting at his chest, surging to his fingertips. Violet flames flared to life.

He screamed in panic. But the flames did not burn him. He stared—first horrified, then awed. The harmless tendrils coursed the length of his tiny arm, like serpents of purple light. He realized they must not be dangerous after all. He reached for the nearest tree and touched it.

Flames gushed from his fingertips as though something had been undammed within him. The fire wreathed the tree's great trunk and spread higher and higher, swallowing the limbs. He screamed. He pulled his hand away—too late. His fire climbed as high as the heavens now. The tree shook and groaned, as though it were calling for help. El'rash'lin ran.

Years passed. He sensed that; sensed, too, that he'd been wounded. They were driving him away. Their thoughts conveyed the same raw hate as their yells. They hated him as much as they feared him. He told them they had no reason to be afraid. He would not hurt them, would not summon the magic they feared so much.

The Sylvs did not listen. They drove him out of the thick, ancient darkness of tree-shade, into the harsh strangeness of the world beyond. Nothing covered him but awful, empty sky. He wandered, half starved, alone and afraid. He came upon strangers—people with burly bodies and rounder faces, who spoke with words he sensed were not his own language though he understood them nonetheless.

He asked them for help. Most ran. Others hefted axes and tried to split him like a block of wood. He wanted to die, but something snapped. Something within him would not let them take his life. It roiled until he could no longer deny it. Finally, in despair, he fought back. He tried not to kill them, tried to soften the magic so that it would only scare them off, but the flames roared beyond his control. Screams echoed in his ears, driving him mad.

I will not fight... I will not kill...

He ran. They followed. In their naked, bestial thoughts, they blamed him for everything: failed crops, abrupt sickness, babies born cold as dead fish. He wanted to tell them their suffering was not his fault, that he did not hate them, that he was only different—not their enemy—but he knew they would not listen. Just as his own family had refused to listen. Finally, exhausted, he collapsed on the banks of a river. He waited to die.

But then *he* appeared: a giant of a man, big as an Olg but with almond eyes, angular Sylvan eyebrows, and a sharp jawline, fire flying from his hands. Tattoos covered him, head to foot. Before him, attackers scattered like so many cinders. Then, face lined with concern, the big man knelt to help him.

"Do not be afraid. You are safe now. I am like you. My name is Fadarah."

He blinked in shock. "I am El'rash'lin..." His voice broke. Fadarah's eyes were violet, like his own, the pupils white as starlight. "Are... are we demons?"

Fadarah smiled. "No, my friend. We are gods."

So many saved now. So many more than they'd ever dreamed.

El'rash'lin watched them gather on the sun-washed plains, eyes filled with tears. Kith'el. Silwren. Iventine. Aerios. All of them—his new family. And Fadarah, their leader. So many. Surely they were safe now. No mob could harm them. They could go somewhere... live in peace.

They settled on the northernmost shore of Ruun, far from anyone. They built a village. They lived there for years before the Sylvs came. It was not enough that the Shel'ai had been driven from the Wytchforest. Sylvs now claimed that all the evils of the world could be traced back to them.

Horsemen, swords, great clouds of arrows.

The Shel'ai fended off wave after wave, violet flames burning the shadows of the dead into the scorched grass, but they just kept coming. Hundreds, then thousands. Finally, in despair, Fadarah ordered them to flee.

For weeks they ran, living like wild animals. They'd wisely targeted the Sylvan cavalry first, decimating them early in the fighting, hoping the footmen would give up. But the remainder of the Sylvan host pursued, only hours behind. Then, at last, the Sylvs grew weary of their own losses and gave up, returning to their own homeland. For them, it could not be called a victory because a handful of Shel'ai remained alive.

The Shel'ai did not celebrate. They wept. Some cried out for revenge. But Fadarah refused. He led them south instead. He told them to have hope. Perhaps Dwarrs were different. Reclusive, taciturn dwellers of hills and caverns, what did the Dwarrs care if the Shel'ai raised a new village in the unused fields? So the Shel'ai headed south, avoiding contact with Humans. They sought refuge in the snowy shadow of the Stillhammer Mountains, a safe distance from the city-fortress of Tarator.

But the Dwarrs answered with threats, and legions of armored men massed on the border. So the Shel'ai went north again. They decided to take their chances with the Humans—but their arrival in Ivairia coincided with the onset of famine and plague. Though the Shel'ai protested their innocence, even their attempts to use magic to ease the Humans' suffering were rebuffed.

Some suggested they seek solace on the Lotus Isles. Others questioned the wisdom of this, doubting that the Humans there would be any different than the Humans in Ivairia.

"We will have no peace until all our enemies are crushed." El'rash'lin heard himself speaking the words.

The others agreed—even Fadarah, the great man sitting alone by the fire, wearing in his expression the awful loneliness of the wilderness.

"Then we will crush them," Fadarah said at last. "But to do this, we must become more than Shel'ai." He rose to full height. "We must become what the Sylvs fear even more than they fear us. We must become the stuff of nightmares. We must become Dragonkin."

El'rash'lin made the discovery. He read of the place in the famous Scrollhouse of Atheion, slipping unseen into the ancient, floating library in the dead of night. There, he scanned yellowed tomes written long before the Shattering War, until he found the legend: Namundvar, the Dragonkin.

On pages over a thousand years old, preserved by magic, the great, dying sorcerer had written how his kind defied the gods, leeching power from the gods' favored creations: dragons. But the dragons had disappeared—dead or vanished, Namundvar would not say—and the Dragonkins' power was waning. Some had even begun to mate with barbaric Humans and Dwarrs, spawning the first Sylvs.

The Sylvs multiplied. They had no magic of their own, but they overran half the Wytchforest through sheer numbers. Then, the Shel'ai—those Sylvs born with sorcery in their blood—began to appear at random. Nobody wanted them. The Sylvs did not trust magic, and the Dragonkin were disgusted that their power had been so diluted. Thus, they all fought each other.

Namundvar knew it was a war none could survive. So he called upon the last of his dying power to carve a breach through the heart of the world, through all that was, to tap directly into the Light.

Let all behold the spring from whence we came; let them know, at last, what unites us.

Namundvar's Well. El'rash'lin pondered the legend. He dared to hope. *Might Namundvar's dream still be realized? Could the endless wars that racked all the races be stopped somehow if people could be shown reason?* He shared the legend with Fadarah. The great man's eyes filled with hope of a different sort. He embraced El'rash'lin like a brother. "You have done it," he said. "We will draw fire and light from this Well. We will save our people!"

They gathered in the deepest secret sanctum of Cadavash—young and old, all the Shel'ai who remained. Four had volunteered: Silwren, Aerios, Cierrath, and Iventine. They stood fearfully in a circle near the Well, Fadarah just a few paces beyond them. In a moment, it would begin. It took only a little magic to unseal the Well, but it would take the combined might of all those assembled to steal from it.

El'rash'lin knew their plan. He knew every detail of Fadarah's strategy. He knew because he had drafted much of it himself, long before. He wept. He had argued against this. But no one would listen.

So instead, without a word, he stepped toward the edge of the Well and joined the others. Fadarah's eyes widened, wet with tears. But El'rash'lin was not doing this for Fadarah. The words of Namundvar's legend echoed in his mind: *Let all behold the spring from whence we came...*

All the Shel'ai ignited and combined the full sum of their powers. Violet light flooded the chamber, playing off ancient paintings. El'rash'lin's eyes had been closed in concentration, but he opened them. He gazed into the Well. He expected to see peace, tranquility, even power. Instead, he saw the weight of his own mistake, surging up from the depths, so great that it crushed the breath from his lungs.

CHAPTER TWENTY
ROWEN'S PLEA

ROWEN GASPED FOR AIR. HE looked around, speechless, and saw that he was standing once more in the basement of the jailhouse in Lyos. Silwren stood in her cell, her face taut with worry—but not for him.

El'rash'lin was lying on the cold stone floor, body shaking, his eyes blank and staring. Rowen knelt beside the fallen sorcerer, filled now with pity for the man whose memories he now shared. He felt for a pulse.

"Silwren, help him." Rowen reached for the keys to her cell and realized they were still upstairs. It did not matter. Silwren touched the locked door of her cell, and it swung open. Rowen blinked. *Why didn't she escape earlier?*

Silwren moved forward and sank to one knee beside her friend. She took his hand in hers. Her eyes closed. A violet glow enveloped her body. Moments later, El'rash'lin coughed and opened his eyes. He glanced up at Silwren, almost without comprehension. Then El'rash'lin faced Rowen.

"Forgive me," he gasped. "I wanted... to show you more, but my strength faltered." His violet eyes rolled back.

Rowen looked urgently at Silwren, but she said, "There's nothing more I can do. He needs rest. Help me hide him."

Rowen grabbed the fallen sorcerer's arms and dragged him as gently as he could into Silwren's cell. She followed.

"It's the magic, isn't it?" Rowen asked. "It's killing him."

Silwren nodded slightly.

"Will it destroy you, too?"

She did not have to answer.

El'rash'lin did not look so hideous anymore. Only tired. The memories of the sorcerer's life still filled Rowen's mind as though they were his own: trees, blood, laughter. Fire. He still had many questions, but he was finally beginning to understand.

"He tried to use his own magic to heal you," Rowen said. "You and the others. That's what left him... like this."

Silwren was quiet for a moment. "Iventine—the Nightmare—woke first. He had delved deeper into the Well than any of us. It warped him. Going so deep into the Light, then being ripped away..."

Rowen thought of his own experience at Namundvar's Well, of that sense of wholeness and tranquility—woven into him, then torn out—and shuddered.

"When El'rash'lin woke, he could have saved himself, but he didn't. He tried to use his own magic to heal Iventine, to save all of us from madness. He thought if he gave us time to heal..." Silwren's voice lowered to a shameful whisper. "I went mad, too. When I woke... I lashed out. Aerios, Cierrath... I killed them."

Rowen saw now why she so frequently bore no expression. Each moment for her was a battle against the same madness that had left El'rash'lin deformed and had turned Iventine into a demon. He wanted to soothe her but could think of nothing to say. He looked down at El'rash'lin instead. "The Light did this to him."

"Not the Light. The subversion of it." Tears clouded Silwren's eyes now. "He spoke the truth when he said he wants to die. So does Iventine, I think. To go back..." Her voice broke. "When Iventine comes, I can't fight him. Do you understand? If I do, it'll be *worse* than death! I'll go mad. I'll lose control of myself. I could kill everyone..."

She broke off, trembling. Rowen took her in his arms. He tried to soothe her, but so deep were her fear and despair that he wondered if she even realized he was still there.

Rowen thought his careful retelling of all he had learned from Silwren and El'rash'lin would leave his audience impressed, perhaps even spur them to action. He'd gone first to Captain Ferocles and Sergeant Epheus, meeting with them in the barracks office of the captain, but neither of them wanted anything to do with it.

"Now we have not just one sorcerer to contend with, but two!" Sergeant Epheus spat.

Captain Ferocles eyed Rowen with disgust. "You're proving to be more of a nuisance than you're worth," he said. "Locke, I do not care about sorcerers' fairytales. I care about Lyos. If these two won't help us, they're a liability. We should kill them now and be done with it." He tapped his sword's hilt meaningfully.

Rowen felt his face go hot. Before he knew what he was doing, he drew Knightswrath and leveled the blade at the captain's throat. Sergeant Epheus leapt to his feet, drawing his own sword, but Ferocles held up a hand to stop him.

"You will *not* harm them." Rowen prodded the captain with his sword tip, hard enough to draw a tiny rose of blood through the man's tunic. "They will help us. You have my word. But threaten them again, you bastard, and I'll have your head!"

Ferocles blinked in surprise. A faint smile formed. He nodded slightly. "Have it your way, Locke."

Fuming, Rowen withdrew his blade and sheathed it. He left without another word.

Epheus made to follow, sword drawn.

However, Ferocles stopped him. "Don't bother," he said with a chuckle. He dabbed blood off his tunic and rubbed it between his thumb and forefinger. "Odds are the good corporal will be dead in a couple days, anyway."

Epheus did not smile. "And the wytches?"

Ferocles answered with a heavy sigh. "They're locked away. They haven't hurt anyone yet. And I suppose it's a bad idea, on the eve of a siege, to waste the number of men it'd take to kill them. Let them live—for now. But when the siege comes, they'll either help us, or we'll kill them, regardless of what Locke thinks about it."

Rowen cursed his temper. He kept looking over his shoulder as he made his way along the cobblestone streets, half expecting to see a squad of soldiers coming to arrest him—or simply to kill him on the spot. But he was alone. In fact, the streets of Lyos were eerily calm.

If the arrival of the Isle Knights had done nothing else, it had at least helped quell some of the people's unease. Crovis had even reassigned the squires—several hundred in number—to assist the Red Watch. These squires, while not yet knighted, boasted the superb training and discipline of the Lotus Isles. Rowen knew this all too well, since many of the squires were familiar to him—though he'd done all he could to avoid them.

Thanks to the presence of the Knights and squires, the riots had finally ceased. Rumors of Cassica's fall and the approaching Throng had spread, but by word of Crovis Ammerhel, the people of Lyos suffered a strict curfew. This made Lyos appear almost deserted, save for the taverns. Rowen thought of his first day back in the city, seeing children playing while mothers tended the small gardens in front of their homes. He wished suddenly for a bit of noise to break the awful stillness: a flute, an angry shout, a child's laughter, anything.

He wondered what had become of Hráthbam. Was the merchant back in Sorocco by then? Rowen missed him, but at least his friend was far from harm. He thought of Jalist too, wondering if the Dwarrish sellsword had indeed joined the Throng. *If so, doesn't that make him my enemy now?*

He sighed and thought of Ferocles. He could not blame the captain for doubting him. He had to admit his story sounded absurd. Epheus had even suggested that this was all some kind of elaborate ruse. But what did the Shel'ai have to gain? Surely, they could free themselves from their prison whenever they wished—just as Silwren had opened her jail cell with a touch. And if they planned to use a Human to help them gain the city's trust, they might have chosen someone more influential than Rowen!

He went to find the Isle Knights. He loathed the thought of speaking with Aeko again after their last meeting, but perhaps she could make better sense of the renegade sorcerers' strange tale. Or maybe she had further news of the Throng.

He found Crovis Ammerhel, Aeko Shingawa, and Paltrick Vossmore—representatives of the three orders of Isle Knights—positioned on the battlements overlooking the gates of Lyos, ringed by other Knights and squires, halfheartedly discussing the city's defenses in the unlikely event that the Throng attacked after all.

Rowen hesitated, fearing the humiliation he'd feel if one of the squires recognized him, but they seemed preoccupied with grooming their armor and trying to look impressive for the female citizens of Lyos. Instead of mail wrought from kingsteel, these squires wore tough leather armor finely embroidered with the sigil of the Knighthood. Also, in place of adamunes, they bore curved shortswords called *tashi*.

Gods, I almost forgot about Knightswrath! The Codex Viticus forbade squires from wearing adamunes. Aeko had not mentioned it when they last spoke, but it would not help his case if they saw him with it now. He shifted his sword belt so the weapon was concealed by his cloak. Then he approached the battlements. With the other olive-skinned Knights deep in conversation, only Aeko saw his approach. She smiled faintly, but Rowen knew better than to address her. He cleared his throat, his face already flushed, and requested a moment of Sir Ammerhel's time.

The Knight of the Lotus fixed him in a haughty stare, looking for a moment as though he would refuse. Then, he bowed slightly. "Of course, Corporal. We are your humble servants."

Somehow, I doubt he means that. For the second time that morning, just as tendrils of sunlight unfurled like bloody ribbons across the battlements, Rowen related his tale. He strove to sound more confident than he had in Captain Ferocles's office, but his voice faltered. Being in the presence of established Knights unnerved him, reminding him of his disgrace. His only comfort was that he doubted Sir Ammerhel even remembered him from the Isles, anyway.

Before Rowen had finished, Crovis Ammerhel raised one eyebrow. Sir Paltrick Vossmore fought back a grin. Aeko looked away. Rowen decided to leave out the part of the story where Silwren refused to fight the Nightmare. When he concluded, Sir Ammerhel cleared his throat and answered formally. "You speak well, Corporal. Tell me, what is it you ask of us?"

Never had Rowen felt so intimidated, but he knew he could not turn back now. He needed the Knights' guarantee that Silwren and El'rash'lin would not be harmed. But he had nothing to bargain with. *Honor be damned,* he thought. He decided to lie.

"Silwren and El'rash'lin have pledged their aid in defending Lyos, just as the Shel'ai aided the Isle Knights long ago in the days of Fâyu Jinn. In exchange, they ask for your pledge that neither the Knights nor the armies of Lyos will engage this demon on their own. To do so, they say, would be suicide." He tried to sound nonchalant as he added, "Also, they would like your word that they'll not be harmed, so that they can carry out their own end of the agreement and keep Lyos safe from harm."

Sir Ammerhel cleared his throat again. "Thank you, Corporal."

Baffled, Rowen watched as the Knight of the Lotus simply returned his attention to the battlements, speaking in hushed tones with Sir Vossmore about the defense of the city, as though Rowen had not said a word.

Rowen summoned his courage, reached out, and tugged on Sir Ammerhel's tabard. Out of the corner of his eye, he saw Aeko give him a warning shake of her head, but he ignored it. "Sir Ammerhel... forgive me, but I must have your answer."

The Knight of the Lotus faced him with naked irritation. "Must you?" He sized up Rowen with a derisive glance. "I thought to treat you with humility, Corporal, but you are testing my patience. Clearly, these sorcerers have bewytched you. And you insult me if you think to come here this morning and share your curse with us!"

Sir Ammerhel showed him his back. "Go treat with sorcerers and the damned if you like. Your soul is not my province. But the welfare of Lyos is, and you have already taken too much of my time." He resumed his conversation with Sir Vossmore.

Rowen stood there for a moment, stunned. He could feel the gaze of the Red Watch, squires, and Isle Knights, all momentarily unified in appreciating his humiliation. Rowen wanted to press the matter further. For one wild moment, he even wanted to fight. But Sir Ammerhel could kill him in seconds.

Finally, he slumped from the battlements. Moments later, he heard Aeko call his name. He ignored her. He could tell by her lighter footfalls and the jingling of spurs that she quickened her pace. He jerked away when she touched his arm, heading instead for the morning bustle of the market. Business opened early in Lyos. Already the scents of fish and herbs filled the air, mingling with the sweetness of freshly baked bread.

Aeko called out his name again. This time, when Rowen ignored her, the olive-skinned Knight of the Stag caught his arm and wrenched him to a halt. With surprising strength, she shoved him away from the crowds, into a dirty alley between two inns.

"That was foolish." She pointed back in the direction of Sir Ammerhel. "What did you think you were going to accomplish there?"

Rowen did not answer. Aeko stood half a foot shorter than he, but the look on her face intimidated him.

"Is it true?" Aeko asked instead. Her almond-shaped eyes narrowed. "Did that wytch and her friend curse you?" Her hand moved for the hilt of her adamune.

"I don't... I don't think so."

"You don't *think* so?"

Rowen threw up his hands. "What is it you want from me, Commander?" He backed away from her. She followed him deeper into the alley.

"I'd like to know why you are so intent on throwing your life away. Did you really think that Crovis Ammerhel, a venerated Knight of the Lotus, was going to accept help from a Sylvan wytch? Or change his mind based on some ranting tale from a mainland corporal?"

Rowen gritted his teeth. "I do not pretend to be wise, Commander. But I am no fool. Silwren may be a wytch, but she is no devil. The same can be said for El'rash'lin. When they say they've come to Lyos to protect us, I believe them."

After a moment, Aeko said, "Then I believe her, too. But it doesn't matter. *None* of this matters, Rowen. What Crovis said is true." She lowered her voice even though the noise of bartering, bustling crowds beyond the alleyway meant they might have shouted and no one would have noticed or overheard them.

"Another bird arrived this morning. Word from our scouts to the west. The Dhargots are sweeping across the Simurgh Plains. Footmen, cavalry, war-elephants..." She winced. "Gods, Locke... They've already taken Syros, and they're marching on Cassica—or what's left of it. Soon, the Shel'ai will have to turn their army around. They'll have to look to their rear, or else they'll lose everything!"

Rowen's heart sank. He wanted to believe her, but El'rash'lin's memories returned to him. "El'rash'lin said this would happen. The Throng made a deal with the Dhargots. Fadarah will clear a path. Then the Dhargots will sweep their legions across the Simurgh Plains, all the way to the coast, and the Isle Knights will have to fight them."

Aeko's eyes narrowed. "El'rash'lin said this... and you're only telling me now?"

"I didn't think you'd believe me."

"You're right. I don't. Why would the Dhargots help Fadarah?"

"The Dhargots get the Free Cities—and the Isles, if they can take them—in exchange for helping the Shel'ai take the Wytchforest. By the time it's all over, the whole damn continent will be drawn into this. It'll mean fighting unlike Ruun has seen since the Shattering War!"

Aeko took a deep breath and let it go. Rowen sensed her frustration. "Apparently, your mind was drifting when we taught strategy on the Isles. Even a Shel'ai knows better than to trust a Dhargot. Why would Fadarah conquer all this land then just give it away?"

"Because it's not enough to have an army. The Shel'ai learned that the hard way. Wherever they go, someone tries to kill them. The only way they'll be at peace is if they break everyone who can hurt them."

Aeko grimaced. "You almost sound like you agree with them."

"I'm not entirely sure that I don't," he confessed.

Aeko shook her head. "Maybe Ammerhel was right to dismiss you after all."

Rowen recoiled as though slapped.

Aeko's face flushed with guilt. "Damn. Forgive me..." She started to reach for his arm then stopped herself. "But it's true, Rowen. Can you even conceive of all the planning and strategy that went into winning these battles? If the sorcerers' goal is to take the Wytchforest, why waste their men's lives on the plains? Did they think we'd care whether or not they put Sylvs to the sword?" She laughed coldly. "There are few in the Lotus Isles who remember the old stories about all the races fighting together as allies once. Most say those stories are just fairy tales. But even if they were true, the Knighthood would never get involved in a war on the opposite end of the continent!"

She's right. But she's wrong, too. Somehow, I know it.

He rubbed his eyes. "You're thinking of this in terms of numbers, Commander." He still referred to her by her title, for despite the occasional warmth in her eyes, he had never felt free nor had he been invited to call her by her given name. "Battalions, swords, how many miles men have to march, how much food it takes to feed and armor them. How much they have to pay the mercenaries to keep them from rebelling. Am I right?"

Aeko frowned. "Of course. That's what *all* generals must think about."

"Unless they're sorcerers," Rowen answered. "El'rash'lin says this is just a ruse. I know it from his own mind. The Shel'ai aren't strong enough yet to take the Wytchforest. Besides, they want more than that. They want *everything!* All of Ruun. They want us all to destroy each other. That's the only way they can ever be safe."

Aeko's expression said she did not believe him, but he was tired of arguing, tired of standing in this alley, which smelled of mud and filth. He was tired of this city. But most of all, he was tired of not saying what he really wanted to say.

"You should have defended me. I was a fine student. If Crovis would not do it, you should have knighted me yourself."

Aeko blinked in surprise. "That's a dead custom. Nowadays—"

"What about the Codex Lotius? What about honor?" He shook with rage. "You're a hero! My brother worshipped you. The peasant girl who became a Knight, who beat five Olgrym single-handed—"

"Three," Aeko corrected. "There were three, not five. One already had an arrow in his leg. And I almost died fighting them. Anyway, I'm not in Lyos because I'm some fearless hero. I am here because

Crovis Ammerhel likes to stare at me. When he isn't belittling my intelligence and questioning my honor, that is."

Rowen's jaw fell in disbelief.

Aeko sighed. "I am sorry I couldn't do more for you. But let me tell you something about my place in the Knighthood while you're finally standing still and listening. Crovis despises me. He would strip my title in a second if he could. I bet he dreams of that even more than stripping my armor! You think the Knights are some kind of goodly brotherhood. They're not. Most of them are like Crovis: honorable to a fault but not like the stories. Not like Fâyu Jinn. Those Knights don't exist anymore—if they ever did."

Rowen could think of nothing to say.

Aeko sighed. "Your brother's name was Kayden—if I recall."

This caught Rowen further off guard. He had spoken with Aeko on the Isles, but he never mentioned Kayden to anyone there. If he won his Knighthood, he was determined that it be on his own merit, not Kayden's reputation.

"I remember him," Aeko said, taking his silence as answer. "You look like him. Crovis didn't want Kayden knighted, either. I had to call in more favors than I cared to spend to get your brother his adamune."

Rowen blinked back tears, cursing a sudden surge of emotion. "Kayden wanted me to come to the Isles, but I didn't have enough coin yet. Then I heard..." He choked then forced a smile. "I had a hard time accepting that. I know it happens. I've known other men who fell out of the saddle while drunk and busted an arm or something. And I saw an old man once who split his skull that way. But Kayden was a good rider. To survive all that training, to go through everything he did, then die like that—" Rowen stopped. Something in Aeko's expression unsettled him.

"The letter," Rowen began. "The Knighthood sent me a letter, saying he died by bad chance. A snake spooked his horse. He fell... split his head on a rock." It seemed to Rowen that even as he spoke, he could hear the speed and tone of his own voice changing. "Commander..."

He trailed off. For a long time, he could not speak. When he finally found his voice, he hardly recognized it. "Who killed him?"

Aeko's answer was quick, as though she were unsurprised by the question. "I cannot tell you."

"Can't or won't?"

"Both," Aeko said, unfazed. "I understand your grief, Rowen. I do. But I have already hinted at too much, and it is not my place to say more. I was not Kayden's commander."

"Then who was?"

"A Knight of the Stag named Matsuo. He was my friend. He died too—along with most of the company."

"Where?"

Aeko tensed. At last, she said, "The Ash'bana Plains, north of the Wytchforest. Near Godsfall. They were ambushed."

Rowen's eyes widened. Godsfall was the land of the Olgrym, probably the most dangerous place in all of Ruun. But the Knights' destination stunned him most of all. "The Wytchforest! What in Fohl's hells were they doing there?"

"They were looking for something." Aeko fell silent.

"No. You have to tell me." When she did not speak, he seized her arm. "What were they looking for?"

Aeko swore under her breath. She twisted free of his grip but did not leave. They stood a while, awash in the distant, chaotic sounds of the market. At last, she said, "They were looking for the tomb of Fâyu Jinn."

CHAPTER TWENTY-ONE
IN THE THRONG

THE THRONG MADE CAMP ON the Simurgh Plains just two days' march from Lyos. Campfires blazed everywhere like flickering orange jewels. Catching the night breeze here and there flew several banners: the crimson greatwolf of Fadarah plus the various emblems of the men's homelands, now used to distinguish one company from another. Despite the fact that most of the men were conscripts from conquered cities, high pay and relatively good treatment—coupled with fear of the Shel'ai—had kept the ranks in line so far.

But Fadarah could tell that was changing. He gleaned thoughts of rebellion in the minds of nearly every man he passed as he made his way through the camp. Still, all who saw him coming looked away quickly. He felt a touch of smugness as he sensed how they feared him. He stood a good foot taller than any other man in the camp, with a powerful build even the most muscular Humans envied. Tattoos covered most of his exposed skin, including his shaved head. While Fadarah doubted that the men of the Throng understood the full implication of those tattoos, camp gossip had at least informed them of the brutal truth: in his youth, Fadarah had tattooed his body with the names of the Olgrym he'd killed.

As he paced the camp tonight, Fadarah also used his magic to amplify his hearing. He could tell that word of the latest developments had spread. The Dhargots were marching onto the plains, threatening the same homelands that the soldiers thought they could protect by pledging themselves to Fadarah's banner in the first place. Some men wanted to rebel outright. Others wanted to try and desert, though anyone caught attempting such a thing was burned alive by wytchfire. No one could believe that Fadarah, who had proven himself on countless occasions to be a cunning strategist, seemed unperturbed by the Dhargots advancing behind them, seizing for themselves all the lands that the Throng had taken just months before.

Even when the occasional Human officer got up the nerve to ask, neither Fadarah nor the other Shel'ai offered any explanation. *Many will not want to fight tomorrow.* He had already paid these men a fortune, but they wanted more than wealth. They wanted their lives. They wanted to go back and defend their homelands from the Dhargots.

Fadarah did not begrudge them this. For all their sins, he could not bring himself to share Kith'el's infamous hatred of Humans. He could imagine what it must be like to have a home and to see it in danger. Any soldier who survived the coming battle would be released. Of course, Fadarah did not expect many of them to survive.

He felt a pang of guilt but reminded himself, as he had countless times before, that he had no choice. If the men were released to go back and defend their homelands, they might actually succeed in slowing the Dhargots' advance. Fadarah's bargain with the one they called the Red Emperor—an alliance that would eventually help Fadarah claim the Wytchforest—meant giving the Dhargots free run of the Simurgh Plains, clear to the Burnished Way if possible.

He looked up. Clouds veiled the heavens, including the great starry swirl of Armahg's Eye, which many of these superstitious Humans called an ill omen. That gave them all the more reason to revolt, and his Shel'ai were already hard-pressed, guarding against deserters. Add to that the strain of keeping the Nightmare in check, and the Shel'ai were nearing their breaking point. But he only needed them for one more day. And so he went to see Brahasti.

The thought of dealing with the exiled Dhargot momentarily sickened him, but for all his despicable qualities, Brahasti was still the best strategist gold could buy.

Fadarah paused outside the man's tent. Guards tensed, their

expressions uneasy, but Fadarah dismissed them. Then he listened and scowled. A woman cried from within Brahasti's tent.

Didn't I warn him about that? Fadarah scowled. Violence born of necessity was one thing, but this was quite another. He and the other Shel'ai did not tolerate such things, even among high-ranking officers like Brahasti. Fadarah threw open the tent flap and strode inside.

Darkness and the reek of sweat filled the tent. Fadarah waved his hand, conjuring a sphere of wytchfire that hovered in the air in front of him. Relics cluttered the tent—trinkets from sacked towns and cities, plus chests of gold coins Fadarah paid to retain the man's loyalty. Looking past these, Fadarah's eyes fell on a straw pallet.

Brahasti lay there: tall, dark haired, and frightfully thin. A young woman was pinned beneath him—probably one of the prostitutes who followed the army, looking for work. Her cheek was bleeding. He was biting her neck now. She stared imploringly at Fadarah.

"Brahasti, get up."

When the man did not answer, Fadarah snapped one hand into a fist, using magic to wrench the man off the woman and fling him to the ground. The woman leapt up, grabbed her gown off the floor and rushed out—still naked—into the night.

Brahasti rose from the ground, also naked, and laughed. "My apologies, General. I didn't hear you come in." He nodded after the woman. "But I'm guessing your entrance made quite an impression on her."

A chill ran down Fadarah's spine. *Strange. After all I've faced, even though I could kill this man with a gesture, something about him frightens me.* "I sent for you an hour ago," Fadarah answered coldly. "If you have such an affinity for torture, perhaps I should impose a Blood Thrall on you."

"You'll find I am not as creative a killer when I am under duress." Brahasti grinned. "Still, I appreciate your fortitude, General. That's why I serve you."

Fadarah took a threatening step forward, a fierce violet glow igniting around his body. "You serve me because otherwise, I'll roast your living organs." He closed his fist and opened it, summoning tendrils of wytchfire so brilliant and hot that Brahasti drew back. "We have business to discuss."

Brahasti still had not bothered to cover himself. "Of course, General. How can I be of service?"

Fadarah considered ordering the man to dress then decided he preferred to leave as quickly as possible. "The army is on the verge of revolt. They'll ask you to lead them against me—if they haven't already."

Brahasti nodded, unfazed. "Shall I refuse?"

"No. Tell them you want to revolt, too, but insist they wait until after Lyos has fallen."

"How long?" Brahasti's eyes danced with cold amusement.

"One week," Fadarah answered. "Say you overheard plans for half the Shel'ai to leave the army on another mission of some kind— meaning it will be easier for you to kill the rest of us. Pretend you're acting out of concern for your men's lives."

"And what will you give me in exchange?"

"First," Fadarah said, "your life. Because if the army does not fight tomorrow, I will blame you. And I promise, you will not die quickly."

Brahasti examined one fingernail. "I understand."

He's not even afraid of me. Kith'el is right. This one is too cruel to control. I could impose a Blood Thrall on him, but he's right. I need a general, not another mindless guard dog like the Unseen.

Fadarah fought the impulse to draw his greatsword and cleave the man in two. Instead, he decided to bribe him instead. The figure he promised was more gold than Brahasti had ever seen—more gold, in fact, than most kings held in their treasuries. Brahasti's face brightened. The Dhargot bowed, a touch of mockery in his voice as he said, "I remain your humble servant, General."

Fadarah whirled and left the tent, dismissing his wytchfire and leaving Brahasti in darkness. His heavy armor clattered as he stomped off into the night. One matter, at least, had been settled. But that left others. As he walked, Fadarah thought of El'rash'lin again. *I miss your cunning, old friend.*

The plan to pit all the peoples of Ruun against each other, yoking their strength while reducing their threat in the process, had been as much El'rash'lin's as his own. If El'rash'lin had indeed gone as mad as poor Silwren, he might very well betray their advantage to Lyos. But there was a way to prevent that. The Sorcerer-General sighed with regret. *Forgive me, old friend, but you've left me no choice.*

Jalist Hewn had joined the Throng shortly after the host had marched from the smoldering ruins of Syros and was slowly rumbling toward Cassica. He was, to his knowledge, one of only a half dozen Dwarr in an army of thousands. This he knew only by rumor; he had never sought out or spoken with the other Dwarrs, nor did that trouble him. Jalist had no desire to seek solace among his own kind. He was used to standing out in a crowd.

"Ants on two legs," Humans sometimes called his kind. While most Dwarrs had red-brown or black hair, which they wore in tight fighting braids, Jalist's shone like sun-bleached pebbles. A squad leader could spot Jalist from a hundred yards away. An enemy could single him out in the fiercest melee—which happened often. Jalist was used to this, too.

Once, years and years before, Jalist had served as a housecarl under King Fedwyr Thegn of Tarator, where his famed long-axe cut bandits clean out of their saddles. But that was long in the past. His only reminder of his old life was the tattoo of a black dragon on his bicep: the personal insignia of the housecarls.

Jalist had thought of the tattoo the first time he saw the Nightmare. He had heard stories but had not yet actually seen it in action. When he did, he doubted the citizens of Cassica were any more terrified than he was.

No ultimatums, no demands—the Throng simply fanned out beyond the walls of Cassica, cavalry and footmen in neat formation. The Shel'ai formed ranks and stared, just beyond bowshot, as though waiting for something. The hired swords milled around behind them.

Then, the Nightmare roared to life. Friend and foe alike pissed themselves when they saw it. A scaled thing, huge but man shaped... and burning. Always burning. Chains and a blackened steel collar held it in check, its eyes slicing about—yellow, cold, thin as daggers.

Then the collar vanished—whisked away by magic, no doubt—and the beast howled.

Jalist had never seen fire demolish stone before, but that was exactly what happened. One blast only, and the walls of Cassica came crashing down.

The Shel'ai swarmed forward, shrouded in their bone-white cloaks, riding their well-bred destriers—Fadarah himself on a huge bloodmare. Jalist followed because he had no choice, swept up with his regiment.

In truth, only one section of wall was demolished, but at the time, it had seemed much worse. Some men were killed in the collapse but not many. The rest huddled, coughing and wide-eyed, and thought they were about to die. Jalist pitied them. But as quickly as it appeared, the Nightmare seemed to disappear—replaced, he swore, by a stooped figure in a cloak, though no one believed him.

Fadarah himself had ridden forward, huge and imposing in his dark armor. A banner displaying his crimson greatwolf snapped overhead. He called out, pledging that any who surrendered would be spared. One by one, Cassica's defenders threw down their pikes and swords. Fadarah was true to his word. His army looted the city while the white-cloaked Shel'ai maintained order, keeping rape and bloodshed to a minimum. Meanwhile, the soldiers of Cassica were herded together on the plains outside the smashed wall.

"You will find me fair as I am cruel," Fadarah had said, his voice booming. "The stories are true. Those who oppose me die screaming. But those who swear fealty to my army see their loved ones spared and their pockets filled with gold. Decide now."

Men exchanged glances, their faces smeared with blood and soot.

Jalist, arrayed with the men of the Throng, took a moment to study the rest of the sorcerers arrayed around the dark-armored general. He had never seen Shel'ai before, but their exotic features mesmerized him as much as their magic. He came back to his senses when he heard the fallen city's defenders mumbling their pledges of loyalty to the Shel'ai.

Jalist had no doubt that many still had half a mind to rebel just as soon they could, but such desires withered with time. Serving the sorcerers turned out to be better than anyone expected. There was always plenty of stew and bread, and Fadarah paid them well. Every hired sword and conscript earned more coins than they could spend. What's more, the sorcerers employed priests and priestesses of Tier'Gothma to tend their wounds, plus minstrels and whores for their entertainment. But something had changed. Jalist considered this as he went to see Llassio.

The lad was a Syrosi pikeman who'd joined the Throng after his own city fell—a freckled, clumsy youth with an easy smile and a guileless nature that made him a target for ridicule among the other sellswords. Though Llassio had technically been with the Throng longer than Jalist had, the lad stood little chance of surviving on his own. Jalist had resolved to keep the lad from harm, though after the fall of Cassica, he wondered if the young man would live to see the sunrise.

Lost in thought, Jalist nearly collided with a squad of Unseen. But he saw them at the last moment and stepped to one side, bowing so deeply that his sand-colored hair nearly touched the ground. The men stalked past him. A few glanced at him and smirked derisively. They wanted nothing more than to start a fight, but the Shel'ai frowned upon such things, and the Shel'ai were the only beings in all of Ruun that the Unseen had to answer to. Jalist scowled at the cruel warriors then hurried on to Llassio.

A gigantic hospital tent had been erected at the center of the camp. The Shel'ai had hired twenty gentle priestesses of Tier'Gothma to employ their skill with herbs and ancient medicines. But their skills had limits. As Jalist entered the tent, his stomach knotted.

Gods, can't they do something about that smell? Jalist knew better than to pinch his nose around corpses. Instead, he breathed deeply and clogged his senses all the way to the brain with the awful smell of shit and rotting meat, so he would get used to it faster.

Everywhere, straw pallets held the wounded and the dying. Jalist's heart wrenched with pity when he heard their groans and whimpers of distress. A few of these men he recognized. While the initial battle for Cassica had been nearly bloodless—at least, as far as the Throng was concerned—there had been trouble after. A battalion of Cassican men-at-arms had not been in the city at the time of the attack—gods knew why—but had appeared late, hot for revenge, after the Nightmare had vanished.

Jalist himself had been nearly killed when the fiery scourge swept over everything. He and Llassio had been part of the force sent to reinforce the subcamp. They were rushing to aid the Unseen battling the rebel men-at-arms when flames burst from what was rumored to be a tent full of demons. Jalist pulled Llassio to the ground and threw his wooden, iron-rimmed shield over them. The shield burned to nothing in his hands. But Jalist pressed himself flat against the earth and the flames washed over him, singeing his leather brigandine but leaving him otherwise unharmed. Llassio was not so lucky. The flames had scoured his body, burned off his tunic, and melted the rings of his hauberk into his skin.

Jalist spotted the hospital bed in which Llassio rested and stopped. For a moment, he wanted to run away. But then, Llassio turned his sweating face and grinned. One blackened hand lifted, beckoning weakly. The Dwarr forced a smile and went to join him.

"Hey, lad. You're looking better." Jalist hoped he sounded convincing. As he spoke, he tried to keep from looking down. The priestesses had done what they could, using tongs and thin, sharp knives to extract the metal rings melted into Llassio's flesh. But they could do nothing about the ghastly, open wounds extending from his collarbone to the top of one thigh. They might have used needle and thread to stitch them shut, but there was not enough skin left to sew.

"I... feel better today, believe it or not." Llassio smiled weakly.

He sounds drugged. Jalist looked up as someone else joined them, an old woman but not a priestess. A good foot taller than he, she wore a bone-white cloak sewn with crimson greatwolves. She smiled at Llassio before nodding politely to Jalist.

Jalist bowed to her. Most Shel'ai treated Humans at best with chilly indifference. Not Que'ann. Gentle and shy, she rarely used her magic for battle, preferring instead to assist the priestesses of Tier'Gothma with healing.

Que'ann whispered soothingly to Llassio as a soft violet glow formed around her. She urged healing energies into Llassio's body.

This further numbed the pain and kept him alive, Jalist guessed, but it could not mend wounds of this extent.

He should never have been moved! But Fadarah had ordered that the campaign continue. So the wounded were loaded in wagons and hauled along with the rest of the army. Que'ann had done much so far to help the dying survive their travel, but she was only easing their suffering. For Llassio, no magic was strong enough—save, perhaps, that of the Nightmare, though Jalist doubted the demon's repertoire included healing.

The youth looked up at Jalist, his face sweaty and pale. "Que'ann says she's going to take me to the Wytchforest when this is all done. Can you believe that, Jalist?" Llassio turned to Que'ann. "No Human has been there for... how long?"

"At least ten centuries." Que'ann answered, her melodic voice betraying her Sylvan accent. "Not since the Shattering War. I myself have not been there since I was little. Perhaps we can go together."

Jalist blinked back tears. Que'ann was lying. "Good, Llassio," he said. The Dwarr squeezed a small patch on his friend's wrist—the only part of his arm that had not been burned. "That sounds good. You'll have to tell me all about it."

Llassio said, "No need. You'll come too. Right, Que'ann? A Human and a Dwarr in the Wytchforest. Won't that be a sight!"

The Shel'ai woman did not answer. The violet glow faded from her body. She had done everything for Llassio that she could. Jalist struggled for words. A throat cleared behind them. When Jalist saw who stood there, he had to resist the urge to draw his sword.

"Good evening, General," he said instead.

Brahasti el Tarq looked past him, nodding to Que'ann instead. Then, he grimaced at Llassio. "Gods, someone should put that poor wretch out of his misery!"

Que'ann frowned at Brahasti. Jalist went further than that. Grief turned to anger, and before the Dwarr knew what he was doing, he gave the Dhargot a hard shove. The general flew back several steps but kept his footing. Indignant, he raised one hand, as though to backhand Jalist across the face, but drew back at Que'ann's warning glare.

"Outside, then," Brahasti grumbled.

Jalist Hewn followed him out, one hand openly holding the hilt of his sword. He had just made a mistake, but he did not care. The black dragon tattoo tensed on his arm. If Brahasti wanted a fight, Jalist would give him one.

But once they were outside, Brahasti's frown became a thin smile. There were no guards nearby but the Dhargot general glanced in all directions anyway, as though making sure no one was close enough to eavesdrop on their conversation.

That told Jalist right away what the general wanted to discuss. Still, he kept one hand on his sword. "Make this quick, General."

"I could have your hand for shoving me, Dwarr. Do you know that?"

Jalist met the general's gaze even though Brahasti was a foot taller.

Brahasti shrugged. "No harm done, though. I can see your poor friend is dying. I will come straight to the point, then."

"Please do."

Brahasti lowered his voice. "We must postpone the revolt."

The Dwarr feigned ignorance. "What revolt?"

"Riccard and Eric deserted this morning," Brahasti said in a low voice. "Lost their nerve—then Eric lost his life when an arrow caught him in the back of the neck. I know that you haven't been with the Throng very long, but you're now the most senior sellsword captain. I've already spoken with the others. They'll follow you. And I'm telling you, the revolt must wait!"

"Wait, hells! This foolishness ends tomorrow, whether you say so or not."

"It's too soon, my friend." Brahasti placed a hand on Jalist's shoulder: an odd gesture, since Jalist stood only as tall as Brahasti's breastbone. "You must trust me. I am thinking of your life as well as my own."

The Dwarr shoved the hand off his shoulder. "You're thinking of your own coin purse."

"It was *your* idea to draw me into this. Why not trust me now?"

Jalist said, "Let's keep this straight, Dhargot: I've *never* trusted you. But you're smarter than I am, and if we're going to do this, we need *your* help."

"So you do. But the revolt must wait." Brahasti lowered his voice further. "In a week, Fadarah and half the Shel'ai are turning back to the Wytchforest. They're taking the Nightmare with them. The rest of us are supposed to stay and guard Lyos. If we attack after Fadarah has gone, we can overwhelm the remaining sorcerers with ease. More lives can be spared. Maybe our own. Then we can go home."

Home... Jalist remembered Tarator. Great stone halls scented by roasted meats and spiced ale. Silk banners proudly displaying the hammer and black dragon of the Dwarrs. The housecarls seated at their place of honor, their laughter and boasting rising from the heavy stone table like music. King Fedwyr, proud and strong atop his dark throne. Beside him, Prince Leander Thegn, the king's eldest son—Leander the Brave, Leander the Horse Tamer. That look the prince gave Jalist when they thought no one was looking. A look soft as lambskin, heady as strong wine.

Jalist concealed his wistfulness behind a scowl. "How do you know this?"

"Because Fadarah asked me to take command of the Unseen while he's away." Brahasti grinned. "For a fortune in coin, of course."

That, Jalist believed. Still, the Dwarr had to be sure. "How do I know that Fadarah didn't bribe you to betray us?"

Brahasti seemed unfazed by the question. "You don't. But if you go through with this revolt tonight, you will do so without my help. And all of you will die, which means the Dhargots will raze your homelands while you rot in the earth."

Jalist pondered this. He did not care about the Dhargots. He cared about the men in his command. Something was amiss. He felt it in his bones. If they did not revolt soon, they would all die.

The Dwarr tried to decipher Brahasti's expression, but he might as well have tried to decipher blank stone. Eventually, Jalist turned to warm his hands by an abandoned campfire. "One week. No more."

Brahasti agreed. "One week. Thank you, my friend." He turned to go.

Jalist grabbed his arm. "I may be new here, and I may not be as young as I used to be, but there's still strength left in these bones. If you're lying, I'll slice off your cock and grind it under my boot heel. Look into my eyes if you doubt me."

Brahasti carefully removed his arm from Jalist's grasp. Expressionless, he nodded. "I would expect no less from you. But remember, Dwarr, our fates are joined. I have as much to risk here as you do."

Yes, as much to risk… but more to gain!

The Dhargot sauntered away, seizing a passing prostitute by the wrist and pulling her after him. Jalist stood there a moment, considering what he'd just agreed to. Almost as soon as he'd joined the Throng, he'd learned of the men whispering of revolt. When several sellsword captains brought Jalist into their confidence, he suggested they invite Brahasti, as well. As much as Jalist hated the infamously callous Dhargot, his worth was obvious. Initially, the sellsword captains refused, but Jalist eventually won them over.

Except now, most of them are dead—and I'm in charge! Jalist had not wanted that. Still, Brahasti himself had pointed out how much concentration it took for the sorcerers to control the Nightmare. That meant the best time to revolt was during the next siege. There must be hundreds in the Throng—men from Syros, Cassica, Quorim, and countless other towns—who wanted to head back and defend their homes from the Dhargots. Once the revolt began, he hoped they would fall in line. Jalist said they should deal with the Unseen first, but Brahasti disagreed. All had heard stories of the Blood Thrall. Killing the Shel'ai might free them. They might even hail Jalist and the others as heroes.

But Brahasti wanted to wait. *He might have a point,* Jalist conceded. *If he's telling the truth, that is.*

He thought about Que'ann. Jalist would try to protect her when the fighting started. But if she chose to remain loyal to her own kind—as Jalist feared she would—then they would have no choice but to kill her.

The Dwarr sighed. He thought of how gently Que'ann cared for the wounded, especially Llassio, her pale hands pressing cool cloths to wounds, her touch kindling magic to soothe pain when her pointed ears caught the faintest moan. How the freckled youth and the other injured men loved her! Remembering his friend, Jalist hurried back into the hospital tent. He reached Llassio's side just as Que'ann was somberly closing his friend's wide, staring eyes.

"I am sorry," Que'ann whispered. She touched his arm, her hand warm, then moved on to tend the next in a long line of wounded.

CHAPTER TWENTY-TWO

KAYDEN'S FATE

A EKO SHINGAWA STOOD WITH ROWEN Locke on an empty marble walkway as the midday sun lit the beleaguered city of Lyos. The arched walkway—one of many throughout the city—stood empty for the moment. That one led to the beautiful Queen's Garden at the center of Lyos, normally crowded, but no one cared about flowers and trees at the moment.

"What I am about to tell you is a secret," Aeko began hesitantly. "If Crovis found out, he could have my adamune. Or my life. I want your oath to repeat none of this."

Rowen said, "You have it."

But Aeko pressed him. "You won't like what I have to say." Her voice lowered. "You might hate me afterward. You may consider me your enemy. That's your right. Still, I need your word on this. Swear it again."

"I swear, damn you. Now get on with it!"

"Calm yourself, and I will," Aeko said. "You know the legend of Fâyu Jinn... how he founded the Knighthood, allied with the other races—even the Shel'ai—and helped drive the Dragonkin from Ruun."

Rowen nodded impatiently. *I also know my brother died five years ago. And I know I don't know why. That's a bit more important to me than fairy tales.*

"And the Oath of Kin," Aeko went on. "The pact between Fâyu Jinn and the Sylvs—"

"That if ever their nations were in dire need, each could call upon the other," Rowen interrupted, quoting the legend almost verbatim. "But you said yourself that most Knights don't believe those stories!"

"And do you remember the legend of the kings' burials?"

Rowen frowned. He thought back to the fairy tales again. "Fâyu Jinn decreed that upon his death, he was to be buried in the Wytchforest as a symbol of his people's kinship with the Sylvs. King Shigella of the Sylvs did likewise and was buried on the Lotus Isles. Their tombs were supposed to be a constant reminder of the old alliance." He snorted. "But it's all a lie. There is no Sylvan king buried on the Lotus Isles. If there was, we'd have found the tomb by now."

Aeko gave him a hard look. "We found it seven years ago."

Rowen blinked.

"We found it on a small island to the east, in the ruins of a city with no name. The tomb was hidden in the rubble—deliberately."

"Who would do that?"

"Good damn question."

Rowen considered this for a moment. "If the Knights wanted to hide the tomb, why not just destroy it?"

"Because it's sealed," Aeko said. "By magic."

"The Shel'ai?"

"Yes and no." Aeko explained, "Remember, the legends tell us that a thousand years ago, Shel'ai fought alongside Fâyu Jinn and the other races against the Dragonkin. *They* could have sealed the tomb. But that doesn't explain why we didn't at least know it was there."

"You think the *Knights* hid it?"

Aeko nodded slightly. "Read our histories, Rowen. You will find almost no mention of the Shattering War. This from a Knighthood that loves words almost as much as it loves itself! Outside the legends, we have no proof that Fâyu Jinn and Shigella even existed or the Shattering War really happened. Until now."

"You really think the Knights would want to hide all that?"

"The few who know about it? Of course!" Aeko laughed derisively. "You've seen what the Knighthood has become. Imagine what men like Crovis would say to an ancient decree saying all Knights were honor bound to lend aid to the Sylvs! Imagine what would happen if we learned the Shel'ai really were our allies once!"

260

Rowen felt lost. He stared past her, into the shadows of the dogblossom trees crowding Queen's Garden. He wanted to run away, to leave all this madness behind him. "So are you going to tell me what all this has to do with Kayden?"

"I'm getting to that," Aeko said. "When we found the tomb, it was sealed by magic. No tool or weapon would open it. But the carvings on the stone claim King Shigella's body is inside. Grand Marshal Bokuden reasoned that if we could prove that Fâyu Jinn's tomb existed too, then maybe the rekindling of the old alliance would be just what the Knighthood needed to heal its reputation."

Rowen glared at her. *You're stalling.* Sunlight played off her long, dark braid. Suddenly, he wanted to vent his impatience by yanking on it.

"Crovis disagreed. But Sir Matsuo volunteered to lead a diplomatic envoy to the Wytchforest. Your brother went with them. When they reached the forest, they were turned away. The Sylvs claimed that Fâyu Jinn's tomb didn't even exist. Matsuo argued then eventually gave up. The Knights started for home. But the Sylvs intercepted them on the Ash'bana Plains..."

Rowen's fists clenched. "The Sylvs killed him?" He took Aeko's silence as an answer. He flushed with rage until he was sure his face matched his beard. "Why... why have I never heard this?"

"Bokuden decided the attack should be kept secret. Many on the Council objected—Crovis among them. But Bokuden is still the Grand Marshal. He swore them all to silence. But it cost him. In time, Crovis will challenge him. And Crovis will win. He's already openly defied Bokuden once by sacking Phaegos."

Just like Sergeant Epheus said! "So Sylvs murdered Knights of the Crane, and the Grand Marshal didn't even seek justice?"

"Bokuden was faced with a terrible choice, Rowen. He could commit an ailing Knighthood to a bitter, impossible campaign against a foreign race clear across the continent—"

"Or pretend it never happened," Rowen finished.

Fuming, he stalked away from her, losing her in the market crowds. She called after him, but he did not answer. That time, it seemed she knew better than to follow. Rowen made sure he was free of her then turned toward the jailhouse.

He did not want to believe Aeko's tales of murder and intrigue, but her story was too strange to be a lie. Rowen touched his sword's hilt. He had never seen a Sylv before, but they must look identical to Silwren and El'rash'lin—save for their eyes. He would know them when he saw them. He would avenge Kayden's murder by torching the Wytchforest himself.

Rowen wondered if El'rash'lin knew anything about Fâyu Jinn's tomb or Kayden and the other Knights' murders. He did not think so. There had been nothing of that in the memories El'rash'lin shared.

Besides, the Sylvs viewed the Shel'ai as enemies. This made Rowen inclined to call them friends—except, of course, that the majority of their kind seemed intent on burning Lyos to the ground. Rowen laughed. *Perhaps it would be better if they did!*

With Hráthbam gone and Kayden dead, he felt hard-pressed lately to find a single person whose life was worth saving. He thought of the prostitute he'd met earlier then reminded himself that he did not even know her name. *All the more reason to get out of here and save my own skin!*

Rowen reached the jailhouse. He braced himself for a cold greeting from the guards, but none stood outside. Red Watch guards would never risk their captain's wrath by leaving their posts—especially during times like these. Rowen reached for Knightswrath, cursed when the hilt felt warm, and stepped through the door.

The smell of blood, filth, and scorched meat filled his nostrils. He wanted to gag. Instead, he stepped sideways and drew his sword, blinking in the darkness. The shutters had been closed, the lanterns extinguished. It took his eyes a moment to adjust. When he did, he saw bodies everywhere. "Gods..."

Movement caught his eye. A dark figure leapt from the shadows. Rowen barely raised Knightswrath in time. A shortsword clashed against his own blade. Then the attacker swung a second shortsword at his thigh. Rowen backpedaled, stumbled, then narrowly parried a vicious lunge at his throat.

Gods, he's fast! Rowen swung Knightswrath in a low, wide arc, trying to keep his attacker at bay. Meanwhile, he squinted in the darkness, searching for more attackers. Dead soldiers littered the floor, their bodies slashed. He saw a slain priest of Maelmohr, too, who must have been here to minister to the imprisoned. In the rows of cells nearby, burned corpses lay twisted and blackened against the walls. Their arms were contorted before them in some vain, final attempt at self-preservation.

His attacker drove at him, fast and coldly disciplined. Rowen had no choice but to give ground, trying not to trip over the dead as he backpedaled. He sensed that his attacker was trying to herd him away from the open door to prevent escape. Had he not instinctively sidestepped upon entering the jailhouse and smelling blood, he would have been killed.

His mind reeled even as he fought off his attacker's leaping blade. The guards and priest had been killed by steel. The prisoners had been killed by fire. But the cells, constructed of stout iron bars, were still locked. That meant the men had been killed by sorcery allied with steel.

Rowen parried another flurry of cuts, struggling to hold his ground. "I take it they left you to kill whoever walked in."

His attacker answered with another flurry of cuts that Rowen barely survived. *So much for stalling.*

A thin black cloth masked his opponent's features. The man's leather armor was black too, making him nearly invisible in the darkened jailhouse. But Rowen made out an emblem—what looked like greatwolves—sewn into the man's armor. The sigil's color matched the blood on the floor.

I'm getting tired, and he isn't even breaking a sweat yet! Rowen backed off. "Who are you?" he demanded.

The man came at him with the speed of a dancer, lunging one blade at Rowen's eyes and the other at his groin. Rowen could not parry both at once. He sidestepped, beat back another cut for his shoulder, then grimaced as one of the shortswords cut a bloody groove in his thigh.

Pain gave him renewed fury. He beat back his attacker, Knightswrath dancing in his hands, but he could not press his advantage. He just was not fast enough. Exhaustion crept up his arms. He barely parried a stab at his face then botched another parry and took a sword point to the shoulder.

Rowen swore in Shao. He backed up as fast as he could, even though that carried him farther from the jailhouse door. Blood ran from his wounds, hot and unstaunched. He expected his opponent would follow and finish him off. Then he heard footfalls.

Down the stairs from the upper level of the jailhouse came a new figure: tall, thin, and dressed in a bone-white cloak sewn with the same blood-colored greatwolves adorning the armor of Rowen's attacker. The cloaked man glanced at Rowen with only mild interest. The man's hood was down, revealing youthful, haughty features and long, tapered ears. Though ten yards separated them, Rowen saw dragonmist in the man's eyes. He cursed again. A Shel'ai. Not Silwren or El'rash'lin but a Shel'ai, nonetheless. That explained the fire.

I know him, Rowen realized, though he could not fathom how. Then he understood: El'rash'lin's memories. *What was his name? Kith'el. No—Shade.*

"Finish him," the cloaked figure ordered.

The dark-garbed fighter hesitated. The man's brow contorted in abrupt, awful pain.

"You'd be better off running," Rowen called out. "By now, half the garrison must be on the way here!"

Shade smiled wolfishly. "Not likely, Human." He faced the dark-garbed fighter again. "Meet me downstairs after he's dead." He left the staircase he'd just descended for the one that led down to Silwren's cell.

I have to stop them!

Rowen raised Knightswrath with both hands, holding the sword straight over his head. The Shao called the position *hoso no-kami.* Guard of the Tower. It was the strongest attack pose but the weakest for defense. But a strong defense against an opponent such as this only delayed the inevitable. "*Singchai ushó fey!* Come and die, you bastard."

But the fighter did not move. The man's eyes went taut with pain again. Rowen frowned. He had not wounded the man. Was this just a ruse to draw him in?

Rowen remembered another old saying of his brother's: *When in doubt, charge!* Rowen charged. To his amazement, the fighter made no move to defend himself. Knightswrath descended in a rusty arc. At the last instant, Rowen changed its course. With two quick strikes, he knocked the swords from his enemy's grasp. The man still had not moved. He simply stared.

Why isn't he fighting—and why didn't I kill him? No time to figure it out. Silwren needed him! He shoved the man aside and rushed for the stairs.

CHAPTER TWENTY-THREE
NO QUARTER

T HE BASEMENT TORCHES STILL BLAZED, but Rowen did not
need them, thanks to the wytchfire. The cloaked figure stood
outside Silwren's cell, his face livid, tendrils of violet flames
coursing the lengths of his arms.

Meanwhile, in the cell, Silwren stood protectively over El'rash'lin.
The latter slept fitfully on the cold, straw-strewn floor, as though
gripped by a terrible fever. Rowen descended the stairs. No one
turned to acknowledge him. Rowen winced from the mild slashes
to his forearm and thigh, but he had no time to bandage them. He
only hoped he would not lose so much blood that he passed out. He
glanced over his shoulder, wondering if the dark-garbed fighter was
following him.

Not yet. I should have killed him when I had the chance, though.
Spotting footprints on the stairs behind him, he realized they were
his own, made from his boot soles soaked in dead guards' blood. He
fixed his gaze on Shade instead. With shaking hands, Rowen held
Knightswrath in a guarded position before him, though the sword
would be useless against wytchfire. He started forward... slowly.

The cloaked figure spoke in a language that seemed both familiar
and foreign at the same time. Rowen thought of El'rash'lin again. He
had the odd sensation that if he concentrated, he might be able to
understand what they were saying. But at the time, he did not care.
He edged closer.

Shade still had not noticed him. A few feet more, and he could
strike the murderer down. Then, Shade turned.

He did not appear frightened by the sight of Rowen's poised blade, only surprised. Or was he annoyed? Rowen could not tell which. Silwren screamed a warning—too late. Fingers coursing with wytchfire flung death through the air.

Rowen cried out in panic. He stumbled backward, knowing he could not outrun the fire. Out of desperation, he raised Knightswrath before him as though it were a shield. Time slowed to a crawl. He knew he was about to become like one of the ghastly dead men burned alive in the cells upstairs.

But the wytchfire met his sword instead. Like a dry rag cast into water, Knightswrath drew the wytchfire into its rusty depths. Rowen did not believe it.

Nor did Shade. He stared at Rowen without comprehension. Then he changed tactics. One slender wrist flicked sharply, and Rowen went sailing backward, flung by some invisible force. He struck the ground hard, Knightswrath clattering from his grasp.

Then he heard another clang of metal, far louder than his falling sword. Desperately, he struggled to rise. Something warm and dark ran into his eyes, burning them. He wiped away blood. Dazed, he looked down the corridor. His eyes widened.

The bars of Silwren's cell had been wrenched open, as though made of tin. Silwren stood in the corridor now, her body awash in wytchfire, eyes blazing white. Shade recoiled before her. He pleaded in their foreign tongue again, lifting his hands. A protective shield of violet flames formed in front of him.

Silwren smashed it aside. The fire engulfing her body intensified. She was wholly white now. Rowen felt the heat on his face. Blinded, he turned away. The sorcerer's cloak brushed over him as Shade was flung toward the stairs. He struck hard. Bones cracked.

Somehow, Shade rose, blood running from his mouth, eyes wide with fear. He struggled up the stairs. His cloak caught on the stone and pulled away from him. He left it behind.

Rowen fumbled blindly for his sword. Finally, his hands closed over the dragonbone hilt. It felt so hot he could barely touch it. He hefted the sword anyway. It felt alive in his grasp, even more so than it had in the depths of Cadavash.

He considered chasing down the sorcerer and finishing him. Instead, shielding his eyes with his free hand, he tried to locate Silwren through the glare. But all he saw was light—light and fire.

Then, as abruptly as it had appeared, the light and fire vanished. Silwren stood in the corridor, a mad look in her eyes, the clothes burned from her body. She stared at him without recognition. He feared for a moment that she would kill him. Then she pitched forward, collapsing into a fragile heap. Beneath her, the floor of the jailhouse looked blackened, as though kissed by a dragon's breath.

Captain Ferocles could hardly believe the story when he heard it. As nightfall spread over the city, a squad of soldiers had left the barracks for the jailhouse at shift change to relieve their comrades. Upon entering, they found guards and prisoners—all dead. They descended into the basement, swords drawn, and discovered Corporal Locke with the Shel'ai.

Ferocles was surprised his men did not kill them. Instead, they sent word. When he arrived, he ordered everyone else upstairs. Locke recounted his story. Despite the tale's strangeness, Ferocles could tell by the look on Locke's face that he was either too stunned to tell anything but the truth, or else he was the world's greatest liar. Ferocles knew they had to act fast. So he sent a runner to the Knights.

"Who do I fetch, Captain?" the runner asked.

Ferocles grimaced at the thought of soliciting the help of Crovis Ammerhel. And Sir Vossmore was obviously no more than Ammerhel's lapdog. "Find that pretty Knight of the Stag and bring her here."

The runner's eyes widened. "Captain... the *woman*?"

Ferocles shoved the man toward the door.

Aeko Shingawa appeared more quickly than he expected, a squad of her most trusted Knights in tow. Despite the abrupt summons, they appeared in full battle dress. Ferocles thought she would blanch when she saw the bloodshed. Instead, her almond eyes narrowed, one hand on her adamune. "Who did this?"

Ferocles said, "According to Locke, it was another Shel'ai."

"Locke?"

"He's in the basement, with the wytch and her friend, both of whom sleep like the dead." He glanced at the blood and bodies still covering the jailhouse floor. "No disrespect to these poor bastards."

"And where is the one who did this?"

"Fled." Ferocles shrugged. "I'd like to think even sorcerers have trouble slipping past locked gates, but I wouldn't count on it."

"Have you sent men after him?"

"Not yet."

"Good. Don't."

Ferocles was glad they had opened the windows. At least a little of the stench had cleared from the air, but his nerves were wearing thin. He gestured at the ghastly mess all around them. "These are my men, Knight! And those prisoners—no matter what they did—were still citizens of Lyos! I'll flay this bastard's guts if it takes the whole Red Watch to do it!"

"It might." Aeko held up her hands. "Peace, Captain. I understand your anger. But our first duty is to keep word of this"—she hesitated, glancing around them—"*incident* from spreading throughout the city, unless you want another riot."

Ferocles glowered at her. "I'd rather drink my men's piss than admit you're right."

"But we both know I am," Aeko said. "If the Light wills it, Captain, we *will* find and kill this sorcerer. I swear it. But first, we must look to the city."

Ferocles stalked past her, barking orders to his men. Most of them milled uneasily outside the jailhouse, talking in frightened whispers. More than a few had already vomited there.

Waving off her loyal Knights, Aeko descended into the lower level to find Rowen Locke. The cells of the lower level were all empty, save for one that contained two prone figures. One—a woman—slept beneath a singed, bone-white cloak sewn in crimson greatwolves and splotched with blood. As Aeko drew nearer, she saw how, even in fitful sleep, Silwren resembled some exotic heroine from an ancient mural. *No wonder Locke keeps risking his skin for her!*

Then she noticed the cell itself. The door of iron bars was not open, as she first thought, but wrenched apart. Rowen Locke sat on the floor with his back to the cell, a sheathed sword across his knees. His head hung low. But he jumped at the sound of her approach, fumbling for his weapon.

"Peace, Locke. It's just me." She looked him over. "You're wounded."

Rowen rose with difficulty, using his sword as a crutch. Aeko's eyes fell on his exquisite adamune and widened. That mattered little to her, but it seemed uncharacteristic of Rowen to violate one of the many laws of the Codex Viticus that he had so eagerly tried to learn on the Isles. She wondered how she hadn't noticed the sword before. Shaking off this thought, she returned her attention to his wounds.

"Just some scratches," Rowen said boldly, but she saw how he winced when he moved. "A cleric of Tier'Gothma already tended them."

Aeko nodded and looked into the cell. She found it unnerving to be this close to Shel'ai. She had never seen them before. Silwren looked peaceful enough, despite the strangeness of the long, tapered ears emerging from her platinum tresses. Then she saw the other Shel'ai, the one who must be El'rash'lin.

The breath caught in her throat. "By the Light..." All that was visible of the man's body was his face and hands, but that was enough. The skin looked as though it had been cut a dozen times then had healed as well as it could over a tattered tapestry of warts and sores. She thought back on Rowen's strange tale—that these two had been infused with power like that of the Dragonkin, only to have that very magic threaten to devour them each time they used it.

Silwren appeared to be in the grasp of a nightmare, trembling fitfully beneath a bone-white cloak, but she was anything but ghastly. *How convenient for Rowen.* Did her beauty mean Silwren had not fully embraced her power or that the Shel'ai's story was a lie?

Aeko decided not to press this for the moment. "I'll hand you a silver cranáf if you can explain this in terms I'll understand."

Rowen answered with a chilling smile that seemed almost mad. She was glad when he sheathed his sword and laid it aside. "You won't believe a word of it."

Aeko said, "I swear by the Light to try."

That was good enough. Rowen told her about arriving at the jailhouse to find the guards and prisoners dead. His pitched duel with the dark-garbed fighter. The sadistic Shel'ai who went down to the lower level, presumably to kill Silwren and El'rash'lin, only to be driven away.

Aeko looked at both Shel'ai again and sighed. Her hand rested on the hilt of her own adamune. In a low voice, she said, "Locke, I don't have to tell you what a terrible mess we are in."

Rowen said nothing.

"I sent word to Crovis. I had to. I'm sure by now, King Pelleas knows about this, too. There's a good chance that neither will believe what you told me. In fact, they may have decided *you* helped these two kill everyone upstairs in an effort to escape."

Rowen reached for his sword again. "Let them think what they like."

Despite herself, Aeko had to conceal a smile. "You understand, they may come for you soon." She gestured at the two sleeping Shel'ai. "You and these wytches."

Rowen nodded tightly.

"And can you say with certainty that these two had no part in the slaughter upstairs?"

"Commander, I swear that on my life."

Aeko nodded, satisfied. "Unfortunately, that changes nothing. At best, we are left with an army fueled by sorcery that will be laying siege to this city the day after tomorrow. And our strongest allies appear to be two renegade wytches who refuse to fight."

Rowen hesitated. She saw him look at Silwren again. *By the Light, is he falling in love with her?*

"They'll fight with the time comes," Rowen said. "I swear it, Commander."

Aeko's eyes narrowed. "You've sworn many things, Locke. Be careful that you do not overextend your honor."

Rowen flinched.

Aeko looked into the cell again, eyeing the Shel'ai. "Two things must be done here," she said at last. "To protect the wytches, we must get them out of here. Take them somewhere Crovis, the king, and the good captain will not find them."

Rowen's expression soured. "I know a place."

Aeko nodded. "The second thing, then, is to protect *you*. I know of only one way to do that. I'll waive your dismissal and make you my personal squire."

Rowen's eyes widened. "Commander..."

Aeko waved him off. "You'll be under my charge, answerable only to me. By Shao law, Crovis cannot touch you without a trial. And King Pelleas will not move against you for fear of alienating me on the eve of battle. There are formal ceremonies and oaths, but we can dispense with those for the moment." She added, "Don't thank me yet, Squire. It remains to be seen whether or not I've done anything but prolong the inevitable." She pointed at the unconscious sorcerers. "Now, remove these two from my sight."

Rowen, roused from his daze, went into Silwren's cell to wake her.

Aeko watched from the corridor, one hand still resting on her sword. Footsteps made her turn. A Knight of the Crane was bounding down the stairs toward her, his face flushed.

"Commander, they send for you. A patrol of Red Watch just clashed with the Throng's vanguard!"

Aeko swore under her breath. She did not have to ask the Knight which side had won. "And Captain Ferocles?"

"Already left for the battlements."

Good. She pointed at Rowen and told the Knight, "Help him. Whatever he needs, no matter how fey it sounds. Henceforth, he is my personal squire, subject *only* to my judgment." She added, "Swear it on your honor."

The Isle Knight's eyes widened, but he nodded without hesitation. "On my honor."

Aeko considered asking about Rowen's adamune then decided she had more urgent concerns. She gave him a parting look of sympathy and rushed up the stairs, into the chaos that awaited her.

CHAPTER TWENTY-FOUR

BROKEN OATHS

TORCHES BLAZED ALONG THE PARAPETS like unfriendly jewels. The battlements bristled with soldiers of the Red Watch and Isle Knights, the latter gleaming in their cold steel mail. Archers and pikemen rushed to and fro, many of them wide-eyed and shouting, as though the siege had already begun. Aeko shook her head with disapproval. *If the people see this, it'll create a panic!*

Sure enough, the people of Lyos were spilling from their homes. Mothers in simple Lyosi sarongs held their crying children while fathers stood agape. All wanted answers. Crowds were forming.

Aeko cursed, touching her sword's hilt. There must already have been rumors flying around, after witnesses saw soldiers and Knights rushing to the jailhouse. Now this. She could assign the squires to help the Red Watch restore order again, but that would take time.

She turned her attention to the gates that opened onto King's Bend. Wounded men streamed in, leading horses laden with the dead. Some of the men shouted. Others cried. Aeko spotted Captain Ferocles and ran to him. "What is this?"

The captain grimaced in the torch glow. "A gods-damned mess, that's what it is! One of my patrols blundered right into the Throng's vanguard. Their sergeant panicked. I'd have his head if the Throng hadn't already taken it." He pointed at a ghastly corpse in the distance, already being pulled down from a horse by a pair of soldiers.

Aeko asked, "How many casualties?"

"Ten dead at least, six more missing." He grabbed Aeko's arm and squeezed so tightly that she was tempted to break his wrist to make him release her. "It wasn't even that demon of theirs! Just one Shel'ai and a vanguard. He cast some kind of devilry on my men's horses—kept them from running. Then the Throng's elite—those devil-fast warriors in black leathers—cut my men to ribbons." His body shook, though Aeko could not tell if it was in rage or fear. "Gods, how are we supposed to fight *that*?"

Aeko twisted free of the captain's grasp, acutely aware of soldiers and citizens alike eavesdropping on the captain's every word. "Captain, lower your damn voice."

Ferocles blinked. "Of course. You're right." He pointed to the gates, still open, revealing the dark, empty horizon beyond Pallantine Hill. "They're not far now. Ammerhel was wrong. They're not turning to face the Dhargots. They're coming for *us*!"

"Tell the king," Aeko said. Doubtless, the king already knew, but just then she wanted the captain—and his temper—somewhere else.

"No need. Pelleas knew your leader was wrong!" Nevertheless, the Captain of the Red Watch hurried off, toward the palace at the city's eastern edge.

Aeko stood where he left her, fists clenched. She spotted Sir Crovis Ammerhel on the parapets above her. Sir Paltrick Vossmore stood with him. Both men were staring at her. Crovis had a faint smile on his face.

Aeko, swallowing her contempt, ascended the stairs and joined them. She bowed. Vossmore returned the gesture. Crovis did not. The latter said, "I thought he was going to strike you for a moment. I'd have taken his hand if he did."

"Thank you, Captain Ammerhel. But I can take care of myself."

Crovis glanced over the parapets, into the night. Aeko followed his gaze to stars and night-darkened plains, a few urusks grazing obliviously in the distance. No Throng, not yet. But she shuddered. She could feel them coming.

"It seems the wytches are even worse at strategy than I thought," Crovis said. "First, they risk our ire with that foul business in the jailhouse. Now, they march on our protectorate, even as the Dhargots sweep up behind them." He laughed. "All the better."

Aeko turned to Sir Paltrick Vossmore instead. The young Isle Knight's usual haughtiness had been replaced by naked fear. He looked back at her. She realized they were thinking the same thing.

Crovis turned to face her, breaking her attention. "We should look to the defenses," he said. "I do not trust these Red Watch commanders to do their job, so you two will each command one third of the city's force. We will allow Captain Ferocles to retain command of the rest." He nodded at Paltrick. "Sir Vossmore, you have the honor of coordinating the courtyard's defense. I will lend you fifty knights and a hundred squires to reinforce the ranks. You are charged with holding the enemy, should the gates be breached."

Paltrick's eyes widened. Then he bowed. "I am honored, Captain."

Aeko's fists clenched. That task should have been assigned to her. Paltrick was a good soldier but inexperienced. She wondered if Crovis was trying to insult her or keep her alive.

She cleared her throat. "Captain, who will command the rest of the company?"

"I will."

Then Aeko understood. Crovis was thinking of the future. When they returned to the Lotus Isles, the story of this battle would be told and retold. Crovis would see to that. Everyone would know that while she lorded over a few squads of frightened footmen and Paltrick probably got himself killed in the courtyard, the great Crovis Ammerhel had acted as the linchpin of the city's defenses.

Aeko wanted to shake him. She wanted to slap the confident smirk from his face. What future would they have if the city fell? Besides that, hadn't the Knight of the Lotus seen the bodies of slain Red Watch? Did they mean nothing to him? But she said nothing.

"Do you think they will offer a parley?" Paltrick asked, voice wavering.

Crovis said, "According to rumors, the Throng offers no terms until the battle's already won—and then, only so they can swell their ranks with conscripts. But this is one battle they will *not* win." He confidently faced the horizon again. "We need only hold them at bay for a few days. Eventually, they will have to march west instead and brace to meet the Dhargots. Besides, we have the Light on our side." He reached out and slapped Paltrick's shoulder in a show of camaraderie. "Have no fear, young Vossmore. This will be like another day in the tilting yards."

Aeko heard the sound of an entire squad's footsteps and tensed. Sergeant Epheus joined them, flanked by men of the Red Watch. All held drawn swords. Aeko braced herself. The sergeant faced her, eyes livid. He leveled his sword at her.

Aeko did not move. Paltrick cried out, alarmed, and reached for his own blade. Crovis was faster. Shoving Aeko out of the way, he slapped the sergeant's blade aside with one gauntleted fist. Then he drew his adamune, its curved blade gleaming lethally in the night. Sergeant Epheus stepped back. All around them, Isle Knights stared in confusion. Paltrick signaled, and they moved in, forming steely ranks behind their three officers.

Crovis never took his eyes off Epheus. "What in Jinn's name are you doing?"

The sergeant pointed at Aeko. "Arresting her."

"I think not, Sergeant. You have no authority over us. But if you have a grievance, voice it now."

Epheus said, "Gladly. I just came from the jailhouse. This addle-brained bitch released the Shel'ai prisoners! She sent them off to gods-know-where with that daft corporal, Locke. For all we know, they've already joined up with the enemy." Epheus started forward again.

Crovis blocked him even as he cast Aeko an icy glance. He did not have to ask her if the sergeant's accusation was true. "I'll take care of this myself, Sergeant. Look to your city."

The sergeant opened his mouth to protest.

Crovis cut him off. "Everyone in the city must be placed under house arrest at once. And tell Captain Ferocles to get back here, where he belongs. You are about to have another riot on your hands."

The sergeant turned to look at the rest of the city. The uncertain crowds Aeko had seen earlier, spilling out onto the cobblestone streets, now resembled a mob. Sergeant Epheus glowered at Aeko, then gave Crovis a nod. Descending the stairs from the battlements, boots sounding off stone, he issued new orders and focused his full attention on preventing another riot. The Isle Knights relaxed. Aeko sighed. Then, she turned to face Crovis Ammerhel.

Crovis spoke in a low voice. "Aeko, what have you done?" Aeko had expected contempt. To her surprise, the Knight of the Lotus's eyes were wide. He sounded stunned, almost hurt.

"What I thought was right."

"May you live long enough to explain that to me." Crovis's expression hardened. He sheathed his sword and he turned his back on her, facing the plains again.

Few stars shone through to the plains north of Lyos, Armahg's Eye a faint, starry smear beneath a thick advance of storm clouds. The moon was a ghostly sliver. In spite of a stream nearby, its waters black as ink, the earth here was rocky and bad for farming. Nothing lived here but a small, wandering herd of urusks, their long scaly snouts always close to the dirt.

That suited Lethe just fine. He was tired of killing.

The Unseen's hands trembled as he stripped off his leather armor and mask and washed the blood and grime from his face. Night air chilled the water; it felt like ice against his skin. He took a deep breath and let it go, glancing up at the veiled heavens. He might have prayed, but he knew the gods would not answer. They never did.

Was that really Rowen? He did not want to believe it. At first, he had not recognized him in the grisly darkness of the jailhouse, simply intent on following his master's orders to kill anyone who entered the jailhouse and thus spare himself the torments of the Blood Thrall. But the Shao battle cry had startled him back to his senses.

My fault. I should have let them kill me... He thought again of the sorcerers' ultimatum, voiced so long ago on the Ash'bana Plains: death or servitude, bound by magic. He thought of his comrades—those who defiantly chose death instead. The sorcerers had given it to them. And what had he seen in the sorcerers' eyes—was it grudging admiration?

But when the choice fell on him, his courage faltered. Like the others, he chose instead to join the Unseen.

More than ever before, Lethe wanted to kill himself. But the Blood Thrall made that impossible. He had already endured all he could by disobeying. He was supposed to have killed Rowen. He hadn't. The resulting punishment from the Blood Thrall had washed over him for what felt like centuries, a burning scourge that seemed to touch every inch of skin down to its deepest layer, before Shade finally dismissed it and ordered him to follow. There had not even been time to catch his breath. Lethe simply rose from his twitching torments on the bloody jailhouse floor and followed, weeping with relief.

Lethe shuddered. He called upon every shred of humanity and self-control he had left and tried to clear his mind. Shade stood nearby, facing the distant walls of Lyos. The Shel'ai appeared lost in thought. He had taken another bone-white cloak from the saddlebags of his destrier. It rustled in the night breeze as he pulled it tightly around his body. Lethe could no longer tell which dark splotches represented the emblem of the crimson greatwolf and which were simply blood stains. *He's in one of his trances again. Probably telling Fadarah what just happened.*

Lethe went to tend the horses. He removed their saddles and fed them oats while they drank from the stream. He brushed and rubbed down his palfrey first, then the rouncey. Both were skittish, but they trusted Lethe. Then, he turned his attention to Shade's fearsome destrier. The coal-black horse, huge and powerful, built less for speed than heavy combat, shied away from him. Lethe had seen his master's chosen mount tormenting the other horses, nipping and kicking at them while their riders were gone.

The destrier might have reared up against Lethe himself, but he caught the bridle and yanked it into obedience. The horse seemed to sense Lethe's temper and gave in.

Lethe glanced over his shoulder and saw that his master had emerged from his trance. "I suppose you think that was necessary," Lethe muttered.

Shade said, "Spare me, Human. Unlike you, I take no pleasure in killing."

278

Lethe paused and lowered the curry comb. "Fohl's hells! You could just as easily have used your magic to slip into that prison undetected. You killed those men for sport." He touched the handle of his shortsword, wondering if his hate was finally strong enough to let him kill this man. The Blood Thrall buzzed to life, informing him otherwise.

Shade faced him soberly. "Not for sport. To prove a point. I would not expect you to understand." The Shel'ai waved his hands, conjuring a violet campfire. He sat by the fire to warm himself. Though his face was like stone, Lethe saw something in his master's eyes—a tiny spark of brutal, almost lustful enjoyment. *Gods, the stories are true. This one loves killing the way rich men love gold. He might hide it, might even regret it sometimes, but it's there.*

Lethe wondered if Fadarah knew. He doubted it. *But I bet that wytch of yours knew. I bet that's why she turned on you.* "That was murder," Lethe repeated. "Tell me you took no pleasure in it, and I'm Zet reborn."

Shade turned to face him, Sylvan features dagger-sharp in the darkness. "Pardon me if I doubt your conscience, assassin. That was mercy, not murder. This is the end. We have pushed as far east as needed. My master wants this city destroyed so that the Isle Knights will be certain to go to war." He hesitated. "And he wants it done quickly."

Something in Shade's voice chilled Lethe's blood. "What does that mean?"

Whatever Fadarah had ordered, Shade looked none too excited about it. "If Silwren or El'rash'lin summons the courage to face the Nightmare, Lyos might actually survive. We cannot risk that. So we must break Lyos from the inside out."

Lethe winced. *More killing.* A cold, familiar hollowness filled him.

"This time, we will not be alone. My master sends two Shel'ai and a squad of Unseen to aid us. They will reach us within a few hours. Once more, we will slip into the city unnoticed. This time, though, it will be more dangerous." He hesitated. "More painful."

"You said you'd set me free. You lied."

"I did *not* lie. I merely have further need of your services—such as they are. But that need will lapse once Lyos has fallen." Shade added, "Besides, you might yet find the quick death you seek. I do not expect many Unseen to survive what we must do tonight."

To Lethe, the words were music. Still, he glared at the sorcerer. Then, for lack of anything better to do, he went back to brushing the horses. He started with Shade's destrier. "I know what you carry, Sorcerer," he called over his shoulder. "Thanks to you, I carry it every day." He braced himself. He expected Shade to unleash the agony of the Blood Thrall. But he did not.

"Who was that man you were fighting?"

The unexpected question cut clean through Lethe's rage and made him shudder. Had his master been reading his mind? He kept his eyes on his work. "Just someone I recognized from my old life."

"Indeed." Lethe could tell by the Shel'ai's tone that he did not believe him.

Lethe snapped. "If you want to know so damned bad, why don't you just read my thoughts?"

"I already have." Shade's voice softened. "For what it's worth, Human, I am sorry." The Shel'ai gathered his bone-white cloak around himself. Then it began to rain. The rain soaked the Shel'ai's clothes, darkening the crimson greatwolves and bloodstains.

The violet campfire flickered but did not go out. In a voice little more than a whisper, Shade said, "I wonder how it happened. How we became monsters." He sat again, pulling up his hood against the rain.

CHAPTER TWENTY-FIVE

DOGBANE CIRCLE

"**G**ODS, I HATE THIS PLACE!" Rowen muttered.

Morning light spilled through the open window of the tiny shack as he opened the cracked shutters, allowing new air to stream in. The air was stale, even after a storm that had washed over the city well after midnight, thundering as it unleashed an unapologetic torrent of rain. Rowen almost could not believe it. He reeled from the stench of human filth and burnt urusk meat: the daily perfume of the Dark Quarter.

The streets—if that was the correct term for the muddy spaces between the uneven rows of shacks, inns, and brothels—were already crowded with cutthroats and beggars. The streets contained children, too—some of them naked, all grubby as animals, running and fighting in the mud. While he remembered that from his own childhood in the slums, he could see that now, many more of them appeared to be Ivairian refugees. Meanwhile, armed men from the gangs prowled, looking for food and trouble.

Rowen winced, wondering if he had made a terrible mistake. But what choice did they have? Aeko was right. If Silwren and El'rash'lin stayed in the inner city, they would be killed. But if they still meant to save the city, they needed to be close when the Throng arrived.

He rubbed his eyes. He had spent the night in restless sleep, plagued by nightmares of fire and death. He woke afraid, not even knowing at first where he was. When he remembered, the fear did not dissipate.

Memories from the night before returned to him. Aeko's Knights, bound by her orders, had donned plain cloaks to hide their identities and sullenly escorted Rowen and the Shel'ai through the rear gates of Lyos, around the city walls to King's Bend, then down the worn, trash-strewn paths into the slums. The Shel'ai were still unconscious. The knights carried them on litters, concealing their identity by covering them like corpses. Rowen led the way, shuddering as much from fear and loathing as from the night air's chill.

The Dark Quarter had changed very little. Rows of shanty-inns and brothels lined the streets, many of them simply going by different names now. Here and there hung the territorial markings of the gangs: the Skullbreakers, the Bloody Asps, the Crazy Knifemen, and others he did not recognize. Those areas, he avoided. Without the Knights for protection, and with the Shel'ai unconscious, he might not last long in some of the worst areas of the slums.

Rowen did not think the small, ratty cottage where he and Kayden had lived as children would still be there. The sight of its cracked mud walls and low straw roof chilled rather than heartened him. It had been turned into a whore shack now. Upon entering the door, he was greeted with the smell of sweat and urine. Naked, brutish men and women lay unkempt on the dirt floor, all of them unconscious. The air reeked of *fran-té*, an acrid, slum-favored plant that, when smoked, produced reeling hallucinations.

With the Knights' help, Rowen roused the people and told them to leave. They did not protest. Rowen was wearing a plain cloak to hide his Red Watch uniform of faded scarlet, but they saw it anyway and thought the Knights were guards as well, coming to drive them away or kill them. Their spirits rose when Rowen handed them a few copper cranáfi instead.

Although none of the Knights knew him, he imagined that they must have sensed by now that he too came from this place of filth. He dismissed the Knights as quickly as he could. They hesitated. Though visibly anxious to leave the Dark Quarter, they doubted it would please their beloved Commander Shingawa if her new squire was knifed the moment they left.

"I'll be fine," he assured them. He glanced back at the makeshift stretchers upon which Silwren and El'rash'lin still slept, fitful and oblivious. Summoning his courage, he said, "I must have your word that you'll tell no one except Commander Shingawa where we are. Not even Sir Ammerhel. Swear it on your honor."

The Knights hesitated. Rowen knew they wanted to refuse, but Aeko had already told them to follow his instructions, no matter how crazed. One by one, the Knights swore. Then they left.

Now, as daybreak spread across the shadowed filth of the Dark Quarter, Rowen wondered if his decision had been the right one. They were still alive, still safe, but how long would it be before the slumdwellers turned on him, or Captain Ferocles sent soldiers of the Red Watch to scour the Dark Quarter until they were found?

Rowen distracted himself by stripping off his faded scarlet tabard and tossing the black falcon emblem into the corner of the filthy shack. Traveling alone in the Dark Quarter while wearing a Red Watch uniform was asking to be stabbed. *Besides, I'm a squire now.*

He decided to check his weapons. He had a small knife hidden in his boot. Otherwise, he had only Knightswrath, since the longsword issued to him when he joined the Red Watch had been confiscated and never returned.

In his daze, and in all the chaos that followed the battle in the jailhouse, he had not bothered to inspect the adamune Hráthbam had given him. He remembered how the rusty blade had absorbed wytchfire that should have burnt him to cinders. He had not spoken of this to Aeko or Captain Ferocles, thinking he must have been mistaken. But he had felt the terrible heat of those flames and knew the already damaged blade must be wholly ruined now.

Returning the knife to his boot, he sat in front of the open shutters of his boyhood shack, letting the morning light wash over him, warming his skin. He laid Knightswrath across his lap. He unsheathed it. Bright, perfect kingsteel flashed in his palms.

Am I still dreaming? The blade looked remade, a lethal curve of kingsteel with distinctive snowy swirls deep in the metal. Spelled across the blade in gilded lettering, the sword's name shone clearer now.

Fel-Náya. Knightswrath. Beneath the name, what Rowen had first mistaken for a darker stain was in fact the exquisite, silver inlay of a dragon in flight. The design must have been the emblem of the swordmaker, but he did not recognize it. He returned his attention to the intricate designs covering the brass crosspiece and dragonbone pommel. These also seemed more distinct, almost lifelike. "Gods..."

He heard rustling behind him. As though waking from a trance, he turned. El'rash'lin sat up then rose painfully to his feet, face pale with weariness and hunger. He looked around and grimaced. "Have I gone to Fohl's hells?"

Despite himself, Rowen laughed. He sheathed Knightswrath, resolving to puzzle over the enigmatic sword at a later time. "Careful, Sorcerer. You're insulting my childhood."

"If *this* is your childhood, Human, we have more in common than either of us thought."

Rowen considered the memories El'rash'lin had magicked into him. He still felt them as though they were his own, which puzzled and unnerved him. Several times since then, he had found himself strangely aching to return to a forest he'd never seen, to a people he did not even know.

They were both orphans, both scarred—both plagued by anguish and loneliness they tried their best to deny. Rowen remembered his own childhood in the Dark Quarter and shuddered. Had El'rash'lin, in imparting some of his own memories, gained some of Rowen's as well?

He wanted to offer some paltry words of comfort, but he could think of nothing to say. Morning light spilled through the cracked shutters, illuminating the dust in the air. He looked at Silwren instead. She was still asleep, face taut with pain and weariness. Rowen gasped. *Am I mad, or does she look maybe five years older?*

El'rash'lin nodded grimly. "She's dying, Human." He coughed. "Although slower than I am, it seems." His misshapen lips broke into a sad smile.

Rowen asked, "Will she become—"

"Like me?" The crooked smile broadened. "In time, yes. Shel'ai were never meant to be Dragonkin. We stoked the fire too high. It devours us from the inside out."

Silwren stirred, but her eyes did not open.

"She'll wake soon," El'rash'lin said. His voice sounded hollow.

Rowen said, "I'll go and get food. Bar the door behind me. Open it for no one but me, or you may have to call upon that magic after all."

He fetched his cloak and adjusted his leather brigandine. He thought about wearing Knightswrath openly to dissuade would-be cutthroats, but the sight of the exquisite dragonbone handle would only encourage them all the more. He shifted his sword belt, partially concealing the weapon beneath his cloak. Taking the dagger from his boot, he slid it into the belt for easier access. Then, with great reluctance, he left the shack of his youth for the Dark Quarter beyond.

Morning wore on, and chaos spread through the muddy streets of the slums. Everyone had heard by now that the Throng was only hours away. Beggars and orphans fought their way up King's Bend, hoping to seek refuge behind the walls of Lyos. But the gates were barred. Along the parapets, both the Red Watch and Isle Knights denied them entrance. Crossbows were fired with warning *crack*s, spilling iron-tipped bolts into the dirt.

The slumdwellers drew back in fear. Rowen's heart sank as he watched them slump back to their homes and muddy streets, dejected. Pity turned to anger. Concealed by the hood of his cloak, he trained his gaze on the battlements again. This time, the wealthiest citizens of Lyos gazed back, derisively.

"They'd rather watch us die than grant us entrance into their precious city." He had not meant to speak aloud, but a passing slumdweller heard and nodded in grim agreement.

"That's our lot. They leave us the worst land for crops, tax half of what we grow anyway, then when trouble comes, they leave us nothing but rocks to fight with!" The man pulled a crooked dagger out of his sleeve and waved it, grinning. "But I make my *own* weapons!"

The man had fashioned his dagger out of a crooked shaft of urusk-bone, crudely sharpened at one end, wrapped at the other with shabby leather for a kind of hilt. Around King's Bend, other slumdwellers carried weapons, too. Those from the gangs carried axes or metal blades, but others had nothing more than farming implements or crude spears of fire-hardened wood.

These people won't last ten seconds when the Throng comes. Even if the Isle men and the soldiers of the Red Watch succeeded in holding the walls of Lyos, even if Silwren and El'rash'lin stopped the Nightmare, the slums would be overrun. Anyone who resisted would be killed.

The Throng was known to show mercy to those who surrendered, but only to swell their ranks with conscripts. But the Throng surely had enough farmers and laborers by now. What was the use in conscripting lawless, sickly peasants who would need to be clothed, fed, and armed first?

He spotted a familiar face—the young prostitute who'd approached him and Hráthbam when they first made their way up King's Bend. The facade of lust had vanished. She wore a thick cloak now and held a crying infant close to her body, her eyes wide with panic. She passed Rowen without recognizing him. He stared after her with pity.

Jinn's name... all these people are going to die! He wondered why they did not flee. Then he remembered why he and Kayden had stayed in the Dark Quarter: where else could they go? The Lotus Isles would not have them. Ivairia was already riddled with famine. Dwarrs were infamous for butchering trespassers whether the lands in question were in use or not. Refugees would have no better luck fleeing west. Even if they managed to avoid the Throng, most of the Free Cities where they might have taken refuge had already been devastated. The rest would burn soon enough, once the Dhargots came.

Rowen's fists clenched. As much as he hated this place, the injustice filled him with pity and rage. Before he realized what he was doing, he'd thrown back his hood and was striding purposely back into the Dark Quarter, pushing through fearful crowds until he reached Dogbane Circle.

The place got its name from street vendors there who dried salted slabs of tough meat cut from stray dogs, alongside the usual fare of charred urusk flesh. The bones and waste, meanwhile, were simply discarded and burned in the circle so that the air always had an acrid stench.

Gangs met here to parley. Dogbane Circle hosted a standing truce, making it the Dark Quarter's equivalent of the great King's Market of Lyos. Slumdwellers gathered there now, but not to shop or steal. Helpless, desperate, they looked to the gangs for protection. Rowen did not blame them. Many of these people had families. The gangs could give them a better chance than they'd have alone.

The problem, of course, was that the gangs knew it. Each gang leader was flanked by bodyguards marked with the tattoos of their allegiance. Rowen saw familiar men, all dirty, some with stringy hair, others missing fingers. The gangs usually fought each other for control of the Dark Quarter. But today, they were smiling.

A raised wooden platform had been constructed from old tables and chairs pushed together. In a few minutes, he guessed, whomever the gang leaders elected would mount the makeshift dais and address the slumdwellers, offering the illusion of protection in exchange for what little wealth the Dark Quarter had. Rowen wondered if, five years ago, he would have acted any different.

He pushed his way into the heart of Dogbane Circle. Steadying his gaze, he threw off his cloak and shifted Knightswrath—still sheathed—to his left hip. Gang leaders' bodyguards turned to face him. They looked him up and down. They frowned. No asp or skull tattoo adorned his arms, no gang sign on his tattered leather brigandine.

Rowen ignored the bodyguards and started toward one of the gang leaders, a man he recognized: Fen-Shea, leader of the Bloody Asps. Before Rowen could reach him, Fen-Shea's men—each tattooed on his left arm with a red zigzag that was supposed to represent a bloody serpent—blocked his path. All drew their daggers. Rowen did not draw his sword. Instead, he called out Fen-Shea's name.

The gang leader frowned. Then, a cold grin spread across his face. "Locke. I figured you'd be keeping your brother company in Fohl's hells by now."

Rowen bristled. He sized up his opponent. Fen-Shea was well muscled with a shaved head, bare chested but for a brace of daggers and what looked to be a necklace made from rodent skulls. "I see you still like to wear your own family around your neck."

Fen-Shea's grin vanished. Some of his own men smiled. Other

gang leaders laughed openly at the leader of the Bloody Asps even though his gang was indisputably the strongest in the slums.

Fen-Shea took a step toward him. In one hand, he held a blackened mace with a long handle wrapped in snakeskin. He said, "I *thought* I saw you awhile back, when that wytch fell from the walls. I didn't believe it. They even say you talked the soldiers into sparing her!" Smiles vanished. Men clenched their weapons. Fen-Shea grinned, enjoying the reaction. "Tell me, Locke, have you come home to die?"

Rowen shrugged. "If I have, it won't be by your hand."

His response drew scattered laughter. Fen-Shea only had to say the word and Rowen would be cut to ribbons. But he wouldn't. Not yet. Fen-Shea had been humiliated. Simply having Rowen killed would not erase that. *At least, that's what I'm hoping.*

"I heard you joined the Red Watch," Fen-Shea called out in a loud voice, prompting a deafening hiss of disapproval from the men around them.

"We all make mistakes."

Fen-Shea snorted. "And you just made another one." He waved the great snakeskin mace in a slow circle, stretching his arm. "You want to apologize... or should I haul those words out of you, along with your entrails?"

Some of the men cheered. Beyond them, the rest of the slumdwellers stared in confusion. Rowen struggled to control his fear. "I have something *else* you can pull on, Fen-Shea." He turned his back on the man and raised his voice so all could hear. "I am *not* a man of the Red Watch. Not anymore. I'm not a sellsword, either. I am Rowen Locke, the new leader of the Bloody Asps."

The chanting of the crowd buffeted his face like desert air. Rowen stumbled, overwhelmed for a moment by the noise. Why had he been so hotheaded? He'd barely eaten or slept in days and was in no shape for a fight, least of all against someone like Fen-Shea.

The leader of the Bloody Asps laughed, sensing his fear. He charged. The great, snakeskin mace whirled at Rowen's head. At the same time, Fen-Shea drew one of his knives and slashed at Rowen's thigh—the one injured in the battle at the jailhouse.

Rowen backpedaled out of range of the knife and used Knightswrath to hammer Fen-Shea's mace out of the way. The shock of the blow swept up Rowen's arm. He cursed. *Why didn't I ask El'rash'lin to heal me?*

But Fen-Shea was taking his time. He circled Rowen slowly, swinging his mace, waving to the crowds and laughing with his men. Fen-Shea's men watched, enjoying the sport along with the other gangs. Even the common slumdwellers seemed to have forgotten all about the Throng and focused instead on the fight before them.

Rowen fought in vain to clear his mind. He'd hoped to take command of the strongest gang in order to broker some kind of alliance to protect the slumdwellers. The law of the slums gave him the right to take Fen-Shea's place if he beat him. But what good would that do? Someone else might just challenge *him*, then. And even if they didn't, would leading the gangs really help him save the people of the slums? *Gods, I didn't think this through—*

Fen-Shea pivoted suddenly and charged. He feigned a lunge with his knife, then threw it instead. Rowen saw it coming. He sidestepped, letting the knife clatter past him. He blocked Fen-Shea's mace again.

Fen-Shea drew another knife from those sheathed along his torso and lunged. This time, Rowen dropped one hand from the hilt of Knightswrath and caught Fen-Shea's wrist. He twisted. Fen-Shea grunted and dropped the knife into the mud.

The leader of the Bloody Asps pulled free and backed away, retreating across the muddy, bone-strewn earth of Dogbane Circle, clearly biting back a scream of pain as he nursed his sprained wrist. This time, Rowen followed. He offered two slow cuts—which Fen-Shea blocked—then followed those with a third, faster cut that would have severed the gang leader's leg at the knee, had Rowen not turned his blade at the last second.

The flat of Rowen's blade swept Fen-Shea's legs out from under him. The snakeskin mace flew out of reach. Cursing, Fen-Shea reached for another knife. Rowen stomped on Fen-Shea's hand, pinning it to his chest. Rowen tucked the tip of his sword under the gang leader's chin. Breathing hard, Rowen looked down at him. "Yield."

Fen-Shea blinked in surprise. He grimaced. Then he nodded.

Rowen stepped back, letting him up. The other members of the Bloody Asps stared at him with surprise and grudging respect. No one had ever beaten Fen-Shea before. They would follow him—at least for now.

The same could not be said for the other gangs. He read the truth in their frowns and uncertain gazes: they thought Fen-Shea's defeat was a fluke. Or, failing that, perhaps the old leader of the Bloody Asps had not been so formidable, after all. Why should they follow a former soldier of the Red Watch most of them did not even know?

The Dark Quarter was divided now. The people were doomed. *Gods, I've only made matters worse!* Then, he spotted Silwren.

She stumbled toward him, barefoot across the muddy ground of Dogbane Circle, still dressed in nothing but Shade's bone-white cloak. She held it cinched across her breasts with one hand, leaving one shoulder bare and pale in the still-young light of day. Her hood was down, revealing her long, tapered ears. Platinum tresses spilled, unkempt and lovely, almost to her waist.

Her violet eyes found his. Her mist-white pupils shone now like the sunlight. For a moment, he was speechless. Then he came to his senses. He shook his head in warning, but it was too late.

A dreadful whisper swept through the crowds. Slumdwellers followed her with steely eyes. Some stared, entranced. Others grimaced and backed away, reaching for weapons. The gang leaders, forgetting Rowen, waved in more men to protect them. Weapons glinted in the sunlight. Those who had no weapons picked up rocks.

Silwren stared back at them, defiantly. "Yes," she called out in a loud voice that echoed throughout the Dark Quarter, "I am a Shel'ai." She came forward until she stood at the heart of Dogbane Circle. She touched Rowen's hand. Then, she ascended the makeshift dais and turned slowly, letting everyone look at her. "You would not find it hard to kill me. But if you wish to save yourselves and your families, you will listen to what I have to say first."

Rowen fixed a stern expression and raised his sword, even though he doubted he could match a Shel'ai's ability to intimidate all the gangs of the Dark Quarter at once.

Silwren said, "In just a few hours, an army led by sorcerers will reach this city. Swords and arrows will not stop them. The demon you have heard about is real. He will smash the great walls of Lyos as if they were kindling. All of you will die," she paused as fear rippled through the crowds, "unless you stand against this together."

She lifted one hand, pointing to the summit of Pallantine Hill. "The people of that city, in whose shadow you live, call you wretched. They look down from their parapets and see you fighting like dogs for scraps, and it sickens them. They speak of killing you. I know. I've heard them." She lowered her hand. "I've heard you speak just as often of killing them. And me. And each other. If *they* are wrong, perhaps you are, too."

The crowd murmured uneasily. Meanwhile, Silwren turned westward, toward a great, dark blur on the horizon. "I am weary of bloodshed born of loyalty, of peace sought only through steel and wytchfire. But I am as guilty as any. So when the Throng comes... if I must... I will give my life to stop this—just as others have risked their own lives to save mine."

She faced Rowen. Her violet eyes seemed suddenly less foreign to him. He saw something heart-wrenching there and nearly wept. A faint smile touched her lips. Though her voice softened, it resounded just the same.

"You could kill me—and each other, as they expect you to. And die soon after, like animals. Or you could make another choice."

Her voice grew louder. "It could be like the tales of old: Isle Knights and Shel'ai fighting together. Homes saved from the torch, thanks not to lofty oaths or threats and promises of payment, but the simple courage of strangers. We could live—if only for one, fine hour—as we were meant to."

Her voice fell silent. In Dogbane Circle, nothing moved. Men shifted uncertainly, weapons in hand. Rowen's gaze moved from face to face. *It's not going to work! She touched some of them—but not enough.*

Then, Fen-Shea stirred. Without a word, the one-time leader of the Bloody Asps stooped, retrieved his mace, and made his way toward the makeshift dais upon which Silwren still stood. He limped slightly. Rowen shook off the spell of Silwren's words and lifted Knightswrath, thinking that the man wanted to fight him again for leadership of the Bloody Asps.

Instead, Fen-Shea came to stand beside him. He slapped Rowen's shoulder and winked. Then he put his back to Silwren and faced the crowds, his fierce look daring anyone to try and harm her.

The crowds began to mutter. A few people fled, but to Rowen's great surprise, a few men of the Bloody Asps walked up and joined them. Then a few more. Then the stringy-haired, wild-eyed leader of the Crazy Knifemen shrugged and joined them, followed by half his men. Other gangs followed suit.

Within an hour, Rowen and Silwren had an army.

Jinn's name, now what? Rowen feigned a look of certainty as he stood on the dais and swept his gaze over the roiling crowds of Dogbane Circle. He was glad the gang leaders had stopped asking questions, Fen-Shea having tasked them with arming everyone he could before he himself left—"To give my wife one last bedding, in case I get my guts cut out," he said.

Rowen's first act had been to advise Silwren to mindspeak with El'rash'lin and warn him to stay out of Dogbane Circle. Despite the miracle worked by Silwren's eloquence, Rowen doubted their tenuous alliance would hold if the already frightened slumdwellers saw the disfigured sorcerer heading their way. He wondered what to do next. He thought he'd seen smoke cresting the battlements of Lyos but attributed it to another riot. Several slumdwellers ventured up King's Bend then returned, reporting that the gates of the inner city had been closed.

Nevertheless, Rowen penned a letter and asked for volunteers to carry it to the inner city's high walls. From those, he chose a gangly, freckled youth—the most innocent-looking one of the bunch—and sent the runner up to the gates, offering a deal: Silwren and their patchwork army would fight for Lyos, in exchange for the king allowing the slumdwellers to take shelter behind his city's high walls.

Rowen did not bother addressing Sir Crovis Ammerhel in the note, since he knew the Knight of the Lotus would refuse. He hoped the king would be more reasonable.

Rowen led Silwren out of Dogbane Circle, toward the outskirts of the slums, to await the runner's return. Crowds pressed in, though Rowen was glad they kept their distance since he still did not entirely trust them around Silwren. He hoped the runner would return with news that the king had accepted his offer but suspected that instead, the king would only request to meet. Even though approaching the walls might mean his arrest—or get him feathered with a dozen arrows—delivering the offer himself instead of sending a messenger might have made a better impression.

Gods! Why did I do that? He answered himself with a glib smile. *My first time leading an army. I guess I'm bound to make mistakes. Still—*

A scream interrupted his thoughts. He saw the runner making his way toward them, supported by two of his friends. The young man howled with pain, a crossbow bolt sunk up to the quills in his shoulder.

"They wouldn't listen!" cried one of his friends. "They ordered him back, but—"

"Some itchy bastard got eager with his trigger before he could take a step," the other finished. "He dropped your note in front of the gates, but gods know if anybody came out to pick it up." The runner howled again.

Damn. Rowen directed his gaze up the hill, toward the gates, but all he saw was the faint glint of sunlight of helmets, cresting the battlements. He imagined a hundred crossbowmen watching them, weapons loaded, just waiting for him to get a bit closer.

He directed his attention back to the wounded runner. Someone offered to go and fetch a healer. Rowen remembered what passed in the Dark Quarter for healers and shook his head. "Silwren?"

She nodded slightly.

Rowen gave orders. The young man's friends held him down while Rowen withdrew the crossbow bolt from his shoulder. Rowen winced—not just from sympathy, but also from dread as the man's screams spread uncertainty through the crowds milling behind them.

Then Silwren laid her hands on the young man's shoulder. A violet glow bubbled from her hands, seeping into the ghastly wound.

The crowd reacted at once. Some screamed. Others ran. But most muttered prayers and crossed themselves with superstitious signs. Yet when Silwren withdrew her hands and the stunned young man rose, unharmed, all of them gasped. A few cheered. *Well, at least they aren't killing us.*

He stepped closer to Silwren. "If we can't convince the king to let these people into the city, we should send them east, toward the sea."

But Silwren shook her head. "I'll lead them against the Throng myself. I want Fadarah to see their faces."

The certainty in her voice surprised him. Rowen eyed the poorly armed people around them, not a one of them in armor. In a low voice, he answered, "They'll be massacred."

"Not if El'rash'lin and I can stop Iventine," Silwren countered.

And if you can't?

Though Rowen only thought the question, Silwren faced him nonetheless. "Then, Human, it will make no difference where or how far they run."

CHAPTER TWENTY-SIX
"IN JINN'S NAME..."

MIDDAY FOUND MEN ALONG THE parapets of Lyos, staring down at something they had never seen before and could not ever have imagined. Men streamed up from the Dark Quarter and crowded King's Bend. They had armed themselves with whatever they could find: knives, farming tools, and makeshift spears. Some proudly carried crude banners before them: the cracked skull, the black knife, the red serpent, and a dozen others.

Captain Ferocles swore under his breath. For days, he had been combating a soaring desertion rate among his men. *Then, last night's disaster. And now this!*

Of course, he had been wondering how long it would take the slumdwellers to riot. He couldn't exactly blame them, given the juggernaut of the Throng rolling across the plains. But he was not about to admit these violent wretches into his city, regardless of Aeko Shingawa's pleas.

He signaled the archers and crossbowmen. They had already frightened off a handful of slumdwellers seeking to gain admittance behind the walls, even going so far as to wound one madman who claimed he'd been sent by the wytch to offer them a deal. But this would be worse.

Slender, steely arrows gleamed in bright, awful rows. Strings tensed, men waiting only for their captain's signal to unleash devastation upon King's Bend. Ferocles hesitated. He was loathe to waste so many arrows on the eve of a battle. And he doubly loathed the idea of heartening the enemy by heaping the corpses of his own people in front of the gates. Of course, these were slumdwellers, not true citizens, but he doubted the men of the Throng would appreciate that distinction.

The king would not approve, either. Not that he's here to tell me that himself... Ferocles frowned. The slumdwellers were moving *away* from the gates. Were they running away? If so, where were the women and children?

He turned back to the Dark Quarter, following the sounds of weeping babies, and saw the women and children solemnly watching from a distance as, with surprising order, the men from the slums marched in haphazard columns partway down King's Bend, then stopped and formed ranks.

"Have they gone mad?" Epheus cried.

Captain Ferocles ordered the archers to stand down. He scanned the haphazard ranks more closely. He spotted three figures at the head of the ramshackle host. He swore under his breath. One stooped figure wore a cloak and hood. Another—a woman—had bright hair that glittered like quicksilver in the sunlight. The third—a man—bore a mess of unruly red hair and carried a flashing adamune before him.

"Go get Ammerhel," he ordered. "And Shingawa, too, I suppose." Sergeant Epheus left at once, sprinting toward the barracks. Meanwhile, Ferocles fixed his gaze beyond the sun-warmed battlements at the strange, grim host arrayed beneath him. Men without armor or fortifications, barely armed, solemnly faced the juggernaut of the Throng as it swelled off the horizon like a great, bristling stain.

Despite himself, he smiled.

Crovis glared at the scrap of paper so hard that Aeko wondered if he would tear it in two. Instead, the Knight of the Lotus laughed. "Is this some kind of jest?"

"I think not, m'lord. Locke is many things, but I doubt he's the type to make practical jokes on the eve of battle." Aeko turned to look out the window of what had been the office of Captain Ferocles before Crovis claimed it for himself. A faint tendril of smoke drifted in through the window, carrying the scent of charred flesh as well as burned wood.

Rowen, what in Jinn's name have you gotten yourself into?

Crovis said, "Well, I'm sure the Red Watch crossbowman's shot served as adequate response. The captain says they're massing on King's Bend. If they want to throw themselves on the blades of the Throng, let them." He pushed the note aside. "We have no time to deal with these two renegade sorcerers now—let alone your squire." He gave her an icy look. "We must see to the defenses before the Throng gets here and make do with what we have left."

"Which isn't much," Aeko muttered.

Crovis raised one eyebrow. "Your point?"

"Just that we're hardly in a position to refuse assistance. *Any* assistance." Aeko picked up the message and reread it herself. "Besides, if we don't let them in, they might turn to the Throng instead."

"So your brilliant advice is that I let this untrustworthy rabble into the city, into the very heart of our defenses, lest they aid the enemy instead?"

Aeko thought he had a point but kept that to herself. "We have nothing left to gamble with, m'lord. We can't hold Lyos on our own. Not now. We both know it. But if Locke is telling the truth—and on that, I can vouch for his honor—then we might still have a chance."

"Or our ruin will come all the sooner."

Aeko nodded. "True. At worst, we'll die a few hours sooner. At best, though, we'll be the saviors of Lyos."

Crovis's eyes sparked with newfound interest. He held out his hand. Aeko returned the message.

"I cannot be seen acquiescing to demonic influences," Crovis said after a pause.

Aeko caught his meaning. She forced a bow. "I will see to it, m'lord. If I am wrong, the shame will be on *my* name, not yours."

Crovis thought a moment longer and nodded. "So be it. See it done—while there's still time. And gods forgive you if you're wrong." He held the message in the flame of a candle until it withered in a fresh curl of ash and smoke.

Rowen Locke glanced back at the walls of Lyos. "Something's happened," he said.

El'rash'lin laughed, the sound muffled by the thin white cloth he'd tied over his face to mask his disfigured appearance. "That's quite the understatement, Human."

"No... I mean, something's happened *in the city!*" Rowen pointed at a thin column of smoke, deep behind the walls of Lyos.

El'rash'lin turned to look. Before he could answer, the gates of the city opened. The army of slumdwellers tensed. Was the Red Watch coming to disband them—or worse?

Rowen drew his sword, brandishing Knightswrath overhead. "Hold your positions!" He lowered his voice so only El'rash'lin could hear. "If they ride out to kill us, can you conjure up something to stop them?"

"What did you have in mind?"

"An illusion of burning Olgrym, the visage of Zet himself, a few million giant ants—hells, Sorcerer, anything!"

El'rash'lin hesitated. "Yes... but it will leave me unable to fight the Nightmare."

Rowen grimaced. He was about to pose the same question to Silwren when Aeko Shingawa rode out of the gates toward them. A full squad of ten smartly armored Isle Knights followed her. "At ease!" he called to his newfound army. He sheathed his sword. "They're friends." *At least, I hope so.* "Let them pass."

Grumbling but obedient, the armed men from the slums broke ranks, letting the Knights on horseback through. Rowen moved ahead of the Shel'ai, toward the Knights. Aeko spotted him and slowed. She tossed the reins of her destrier to the Knight next to her and dismounted. After the previous night's rain, her boots sank into the mud of King's Bend.

In addition to her chain-mail hauberk and azure tabard, the Knight of the Stag now wore breast- and backplates, pauldrons, rerebraces, couters, vambraces, gauntlets, tassets, and greaves. Each piece of strong, exquisite armor was emblazoned with stags and balancing cranes and the distinctive, snowy scrollwork of kingsteel.

The Knights behind her wore kingsteel plate as well. All carried adamunes. In addition, some carried broad, fearsome polearms that gleamed wickedly in the sunlight. Most of the Knights were no older than Rowen. They glanced uncertainly at the throngs of shabbily dressed, armed men milling around them.

I wonder how many of them used to be poor... and how many haven't been this close to poverty in their whole lives!

Aeko freed her boots and steel greaves from the mud with a look of irritation. Rowen fell to one knee before her. "On your feet, Squire," she snapped. She stared past him, at the Shel'ai. "Someone explain this!"

El'rash'lin stepped forward. "The king would demonstrate sense and compassion if he let these poor people behind the walls. He would also gain a few hundred fighters."

Aeko Shingawa flinched. "King Pelleas is dead." She gestured back up King's Bend, at the smoke still rising from Lyos. "He was murdered last night."

Word of her pronouncement spread among the listening slumdwellers.

Rowen blanched. "How..."

"Hacked to pieces in his bed," Aeko said. "They came out of nowhere. Shel'ai, plus a squad of Human warriors. They slipped into the palace, slaughtered almost everyone before the alarm was raised. After that..." Grief shone in her eyes. "We lost a lot of Red Watch and Isle men—including Sir Paltrick Vossmore, my junior officer." She cleared her throat. "The city's been in chaos ever since. We've taken command as best we can. But now we know what we should have guessed days ago: steel alone won't beat the Throng."

Aeko went to stand before Silwren. Dark-haired Human and pale Sylv, Knight of the Stag and renegade sorceress, they regarded each other in silence. Then Aeko bowed. Taking her cue, the other Knights bowed from their saddles. Aeko stood lance-straight and said, "Silwren of the Shel'ai, on behalf of Sir Crovis Ammerhel, Knight of the Lotus, I come to you—and your companion—to formally request an alliance, and to offer you our full amnesty and protection. We swear this on our honor, in Jinn's name."

Rowen's world seemed to move at a breakneck pace after that. Aeko personally escorted them through the open gates and up the stairs to the battlements, where Sir Crovis Ammerhel waited. Meanwhile, her squires and Knights herded the slumdwellers into the city, past the disapproving gazes of Captain Ferocles, the Red Watch, and the wealthy citizens of Lyos. The Islemen led the motley host straight to the armory and outfitted them with weapons and whatever mismatched armor could be found. Though tempted to remain with Silwren, Rowen knew that Aeko's vow now protected them just as surely as the Knights' steel, so he stayed with the slumdwellers instead.

By order of Captain Ferocles, every other able-bodied man was sent to the armory as well. Rowen saw men close their doors, as though intending to hide inside their homes, only to look out their windows, see mere slumdwellers bravely arraying themselves for battle, and hurry out to follow suit, ashamed.

Along the battlements, archers took position near murder holes, beside trebuchets and ballistae that looked as though they had not been fired in years. Elsewhere, those who could not fight were tasked with filling buckets of water, in case the enemy hurled fire over the walls. Chief among these were the women and children from the Dark Quarter, along with the wealthy women of Lyos. All had been granted sanctuary by the clerics of Lyos, but most refused to sit idly by while the men fought and died.

Rowen did what he could to help. Years as a sellsword had taught him a little about the engines of war—knowledge that the defenders of Lyos sorely lacked. He directed the positioning of the trebuchets and ballistae then helped instruct teams of men in how to load, aim, and fire the massive weapons. When he was done, he went to find Aeko on the battlements overlooking King's Bend.

The Knight of the Stag stood beside Crovis Ammerhel, the latter still speaking in heated tones with Silwren and El'rash'lin. Rowen listened a moment and guessed they were trying to figure out how to incorporate magic into the city's defense strategy. With King Pelleas dead, the Knights had assumed command of the city. Ferocles insisted all the murderers had been trapped in the palace and killed. Still, the murderers' grisly work had not included killing just the king, but the queen and their children, too. Nearly the entire royal line had been butchered in their beds. A messenger had been dispatched for Phaegos, summoning the last surviving son of Pelleas, but it would take days for him to arrive.

This left matters in the hands of Aeko and Crovis. Rowen sensed the tension between the two Knights, but for the moment, it seemed they had laid their animosity aside for the sake of duty. Rowen joined them quietly. Aeko cast a quick glance at her new squire and smiled—though so far, his title had been purely ceremonial since Aeko preferred to sharpen her own weapons and polish and don her own armor—then returned her attention to the conversation.

Their first concern was to ascertain how the murderers had breached the city and to prevent it from happening again. El'rash'lin confirmed that a Shel'ai—with the use of magic—might muddy the senses of a couple guards and enter a place undetected, a handful of armed men in tow. But secreting an entire company of swordsmen through either the front or rear gates, past dozens of watching eyes, was impossible.

"Maybe they came through the aqueduct," Rowen offered. The aqueduct was covered to prevent an enemy from poisoning the city's water supply, guarded as well by squads of bowmen along the walls, but perhaps the Shel'ai had secretly breached it.

Crovis glowered at him. "With weapons and armor on their backs? They'd need gills and the strength of oxen."

El'rash'lin grew thoughtful. "Shel'ai can use magic to survive in unfamiliar elements for a time—even underwater. It is also possible to cast such spells on someone else. But the pain would be maddening."

Rowen swore. The famous aqueduct of Lyos fed fountains, wells, and bathhouses all over the city. If what El'rash'lin said was true, it would be impossible to seal or guard them all.

"Can your magic aid us somehow?" Aeko asked.

Silwren shook her head. "It takes too much effort to control the magic. We might do more harm than good."

Crovis faced her. "Do you intend to offer *any* substantial assistance, or shall I dissolve this alliance right here and now?"

El'rash'lin fixed the haughty Knight with a sobering gaze. "When the time comes, we will do what must be done. Rest assured, Lyos will not fall to sorcery. As for swords—you must contend with those yourself."

Crovis fumed for a moment then stalked away, as though to inspect the battlements' defenses.

Aeko bowed to El'rash'lin. The latter had removed his mask upon entering the city. If his disfigurement unsettled her, she did not show it. "Forgive the captain. It wounds his pride to ask for help. I do not think he would have asked at all, were it not for the panic after the king's murder."

El'rash'lin eyed her sadly. He started to answer then stopped, took Silwren's arm, and drew her away.

Aeko said to Rowen, "Crovis does not approve of their plan. And by the Light, I don't either."

"Is this a new plan all of you dreamt up while I was in the privy?"

Aeko smiled faintly. "No, the same one. When the Throng comes, El'rash'lin will go out to meet the Nightmare—alone. Silwren will stay on the walls and use her own magic to help him, to keep him from losing focus somehow. They think they might be able to hold back Fadarah and his Shel'ai, but that's the best we can hope for. We'll have to face Fadarah's warriors on our own."

Rowen thought of Jalist again. He looked westward and shuddered. The Throng spread across the horizon, close enough that he could see individual banners, horsemen, siege towers, and company after company of footmen.

"You've seen more of magic than I ever will," Aeko said. "Do you think those two can do what they promise? Can they destroy the demon?"

Rowen winced. He wanted to tell her that it was not a demon. It had a name. It had been a man, once. His friend. *No, those are El'rash'lin's memories—not mine.*

Aeko took his silence as an answer. Her sharp eyes surveyed the battlements. "The men's spirits have improved, at least."

Banners rippled in the breeze—not just the Lyos falcon and the balancing crane of the Lotus Isles, but the crude symbols of the Dark Quarter, too. The new alliance had filled people with hope. Sunlight flashed off armor as men went about their feverish preparations. Men of the Red Watch labored alongside squires and Isle Knights. Rich citizens of Lyos took up weapons, assuming posts alongside slumdwellers. All, for a moment, were equals. It could not last forever, but would it last even as long as the battle?

He remembered Silwren's words in the Dark Quarter. Perhaps this would be their finest hour after all—though he doubted many of them would live to appreciate it.

CHAPTER TWENTY-SEVEN

THE NIGHTMARE

AEKO ESTIMATED SIX THOUSAND MERCENARIES, all marching under different banners, and four hundred horsemen with spears and shields. She saw the outlines of trebuchets and siege towers, too. These worried her far more than the enemy cavalry, which would have to dismount sooner or later since horses were practically useless in a siege.

Unless their demon tears our walls down. There was no sign of it yet. But here and there at the head of the approaching host, Aeko caught sight of tall, lean figures in bone-white cloaks and hoods. Even from this distance, she could make out the extravagant crimson greatwolves sewn into cloaks and banners. Around these men rode others dressed head to toe in black.

Given the Nightmare's penchant for tearing down walls as though they'd been built from a child's wooden blocks, Aeko had suggested they not array themselves along the battlements, massing instead in the courtyard or even along some makeshift fortification deeper within the city. But Crovis refused, very nearly accusing her of cowardice.

So here we are. Aeko tapped her sword hilt. *Let's hope our new allies can stop the Nightmare before he turns the walls of Lyos to dust... and us with them!*

She turned to Silwren. "Will Fadarah try to parley with us?"

The Shel'ai regarded Aeko with her ghostly, disconcerting eyes. "They never offer truce until after the walls are breached."

"So I hear."

Crovis Ammerhel overheard and faced Silwren. "Keep your word, and the walls will stand." He touched his sword. "Keep it not, and I'll have your head."

El'rash'lin said, "Captain Ammerhel, if we fail, I doubt you will have that pleasure." The stooped sorcerer coughed then straightened. "The magic we wield is the same as the Nightmare's. We survive it only because we do not use it. If we unleash what we must to win this battle, it may kill us."

Crovis said, "Then I shall pray for your souls."

Aeko flinched at her superior's callous tone, but the disfigured sorcerer appeared unfazed. "You would do better to pray for our deaths, Sir Knight. If the magic drives us mad—as it might—then all of Lyos will become a smoldering graveyard."

Aeko saw by Crovis's scowl that the Knight of the Lotus did not believe a word of it. But she met El'rash'lin's gaze herself. Her revulsion melted. Fear and pity swelled inside her. "Perhaps we should attempt to parley first," she suggested. "We could ask for their terms—"

Crovis said, "Isle Knights do not beg for terms. For implying as much, I am within my bounds to accuse you of cowardice in the face of the enemy."

Out of the corner of her eye, Aeko saw Rowen cast her superior a murderous look. The others shifted uncomfortably, especially the Isle Knights. Aeko bowed. "I spoke in haste. Forgive me, Sir Ammerhel." She straightened but kept her eyes low, as she knew she must.

"Indeed," he answered. "Pray there will be time to make amends."

"Thank you," she forced herself to say, her face burning.

For a long time, all eyes stared over the battlements. The Throng drew steadily closer. Unease spread along the walls. The well-disciplined Isle Knights kept their composure. Meanwhile, the rest of the city's defenders struggled to do the same. Lyos had not been besieged for as long as anyone could remember. Now, their king was dead, and an army bolstered by sorcery was drawing close. The men's spirits—which had seemed so strong just hours before—began to erode.

Foreseeing this, Aeko had convinced Crovis to reassign most of the squires among the native defenders of Lyos, to give them courage. Unfortunately, many of these squires were equally untested.

Here and there, men threw down their weapons and ran. *Where do they think they'll hide—the sewers? Inside a well? Where will they hide where the Throng won't find them?*

Captain Ferocles swore. "If you'll excuse me," he grunted. He drew his sword and stalked off, shouting orders. Sergeant Epheus followed.

"Deserters," Crovis Ammerhel muttered with disgust. The Knight of the Lotus said to Silwren, "I am told your kind can speak with their minds. If you wish, you may relay this offer to your former master: tell him I will accept his surrender now, should he wish to give it."

Rowen Locke edged closer to Aeko and whispered, "Is he mad?"

Aeko did not reply. Despite the lingering warmth in her cheeks, she smiled at her captain's bravado.

Silwren said, "I am already speaking with him." Her voice was halting.

Crovis Ammerhel scowled. "What does he say?"

The tears building in Silwren's violet eyes began to flow down her cheeks. The sight of so Human a gesture emanating from the ghostly eyes of a Shel'ai alarmed Aeko.

"He asks—" Silwren's voice broke. She regained her composure and started again. "He asks why we betray him. He asks how we can do this... to our own people."

Crovis Ammerhel drew his sword, the magnificent curved blade sparkling in the afternoon light. "Tell him you have chosen to ally yourself to the Light, to forsake the foulness of your wytchcraft. So, too, could his own sins be forgiven, by the Light's grace."

Silwren did not answer. Instead, she reached out her hand. El'rash'lin took it in his own. He said something in Sylvan. She hesitated then nodded.

The sorcerer turned to face Sir Ammerhel. "Open the gates," he said simply. "I will go out and meet them."

The Knight of the Lotus looked skeptical but gestured to one of the Isle Knights standing nearby. "Open the gates. The sorcerer goes out... *alone*."

El'rash'lin and Silwren embraced. Silwren would not let him go.

Finally, El'rash'lin gently pried himself free. His disfigured face broke into a sad smile. He whispered something into one of Silwren's long, tapered ears, bowed to Rowen, then started down the stairs.

Rowen said, "I'm going with him."

Aeko grabbed his arm. "You're staying right here. That's an order."

Rowen blinked in surprise but obeyed.

El'rash'lin had reached the courtyard now, flanked on all sides by Isle Knights. His body already looked stooped again, as though merely descending the stairs had sapped his strength. How could such a wretched figure be their savior? *Then again, most of what I've seen lately makes no more sense than that.*

The Isle Knights signaled to the gate guards. They reluctantly hefted a stout, eight-foot crossbeam out of the way and pushed open the great oak gates of Lyos. El'rash'lin shuffled out, alone, and started down King's Bend. The gates of Lyos closed behind him.

Far away, beyond the base of Pallantine Hill, Fadarah had dismounted his red-flanked, yellow-eyed bloodmare and stood alone at the head of his host, deep in mindspeak. *"I have spoken with Silwren and El'rash'lin. They will not see reason."*

Shade answered, presumably from the place where Fadarah had sent him—east of the hill, near a break in the soil that led down to a great, underwater sea. *"The fault is mine, General. I sought her out, but I spoke in anger."*

Fadarah said, *"So you did. But she loved you once. If she will not listen now, then the fault can only be her own."* He faced Lyos. The Throng had halted near the base of the hill, still well out of range of archers and siege engines. Neither side sent emissaries.

Fadarah studied the challenge before him. The only way for an army to reach the walls of Lyos was to advance all the way up the winding road to the hilltop, trying all the while to keep their own siege engines from getting mired in mud, meanwhile weathering storms of arrows from the walls.

Azure banners of the Isle Knights fluttered from the parapets. Fadarah realized for the first time that the color of the Knights' banners perfectly matched the color of Sylvan eyes—those who weren't Shel'ai, that is. *All the more reason for them to burn.*

Fadarah focused once more on the slow-moving juggernaut that was the Throng, supervising its endless columns of cavalry and footmen. Shade's slaying of the king and most of his family had weakened the will of Lyos but not broken it, as Fadarah hoped it would. But it made no difference. Fadarah had just given Shade a fresh host to command, which included the majority of the Unseen, plus a handful of Shel'ai. Even if El'rash'lin and Silwren managed to thwart the Nightmare, Shade could finish Lyos himself.

Fadarah asked, *"Are you ready, my son?"*

"We await your command."

"It is given." He broke off from the mindspeak. He trained his eyes on the hill again. A single figure had appeared, shuffling weakly down the long, winding trail toward them. "El'rash'lin, my old friend..."

No, El'rash'lin was his enemy now. The man could have no purpose in mind save to fight the Nightmare, to thwart the strategies he himself had helped invent. But where was Silwren?

Then Fadarah understood. He imagined her on the walls, preparing to use her own magic to bolster El'rash'lin's focus. She would keep him from losing his mind in much the same way the sorcerers of the Throng controlled the Nightmare.

Fadarah closed his eyes. With his mind, he spoke to all the other Shel'ai, telling them to prepare. In a moment, they would rouse the Nightmare. In a moment, they would unleash their full fury upon these plains. Lyos would crumble—as would El'rash'lin. It could be no other way. He knew they understood. Still, Fadarah wept as he gave the order.

"Bring forth my Nightmare..."

Jalist Hewn was standing in the foremost row of pikemen, near the remainder of the Unseen, when the Nightmare was summoned. At once, the Dwarr's blood ran cold. The monstrosity appeared out of nowhere, as though somehow spared the sane laws that governed the world of men.

It plodded through the ranks—a great, dark, smoldering thing, ringed by sorcerers in cloaks and hoods. Unease swept through the army, worse than usual. The men were tired, after all, and scared for their homelands to the west. They were unnerved, too, that so many Unseen had been sent to take the city from within—an unusual tactic for Fadarah.

And now, the Nightmare. Jalist clutched his long-axe until his knuckles turned white. Well over a dozen times had he lived this moment in his dreams, but still his heart filled with such panic that he wondered for a moment if it would wrench itself from his chest.

"Steady, lads!" he called, as much to embolden himself as those around him. "Think of Llassio. If he could die with honor, the least we can do is gawk at this abomination without pissing ourselves!"

The men around him laughed uneasily. But the Dwarr's words had an effect. Men straightened and lifted their eyes, gaining a thin measure of control over their fear.

Besides, all we have to do is watch. No rebellion today. He was glad that most of the men around him were veterans. They knew what to expect. The Nightmare would slough up to the walls, bring them crashing down with a jolt of raw magic that blasted stone into dust, then vanish. The Shel'ai would order the ranks forward. The city, unquestionably conquered, would surrender what remained of its army, and that would be that. *So why do I have such a terrible feeling about this?*

Jalist thought of Llassio, buried just the night before. The Dwarr's strong hands were still blistered from digging the grave. He had dug it alone, refusing all offers of help. *Something tells me you're the lucky one, lad.* Other images flashed through his mind: his one-time home in Stillhammer. Leander, the gentle Dwarr prince.

Jalist clenched his eyes shut for a moment then opened them. He had the awful feeling that he would never see Leander again. He would never go home. He and all the other fools around him were about to die.

"So be it," Jalist muttered to himself.

An autumn breeze stirred his sand-colored hair, his neatly braided beard. He touched the ornately carved handle of his long-axe and fixed his eyes on the scene before him. The city on a hill. He was far from the mountains, he knew, but at least he would die on stone.

Rowen stared as chaos overran the battlements. Everywhere, men of the Red Watch shook with fear. Even the Knights stared, horrified, at what approached them. Men already poised to flee their posts did so now, running for their lives. Rowen realized, dimly, that they were only seeing the Nightmare as Fadarah intended them to see it. An illusion. But that did not help.

For weeks, he had heard about this demon, but nothing had prepared him for this. Not a man but a beast—huge, awful, burning. Smoke leaked from gaps in its scales. Its hooves left smoldering footprints.

Rowen looked away. He forgot everything: El'rash'lin, Aeko Shingawa, the city behind him, even his own name. A mad darkness flooded his brain. He closed his eyes and waited to die.

Then, slowly, the darkness faded. A strange light filled his mind—faint at first, then stronger. Rowen did not know at first where it came from, but then a face formed in the light—a face both strange and familiar. A man with ghostly, violet eyes. Young, gentle, sad. Rowen felt as though he was in the Wytchforest again, staring down at his own reflection. *No. It's El'rash'lin...*

Rowen opened his eyes. The squire blinked in surprise. Before him lay King's Bend, El'rash'lin, the army. And there was the demon—except that in place of a towering, scaled monstrosity, stood a man—cloaked and hooded, hideously twisted and deformed like El'rash'lin, but just a man.

"We have dispelled the illusion," Silwren whispered.

Along the battlements, panic slacked, replaced by puzzlement. Rowen trained his eyes on El'rash'lin now. The stooped figure halted on King's Bend, halfway between the city and the army below. He stretched, slowly, to his full height. He waited. Iventine—crazed—rushed up to meet him. The men grappled, wytchfire gushing from their fingertips.

Men watched from the plain and the battlements of Lyos alike as the ravaged sorcerers fought. Flames crackled in bruise-colored tendrils, alive and strong despite the frailty of the men who conjured them. Rowen watched, helpless. Then he looked to Silwren for help. But her eyes were closed now, deep in concentration. A violet glow enveloped her body. Everyone but Rowen drew away from her in fear.

She must be lending her strength to El'rash'lin. He wished he could do the same.

"Silwren, I'm here," he whispered. He did not know if she could hear him.

Jalist Hewn stared. There, on the slopes of Pallantine Hill, the whole world seemed to have gone mad. The Nightmare that had plagued his dreams had disappeared. In its place stood a misshapen sorcerer of awful power. He was battling another Shel'ai—an equally disfigured man Jalist did not recognize.

"I think I've lost my mind!" someone muttered.

"Lost mine first," Jalist said. He wondered why the Shel'ai of the Throng were just standing there. Why didn't they rush to the defense of their demon? Why weren't they ordering the Throng forward?

Jalist fixed his eyes on the nearest sorcerer. The man's hood had fallen, revealing a face wracked by fierce concentration. Beads of sweat formed on his brow, his eyes clenched shut.

Jalist spotted a second Shel'ai not far from the first, flanked by a protective ring of Unseen. This sorcerer's hood was still raised, but Jalist saw the man jerk, as though his whole body had gone so tense that it spasmed. Then he understood.

Brahasti was right. If they break their concentration, they'll lose control of the Nightmare. Jalist's mind raced. Shade and ten other sorcerers had already gone to slip into the city, taking the bulk of the Unseen with them. Something had already happened to the Nightmare, weakening it. All the Shel'ai left among the Throng were occupied, including Fadarah.

To the hells with Brahasti. It's time! Jalist hefted his long-axe, thrusting the steely blade into the yellow glare of the afternoon sun. With all his strength, he shouted, "Now, lads! For Quorim! For Cassica! For Syros! For all you've lost and all we've yet to lose...*fight!*"

He charged. The Dwarr feared no one would respond, that he would die alone like the fool he was. Then he heard a great, furious shout as the army came to life. Some threw down their weapons and ran. Within moments, whole companies were deserting. But others echoed Jalist's cry then surged forward, weapons glinting. No longer was their target the people of Lyos, but their Shel'ai captors.

Blank faced, the remaining Unseen braced to stop them. Jalist had expected this. The awful Blood Thrall forced the Unseen to defend their masters from attack—even though they hated them more than anyone. *Don't worry, lads. Our blades will set you free.*

He faced the nearest shadowy fighter. They traded swings, then Jalist ducked beneath a shortsword and came up fast, swinging his long-axe in a vicious, sweeping cut. His Unseen opponent staggered and fell, throat open, eyes wide with gratitude.

Jalist leapt over him and chose another opponent. When his long-axe stuck in a man's shield, he drew his broad-bladed shortsword instead. He finished off this opponent then paused a moment to take stock of the situation.

The Throng roiled now, in full revolt. Most of the men had fled westward, deserting back toward their homes, but hundreds remained, hot for revenge. They charged the Unseen, hoping to cut their way through and hack the Shel'ai to pieces. Then, a terrible flash of wytchfire lanced through the ranks, burning pikemen like candlewicks.

Jalist cursed. They were too slow. The revolt had broken the sorcerers' concentration, all right. Only now, the Shel'ai were turning their magic on the mutineers!

Violet flame billowed over Jalist's head, followed by more screams as the fitful magic slew anyone who happened to find themselves in its path. Jalist spotted the sorcerer just a few yards away, guarded now by just a single Unseen warrior.

Jalist wrenched his long-axe free, lowered his head, and charged. The Unseen warrior spotted him and braced. But Jalist was not in the mood to duel. He threw his broad-bladed shortsword, and the Unseen toppled, eyes brimming with that same awful gratitude. The Dwarr leaped over the body, returning both hands to his long-axe.

The cloaked Shel'ai twisted toward the sound, unleashing a second storm of wytchfire. But he was not expecting someone of Jalist's short stature. The Dwarr ducked well beneath the flames and swung. The sorcerer crumpled.

"Not so powerful now, are you!" Jalist swung his axe twice more. Then he looked about, searching for another enemy. Other Shel'ai battled in the distance, refusing to die quietly, wytchfire streaming from their fingertips. But all were far away now. He was tempted to yank back the hood and see the face of the one he had just killed.

What if it's Que'ann? Shaking his head, he straightened, chose the nearest enemy, and charged, howling like a madman.

CHAPTER TWENTY-EIGHT
TURNING TIDES

IGH ATOP THE BATTLEMENTS OF Lyos, standing next to Silwren, Rowen Locke watched in disbelief as the Throng turned on itself. Hundreds of men fled westward while others surged toward the hill, battling the Shel'ai and their dark-garbed bodyguards. Screams and the din of battle filled the air. Rowen spotted who he thought must be Fadarah himself: a huge man, big as an Olg, dressed head to toe in black armor. He stood at the head of his great host. One hand carried a great sword while the other crackled with wytchfire. Then he lost sight of him in the swirling chaos of battle.

Meanwhile, El'rash'lin and the Nightmare continued their mad battle on King's Bend. Wytchfire flew from their hands, their bodies bathed so brightly in magic now that men turned away, blinded. Though there were no houses on King's Bend, abandoned carts and vendors' tables went up like dry kindling.

Rowen shouted to Aeko, "We have to get down there and help him!"

"And how, Squire, do you suggest we do that? We'd be burned alive once we got close."

Rowen was tempted to grab a longbow, but the Nightmare would be a hard shot even standing still. Besides, the battling sorcerers blazed so fiercely now that he could no longer tell who was who. Nor, he realized, could they ride out to join those rebelling against Fadarah since the two Dragonkin were battling in the middle of King's Bend.

Silwren remained deep in her trance, her face strained with exhaustion.

Frantic, Rowen looked toward King's Bend again. The blazing Dragonkin continued to grapple, awash with fire and light, but he could not tell how the battle was faring. Then, an awful cry split the air as one of the blazing figures toppled, his body smoking. The other reeled over him and stumbled but did not fall. At the same time, Silwren whimpered and slumped toward the battlements. Rowen caught her as she started to fall over the edge and lowered her to the ground.

"What do you see?" he asked Aeko.

The Knight of the Stag peered over the walls, speechless. A moment later, she started to answer, but a new cry drowned her out. Sword clashes and screams. *That's not coming from below...*

Sir Crovis Ammerhel drew his sword. "They attack the city from within!"

Aeko grabbed her captain's arm. "Your place is on the walls. Let me go."

Crovis glared at her. Then he nodded. "Take thirty Knights with you."

"Captain—"

"I'll send more if you need them," Crovis promised. "But I must wait to see what happens below before I weaken the front defenses."

Aeko gestured for Rowen to follow and started for the stairs. Rowen hesitated, glancing down at Silwren, still anxious to learn El'rash'lin's fate.

"Go, Squire," Crovis said. "Your wytch is safe with me. I swear it on my honor."

That will have to do. Rowen rose and hurried after Aeko, Knightswrath in hand.

Further into Lyos, the Knights discovered a nightmare of a different kind. Enemies had sprung as though from nowhere. Shel'ai in damp bone-white cloaks stalked the cobblestone streets, burning all in their path. Already, lines of houses blazed. Mothers clutching their children ran for their lives. Flames wreathed Queen's Garden.

"We need *all* the men here, now!" Aeko seethed. He imagined what had happened: the enemy had come through the aqueduct again since Aeko did not have enough men to guard all the wells. Some had probably already killed the Red Watch guarding the rear gates and opened them. Lyos was being attacked on two sides. "We need Silwren!"

Unseen swept up the streets, dozens strong, mad for blood. She shuddered, thinking of the temples they must have already ravaged. Ahead lay yet another temple—this one devoted to Tier'Gothma. It was filled, she knew, with refugees from the Dark Quarter—those too young or infirm to fight.

Aeko ordered Rowen back to the walls. "Tell Crovis to send *all* the Knights at once—plus whatever else he can spare. And bring Silwren if she's still alive. Archers, if she isn't." Rowen hesitated. Aeko shoved him. "Go!" This time, Rowen obeyed.

The Unseen had slowed at the sight of the Isle Knights. The two forces faced each other. Aeko raised her sword and saluted, momentarily holding the crosspiece of her adamune at nose level, the edge perfectly vertical between her eyes. To her surprise, many of the Unseen returned the gesture in the same Shao style.

She had no more time to ponder this before they charged.

Rowen found the walls all but abandoned. Silwren lay slumped in the distance, just where he'd left her. A handful of Red Watch and armed slumdwellers milled about, uncertain.

Where in Jinn's name did Crovis go?

Rowen sprinted up to the battlements where Silwren lay and looked out over the twisting road below. He saw no sign of El'rash'lin or the Nightmare. But Crovis Ammerhel galloped down King's Bend at the head of his Knights, charging the remains of the Throng. "Gods, what's he doing? We have to clear the city first!"

Captain Ferocles and Sergeant Epheus shouted in the courtyard below. He guessed they were trying to take command of the soldiers left behind. Rowen called to the slumdwellers nearby, ordering them to go and help. Then he turned his attention back to Silwren. He shook her. "Silwren, we need you!"

She opened her eyes. "El'rash'lin. Dead..."

Rowen blanched. Grief swelled within him—grief over the death of a violet-eyed boy—but he fought it back. "They're inside the city. Do you understand? They're burning the temples where the refugees are hiding. They're killing everyone we saved!"

Silwren blinked, as though waking from a dream. She stood on her own. Something terrible kindled in her eyes. She said, "Take me there."

Jalist Hewn awoke from his blood-daze to see the gates of Lyos swinging open, just a few hundred feet up the road. Armored Knights in azure tabards streamed out, row upon row of red-garbed soldiers trailing behind. He frowned. "What in Fohl's hells?"

Just ahead, the last of the Unseen were fighting a pitched battle against the rebelling Throng, trying to hold off the latter long enough for Fadarah and the remaining Shel'ai to get away. Jalist had intended to do everything in his power to stop this. But the sight of armed men thundering down King's Bend brought him back to his senses. The Isle Knights did not mean to join them. Instead, they meant to attack the Throng. "Gods-damned fools!"

They could not run. The Knights could easily ride them down, their spears and curved swords hacking them to ribbons. He looked around, wishing for the first time that Brahasti were here, but the sadistic Dhargot was nowhere to be seen. Men turned to him, looking for guidance. He grimaced. Only one choice remained.

"Well, lads, let's hope there's some truth behind those stories of Islemen's honor." He threw down his long-axe. The men hesitated, exchanging glances, then followed suit. One by one, they cast down their weapons.

The charging Knights slowed. Jalist raised his open hands in a sign of surrender. He spotted the Knights' captain—a proud man in a brilliant steel helm—and approached him. The Knight's destrier reared, hooves flailing over the Dwarr's head. Jalist was glad, once again, for not being taller.

The Knight removed his helm, revealing a coldly handsome, olive-skinned young man. "Do you surrender?"

Jalist glowered up at him. "No, we threw down our weapons for exercise. Want to see us pick them up again?" He fought the impulse to drag the Knight from his horse. "We were *rebelling*, you dunce!"

The Knight-Captain stared back, unfazed. "You knowingly took up arms against a protectorate of the Lotus Isles. Consider yourselves prisoners."

"Call us what you like," Jalist spat back. "Just gut those damn Shel'ai before they get away!"

The Knight-Captain smirked. "Oh, I'm sure I can find something for my sword to do." He waved to the rest of the Isle Knights. "Gather their weapons! Search them carefully. Kill any who resist."

Screams and smoke ruled the air. The people of Lyos fled the heart of their own city as the Unseen swept up the streets, running to the walls instead. They sought the protection of the Isle Knights and the Red Watch—only to find the crenellated battlements all but deserted.

Rowen ran in the direction of the fighting, pulling Silwren after him. His stomach lurched as he dodged the bodies strewn about the grand cobblestone streets and marble walkways. They reached the Queen's Garden and slowed.

Ahead of them, at least a dozen dead Knights filled the streets. Heaped all around them were the slain bodies of their foes: men in black armor sewn with crimson greatwolves.

"Aeko..." Rowen ran forward, searching the grisly battlefield for any sign of the commander. But Aeko Shingawa was not among the dead. Silwren touched his arm. She pointed.

In the distance, three Unseen milled in the shadow and smoke of the burning garden. With them stood a Shel'ai in a bone-white cloak. Rowen bristled. He reached for Knightswrath, but Silwren locked her thin hand on his arm, stopping him. Her violet eyes flashed with murder.

"Rowen, get behind me."

Such was her tone that he obeyed. In the distance, the Shel'ai stared at them with open derision. The man spat something in Sylvan. Silwren answered by summoning wytchfire, letting it course the length of her arms, crackling at her fingertips.

The opposing sorcerer flung wytchfire of his own. Rowen recoiled, but Silwren waved, and the sorcerer's wytchfire melted into thin air. Then, she unleashed hers. It washed over everything, pouring from her body until she howled with rage and pain.

Blinded, Rowen drew away from her. When at last she lowered her hands, wytchfire fading from her body, the sorcerer and the dark-garbed warriors had been replaced by ashes that mingled with the cinders of the burning garden.

"There are more," Silwren said. "We must kill them all."

CHAPTER TWENTY-NINE
THE KNIGHT OF THE CRANE

I N LYOS, THE FIGHTING CONTINUED street to street, temple to temple, house to house. Shade, ten Shel'ai, and a hundred Unseen were already deep inside the city. Shade had counted on fighting armed men, not defenseless women and children. But Fadarah's orders were clear: Lyos had to be utterly destroyed. Showing mercy now would only hamper their campaign later.

Fadarah had already warned him of the revolt outside the city. Shade's head spun from the realization that their plans had been unraveled, all due to Silwren and El'rash'lin. Because of them, innocent people were dying.

"Not my fault." Shade unleashed wytchfire, scouring one house after another, wincing from the smell of scorched wood and burned flesh.

Desperately, he had tried to mindspeak with his wife before the fighting began. She refused to answer. They had shared so much, surviving together, and she would not even acknowledge him.

Hurt melted into bitterness. Bitterness became rage. Rage turned to murder.

Shade scattered the Unseen now, issuing their final order: kill and kill until they themselves were cut down. They accepted the order with relish, knowing that release from the Blood Thrall was finally at hand. But he kept Lethe close by. The Unseen wept openly—but killed and killed, as he was ordered.

Not my fault.

Aeko Shingawa led the fight. Blood speckled her olive skin. Gore ran from her adamune. During a brief lull in the fighting, she looked up and noted that smoke choked the sky. A quarter of Lyos was burning now. But at least the invaders did not go unchallenged.

In the distance, a squad of archers took up neat positions at the end of a street and provided cover for fleeing people, raining wave after wave of death on advancing Unseen. Earlier, slumdwellers had banded together and actually managed to kill a Shel'ai by flinging pikes, rocks, and daggers.

But it's not enough...

Aeko had already arrived too late to prevent a squad of Unseen from sweeping through a temple of Maelmohr and murdering everyone inside. But when the Unseen emerged—some weeping, others smug with bloodlust—they'd met the swords of Aeko, her Knights, and a squad of Red Watch commanded by Captain Ferocles. The fighting was brief but furious. By the time it was over, Aeko had lost three Knights. Half the Red Watch had been slain—as had Captain Ferocles himself.

Now, Aeko tightened her gauntlets. In the distance, she spotted a party of Shel'ai and Unseen heading toward a refugee-filled temple of Tier'Gothma. Blocking them were Fen-Shea and his Bloody Asps. Aeko led her Knights to reinforce them.

Steel rang. Wytchfire blazed over stone. Men fell, dying. Fen-Shea's great mace shattered in his grasp. He would have died, but the Isle Knights arrived in time. They raced across a marble walkway and flanked the enemy. One Shel'ai fell, then another—each taking Knights and gang members with him. Then Aeko slipped forward, raised her sword in *hoso no-kami*, and cut a third Shel'ai nearly in half.

The last sorcerer unleashed a fearful gush of wytchfire at her. Aeko pitched forward, trying to dodge. The devilish flames singed her armor. The Shel'ai prepared another strike then stiffened, one of Fen-Shea's knives in his back.

Aeko nodded her thanks. The grim-faced leader of the Bloody Asps answered with a wink. She stopped to catch her breath, glancing at the body-strewn walkway. Why weren't more Isle Knights arriving to help? Then she guessed.

By the Light, Crovis will pay for this!

Sergeant Epheus stood nearby, flanked by a handful of Red Watch, all fighting to catch their breath. She waved. Then she led her remaining few Knights, plus Fen-Shea and the last of the Bloody Asps, back into the fray.

Lethe lifted his shortsword. "Here they come again." He spoke the warning only because he had been ordered to. He stood with Shade in a street near the rear gate.

The guards there had already tried three times to reach Shade. Each time, he drove them back. His master could have broken past them and made it out of the city, but Shade was not finished yet. He wanted to toy with them. A fey smile shone on the Shel'ai's lips.

Lethe watched the men of the Red Watch gather in the distance, nine strong, armed with pikes and shields. They had started out with twenty.

The game reminded Lethe of a cat tormenting a dying mouse. "Enough of this! Finish them, and let's be gone from here."

Shade ignored him. Focusing on the soldiers instead, Shade feigned exhaustion. The soldiers advanced slowly, shields locked, then quickened their pace when they saw the sorcerer leaning wearily against the wall of an abandoned cottage, not a single wisp of fire curling from his wrists. Lethe glanced at the soldiers with pity. He wanted to warn them, but a stranger's life was not worth the torments of the Blood Thrall.

Shade waited.

When the men were almost upon him, he straightened to full height and lifted his hands. Wytchfire blazed to life. The men screamed as Shade's magic washed over them, burning through shields and armor alike. In his fury, Shade burned the bodies, too. He left nothing but ash.

Lethe spat at Shade's feet. "Are you sated, or should I find you something else to kill? Perhaps there's an orphanage somewhere nearby."

Shade winced. The rage in the sorcerer's eyes melted into hurt. Lethe wondered if he'd somehow gotten through to him. Then he followed his master's gaze and saw a woman step into the street. Hair like quicksilver fell past her slender shoulders. Her grimace might have been chiseled from stone. Wytchfire crackled and writhed at her fingertips.

Shade said, "Hello, my love," and unleashed a torrent of flame in her direction.

Lethe lost sight of the woman for a moment. Then the fire cleared. She stood unharmed. A new figure joined her: a man in a tattered brigandine, holding a curved sword wet with blood. *Rowen...*

The woman said, "Kith'el, this must end."

Shade said, "On that, at least, we agree." He threw more fire at her. This time, the woman waved her hands, and the fire changed direction as though swatted away, burning the stone face of a temple statue instead. Cinders sailed like dying stars through her hair but left her unharmed.

"El'rash'lin is dead," the woman said. "That should mean something to you."

"*Many* have died. Many more will." Shade unleashed another gush of fire.

The woman lifted her hands and absorbed it into her palms. That time, she flinched with pain. "How many have we buried and burned already? This must stop."

Shade sneered. "Too many to count. Too many to mourn." He drove at her again, hurtling wytchfire at her face and heart.

She waved it away, stumbling as she did so. Rowen moved to catch her, but she pushed him back, trying to keep him behind her. "There are never... too many to mourn," she answered weakly.

Shade laughed. "But I am weary of mourning, my love!" His voice rang with mockery. "I know you could kill me. But you won't. Shall I repay your mercy in kind?" He turned to Lethe. "Kill the Human. But first, take your mask off."

Lethe's eyes widened. "Please..."

Shade repeated the order.

The Unseen started forward, his body no longer his own to control. Sword in one hand, he used the other to tug the black cloth from his face and drop it onto the bloody street.

Rowen watched Silwren's eyes widen. She whispered, "Kith'el, no..."

Shade answered with fire. Silwren met it with fire of her own. Rowen wanted to help her, but this was her fight. He fixed his gaze on the dark-garbed fighter instead.

Given the man's armor and the way he moved, he must have been the same man he'd battled in the jailhouse. The same man who could have killed him but hadn't. There would be no quarter.

"*Singchai ushó fey...*" He only whispered it. Then, hefting Knightswrath, he ran to meet his attacker. He stopped halfway.

Dimly, he smelled Lyos burning around them, heard the din of fighting as the Knights and the Red Watch sought out the remaining Unseen. But more than anything, he saw the face of his enemy—this time, unmasked.

Green eyes, auburn hair. A face knife-scarred on one cheek in the act of saving Rowen from a would-be child raper, years and years ago. "Kayden..."

CHAPTER THIRTY

MERCY

THEY MET WHERE THE STREET widened to accommodate a well. Dead men littered the ground. There, only days before, the living had idly quenched their thirst after labor. Mothers had drawn water to bathe their children.

Rowen shook his head. "Gods, this cannot be..." Knightswrath dipped before him.

Kayden did not slow. He passed the abandoned well, his shadow rippling over broken stone and spilled blood. "Lift that sword, little brother. Or I'll kill you where you stand!" The former Knight's eyes broiled with despair.

Rowen backed up. "Kayden, wait! Tell me—"

Kayden swung his shortsword. Rowen blocked but did not swing back. Instead, he retreated down the burning street, further from where Silwren and Shade battled in the distance. Kayden followed. He lunged at Rowen's throat.

Rowen parried and circled, trying to keep his opponent at bay. "Kayden!"

The former Knight's eyes welled with tears. "They bewytched me. My choice, though. I should have picked death. I didn't. I was scared. My fault. Ask Silwren when it's done. She'll explain." He swung. "No choice now. You must"—he lunged—"kill me!"

Rowen parried and sidestepped. He glimpsed an opening for his brother's neck but did not take it.

"I can't fight it again. Kill me, or I'll kill you!" Kayden drew a second shortsword with his free hand. Steel sparked and clattered in the burning street. Kayden drove Rowen toward a wall, twice nearly killing him, never once hesitating. Rowen pleaded, certain this must all be a dream. A nightmare. Then, one of Kayden's shortswords slashed his arm. Pain and blood brought him back to his senses.

"What must I do?" Rowen cried.

Kayden faced him, anguished. "Set me free..."

Rowen blanched. Then, slowly, he nodded. He thought back to all the battles they'd fought together, the countless times they'd sparred. Kayden was better now, but Rowen still knew his brother's style, his weaknesses. He raised Knightswrath overhead. Fire glinted off its ancient blade. They met.

Again and again, swords clattered. The men fought with dreadful calmness now.

Kayden charged. His shortswords flashed. But he held one too low, the other too high. Knightswrath sang a deadly arc. Kayden stiffened. He made no move to staunch the blood swelling from his throat. Instead, he dropped his shortswords with a heavy clatter and started to fall. Rowen threw down his own sword and caught him. "Kayden..."

Rowen stumbled from his brother's weight but managed to keep his head cradled as he knelt. Kayden opened his mouth to answer but instead coughed on his own blood. Then he died, his eyes overflowing with gratitude.

Night darkened the Simurgh Plains for the first time since the Battle of Lyos. There, miles from the city, Fadarah held the lean, cowering figure of Brahasti el Tarq by the scruff of his cloak and shook him. Dirt and blood smudged the Dhargot's face. His extravagant robes hung in tatters. Fadarah flashed back to the sickening sight of Brahasti brutalizing the whore in his tent.

The Dhargot knew better than to resist. Even without magic, the half-Olg could rip him limb from limb. Fadarah glared down with blazing violet eyes, his tattooed face contorted in rage. Still holding the Dhargot with one gauntleted fist, Fadarah splayed the fingers of his other hand before Brahasti's face. Violet flames crackled to life at his fingertips.

Brahasti's face went pale. "General, please…"

Fadarah hoisted the man off the ground and tossed him like a child's toy. Fadarah did not have to look at the faces of the other Shel'ai to know they disapproved—but only because they wanted Brahasti dead. He could not blame them. Fadarah narrowed his eyes, flames still sparking from his fingertips. "Speak."

For once, Brahasti's expression conveyed no arrogance. "Forgive me, General. It wasn't my fault. That Dwarr man-lover, Jalist. *He* signaled the revolt!"

Fadarah took a menacing step toward the Dhargot as the latter struggled to rise. "Am I to believe that they revolted, even after you ordered otherwise?"

Brahasti nodded quickly. "I swear it!"

"And you did all you could to stop them?"

"Yes, General!"

Fadarah countered, "Then why are you still alive?"

Brahasti hesitated, visibly unsure how to answer. One of the Shel'ai standing behind Fadarah moved quietly to the towering sorcerer's side. She threw back her hood, the light of Armahg's Eye shining through her short, flaxen hair. "Let me kill him, General." She lifted one delicate wrist, her hand awash in flames.

"No, Avesha."

"General, this man betrayed you! He cost the lives of twenty-three Shel'ai!"

"You can read his mind as well as I can. There was no profit in betraying us." Fadarah remembered Brahasti's chests of gold coins, the wealth the man had pilfered from the conquered cities of the Simurgh Plains. All of that had been left in his tent when the Throng disbanded. Once again, Brahasti was penniless. That, at least, was a pleasing thought.

Brahasti nodded emphatically. "General, I sought you out myself! When the revolt began, I could have joined them or fled—"

"I would have found you," Fadarah interrupted. "There is no place in the world where you can hide from me." Even as he spoke, Fadarah thought that Avesha was right: he should kill him. But he had other tasks for which Brahasti might still be of use. "Go."

Brahasti bowed. "Thank you, General." He tried to look dignified as he hurried into the nearest tent.

"Keep an eye on him," Fadarah said to Avesha. "If he strays from the camp, burn one of his ears off."

Avesha nodded. "Yes, General."

Fadarah pushed the Dhargot from his mind and turned to survey the remainder of his once-great host. The mighty Throng was no more. Less than a dozen Unseen remained, faces as grim and murderous as ever, for they knew how close they had been to release. But that did not trouble him.

Fadarah thought of old friends not among those assembled, brave men and women he himself had rescued after they were driven from the Wytchforest: Que'ann with her gentleness, Aerios with his quick wit, Cierrath with his tireless, unflappable loyalty. He realized with a chill that he would never see them again. They were lost, at best cast back into the Light.

He thought of Namundvar's Well, of the magic they had leeched. The abomination of the Nightmare. So much death. *What must the Light think of us now?*

Fadarah moved away from the others, to the edge of their makeshift camp, and began to strip off his heavy plate armor. His servants had all either fled or been killed, so he stripped off his armor himself, casting it piece by piece onto the darkened plains. He flexed his great muscles, trying to fight off the awful numbness he felt. *No. I must not give in. So much has already been gained.*

Someone approached and knelt before him.

"You need not worry, Kith'el. I am alive and unhurt." Fadarah added, "Though I am surprised to see that Silwren let *you* live."

Shade flinched. "As am I, General."

"Did you encounter resistance on the plains?"

"No. The Isle Knights follow the false trail left by Avesha's magic."

"And Silwren?"

Shade did not answer.

"She let you live for a reason," Fadarah guessed.

"Yes, General. We fought. I was... not myself. I felt crazed... almost like I had when I was young and—"

"That would explain your disobedience," Fadarah cut in. "When

328

the Throng revolted, I ordered you to abandon Lyos. You stayed. Your anger cost ten Shel'ai their lives."

Grief choked Shade's voice as he said, "I know, General." Shade paused. "I submit myself to your judgment. If you wish me dead—"

"Oh, I think you will punish yourself far more harshly than any of us ever could," Fadarah said. "And Silwren's message?"

Shade blinked. "She said the next time she saw you, she'd burn you to cinders."

"I trust she meant that threat for you, too?"

Shade lowered his head, still kneeling, and stared at the dark earth.

"Yet she let us live. Silwren could have killed us, but she didn't. There may yet be hope for her." He sighed. "I sense there is more you wish to tell me."

"I must ask... forgiveness for yet another transgression, General. This may be the worst of all." Shade paused, trembling with shame. "I first saw it in the jailhouse at Lyos, but in my fury, I didn't recognize it. Then I saw it again on the streets when I fought Silwren. I don't know how she found it, but—"

Fadarah's eyes narrowed. "What did you see?"

"The Sword of Fâyu Jinn. The last we heard, it had vanished from Sylvos. We searched everywhere but..." Shade hesitated. "General, they have it."

For a long time, an ominous silence hung about the Sorcerer-General like a dreadful shawl. "I trust its full might remains unkindled, or else we would not be here."

"But if Silwren should—"

"She won't. She knows the price. No matter what side she has chosen, *that* will always be beyond her." He paused. "Though if she knows, surely El'rash'lin did, too. Strange that neither of them took action. Perhaps we overestimated their resolve... and their courage."

Shade opened his mouth to reply, but Fadarah dismissed him with a wave. The Sorcerer-General stood alone for a while, contemplating Shade's words. Then he heard heavy footsteps as someone else approached. He stifled his irritation at the interruption, but then his eyes widened.

Fadarah made no effort to summon wytchfire, knowing a lone Human posed no threat. Instead, he scrutinized the man as he emerged from the shadows: tall and burly, dressed in midnight-blue silk, dark skinned like a Soroccan. "You are either the most foolish or the most unlucky Human who ever lived."

"That's hardly an appealing set of choices," the man said. He wore a scimitar at his side but made no effort to draw it. He did not appear surprised or even troubled by the sight of Fadarah.

Fadarah considered using magic to wrench the man's true intentions from his mind, but he guessed them easily enough. "You have come to kill me."

"So much for the element of surprise."

Fadarah said, "You never had a chance, anyway." Out of the corner of his eye, he saw several Shel'ai drawing near, alerted by the sound of voices. He used mindspeak to order them to stand back. "Tell me your name."

"Hráthbam Nassir Adjrâ-al-Habas." The Soroccan answered with a slight bow.

"And the reason a lone Soroccan is wandering the plains in search of a man who could kill him with a touch?"

"Repayment," Hráthbam answered. "We Soroccans honor our debts."

"And to whom are you indebted?"

"A man you used to know," Hráthbam answered. "A good man. His name was El'rash'lin."

For the first time in years, words eluded Fadarah.

"I met him on the plains," Hráthbam continued. "He saved my life. Only it turns out that magic is a funny thing. In saving me, he created some kind of bond between us. I don't know if that was his intention... but he did it nonetheless. I tried for weeks to deny it. I even tried to go home." He laughed. "We Soroccans have a saying about trying to outrun your own shadow." His gaze hardened. "El'rash'lin is dead."

"So he is." Fadarah was glad the darkness hid the spark of grief in his eyes. "I take it you came to avenge him?"

"Life is a matter of choices. There were others I hoped to place before that one."

"How did you find me?"

Hráthbam surveyed their dark surroundings, especially a dense copse of trees in the distance. "This is where you met El'rash'lin for the first time. Some of his memories are mine now—no matter how I try to ignore them. Something told me you'd be here. Maybe it was luck. Maybe it was the gods. Either way, I came here to do what El'rash'lin would have done."

"El'rash'lin would have killed me?"

"If he had to. But first, he would have embraced you as a friend, as a man he thought of as a father. He would have talked to you. He would have tried to make you see reason."

Fadarah scrutinized the Soroccan again, studying the man's dark, stoic expression. "You have courage, Human, but this argument is older than you are."

"Of course. But a debt is a debt. I had to try." Then Hráthbam blurred into motion. Instead of bothering with the heavy scimitar, one hand drew a little knife from his sleeve and flung it at Fadarah's throat.

The Sorcerer-General caught the knife in his fist. His other hand lifted. Wytchfire crackled at his fingertips, but he did not unleash it.

Other Shel'ai raced toward them, but Fadarah ordered them back again. His gaze narrowed. The Human stared back, unafraid, not even trying to run.

Fadarah chuckled. "A fine effort, Human." Fadarah tossed the knife at Hráthbam's feet. His half-Olg skin, tough as leather, barely bled. "Go."

The Soroccan hesitated a moment. He stooped, picked up the little knife and tucked it back into his sleeve. Then he turned and disappeared back into the night.

The other Shel'ai hurried to Fadarah's side. Avesha glared after the Soroccan with murder in her eyes. "General—"

"Courage is courage," Fadarah said. "Let him go."

Avesha started to argue, but Shade touched her arm. The Shel'ai withdrew, leaving Fadarah to his thoughts.

The last of the Unseen formed a perimeter around the camp. The men looked more ragged than ever, nearly bestial. All hope for a quick death had been lost. They had accepted their fate, a curse from which they would never be freed.

Hours passed. The cloudy sky had cleared, letting starwash light the empty plains. At last, the rest of the Shel'ai had gone to sleep, surrendering themselves to dreams plagued by anguish. Fadarah, still wide awake, crept into the tent of the Nightmare.

He waved his hand, and a sphere of violet light formed out of thin air, hovering. Fadarah studied him—the demon who had single-handedly conquered most of the Simurgh Plains, now just a gaunt, twisted, naked figure decaying from the inside out. He refused the impulse to look away. "Forgive me, my friend..."

Doubly ravaged from extensive use of Dragonkin magic and the battle against El'rash'lin, Iventine's body was more disfigured than ever, covered in sores, his chest unnaturally concave, limbs unnaturally twisted as though the bones had left the womb malformed. Neither time nor magic would heal him. What little remained in the man's facial features that had been recognizable was gone, like his personality, never to return. Even in his deep sleep, Iventine twitched with madness and pain.

El'rash'lin's torments weren't much better. But at least El'rash'lin was free. Overwhelmed by Iventine on the road outside Lyos, El'rash'lin had been burned and burned until not even ashes remained. The wild expenditure of so much magic had left Iventine comatose, weak as a child, so that Avesha and a pair of Unseen bodyguards had had to carry him away.

Still, Iventine won. Again. But with each victory, Iventine only lost more and more of himself. Fadarah sighed with pity. He had no more tears left in him tonight. But he had, at least, this simple mercy.

He laid one great, tattooed hand on Iventine's chest and felt a faint, haphazard heartbeat. "Sleep, Iventine. It's done. Others will finish what we have started."

Fadarah closed his eyes. For several long moments, he imagined Iventine's heart beating nakedly against his palm, flouncing like a bloody fish. Then, slowly, Fadarah tightened his hand into a fist. He squeezed. The beating slowed, slowed, stopped.

Fadarah took a deep breath, held it, then let it go. Almost as an afterthought, he extended his consciousness until he felt the heartbeats of all the remaining Unseen warriors outside. To these, too, he granted release.

The tent was silent now. He opened his eyes. The stillness frightened him, but he waved his hand, dismissing the violet light. A chill swept through the open flap of the tent. Fadarah walked out into the night. He hoped Iventine's face bore, at long last, a look of peace. But he refused to turn and see for himself.

CHAPTER THIRTY-ONE

"BY THE LIGHT'S GRACE..."

THE PEOPLE OF LYOS BURIED their dead in the funeral fields east of Pallantine Hill. Rowen, harkening back to his younger employment as a gravedigger, toiled with them to bury the horrors along with all that raw hurt. Soldiers, slumdwellers, and nobles were laid side by side beneath the fresh-turned earth. Captain Ferocles lay among them, buried without eulogy by the grief-stricken survivors of his company. Epheus commanded now, though his appointment as the new Captain of the Red Watch brought little cause for celebration.

A pall hung over the city of Lyos. Prince Typherius, the only member of the royal family left alive, had already committed the bodies of King Pelleas, the queen, and the rest of his family to the grim vaults beneath the palace.

He was not alone in his grief. No one in Lyos or the Dark Quarter had escaped the bitter tang of loss. Nearly all of the Bloody Asps had been killed. Other gangs had sustained heavy losses, too, trying to purge the Shel'ai and the rampaging Unseen from the city. A quarter of Lyos had been burned—temples, gardens, and homes alike. Two thousand lay dead.

But the city still stood. The banner of the falcon flew proudly from the parapets as the ravaged streets were cleared. Soon, inns that had once been filled only with weeping and fearful whispers echoed with merriment. Men told stories of Aeko Shingawa, the valiant Knight of the Stag who had fought to save Lyos from ruin. They told stories of

El'rash'lin and Silwren, two Shel'ai who turned against the evils of their kind and saved them all from certain death.

El'rash'lin, the disfigured sorcerer who—in a final act of courage—met the Nightmare on King's Bend and prevented the demon from tearing down the walls.

Silwren, who spoke in Dogbane Circle and united the frightened people of the Dark Quarter; who drove the enemies from the streets of Lyos then tirelessly visited each of the temples afterward, using her magic to heal the injured, her violet eyes and platinum tresses a common sight long after the clerics had succumbed to exhaustion. Her touch had saved many who would otherwise have died. In the aftermath of so much destruction, her unexpected gentleness gave the people hope. They no longer feared her.

But mostly, they told stories of him, despite all his attempts to discourage them: Rowen Locke, the slumdweller who joined the Red Watch, who briefly led the Bloody Asps of the Dark Quarter before returning command to Fen-Shea. Rowen Locke, who defended Silwren when others wanted her dead. Rowen Locke, one-time squire to Aeko Shingawa.

Rowen Locke, Knight of the Crane.

Word spread, despite Rowen refusing Aeko's offer. For weeks after Kayden's death, he remained inconsolable, spiteful toward all the Knighthood had come to represent. He was, Aeko said, the first squire in centuries who refused to be knighted. She claimed that was a good sign.

Silwren found him standing alone on Beggar's Drop—the same place where, not long before, she had sought to end her own life though her innate magic had acted of its own accord to cushion her fall.

She smiled. So much had changed since then. Even her battle with Kith'el and the pain caused by El'rash'lin's passing had been eased somewhat. She had gone among the people of Lyos, using her magic to heal. It felt good to use her gifts for something other than killing—even though the efforts strained her control, carving wrinkles into her face and leaving blisters on her hands.

She touched Rowen's arm. He turned, alarmed, and stared at her. He seemed torn over whether or not to hate her. After all, she was a Shel'ai—one of those who had enslaved and tormented his brother. But he had El'rash'lin's memories, plus what he'd seen with his own eyes: Silwren tending the wounded, comforting the dying. She read his mind and sensed the rage in him, the raw hurt, but he was willing to listen. *That must be enough.*

Slowly, she explained the irreversible Blood Thrall. Once chosen, it could not be refused. No matter Kayden's will, at best, the Blood Thrall would have remained a dull, daily torment from which he'd finally been saved.

"How could the Shel'ai do this? How could anyone be so cruel?"

Silwren countered. "When in history has there been a war devoid of cruelty?"

Rowen touched his sword. "Did you know?"

Silwren's eyes fell on Knightswrath. She'd not yet told the Human what he carried. She'd spoken about it with El'rash'lin, deciding to keep that secret for now—but El'rash'lin's final request had been for her to try and help Rowen understand. *But am I ready for that? Is he?*

For now, she answered his question. "It happened after El'rash'lin left, while I slept. Had we been there, we would have stopped it. I can only ask that you believe me."

Reading Rowen's mind, she sensed him remembering passages from the Codex Lotius—statements of honor and sacrifice—and how Silwren had fought against her own kind, even the one who had nearly been her husband, for what she thought was right. Guiltily, she withdrew from his mind.

"How did Kayden end up with the Shel'ai in the first place? Aeko says they were ambushed by Sylvs. That it was arrows—not magic—that wiped out his company."

"The Shel'ai pretended to be Sylvs," Silwren said. "They killed the Knights, hoping to create animosity between Sylvos and the Lotus Isles. That way, the Knights wouldn't help the Sylvs once the forests were invaded."

"And some, they took as prisoner," Rowen finished. "And by some curse of the gods, I'm the one who found Kayden!" He shook his head, overcome by grief and disbelief.

"Perhaps it wasn't a curse," Silwren said. "Perhaps it was not chance, either. Perhaps you were *meant* to find Kayden, to save him. Remember Namundvar's Well," she pressed. "You looked into the Light, Rowen. You felt it just as I have. You ache now to be apart from it, but the Light is inside you—in everything. Isn't that what the Knights teach?"

Rowen smiled bitterly. "The Knights are armored dung. The sooner they're wiped off the face of Ruun, the better."

Silwren rested her hand on his sword arm. "The Knighthood needs you, just as the Shel'ai need me. The world has gone mad, Human. We must remake it."

Rowen did not answer. She stayed with him for a long time. She did not have to pry into his thoughts to know what he would do. Together, they watched sunlight spill off the parapets, lighting the slums below.

The ceremony was held in the Dark Quarter. They might have arranged it in the Queen's Garden—had it not been burned. The last Prince of Lyos offered the use of his palace, but the knights refused. A grim silence still hung over the palace in the wake of the king's murder, and this was to be a joyous occasion. So, on Aeko's suggestion, they chose the Dark Quarter instead.

For the first time in Lyos's history, Dogbane Circle found itself cleaned, the earth scattered with white and crimson dogblossoms brought back from the Lotus Isles. A new dais was constructed from white oak. Aeko stood there in smartly polished battle-dress, her azure tabard rippling in the morning light. Bright banners billowed overhead, proudly displaying the dearest symbols of the Knighthood: the lotus, the stag, and the balancing crane.

Crowds filled the circle—not just Isle Knights, squires, nobles, and soldiers, but citizens of the Dark Quarter, too. All came to watch Aeko recite hallowed passages from the Codex Lotius then address the kneeling, white-robed figure of Rowen Locke. Ignoring Crovis Ammerhel—who simmered next to her—she spoke of honor, humility, and the legacy of Fâyu Jinn. She spoke these words to one who had been an orphan, a pickpocket, a sellsword—certainly not the pedigree the Knighthood usually looked for. Other Knights bristled with the insult but said nothing.

"Do you accept the charge granted unto you by the Light: to safeguard the weak, to honor your enemies, to uphold the laws of the Knighthood and defend them with all your blood and breath?"

Aeko had spoken these words countless times on the Lotus Isles, knighting the worthy and unworthy alike, often for reasons that were merely political. The words often seemed like meaningless dogma, the bombastic recitations demanded by formality and tradition.

But not today. For all her efforts to maintain a solemn expression, Aeko could not help smiling at her kneeling squire as Rowen looked up, overwhelmed by unashamed emotion, tears running down his cheeks. He tried to speak. His voice broke. Clearing his throat, he said, "I do."

Aeko's smile broadened. Standing to her right, Silwren handed her something with great reverence: Rowen's bright, unsheathed sword. Normally, squires were given adamunes when they were knighted, but Rowen already had one. So Aeko simply moved to return it to her kneeling squire.

"Then, in the sacred name of Fâyu Jinn, by the Light and all the pantheons of the heavens, I charge you and summon you to—"

She gasped. Her eyes caught the name of the sword in her grasp, freshly visible in the morning light.

Standing next to her, Crovis Ammerhel saw it, too. The Knight of the Lotus paled. "*Fel-Nâya...*"

"Knightswrath," Aeko gasped. She turned from Rowen to Silwren.

Silwren said nothing, but her violet eyes flowed with tears of pride. Aeko wondered if the Shel'ai hadn't recognized Rowen's sword from the beginning, even when she and the other Knights did not.

Uneasy murmurs swept through Dogbane Circle. Why had the Knights stopped? Was something wrong? Still kneeling, Rowen frowned, confused. He had been about to accept Knightswrath, thinking the ceremony nearly finished.

"That sword cannot pass to a mere Knight of the Crane!" Sir Ammerhel whispered hotly, audible only to those standing nearby. "The Codex Viticus—"

"I am aware," Aeko answered.

"I am the commander of this battalion," Crovis pressed, leaning so close to Aeko that she felt his spittle on her cheek. "Lady Shingawa, I should not have to remind a Knight of the Stag of her duty. Hand me the sword before this gets out of hand."

Aeko wondered what Silwren would do if Crovis attempted to seize Rowen's sword by force. If the wytch attacked Crovis, Aeko would be honor-bound to defend him. But what about Rowen?

Aeko's fixed gaze fell on Rowen. He was *her* squire, after all. She was knighting him herself, on her honor, without first acquiring permission from Grand Marshal Bokuden, Sir Ammerhel, and the rest of the Knights' Council. While her actions were not strictly forbidden, they were a flagrant breech of etiquette as set forth by the Codex Viticus and observed by the Isle Knights for centuries.

Then it hit her. Her actions, originally intended not just to honor Rowen but to serve as an act of defiance against Crovis, had a dual benefit: she was the presiding officer of these proceedings. Crovis could not interfere.

Aeko's smile returned. She began again. Clear and strong, her voice echoed through Dogbane Circle and the slums beyond. "Then in the sacred name of Fâyu Jinn, by the Light and all the pantheons of the heavens, I charge you and summon you to fulfill your oath. Rise... *Sir* Rowen Locke, Knight of the Crane!"

She pressed Knightswrath into his hands.

Rowen rose. Aeko bowed. All the other Knights followed suit—even Sir Ammerhel. Rowen stared, dumbfounded, as those about him fidgeted.

"Bow, you dunce!" Aeko whispered with affection.

Startled, Rowen bowed to the Isle Knights then straightened. Dogbane Circle erupted into wild applause.

As soon as she was able, Aeko seized him by the arm and pulled him aside, maintaining a strained smile until they were clear of well-wishers. Silwren followed but said nothing. Aeko stopped smiling. But before she could wring his neck, Rowen spoke.

"What did Ammerhel mean about this sword passing to a *mere* Knight of the Crane? I know that squires can't carry adamunes, but you knighted me! If Ammerhel wants my sword, he can have it. That's his right." Rowen shrugged. "The dragonbone's worth a lot, I know, but I'll be happy with *any* adamune."

Aeko frowned. Crovis had stomped away as soon as the ceremony ended, drawing most of the Isle Knights with him. Only a few—*her* supporters, the youngest and poorest knights of the battalion—remained in the Dark Quarter.

Too few... Even now, Crovis could be plotting to have her or Rowen—or both of them—arrested. They had to move quickly. But first, Rowen had to understand what was at stake here.

She tapped his sword's hilt. "Locke, don't you know what you have there?"

Rowen blinked. "My last employer won it in a dice game. When he gave it to me, I thought it was rusted solid, but—"

"We talked in the garden about the legend of Fâyu Jinn's burial—how he decreed that he should be entombed in the Wytchforest as a sign of the old alliance between the Sylvs and the Lotus Isles."

Beside her, Silwren stirred but remained silent.

Aeko continued. "Another part of the legend was kept secret, known only to the highest-ranking Knights—the *name* of Fâyu Jinn's sword, supposedly entombed with him, the ancient sword made by Shel'ai in the days of the Shattering War." She paused meaningfully. "Fel-Nâya." Aeko couldn't quite decide whether to embrace him or strike him. "Locke, how can somebody this lucky—or this blessed—be this dense? By the Light, you're carrying the lost sword of Fâyu Jinn himself!"

CHAPTER THIRTY-TWO

THE EXILE, FULL CIRCLE

E VERYTHING HAPPENED SO QUICKLY AFTERWARD that Rowen could hardly catch his breath. For two days, Aeko and her most trusted Knights kept Rowen hidden, shifting him from inn to inn, from Lyos to the Dark Quarter then back again, so that Crovis could not find him. The Knight of the Lotus might have ruined her for that, but Aeko soon found an unexpected ally.

Typherius, the last surviving son of Pelleas, returned from Phaegos to assume kingship of Lyos. The new king—tall and thin with dark, sad eyes—was no great friend to Crovis, who years ago had infamously ordered the near-sacking of Phaegos over some imagined insult. At Aeko's suggestion, the new king suspended all Isle Knights' authority within his city. Then, he convened a council to decide the matter. Aeko got word to Rowen. He appeared at the palace for only the second time in his life—this time flanked by Silwren and a dozen of Aeko's most trusted Knights.

Though Crovis had not been invited, he strode into the hall almost as soon as the meeting began. "For days, this man has hidden from me." He pointed accusingly at Rowen. "This man, this new Knight of the lowest order, has seen fit to steal a priceless relic thought lost centuries ago! That relic must be returned to the Knights' Council at once. Likewise, this man's honor should be investigated with the utmost prejudice—as should those who have vouched for him." He included Aeko in his gaze.

Rowen bristled, but Aeko rose and spoke in his defense, pointing out the absurd unlikelihood that Rowen—alone—could have breached the great Wytchforest and carried off the sword right out from under Sylvan noses.

"The sword was rusted when it first appeared," she reminded them. "Now it gleams as though newly forged. Could that not be a sign from the Light that it is to remain in Sir Locke's possession?"

Crovis scowled, as did the Knights around him. "The sacred sword of Fâyu Jinn cannot rust. To imply otherwise is blasphemy. Besides, I remind you, there are no witnesses to any of this."

"My former employer, Hráthbam, saw," Rowen countered.

Crovis sneered. "Convenient that the only witness isn't here!"

A ripple of laughter filled the chamber. Rowen blushed with rage and shame. Silwren stood and said, "I witnessed this as well. Has the Knight of the Lotus forgotten, or does he merely call me a liar?"

Crovis faced her with strained politeness. "You misunderstand me, milady. I meant no reproach. This is a matter for the Knighthood, and as such, we must make our ruling based on our own laws and precepts, as set forth by the Codex Viticus. Your credibility as the savior of Lyos is not in question. However, the sword of Fâyu Jinn is another matter." He added in an icy tone, "I trust you will forgive any offense."

Silwren raised one eyebrow—a simple gesture of malice—but King Typherius intervened. He rose from his chair, and all fell silent.

Rowen studied the grim expression of the man who had been a lesser prince just weeks before, who had ascended to the throne of Lyos only after the rest of his family was murdered. *I wonder if I have the same look on my face.*

The new king said, "We are, of course, deeply grateful to all the Knights who bled to save this city. We are also grateful, Sir Ammerhel, for the generous assistance lent by your order these past few weeks in our reconstruction efforts."

Crovis bowed. "We are your servants, Majesty."

Rowen fought off a grimace. While relief had come from the Isles, he had already heard rumors that the Isle Knights–under Crovis's orders—had bled the coffers of Lyos dry as compensation for their slain brethren. The wry look on Aeko's face told him she was thinking the same thing.

"Even with the battle ended, we face a number of troubling questions," King Typherius continued. "What to do with the Throng prisoners, for one. Sir Ammerhel insists they should be taken back to the Lotus Isles and held there until they can be ransomed back to the sorcerers. This, in spite of the fact that their revolt against Fadarah and the sorcerers is probably the only reason all of us are standing here today." He paused meaningfully. "Captain Epheus has already reminded us that they are prisoners of Lyos—not the Knighthood— and should be subject to *our* justice. I agree with him."

Rowen glanced at the new Captain of the Red Watch, seated and scowling at the king's right hand, then back to the king himself. Despite the king's strained smile, he pressed his fingertips against the table so hard his knuckles turned white. *He's stalling.*

"There is also the question of the sorcerers," Typherius continued. "With the obvious exception of Silwren, they remain our enemies. Silwren tells me she has sensed the death of what we call the Nightmare, but Fadarah and many of his ilk live on."

"You need not trouble yourself with them, Sire," Crovis interrupted. "Without an army or their demon, they pose no serious threat."

Same thing you said about the Throng, Rowen thought.

The king continued. "Nevertheless, Lyos must repair itself quickly *and* look to brace itself against whatever future storm may assail us, whether it comes from the sorcerers or the Dhargots."

Crovis had nothing to say at the mention of the armies from the Dhargoth Peninsula which, according to reports, were sweeping eastward.

"And now," Typherius continued, "we have the sword of a lost hero, reappeared as though out of thin air. A priceless symbol, a relic from a bygone age. And the great Isle Knights, so wise and learned, squabbling over what to do with it."

Despite the azure tabard he now wore, Rowen smiled at the king's thinly veiled rebuke of the Knighthood.

Crovis cleared his throat. "What are you suggesting, Sire?"

"I lack my father's wisdom, not to mention his temperance. I never wanted to be king. That's no secret. I would have been quite content to remain in Phaegos." He cast a pointed look at Crovis. "But I would be a poor ruler if I did not say what should be obvious to anyone with eyes. There are powers at work here... powers I do not understand. I have never believed in fate, but even I cannot deny the impossibility of all these coincidences."

Rowen winced. *Are these the same coincidences that led to my brother being enslaved, cursed, then given back to me just so I could free him from his misery?*

The king said, "I see prudence in the advice of Sir Ammerhel: the sword of Fâyu Jinn should be taken back to the Lotus Isles for safekeeping. But my heart says otherwise." He paused, letting the Knights bristle. "Once, thinking I would never be king, I spent my time with fairy tales instead of studies. If I recall the legends correctly, Fâyu Jinn decreed that should the Knights ever ask the Sylvs for aid, that aid would be granted. I understand from Lady Shingawa that a previous delegation to the Wytchforest was rebuffed. I wonder, though, if they would be so quick to turn away an Isle Knight carrying the sword of Fâyu Jinn."

Crovis rose, livid. "Forgive my tone, Sire, but I most strongly disagree. To return the sword to the Sylvs would be a waste. Have you forgotten that they killed the very delegation you speak of?"

Typherius pointed to Silwren. "According to her, your Knights were not killed by Sylvs but Shel'ai disguised as such."

"Either way, the Sylvs are a treacherous race. They might very well kill any Knights who appeared, thinking they'd *stolen* the sword."

"Or perhaps they would take them seriously when they proposed an alliance," Typherius countered.

"*What* alliance? What need have we to ask the Sylvs for help? The war is over!"

Many other Knights grunted their approval. The eyes of King Typherius narrowed dangerously. "It seems I can read a map better than you can, Sir Ammerhel." He gestured at the table before them, indicating an unrolled depiction of the Simurgh Plains all the way to the Dhargoth Peninsula. "The Dhargots are marching east in droves. The sorcerers are still at large. I've asked you before, both privately and in open council, if the Knighthood would pledge to defend its protectorates should the Dhargots sweep this far east... the Dhargots you insisted to my father would prevent the Throng from ever reaching Lyos, I might add. You refuse to answer. In light of this, I'd say you have a rather dubious understanding of war."

Angry murmurs swept through the chamber. Rowen almost laughed. Then Aeko stood. "With reluctance, I must concur with his majesty. The Dhargots are the true threat now—perhaps more than the Throng ever was. I remind this council that according to Silwren, Fadarah's plan is and always has been to prevent the Isle Knights from allying with the Sylvs and to use the Dhargots to stir up a war that might sweep across the whole continent until we destroy ourselves. It's reasonable to question such claims. But to utterly ignore them is foolish." She hesitated. "Though perhaps I should not be surprised, given who I am addressing."

The Knight of the Lotus rose to his feet. Some of his fellow Knights started to draw their swords, but Crovis shouted for them to stop. Sir Ammerhel fixed Aeko with a withering stare. "Battle has a way of eroding the senses, even after it's concluded. Perhaps you do not realize what you are saying. I offer you the opportunity to withdraw your words without reprisal."

Rowen rested his hand on Knightswrath's hilt. Silwren touched his arm.

But Aeko met Crovis's stare with a smile. "Thank you, Captain. I respectfully decline."

Crovis's eyes widened. His face flushed, and he sputtered. He took an angry step toward Aeko, one hand on his sword's hilt, but several of his fellow Knights stopped him. Crovis stomped out of the council chamber, shouting in Shao. Many Knights followed. In their wake, Typherius drew his advisors aside for a hushed, heated discussion.

Rowen rose, leaned toward Aeko, and whispered, "I think you just made a powerful enemy."

"But I angered him long enough to make him forget you for a moment," Aeko answered, deadly serious. "By the Light, if you don't give Crovis the sword, he'll see that it's taken from you as soon as you set foot on the Lotus Isles. He might even risk rankling Typherius and taking it from you while you're still in Lyos." She squeezed his arm. "You are not my squire anymore. Crovis is your commanding officer. If he demands the sword and you refuse, he'll arrest you. I am not strong enough to prevent that. Do you understand?"

Rowen looked down at the sword girded at his waist. He looked, too, at his new armor and tabard. "What will happen if I give Crovis the sword?"

Aeko flinched. "He will declare that it passed into his hands by divine providence. Coupled with his capture of what remained of the Throng, his supporters will see him made a hero. Bokuden will not be able to stop him. Crovis will be made Grand Marshal before year's end."

"And the Dhargots?"

Aeko hesitated. "I can't say. But Crovis isn't so foolish as to commit the Knighthood to a war it can't win. And he certainly has no interest in an alliance with Sylvs!"

Rowen felt his stomach drop. He thought of how vainly Crovis had ridden from the gates to capture the already-deserting Throng after the Nightmare fell, the demonic figure sorely wounded—thanks to El'rash'lin. Crovis' decision had left the city ill-equipped to repel the Unseen and Shel'ai attacking it from within, but it had given Crovis an excuse for glory. He thought of Phaegos, which Crovis had pillaged to fill his coffers. What would happen to the Knighthood if a man like Crovis were placed in charge?

Rowen shook his head. "Crovis cannot have the sword. We both know that."

Aeko eyed him carefully. "Then you must never return to the Lotus Isles."

Rowen leaned on the table with one hand, trying to clear his thoughts. In the distance, King Typherius and his advisors were arguing. Silwren stood nearby, her expression sympathetic. Around them were those few who sided with Aeko: all Knights of the Crane, veterans of the battle on the streets of Lyos.

"The Knighthood is divided," Aeko whispered. "We are the weaker side. But I'll do what I can to make them see reason. You have my word on that."

"And if they don't?"

"Then," Aeko said, "your Knighthood will be stripped from you.

You'll be called an enemy of the order, and all Knights will be honor-bound to capture or kill you, given the chance."

Rowen eyed the balancing crane on his tabard again. "What if I challenge Crovis to a duel? He'll have to accept, won't he? If I kill him..." Aeko's skeptical look made him trail off.

I wouldn't last five seconds against Ammerhel. He clenched his eyes shut, steadied himself, then opened them. "Fine, then. The sword can't go to Crovis. So I'll leave Lyos at once. Knightswrath goes with me."

Aeko touched his arm, sadness in her eyes. "Where will you go?"

Rowen felt his gaze drawn to Silwren. "Where Typherius suggested," he said without thinking. "The Wytchforest. If Crovis wants to follow me *there*, he's welcome to try."

Aeko stared at him. Then she smiled and embraced him. She whispered, "You're a damn fool. But you're still the closest thing in this chamber to a real Knight." When they parted, she waved for her Knights to follow her. As one, they strode out of the hall after Crovis.

Rowen watched them go. He felt incredibly alone.

Silwren moved closer. "I will go with you," she whispered. Her violet eyes reminded him of El'rash'lin. He imagined how traumatic it would be for any Shel'ai to return to the homeland from which they had been exiled, to say nothing of the risk.

Touched, Rowen was about to respond when the king joined them. Rowen started to fall to one knee, but the king stopped him. "No time for that, I'm afraid. If you're interested in avoiding bloodshed, I suggest you leave through the rear gates, the sooner the better. Captain Epheus will take the Throng prisoners to the front gates and release them. That should prove a suitable distraction for Sir Ammerhel." The king wished him luck, but Rowen was too stunned to reply. Typherius left, his advisors in tow—all save Captain Epheus.

The former sergeant faced Silwren uncomfortably. "I have forgiveness to ask of you."

Silwren smiled. She squeezed his hand. Epheus jumped at her touch but did not recoil. Then the captain said to Rowen, "I almost forgot to tell you. One of the prisoners wants to talk to you. A Dwarr. The one who led the revolt, I think. He says he knows you."

Rowen stared. He had not dared to hope. "What's his name?"

"Hugh," Epheus said. "No, Hewn. I think that's it."

"Jalist?"

"You know him?"

"Back when I was a sellsword. He worked with me and Kayden..." He broke off painfully. "Another madman won't hurt. If you're releasing him anyway, tell the Dwarr to meet us at the cave. He'll know what I mean."

The captain nodded and left at once.

With one gauntleted hand, Rowen smoothed his tabard, glancing down at the balancing crane again. He started to laugh. He had been a Knight for less than a week and already he had made enemies. *They will hunt me. By tomorrow, I might be dead. Or worse.*

He started for the door. *One thing at a time. Escape first. Panic later.* As he passed through a dusty slant of window light, he thought the faint red swirls in Knightswrath's dragonbone hilt looked more like ancient bloodstains. Silwren followed him, her expression fixed and unreadable, the pupils of her eyes nearly matching the dusty light around her.

Can I trust you? Are you really so different from the bastards who tortured Kayden?

He remembered that she could read his thoughts if she wanted. Blushing, he cleared his mind by fixing his eyes on the door instead. Then El'rash'lin's memories unexpectedly stirred to life, and he imagined that in place of the ring of cold boots on flagstone, he was a child again, walking barefoot through the Wytchforest. The sun dipped behind an endless span of trees. A fragrant breeze stirred the leaves.

He imagined he was going home.

EPILOGUE

THE SYLVS CALLED IT GODSFALL. It stretched for miles to the north and east of the Ash'bana Plains: a glassy, blighted place. Legend said Godsfall received its name because when Zet's great, burning corpse fell from the heavens, that was where it landed. That was where it burst, and from his corpse, all life emerged.

But that came later. First, there was fire. Zet's fall smote a great crater into the ground, ravaging the soil and turning it to onyx. Flames burned for days, in the air and on land, scouring the surrounding countryside. So terrible was the devastation that even dragons—known once to have roosted in these parts by the bones they left behind—fled south, never to return.

Men said that in all of Ruun, no land was as harsh and unforgiving as Godsfall: a dark, rocky place pocked with chasms and crags. No weeds grew there, no wildflowers, not one single blade of grass. No wild animals roamed, and even the sun was obscured by clouds boiling with dank, acrid rain. But this was Doomsayer's home.

For centuries, the Olgrym's nearest enemies—the Sylvs, in the Wytchforest to the south—speculated that they subsisted on the bodies of their dead. How else could they find sustenance in a place without beasts or farmland? The Sylvs were partly correct. Yes, Olgrym ate their dead, but cannibalism was just a part of their religious rituals. Sometimes, they hunted the Ash'bana Plains for sport, even feasting on the Wyldkin they fought there. But mostly, they ate thorns.

No Sylv had witnessed this—not in centuries. But the bloodthorns grew everywhere, red as their name implied, rising between slabs of black, glassy rock. They were poison to anyone else, but Olgrym lived off them. And grew strong.

Doomsayer appreciated this as he raised another bloodthorn to his mouth. Powerful jaws split through it, releasing a foul nectar that he swallowed only through great discipline. Legends claimed that once, Olgrym had been frail and thin, the weakest of the races born by Zet's passing. After years of strife and endless fighting, they were the strongest.

Olg males gained six feet in height by their tenth year. By sixteen, most towered eight feet or more. They had yellow eyes. Their skin, ash colored, stretched so tight that here and there, raw bone protruded through flesh. Their arms grew thick as tree-trunks. One solid swing from an Olg's two-handed sword could cut a man in half.

But Doomsayer was even stronger than that. He walked alone as the sickly sun filtered through the boiling clouds that always loomed over the dark crags of Godsfall. The weak light lit the horrid burn scars covering all of his exposed skin, reflecting his clan's ancient tradition of coating their armor—or even their bare flesh—with a thin layer of oil and lighting it on fire before charging into battle, the sight of which was known to send even the stoutest enemies fleeing in terror.

Just after dawn, Doomsayer was already awake. He traveled without guards. Men of his race won distinction by murdering their superiors, thus he trusted no one, even the men of his own Felmaul clan.

Unlike the Skullshard clan, who lived at the lowest point of Godsfall's massive crater, or the Ash Hands who sulked in caves, the Olgrym of the great Felmaul clan lived in a kind of fortress: Felmaul Hold. It sat on a jagged peak overlooking the crater—"So that all other clans must look up at us," Doomsayer liked to say. The fortress was massive but crude, consisting of a mountain of carefully piled rocks walled by ancient, petrified trees.

His Felmaul Olgrym had found the petrified trees along the rim of the Godsfall crater centuries ago and carried them—one by one—to the summit of the piled rocks. Though oppressively heavy, the trees were hauled, staked vertically in the earth, and lashed together to form a crude but indestructible wall. In place of a gate, his tribe used the gigantic skull of a dragon, its great mouth open.

To seal the crude gate, the Olgrym maintained a rudimentary system of pulleys that caused the dragon's ancient, toothy jaw to slam down. So heavy was it that, without pulleys, it would take a dozen of the strongest Olgrym to pry the dragon's mouth open again. One could not leave or enter Felmaul Hold, save through the mouth of the dragon.

The skull was just one of many dragonbones the Olgrym had found scattered amid the blasted stones of Godsfall. The Olgrym kept the dragonbones as hallowed relics, sometimes praying and sacrificing to them, but none were more sacred than this skull. The dragon's jaw was large enough that even Doomsayer could pass through without the need to duck. As he left Felmaul Hold, he turned and paused a moment to appreciate the dragon skull's eye sockets, each of them nearly as wide as he was tall.

He wished again that he could have seen this great beast when it was still alive. What a sight that must have been! The dragon's wing bones had already been pilfered by other Olg tribes, but based on skull size alone, the beast would easily have covered the whole fortress in its ominous shadow.

According to legend, the entire continent had once swarmed with dragons, the first true inhabitants of Ruun. Now, terror was the province of the Olgrym—and, on rare occasions, their allies.

Doomsayer had earned his name by foretelling the rise of his race and the downfall of the despised Sylvs: two events which, at last, seemed poised to happen. Doomsayer halted at the edge of his land, shadowed by Felmaul Hold, watching as a lone sorcerer approached Godsfall.

The man—dressed in a cloak the color of sun-bleached dragonbone—dismounted his destrier and made his way, unafraid, toward the towering Olg. Doomsayer noted the man's tapered ears and sharp, pretty features. He resisted the impulse to seize the nearest rock and dash the man's brains out. Despite appearances, this man was a Shel'ai, not a Sylv. Besides, he was a guest.

Instead of bowing, the sorcerer nodded curtly. Doomsayer nodded back, dark locks braided with animal skulls shaking and clattering around his towering frame.

"I am called Shade." The sorcerer's voice echoed off the glassy rocks of the wasted land beyond. "I come on behalf of Fadarah to marshal your legions against the Wytchforest. It is time." He paused. "The Sylvs are laughing at you."

Doomsayer's bony fists clenched. "They will not laugh for long."

Shade watched the great chieftain stalk away, already rousing his Olg warriors in their crude, guttural language. He shuddered. He disliked being this close to Olgrym, but given the nature of Fadarah's tattoos, it was best that someone else serve as the messenger.

It's only a matter of time now. Shade still had doubts as to whether or not the Dhargots would honor their agreement to help the Shel'ai invade Sylvos and drive toward the World Tree—but it made no difference. With the Dhargots fighting the Isle Knights, the Oath of Kin stood even less chance of being invoked than it already did. And best of all, Fadarah had kept this alliance secret, guarded and hidden even within his own mind. Shade had only learned of it after the defeat at Lyos.

That means Silwren knows nothing of it. There will be no one to warn the Wytchforest—and no one who would listen to her, anyway.

"We have made an alliance with Olgrym," he whispered to the cold air. "Gods save us." He remembered Fadarah's promise: this next phase of the war, pitting Olgrym against Sylvs, would end with both ancient foes all but ruined. Sylvos would be theirs for the taking—as would virtually any other realm they wanted. *There will be no one left to threaten us. No one left to hurt us—*

The blare of Olg-horns startled him. Shade had heard those horns before: not low and ominous, like the sound of Olgrym war drums, but shrill, erupting from crude horns fashioned from the bones of dead dragons. A new sound joined the nerve-rattling trumpets: the steady, growing chanting of madmen.

Shade turned his gaze southward, to Sylvos—the Wytchforest—

that distant, leafy blur on a horizon that had once been his home, even the fantastic height of the World Tree, concealed by clouds. He thought suddenly of Captain Lethe and wanted to weep. Instead, he wheeled his mount and rode into the blood-red setting sun.

APPENDIX

THE CODEX LOTIUS

I.   Honor, like dogblossom, blooms best when mired in filth.

II.   A true Knight would fall upon his own sword before bowing in defeat.

III.   In beasts, excellence is displayed through strength; in men, through honor.

IV.   When two fighters meet—and no mercy is requested—one must fall.

V.   Give aid and mercy when asked—but mostly, when they are not asked.

VI.   Seek Light not in the sky but in the soil, the split tree, the rock when it turns.

VII.   He who calls strangers his enemies will soon have too many enemies.

VIII.   One cannot take on the countenance of one's enemy without becoming that enemy.

IX.   Do not fear being wronged; fear becoming what wrongs you.

X.   Good men feel thrice the pain they visit upon others.

XI. Why does the sighted peasant follow the blind king? Because he thinks he must.

XII. He who waits for the gods to tell him where to move will, in time, grow roots.

XIII. Speak plain, speak true, and honorable souls will listen.

XIV. Even the most desperate beast knows what it needs; often, desperate men do not.

XV. All enemies believe themselves right. All are fallible. All are loved.

XVI. It is better to deliberate than to repent.

XVII. There can be no courage without fear.

XVIII. Courage is not prudent. It is fear reborn. Learn to distinguish this from madness.

XIX. Be wary of peace; peaceful, too, are the greatwolf's jaws before they strike.

XX. The false consistently outshine others in their words but rarely in their deeds.

XXI. One must either shun lies or risk embodying them.

XXII. It is good to prevent injustice; but if one cannot, one must not partake in injustice.

XXIII. To pray, unlearn words; to fight, unlearn anger; to love, unlearn desire.

XXIV. Crave only what you own. Own only what do you not crave.

XXV. Tend the blade but trust the scabbard.

ACKNOWLEDGEMENTS

Thank you, Alysha, for your support of my writing.

I'd like to thank my editors, Alyssa Hall and Kelly Reed, for their hard work on this manuscript and for helping a boyhood Tolkien fan realize his dream. Also, thank you to the rest of the team at Red Adept for making the book shine.

ABOUT THE AUTHOR

Michael Meyerhofer grew up in Iowa where he learned to cope with the unbridled excitement of the Midwest by reading books and not getting his hopes up, Probably due to his father's influence, he developed a fondness for Star Trek, weight lifting, and collecting medieval weapons. He is also addicted to caffeine and the History Channel.

Michael Meyerhofer's third poetry book, *Damnatio Memoriae,* won the Brick Road Poetry Book Contest. His previous books of poetry are *Blue Collar Eulogies* (Steel Toe Books, finalist for the Grub Street Book Prize) and *Leaving Iowa* (winner of the Liam Rector First Book Award).

He has also published five chapbooks: *Pure Elysium* (winner of the Palettes and Quills Chapbook Contest*),* *The Clay-Shaper's Husband* (winner of the Codhill Press Chapbook Award), *Real Courage* (winner of the Terminus Magazine and Jeanne Duval Editions Poetry Chapbook Prize), *The Right Madness of Beggars* (winner of the Uccelli Press 3rd Annual Chapbook Competition), *and Cardboard Urn* (winner of the Copperdome Chapbook Contest).

Individual poems won the Marjorie J. Wilson Best Poem Contest, the Laureate Prize for Poetry, the James Wright Poetry Award, and the Annie Finch Prize for Poetry. He is the Poetry Editor of *Atticus Review.* His work has appeared in a number of journals including *Ploughshares, Hayden's Ferry Review, North American Review, River Styx,* and *Asimov's Science Fiction Magazine.*

www.ingramcontent.com/pod-product-compliance
Lightning Source LLC
Chambersburg PA
CBHW030918260626
47169CB00002B/300